MASTER OF THE SIDHE

The battlefield came into sight. As Lugh Lamfada and the Riders of the Sidhe topped the southern hills, he looked down on the plains below, frozen for a moment by the horror of the situation.

The de Dannan warriors were in headlong flight from the twisted Fomor and their monstrous machines. Soon the army would be overrun. Afraid or not, Lugh was their chosen champion. He must do what he could to save them.

"Riders!" Lugh cried, raising the enchanted sword Answerer high above him. "Attack!"

As Lugh's band drove in against the front line of the machines, the de Dannan warriors scrambled to safety. The lances of the Riders dropped forward in one graceful move, as if they meant to joust with the evil engines.

Lugh found himself at the center of a closing circle of the immense machines. He looked around him at the whirling, snapping, chewing blades converging, and wondered if the Silver Warriors could withstand them all.

"Good enough," he told himself, trying to feel optimistic. "At least I've gotten their attention."

MASTER
OF THE
SIDHE

Kenneth C. Flint

BANTAM BOOKS
TORONTO • NEW YORK • LONDON • SYDNEY • AUCKLAND

MASTER OF THE SIDHE
A Bantam Book / September 1985

ISBN 0-553-25261-5

Published simultaneously in the United States and Canada

Bantam Books are published by Bantam Books, Inc. Its trademark,
consisting of the words "Bantam Books" and the portrayal of a
rooster, is Registered in U.S. Patent and Trademark Office and in
other countries. Marca Registrada. Bantam Books, Inc., 666 Fifth
Avenue, New York, New York 10103.

PRINTED IN THE UNITED STATES OF AMERICA

O   0 9 8 7 6 5 4 3 2 1

MASTER OF THE SIDHE

Book One
THE BATTLE FOR EIRE

Chapter One
THE STRONGHOLD

A hundred torches and a large central fire filled the great hall of Tara with a ruddy glow. It fluttered nervously in the fretful gusts of autumn wind that batted at the fortress hill of kings.

The many wavering lights cast multiple shadows of the thick roof pillars against the outer walls of the immense circular room. They created patterns that writhed and altered constantly in a grotesque dance whose music was the keening of the wind itself.

Not many days before, the hall had been the scene of a victory celebration, filled with the rejoicing people of the Tuatha de Danann. Now, no Bards sang, no harps played, no ale was passed. The long tables ranged about the fire pit were empty. The hall of Tara was deserted except for a single group of men gathered on the dais of the High-King.

Some fifty men were on this royal platform, seated or standing around the table where the High-King and his champions sat when feasting. They made a spot of brightness in the gloom of the cavernous space, a grand collection of colors and textures in the tunics and woolen cloaks, the finely wrought brooches and sword hilts of the chieftains, the multihued robes and golden torcs of the Druids. All were intent upon the large chart of the island called Eire spread out upon the planks.

Nuada, High-King of the Tuatha de Danann clans, stood over it. The firelight painted the strong features of his long face in broad, emphatic strokes of light and dark, turning his eyes to flames gleaming in the deep shadows behind his shaggy brows. He indicated locations upon the chart with the slender, glinting point of his own sword as he spoke, his voice booming hollowly in the vast space.

"Our rising against the Fomor has succeeded—so far. We've broken their companies at every place they've tried to

3

stand." The sword tip touched lightly at several points across the upper third of the isle. "Now they seem to have given up resistance altogether and are fleeing toward the north."

He lifted his gaze and cast it around at the circle of stolid faces. The gathered leaders were of a type with their king, long-featured, intense, tall and lean of body, golden-haired. And the eyes of all glowed alike with victory.

"But we mustn't be too ready to believe we've won yet!" he cautioned them sharply. "Until the Fomor are defeated totally, their last warrior driven from Eire, we'll not be done with them or properly revenged for the years we lived as their slaves!"

There were murmurs and nods of agreement at that. None there had not felt the cruelty of the Fomor, and none underestimated the brutal power of that enemy.

"Our scouts have told us that right now they're gathering," he continued. His sword point stabbed down into the chart, impaling a spot on the northern coast. "Here. Their last and largest city in Eire."

He looked to the others again, his voice taking on a grim intensity. "I don't have to tell you that if they choose to stand against us there, the battle will be a long and bloody one. There'll be no making peace. The Fomor will have their backs to the sea and they'll fight with the savageness of the beasts they are."

One of the warriors exchanged looks with his fellow chieftains, then spoke in reply.

"My King, our people are ready. They are armed and trained and their full strength is restored to them. They want nothing more but to finish this war and have Eire at last!"

The High-King nodded. He had expected nothing else.

"Very well. Then be prepared to march. We have had word from the Fomor that they will accept a truce and discuss terms of surrender. Lugh Lamfada and our other comrades have agreed to go to their city and meet with them. But if they refuse to make terms, we will have to fight."

"I hope our friends survive," said a cunning-looking little Druid who sat beside the king. "The Fomor are treacherous."

Nuada's expression gave way to a grin at that.

"Findgoll," he replied, "knowing Lugh and his company as we do, I think it's the survival of the Fomor we should be wondering about."

*   *   *

The little band strode purposefully down from the last high ridge of hills toward the Fomor stronghold. It lay far below, at the base of a wide trough of land that ran to the sea, a square patch of filthy linen dropped on the soft green plain along the shore.

It was an odd collection of people who now approached this goal, although the couple who led it did little to create this impression. They seemed a quite pleasant, harmless sort of pair. The young man was cleanly and boldly featured, his fair hair swept casually back in a thick wave, while the woman had an open, guileless face accentuated by large, bright green eyes and a fine dusting of freckles across her small nose and high cheeks. There was nothing about them to suggest that he was Lugh Lamfada, Champion of the de Dananns and she the veteran warrior called Aine.

It was the three who followed them who created the air of strangeness.

One of this trio was the Dagda, most powerful of the de Danann's warriors. He was an enormous man, with a body hard as bog oak and a face like a rocky cliff softened and seamed by years of Eire's rain.

Beside him strode Morrigan, another woman, though this was barely discernible. Her lean body was closely furled in a black cloak, and her glowing blue-black hair was pulled back tightly, emphasizing the gauntness of her face.

On the Dagda's other side loped the one known as Gilla the Clown. A baggy, battered cloak of faded stripes billowed around his long, loose-jointed frame. Outsize shoes flapped loudly on his feet. A tangle of beard and hair masked all of his face save for his eyes, his nearly constant grin, and the tip of a long nose that jutted from the growth as if striving desperately for air.

As the five drew nearer to the Fomor city, the patch of linen began to resolve itself into separate buildings, tiny squares of dirty white set in rows, dividing the whole area into exact sections. All was shrouded by a thick yellow-gray haze that hung low above it.

Something swooped suddenly down from the sky and directly at the travelers. In a flurry of wings it swiftly checked itself and settled to a landing on the arm Lugh lifted toward it. It was a small falcon, and it ruffled its feathers in a nervous gesture as it turned a sharp gaze toward the young warrior.

"I've been over it, and I don't like it at all," the bird

announced in a sharp, uneasy voice. "The look of the place is bad enough. But the smell!"

This talking bird was in fact a Pooka, one of that extraordinary family of beings who could assume any shape at will except that of a human.

Lugh had to admit the Pooka was certainly right. Even at this distance the breeze off the sea managed to waft the awful stench of the city up to them. It was most reminiscent of something long dead left under a hot sun.

"I don't much like it either, Shaglan," Lugh told the Pooka firmly, "but it's my feeling that we must do this. We can't let the bloodshed continue if there is any possibility this can be settled peacefully. If Bres is willing to talk with us, we have to try convincing him to surrender."

"Well, it's the maddest thing we've ever done," the Dagda growled. "And going in there without my war-ax, I feel like a naked babe in a wolves' den!"

He wasn't alone in that feeling. None of the party carried sword, spear, ax, shield, or any other weapon, as a condition of the truce with the Fomor.

The outer limits of the city were just ahead now. The roadway they followed entered it through a break in a row of close-set square buildings. At their approach, a group of figures moved into this opening and stopped, blocking the way.

"Our welcoming party," Lugh commented, examining them with interest. "Who are they?"

"It's the Serpent's Head Clan," the Dagda supplied. "One of the hardest in the Fomor companies. Very difficult to kill."

They were all tall and cylindrical in body, well-muscled, and wiry in build. The blood relationship was clear in the facial characteristics that had given them their name. Their heads were flat and broad, nearly without chins or foreheads. Most were bald. Their eyes protruded from the sides of their heads and their noses were only thin, moist, pulsing slits above wide, lax mouths.

"A lovely family, they are," Gilla told the Dagda cheerily, drawing only a glare from his large companion.

As the little band came to a halt, one of this clan moved forward. One side of his face was covered by a scabrous mass of dead white tissue, leaving him only one eye. But this protruded so far from his head that he could direct it forward or backward. He lifted a heavy, barbed spear before him and challenged the arrivals in a low, lisping voice.

"Are you the ones come to see King Bres then?"

"We are," said Lugh.

"Are you unarmed, as agreed?"

"We keep our bargains," the Dagda told him irritably.

The single eye swiveled toward him. "We'll see," the Fomor said. "Let's have a look."

Reluctantly, Lugh and the Dagda pulled back their cloaks so the clan leader could peer about for hidden weapons. Gilla the Clown readily lifted the skirts of his voluminous coat and smiled his most inane smile. The Fomor passed him over quickly as an obvious lunatic. Morrigan unwrapped her cloak to reveal a gaunt but sinewy body that the searcher found amusing. He turned to his companions.

"Look at this one. All bones, she is."

She fixed him with the glittering stare of a raptor spotting prey, but made no reply.

With Aine, the Fomor suddenly grew much more interested. For she threw back her coat to expose a woman's form that belied her girlish look. And the short, belted tunic that she wore did very little to disguise it.

"Well, well!" the Fomor said. "This is better! This one will take a bit more searchin'."

He started toward her, hands out, saliva dribbling from the corner of his sagging mouth. Aine stepped back, warning him in sharp tones: "Keep back, snake, or I'll pop out that only eye of yours!"

He laughed and kept moving forward, but in another instant he was on the ground, rolling about, screaming, flailing wildly to drive off the attacking falcon that had launched itself upon him.

"Get it off! Get it off!" he wailed, trying to keep the tearing claws away from his eye.

"We're here under a truce to see Bres," Lugh told him coldly. "Leave off your games and take us to him now!"

"I will! I will!" the hapless being promised. "Just get the bird off!"

"Bird!" Lugh said simply, and the falcon instantly broke off its attack and flapped back to his arm.

The disheveled warrior got up, eyeing the falcon warily.

"All right then," he said sullenly. "Follow me."

They moved after the Fomor, passing the outer line of

buildings. Beyond it they entered one of the city's main thoroughfares and found it a scene of confusion and horror.

The street was congested with uncountable milling Fomor. The appearance of the beings who made up this close-packed mass made the Serpent's Head Clan seem almost pleasant in comparison. For the Fomor of Eire were a people doomed to bear the burden of an ancient curse, and its mark was clear upon them. Each one was touched by it in face or form, and some in both.

Backs were twisted, shoulders bent, limbs stunted or distorted into gnarled claws or clublike hooves or webbed fins. Some lacked arms or legs altogether and made do with crude substitutions of metal and wood.

The faces were of a variety that a human might find in only the deepest and most perverse of nightmares. The greatest number were victims of malformations that gave them the look of beings other than man. Sea creatures seemed to predominate, with an abundance of popping eyes, pulsing gills, and hairless faces lacking ears or noses. Reptilian characteristics were also much in evidence in squat, toadlike heads and drooping mouths. And there were some who simply lacked the essential parts to make up any kind of face, though most of these wore face coverings to hide what even their own brethren couldn't stomach.

It was altogether as if some particularly malicious creator had poured their essences into the cauldron of life with those of whatever loathsome creatures could be found, given them a vigorous stir, then poured out the resulting mixture haphazardly.

Still, for all the terrible nature of their deformities, there was nothing pitiable about the Fomor, and there was certainly nothing weak. They were hard and ruthless warriors, heavily armed, more than able to cope with and even use their handicaps to their advantage: their awful appearance had long served to intimidate their enemies.

But now, for the first time in their memories, they had met defeat, and it had sent them all here, to this final refuge. The influx of hundreds of Fomor from all of Eire had created a situation of overcrowding and disorder. Many arguments, scuffles, and outright fights with weapons were taking place among the violent beings. And at one spot a dozen warriors were engaged in a bloody melée over a pile of booty looted from the once-enslaved de Dananns.

The dreadful nature of the beings was only intensified by the loathsomeness of their setting. Lugh and his companions walked a street turned to an open sewer by refuse, past alleyways clogged with mounds of trash. They breathed a heavy, smoky air made foul with the odor of rot.

Still, it was clear that there had once been a much different intent for this city. Each of the structures the band passed was neat, square, and built of a once-white, once-smooth material. Row upon row of them were laid out in regular intervals, divided evenly by cross streets forming precise right angles. Obviously, a systematic and highly disciplined mind had been behind the creation of such a place. And, just as obviously, that mind had long been lost to the previous occupants.

The little group of visitors stayed very close together as the escorting serpent-headed warriors led them inward, past block after block of the identical buildings. They searched about them constantly for any sign of trouble, but the Fomor seemed little interested. Beyond casting an angry look or derisive word at them as they passed, the warriors did nothing to hinder them. The truce was apparently in effect.

As they moved ever deeper into the heart of the city, a change became evident. The buildings were becoming progressively larger, stretching upward to two, three, and finally four stories. Girths increased in proportion until whole blocks were filled by just a pair.

Their height and their closeness to the avenue created a canyon effect, casting a deep gloom below. It was an unpleasant reminder to the visitors of how far they had penetrated the enemy's camp and how vulnerable they were there. Lugh looked about him at the looming walls and felt a twinge of misgiving. Had the Dagda been right? Had they finally taken a risk too great, gone too far?

But then he saw the broad, absurd grin Gilla was directing at him. As so often before, the peculiar Clown's presence was enough to restore the young Champion's confidence and renew his zeal for adventure.

Abruptly, the party found itself at its goal. They passed a final block of the taller buildings and came out into a large open space

It was a square paved with a smooth stone, closed in by the high stone walls of the surrounding structures. On two sides of it the walls were continuous and featureless except for rows of timber-shuttered doors along the bases. But in the side directly opposite the avenue by which the little band entered the square, the opening of another street was visible.

Lugh and his companions stopped on the edge of this open space and stared across. Their attention was fixed on a group of Fomor warriors gathered just inside the mouth of that other street. Especially, it was fixed on one man who now strode boldly forward from the rest into the square.

All of them knew well enough the face of their old enemy, Bres.

Chapter Two
RUNNING THE MAZE

He walked out a third of the distance into the square and stopped there, taking up a commanding pose, hands on hips, head up, eyes sweeping arrogantly across the group facing him.

He was tall and strongly built, clad in the colorful garb of a warrior chieftain. A cloak of brilliant red hung casually about his wide shoulders, thrown back to reveal a gold-trimmed tunic and the jewel-studded hilt of a sword. Curling masses of black hair formed a mane about a massive head whose strong, roughly chiseled features added to his air of toughness.

Once he had been the de Danann's High-King. He had used his power to strip them of their pride and strength and keep them subservient to the Fomor. Then Lugh had discovered Bres's secret. He was himself half Fomor in blood and wholly so in mind. Dethroned by Nuada, driven from Tara by a de Danann uprising, he had taken control of the Fomor army. He had led it in a war with a single goal: the annihilation of the entire de Danann race.

So far his plans had been thwarted, but the resilient Bres was not to be beaten easily, as Lugh and his friends had discovered more than once. His aura of dominance and power was as strong now as ever before.

"He means for you to go out there and meet him," the one-eyed escort told them, gesturing with his spear. "Go on. You'll be safe there." And he withdrew into the avenue

Lugh and his friends exchanged questioning looks. The Dagda shrugged.

"Well, they at least can't come upon us by surprise here."

Lugh nodded in agreement. He started forward, the others closing in around him.

The square was no cleaner than the rest of the city, and the smell of it was worse. Straw was scattered on the yellow-stained pavement, and the place was littered with the remains of food and dung, as if it were used for penning animals.

Like Bres, they moved a third of the way into the area and stopped, forming a line to face him.

"I hoped you'd be the one to come, Lugh Lamfada," he said with satisfaction. His voice was surprisingly soft and slow, but carried an intensity that made each word clear. He cast a disdainful gaze across the others. "But why do you still travel with such a strange company?" He looked at Morrigan and the Dagda. "These two aging 'Champions' must be more a burden than a help. After all these years, they can't have any real powers left."

"There's still enough life in us to see you finished, Bres," the Dagda growled in reply.

Bres only laughed with scorn at that and turned toward Gilla. "And this absurd Clown seems as useless. He must be very amusing to you."

"I keep them laughing all the time, that I do," Gilla agreed affably. "But I can't come close to doing it so well as you, Bres. Why, that time your own horse threw you in the mud—"

"Enough!" Bres said sharply. His dark eyes flashed the Clown a look of open hatred. Then he turned from Gilla to Aine and the manner softened.

"Dear Aine," he said, eyeing her affectionately. "Such a lovely and ruthless woman you are." Regret filled his voice. "Ah, such a fine mate you might have made to me. You could still leave them, you know. Join me!"

This was more than enough for Lugh. He stepped forward, cutting off Bres's view of Aine.

"No more of this, Bres," he said brusquely. "You agreed to meet us. Will you hear our terms or not?"

"Quick to the point, boy, as usual," Bres said. "All right. Let me hear what you have to say."

"We have to know what your intentions are," Lugh stated frankly. "We've come to give you the chance to surrender. If you agree, you and these Fomor can leave Eire in safety." He paused. "You can save many lives, Bres."

"You're very full of yourself, aren't you?" Bres said derisively. "You've won a few battles, and now I'm to just let it go, let Eire go? My Eire? You're a greater fool than I thought you were!"

"You're the fool, Bres, if you believe you can bring this sorry lot to fight again!" the Dagda returned with heat. "They're broken!"

"Are they?" he shot back vehemently. "Well, I have every Fomor warrior left in Eire gathered here now, ready to face you again. And when I meet the de Dananns this time, I'll have the force to crush them. That I promise!"

The Dagda shook his head, clearly skeptical. But Lugh felt something else. Since the first time he had met Bres, he had the odd sensation that he could understand how the man thought—and right now he was certain Bres meant exactly what he said.

"There is no more need for fighting, Bres," he reasoned earnestly. "We can reach some agreement if we try."

"All I'll accept is your destruction and my control of Eire," Bres told him fiercely, the hot light of fanaticism glowing in his eyes.

"Please, remember that you're half de Danann," Lugh implored, desperately trying to reach him. "Don't let the Fomor blood control you. I can feel a de Danann spirit still alive in you. You know I can. You feel it too. Let it take you."

Like the young Champion, Bres had long felt this sense of oneness, as if something linked their minds. As their gazes locked, the words of Lugh stirred something submerged and nearly lost.

Bres shook his head angrily, breaking off the contact.

"You'll not use that Champion's power of yours to sway me, boy," he sneered. "The Fomor will is too strong. Your de Dananns are lovers of peace, of beauty, of the mind. It has made them weak, and it will destroy them yet."

Lugh sighed. He saw there would be no reasoning with

Bres in this, and his heart fell. He had hoped that all the dying, all the fighting and suffering would end here, and his own task would be fulfilled at last.

But his despair was short-lived. He was still the Champion by his own choice, and if Bres meant to continue, he would too.

"If you are determined to fight, then our talk is ended," he said with a chill formality. "We take your answer to Nuada. Good-bye."

He nodded to the others and they turned to start away, but the voice of Bres, soft, cool, and faintly mocking, stopped them.

"I'm afraid you won't be going to Nuada or anywhere else."

They swung back toward him.

"What do you mean?" the Dagda demanded. "We're under a truce here!"

Bres shook his head in disbelief. "I don't follow your absurd codes. I use them—to take advantage of simple fools like you!"

From behind them came the sudden shriek of grating metal. They whirled toward the noise in time to see an iron gate drop down from high above the avenue, sealing the opening with a grate of heavy bars.

The five trained warriors reacted as one, spinning back to drive at Bres. But the Fomor leader had anticipated their move and used the distraction to run for the opening to the far avenue.

The de Danann Champions had covered only half the distance to it when Bres passed through, and a second gate slipped down, closing the gap with a final sounding clang.

Bres looked back at them through the close-set metal bars and smiled.

"A trap, you see. This square is actually a yard for exercise." He was taking great pleasure in explaining. His voice was slow as he savored every word. "The Fomor, as you know, are afflicted with a terrible curse. Some of them are so grotesquely deformed by it that they have ceased to be men at all. The other Fomor, in their benevolence, give these poor creatures a home here, in these buildings surrounding you." Bres smiled. "And now, you are going to meet them." He raised his voice. "Open the doors!"

In the walls on either side of the square the row of

wooden shutters rose, exposing the openings into the structures. At first, nothing was visible but blackness . . . then, slowly, something began to stir. Wails, horrible screams as of beings in torment, issued from the holes. And finally, figures began to emerge into the open.

At first only a few ventured out, testing the air, hesitating, blinking at the light. Then more followed, faster and faster, until they gushed forth, spreading out across the square. The band of heroes, hardened as experience had made them to the horrible, drew back at what they saw.

The Fomor in the city's streets had often been monsters. But those that swarmed into view now were far beyond any of them. Bres had certainly not exaggerated. Few of the things bore even a vague resemblance to human beings.

There were so many that they clambered upon one another as they pushed forward. All were naked, their misshapen bodies pallid, streaked with their own filth. Young Lugh could relate them to nothing save the writhing mass found beneath a suddenly upturned rock.

Some skittered spiderlike on spindly limbs, some crept on shortened stubs or dragged themselves with whatever appendages they had. The worst were like some kind of larva, nearly limbless, hairless, soft and waxen white, almost boneless as they squirmed along the ground. Their faces were like wet clay, eyes peeping from the sagging, oozing folds, round mouths sucking constantly.

"They have no minds, really," Bres continued in an easy, conversational style. "Just a sort of primitive drive for survival, mostly for food. Oh, did I mention? The Fomor feed them right here." He glanced up to the sky. "And about this time of day, I think." He laughed. "I watched them eat once. Revolting but amazing. They'll eat almost anything!"

By now the creatures had filled the whole outer edge of the square and had become aware of Lugh and his companions. The countless bizarre faces were turned toward them. Mewling sounds of hunger arose. The mass began to ooze in toward them.

The little band moved back to the center of the square as a collar began to tighten about them.

"Form a defensive ring," Lugh told the others. "Gilla, time for your trick, I think."

"I thought it just might be," Gilla replied.

He reached into the billowing folds of his coat and pulled

forth an object, which he launched through the air toward Lugh. It was a sheathed longsword and harness. The finely worked silver of its hilt and scabbard sparkled as it arched across to land in the young Champion's outstretched hand.

Other weapons followed it from the marvelous cloak of Gilla. Swords went to Aine and Morrigan. An enormous double-bladed ax was tossed to the Dagda, and a final sword was drawn out for the Clown himself.

Bres watched this performance with shock.

"You promised to come unarmed!" he shouted in outrage.

"We aren't quite the fools you think, Bres," Lugh called back. Then, to the falcon, he murmured: "Shaglan, get down and change. Find something to clear our way to the avenue."

The Pooka fluttered to the ground inside the pentagram the heroes formed. Lugh quickly donned his harness and drew his weapon from its sheath. The revealed sword flashed as light caught its magically fashioned blade. This was the Answerer, a gift to Lugh from the Enchanted Isles, and he could feel its power course through him as it came into his hand.

He set himself with the others to face the mass around them, swinging the Answerer before him. The blade drew a fan of light in the air and the creatures cowered. But their hesitation was not for long. They were too many, and their hunger overcame any fear.

"I can truly say this is an ugly mob," Gilla observed lightly, looking around at the circle of faces as it closed in.

But then the beings were reeling back, staring up in fear at the thing that had suddenly risen within the defensive ring. It was a bear, twice the height of a man and snarling with a very convincing ferocity.

"Shaglan, to the gate!" Lugh shouted. "We'll follow!"

The bear dropped to all fours and headed off in the direction indicated. The Fomor creatures decided not to hinder it. In fact, they scrambled onto one another in their frantic efforts to be out of his way. He loped along the opened passage, his companions close behind and swinging their weapons around to keep the massed beings back.

The few Fomor warriors outside the gate retreated as the bear slammed against it and shoved its paws out between the bars to rake at them with long claws.

"It's your turn now," Lugh told the Dagda. "Get us out!"

The giant warrior seized the thick iron rods, set his legs, and heaved. The muscles of his back and neck grew tense, tendons standing out in sharp relief. His neck muscles strained like taut cables. His face was set, eyes closed, as the Dagda concentrated all his powers in a single effort.

The bars resisted stubbornly for a long moment, then gave way, squealing as the metal buckled, bending outward, opening a wide gap in the gate.

Across the square Bres howled in fury and swung on his officers.

"They're breaking out! Get around there! Stop them! They can't leave this city alive!"

The Fomor rushed to obey. But it was already too late to stop Lugh's party. Lugh had leaped immediately through the gate's hole, driving upon the Fomor beyond in a furious attack while his friends climbed through to join him.

Together they slashed the Fomor line apart and charged into the open avenue beyond. The remaining Fomor moved to follow, but suddenly found themselves deluged by a new problem. The creatures in the square had seen their own chance for freedom. They were pouring through the broken gate, falling upon the hapless warriors who tried to stem their flow.

Thus rid of their pursuit, the fugitives dashed up the avenue. The few citizens they passed scattered in terror. For now Lugh and his friends were free, but safety was still very far away.

They rounded a corner into a wider, more crowded thoroughfare. Not far ahead of them a four-wheeled cart harnessed to a pair of powerful draft horses stood at the roadside. Two burly Fomor workmen were unloading great wicker baskets of fish from it.

"Just the thing!" Gilla happily declared. "Come on!"

He led the way toward the cart, pushing through the swarm of startled Fomor, and leaped onto its back. A boar-faced workman was just bending over a basket, and one kick from Gilla's huge foot sent him flying out headfirst. The second workman, a turtle-headed Fomor, looked around as a basket loaded with still-lively crabs was smashed into his face, sweeping him from the cart.

"Get aboard!" Gilla called to his comrades, moving to grab the reins. "We're going!"

None of the Fomor who gaped with amazement at this

scene moved to interfere as the others climbed aboard.

"Shaglan, follow close!" the Clown shouted to the bear and urged the horses forward.

They started off, giving the cart a yank, spilling baskets of fish—and nearly the Dagda—off the rear. Gilla headed them up the avenue, pushing them to a full-out gallop. The Pooka ran along behind, the size and strength of his bear-form allowing him to keep up easily.

The Clown kept up this breathtaking pace as he steered the cart along. The Fomor in the streets heard the rattle of its coming, saw it descending on them, and dove for safety. The rubbish-clogged streets were often too narrow, and Gilla was forced to weave his way through a confusing maze, always moving outward, slowing for nothing. The car careened around garbage piles, bounded over trash and occasional Fomor pedestrians who weren't quite quick enough. It barely missed the corners it squeezed past, colliding at one point with a wall that ripped the timber from its side.

Then ahead, a giant mound showed, blocking the way. They couldn't stop. There wasn't room to turn. So Gilla urged on the horses even faster. They slammed into the mound, the horses leaping most of it, dragging the cart along. It flew up, tearing through the pile, crashing down in the street on the far side, still rolling.

Gilla whooped with delight. "Quite a ride, eh?" he called back to the others.

"I may make you eat this!" the Dagda threatened, picking off the rotting vegetables he had been splattered with.

But the Clown's next move wasn't so fortunate. The cart raced into an intersection and the way ahead was again blocked, this time by debris that rose higher than the buildings on either side. Gilla reined the horses sharply around. They made the turn, but the cart didn't. It tilted sideways, hanging for an instant on two wheels. The passengers leaped clear as it was yanked over by the plunging horses. It crashed down, skidded, and then the harness broke. The released team went galloping madly on alone.

The heroes were scrambling up and nursing bruised spots when Shaglan, a bit winded now, reached them.

"You madman!" the Dagda shouted at the Clown. "Now what?"

"Be calm," Gilla soothed. "We've made it. The way out is right before us!"

He pointed up the street. Between the buildings only a block ahead the open country was visible. There was just one small problem left.

The Snake's Head Clan was there, blocking the way.

Chapter Three
APPEALS FOR HELP

The rest of the family had apparently been called in to help. Fully fifty of the reptilian beings formed a solid wall across the avenue. The crash of the cart had already called their attention to the little band, and a spiky hedge of weapons grew up suddenly before them.

"Bres wasn't taking any chances on our escaping," Lugh remarked.

"Ah, it's simple enough," the Dagda said, hefting his ax. "There are only a few of them. We'll just cut our way out."

But a roar from behind them caused them to look back. Up the avenue after them was charging a large mob of enraged Fomor warriors, brandishing an assortment of lethal implements.

"How nice of them to join us," Gilla said to the Dagda cheerily. "And isn't it a fine, fresh day for a bit of a run?"

The big Champion only shot him a dark look in reply.

"They look very determined," Lugh observed. "I think they might be upset."

"They're fast too," Aine added.

She was certainly right there. For all of their deformities and bulk, the Fomor were moving up the refuse-clogged street with tremendous speed.

Seeing their fellows closing in from the other side, the Serpent's Head Clan now began to move forward too. They would crush the little band between two walls of iron like a vise.

"Back to back," the Dagda said.

They paired off—Shaglan and Gilla, the Dagda and

Morrigan, Lugh and Aine—each two facing the enemies on a different side

"Well, that's it then," Lugh said with a warrior's stoic acceptance of death. "They've trapped us fairly this time. But we'll make a fine fight of it." He drew himself up in a good, heroic pose and set his young face in the grimmest lines he could. His voice was touched with regret as he went on. "I'm only sorry about us, Aine. I'd always hoped we'd have some time together after this was over. Some time when the two of us could have . . ."

"Oh, please, will you just be still?" she told him in a rather brusque way.

Startled by this harsh response, he looked around at her. She was standing in a strange, stiff attitude, head back, eyes closed.

"What are you doing?" he asked in bewilderment. "We *are* going to be attacked any moment, you know."

"Of course I know," she said tersely. "I'm calling some help for us. Now, let me concentrate!"

He had forgotten the power that Aine possessed. She could call to her and command nearly any beast with it. But what kind of animal could she call to help them there?

His answer came from the streets and buildings all around them. The sound was first: sharp, high-pitched squeals rising and joining into one piercing sound. Then they came into view, drawn from the filthy, choked alleys and the piles of trash by their mistress's call. They poured into the avenue from everywhere, forming a living carpet that rippled across the ground, an uncountable horde of huge, sleek, sinewy rats.

"Move close to me," Aine told her friends.

They don't need much urging to crowd in as the rats surged around them.

The attacking Fomor were caught by the flood before they could understand what was happening. Like sea waves, the torrent of rodents crashed upon them, over them. The small animals overwhelmed their hulking victims by sheer numbers and the savageness of their onslaught. They bore the warriors down, covering them with the rippling sea of their bodies.

Fomor thrashed and heaved desperately beneath, screaming in agony as hundreds of jaws tore at them. At one point a hand was thrust up from the squirming mass, fingers in tatters or chewed away, rats hanging by their teeth from the flesh of the arm, pulling it back down out of sight. Nearby a head appeared above the surface for a horrible instant, torn, eyeless, mouth round in a last cry.

Those Fomor who managed to get free of the rats fled in terror. The Serpent's Head Clan fought on most doggedly, but even their survivors finally quite the massacre. Suddenly, there was no opposition left in the avenue.

"I think we should go now," Aine told her companions, who watched the incredible scene with fascination and revulsion.

"What, just walk through them?" the Dagda said uncertainly.

"It'll be safe," she said. "They won't hurt us."

"You may say so," he said, "but I have to tell you, I've never much liked rats, and seeing this does very little to change my feelings."

"It's all right, really," she assured him. "Just follow me—and stay very close."

She led the way along the avenue, making her way through the billowing waves of rats. The animals fixed the little band with their dark, glittering stares as it passed by, only edging out of its way. Aine walked along quite calmly, but her companions crept along very gingerly, fearful of treading on a rodent by mistake.

Lugh looked around him at the scores of mounds the rats now were forming. Under each, he knew, a Fomor body lay. So fast did the voracious rodents strip the carcasses of flesh that he already saw the white gleam of bones among the pulsing, furry heaps.

He shivered inwardly and turned an appraising eye on Aine.

"Bres was right, calling you ruthless," he told her.

"It's not a thing I'm ashamed of," she replied frankly. "And you can't say you didn't know it of me."

He looked at that sweet, young, guileless face and then considered the brutal death she had administered so calmly.

"I knew it," he said. "I'm just not certain I wanted it to be true."

"And if I was your vision of the poor, pale, innocent girl," she returned, "you'd have been dead yourself many times before now."

At that he was forced to smile. She was certainly right.

They passed through the rest of the horde of rats and

reached the city's edge at last. No new bands of Fomor appeared to hinder them as they moved out into the open land beyond. They broke into a trot, headed back upward to the safety of the inland hills. Behind them the Fomor stronghold sank back to a patch beneath a filthy yellow haze.

"They escaped?" Bres ranted, fixing his glare on the hapless Fomor officer.

"They moved too fast, my King," the man said in excuse. "And they had powers! Those rats—"

"I don't want to know the details of your failure," Bres told him callously. "Once more these mindless vermin you call warriors have been defeated by that boy and his odd group of friends."

The officer was tempted to point out that Bres's own trap had been somewhat of a failure as well. But he prudently held back.

"Now they'll be warning Nuada that I plan to challenge the de Dananns again," Bres went on, half to himself. "They'll march on us here as soon as they can host. I'll have to act quickly."

"Act, my King?" the officer said in puzzlement. "How?"

Bres gave the man a pitying look. "You poor fool. You and the others would just keep on fighting until you were all destroyed. You don't realize that the Dagda was right. We are too weak to win or even survive another battle with the de Dananns. No, we'll need help to win, and I intend to get it."

This only deepened the officer's bewilderment. "But every Fomor in Eire is already gathered here! Where would you get help for us?"

"From the Tower of Glass," Bres said with great confidence.

The Tower of Glass! Those words had the intended effect on the officer. He repeated them in the hushed tone of reverential awe. The Blessed Tower. The place of purity and light that these creatures of Eire knew only from the tales of their elders. The Dwelling of the Powers.

"Why should they help us?" the officer asked. "They never have before."

"Because if they mean to see Eire held, they've no other choice," Bres returned. "I'll go to the Tower myself and tell them that. I'll bring them to support us, that I promise. Now, ready me a ship. There's no more time. I must sail for the Tower at once!"

*   *   *

In the hills above the city the band gathered to rest and make its plans. The seemingly limitless depths of Gilla's cloak supplied food and full skins of ale.

"It was a near thing, leaving that place alive," Shaglan said, shaking his head. He was now a large and very shaggy dog, an animal shape that pleased Aine and which he thus assumed often.

"It was nothing at all," Gilla said airily. "My plan worked as I knew it would. They always do."

"Your plan," said Aine, and laughed derisively. "We'd not have made it away without my calling in those rats."

"Of course not," Gilla readily agreed, grinning at her. "And that was part of my plan too, of course."

"You are entirely too sure of yourself, Clown," she scolded. "Someday you'll be brought up short by your own cleverness, and I hope to see it."

"Just so it doesn't kill us in the bargain," Lugh amended, smiling.

"Well, no matter what saved us, it's clear enough you would have died for certain if you'd gone alone," the Dagda told the young Champion. "It's good we didn't listen to you."

"I thank you for your friendship and your courage," Lugh replied sincerely. "And I knew it was dangerous to see Bres, but I had to try."

"When will you see that Bres cannot be treated as if he were an ordinary man?" the Dagda asked. "He's got the Fomor blood. He can't be changed. He's got to be destroyed."

Lugh shrugged. "Maybe. The choices are gone now, anyway. He's going to fight, and there are enough Fomor there to make it a hard battle. We have to send word to Nuada."

He looked to the silent, black-cloaked woman. "Morrigan, you must fly to him. Tell him to bring the army here at once."

She nodded. Her voice came dry and crackling. "I will go."

She rose to her feet, drawing the long, thin body stiffly up, unfurling the cloak to hold out like giant wings on either side.

An aura of light appeared around her, causing her outlines to shimmer, grow blurred, and finally disappear within the swelling blue-white glow. The brightness of the pillar of light grew to a near-blinding peak, then shrank down suddenly, concentrating into a small globe of brilliance. In moments this began to subside, revealing a new outline which resolved into a recognizable form as the glow faded.

A large blue-black raven now stood in the Morrigan's place.

"Tell Nuada we'll keep watch on the Fomor until the de Dananns come," Lugh said to it. "We'll join him at the Magh Turiedh plains just to the south."

The raven gave a sharp caw in answer and lifted the wide spread of wings. A few flaps lifted the body, the powerful strokes pulling it up and away from them until, in moments, it was soaring away across the sky, a rapidly dwindling speck.

Shaglan gazed after the Raven-Woman, then spoke with a grudging admiration.

"She flies well enough. Better than I do. But then, it is the only other form that she can take." He smiled around at the others. "More practice."

"Say, look there," Aine said, pointing down toward the Fomor city.

A Fomor sailing ship was now in view, making out of the city's harbor into the open sea.

"What's that about?" Lugh asked curiously.

The Dagda shrugged. "Just one of their fishing boats. Even the likes of those creatures have to keep eating."

But none of them noted the unusually grave expression on the face of Gilla the Clown as he watched the small vessel sail northward, shrinking out of sight.

Chapter Four
THE TOWER

The Fomor craft sailed steadily northward, making its best speed. Behind it, Eire had faded to a haze. Ahead, its destination was now in view.

It seemed to rise up from the waves as the ship approached. In the slanting rays of sunset, striking through the clouds lining the world's rim, it glowed crimson, like a blood-ied spearhead thrusting cruelly outward from the darkening body of the sea.

It was a tower, rising starkly, abruptly, from the sur-rounding level expanse to a height of over thirty stories. The four sheer walls that formed its sides appeared made of single sheets of polished glass which reflected the sea and sky and clouds with a mirror clarity, precisely and coldly.

As the ship swept in closer to its goal, more details of this massive structure became visible. At the bottommost few levels the glass gave way to walls of a smooth, gray-white stone. They formed a solid-looking foundation to anchor the bright Tower, like a candle's holder. And this base was itself firmly implanted in the barren, sea-scoured rock of a tiny isle, seeming almost to grow from it.

It was a startling and unexpected thing to find here, so near the soft, natural beauty and primitive life of Eire. It presented itself with arrogance, proudly alien, dominating the forces of the sea. It was indeed a fit dwelling place for power.

The ship from Eire circled the small isle to the westward side. There the ragged shoreline bent inward, forming a cove. The sea licked up to the stone base of the Tower. Large quays of the same stone were visible along the base, and a series of long docks thrust far out into the waters of the cove. At the docks, over a score of ships were drawn up.

They were several times the length of the arriving craft and twice its width. Their hulls were sleek, formed of a smooth black metal like polished iron. As they lay lined up along the docks, dully reflecting the sunset's glow, they looked like a row of weapons, like well-honed swords waiting to be lifted for a slashing blow.

The ship from Eire sailed on into the cove, heading for the quays. From its deck, hundreds of figures could now be seen swarming upon them. They seemed to be men, normal in size seen swarming upon them. They seemed to be men, normal in size and shape. But in dress they were far different from the people of Eire. There was no ragged Fomor dress, no de Danann finery or flashing jewels. All were clad alike in close-fitting trousers and tunics of a silver-gray.

Some of them worked at tasks upon the ships. Others moved materials in and out through three enormous door-ways in the Tower's base. So diligent about these labors were

they that even the ship's arrival caused only a few to interrupt their efforts to glance toward it, and then only for an
instant. The visitor lowered sail and slid into an empty berth
at the quays without the slightest show of welcoming or
excitement.

Bres didn't wait for the ship to be tied up or the gangway
run out. He leaped impatiently across the bulwark onto the
quay and started along it at a rapid stride, headed for the
nearest of the doorways.

He glanced up at the towering structure as he walked. Its
gleaming length loomed above him now, seeming to lean out
over him threateningly. From so close it was noticeable that
the glass surface of each side was not really a single sheet but
formed of enormous interlocking panels of a diamond shape
joined so finely that only a delicate, precise network of lines
was visible. From his angle this pattern seemed to overlay a
chilly reflection of a somber gray sky.

As Bres neared the doorways, a party of men appeared
from it. There were a dozen uniformed men in two files, led
by another who strode a bit ahead. The men in ranks, unlike
the others on the quay, were helmeted with skullcaps of a
dull silver and armed with sheathed swords and curious spears.
These last were heavy weapons with shafts as thick as a wrist
and large metal globes at the end in place of points. This
formidable party tramped purposefully down the quay toward
Bres with a hard, high-stepping march. Their leader called
them to a halt before him and drew himself to rigid attention
facing the visitor.

Bres stopped, eyeing the leader narrowly. He was quite
young, swarthy, with handsome but crudely drawn features,
like his men's. His officer status was proclaimed by the single
bands of silver about each upper sleeve. For his youth, he
had the disciplined bearing of one long trained, holding himself rigidly, his expression set in a soldierly impassiveness.

"Welcome to the Tower," he declared in a brisk, flat
tone. "We have been sent to give you escort . . . ah . . ." He
hesitated. A faint anxiety softened his iron look.

"You will address me as High-King," Bres supplied irritably. "Now, take me to Balor—immediately."

"Yes . . . High-King," the officer responded. "The Commander is waiting to receive you. This way please." He lifted
a directing arm.

"I know the way well enough," Bres told him brusquely, and pushed past, not awaiting their escort.

Taken off guard, the officer quickly ordered his men to turn and follow while he trotted off ahead in an effort to catch up with the swiftly striding Bres. But Bres was still leading them as they reached the first of the doorways and passed into the Tower.

They entered a space that was cavernous. The late sun cast a wedge of yellow light far into the room, making what lay beyond seem all the more dimly lit in contrast. The ceiling high above and the distant outer walls were lost in shadow.

The vast floor area was cluttered with materials of all sorts—boxes, barrels, sacks, jars, baskets, bundles—piled in mounds and ridges and mountains to create a bewildering landscape. And here and there amid the jumble, shrouded in cloth and shadows and the dust of ages, sat massive, indefinable but ominous shapes, like monstrous beasts crouched in hiding

The little column threaded its way through this mazelike place, finally arriving at a far corner. There an opening in the thick wall revealed a broad stairway. Not slowing his pace, Bres started up it, his supposed escort clattering loudly up behind.

The stairway took them around two sharp turns and up three flights before it brought them out into a long, blank-walled corridor. This they followed until it opened abruptly into a realm of stark white light.

They were now on the lowest level of the Glass Tower itself. The area they entered was the floor of an atrium that rose upward through the center of the entire Tower, a square, thirty-story column of open space, soaring away to a tiny dot of brightness high above.

Around this atrium ran galleries, level upon level, each lined by a rail of gleaming silver metal, each separated from the gallery above it by a band of smooth, spotless white wall. From bottom to top, each level was exactly the same, each of the precise, sharp-cornered, clean proportions as the next one above it, all forming a perfectly balanced whole. And all was lit with an even, hard glow of icy whiteness that seemed to come from everywhere at once and left no shadows.

On the atrium floor and the levels above, more hundreds of the uniformed men of the Tower swarmed, all apparently engaged in business of enormous urgency. Their expression-less faces, drained of human color by the uncompromising light, took on the dead grayness of their dress, giving them the look of graven-stone playing pieces moving on the board of a gigantic chesslike game.

In each corner of the atrium a large square column of the same unadorned white rose upward, connecting all the levels as if supporting them. Bres and his company started across the floor toward the nearest one, the visitor pushing his way aggressively through the bustling crowd from whom he drew only faintly curious looks.

Bres reached the column well ahead of the others and circled it to one of the inner sides. Here, a large door of the brushed silver metal was set into its surface. With an angry gesture he slapped at a small lever set in the wall beside it, and then glared expectantly at the door.

Nothing happened.

By now the officer and escort had caught up with him. A little breathlessly the young officer explained. "It's likely in use, High-King. The lifts can take some time to arrive."

This did nothing to pacify the visitor. He growled and slammed a large fist against the shining panel. Amazingly, this seemed to work. As if intimidated by the violence, the door flew up at once. It revealed a tiny room packed with Tower men.

They gave the scowling Bres sidelong glances of suspicion as they moved from the car past him, quickly dispersing into the crowd upon the floor. Bres stepped into the now-empty room, and the officer drew himself to rigid attention again.

"We will leave you here, High-King," he said with just a tinge of relief in his disciplined voice. "You will be met above. Just push the upper lever on your left and the lift will—"

"I know how the bloody thing works, boy!" Bres grated, and stabbed out with one finger at the topmost of a row of levers inside the door. The panel banged down before the officer's face and, with a metallic rattle and a little shake, the room lifted.

It rose through the hollow center of the column on thick cables pulled by a mechanism at the distant top. It slid upward along the shaft slowly and quite smoothly, save for an occasional shudder or protesting groan of machinery. Each of these, however, caused the publicly fearless Bres to blanch and glance around at the tiny, entrapping space uncertainly.

But his journey finally ended in a last, loud skreel of metal and a final jerk. The door again slid upward, and he found himself facing Sital Salmhor, a man whose many golden sleevebands proclaimed his exalted rank.

He was a fussily neat figure, round-chested, narrow-shouldered and thin-waisted, clad in a well-fitted and immaculate uniform. His features seemed carefully matched to his wedge-shaped face. The mouth was tiny and pursed, the nose long and flaring, the eyes set wide and topped by arching brows, raised now as he ran a chill and haughty gaze over his visitor.

"Well, Bres," he said in a prim voice, "so you did manage to survive again. How . . . nice."

"I survived," he answered curtly, "and no thanks to you for it. Now I mean to see Balor."

"He saw you sailing in," the other answered calmly, ignoring Bres's impatience. "He's waiting to see you."

"Is he now?" Bres replied in tones heavy with sarcasm. "Well, that's surely most kind of him. Take me to him then, and quick!"

The officer's look grew icy at that, showing openly his distaste for this uncouth visitor's commanding manner. Still, he obeyed, turning and leading the way, but at a stately walk that maddened Bres.

They crossed the gallery along one side of the atrium. They were at the very top of it now. Above was the ceiling, grown to a single huge panel of the white light. Beyond the silver rail was a long drop to the floor, shrunken in turn to a tiny square thirty levels below.

They reached a corner of the balcony and entered a hallway that led back from the atrium into the surrounding Tower. It took them into a narrow room, blank-walled and empty but for some rows of benches and a pair of helmeted soldiers who guarded huge double doors. At the approach of the two men they snapped to attention. Then, at the officer's signal, they moved briskly to pull the portals open, allowing Salmhor and Bres to stride on through.

The room they entered was another large one, three stories in height. Its outer walls, forming a corner of the Tower, were glass. Beyond them a gray curtain of hanging clouds was visible.

Upon a massive, square-edged throne set in the angle of the glass walls was a giant figure. It was human-shaped, though several times a man's size in height and girth. The form was completely sheathed in black metal armor, the hands were gauntleted, and the head was covered by a barrel-shaped helmet. Against the backdrop of the ominous sky the dark being seemed all the more formidable.

Bres was seemingly unimpressed by its appearance. He strode boldly toward it, stopping midway in the room to glare up at it challengingly, legs set wide as if for a fight.

The face he gazed into was a blank one. The black helmet was featureless except for a curved metal visor at the front, and this was down. The being was motionless, giving no sign or sound to acknowledge Bres's presence.

After a long moment's wait with no response Bres called out irritably, "Balor, I am here! I demand to speak to you right now!"

"You demand?" a voice clanged out from the giant like a hammer striking a shield of iron. "And who are you to demand anything from me?"

The visor rose a fraction, opening a hairline slit below the metal curve. But through this narrowest of apertures burst an incredible blaze of ruby light, flashing out in a beam that slanted down toward Bres, bathing him in its glow. The visitor was instantly soaked in sweat from the near-scorching heat that played about him. This power from just a fraction of the shuttered eye hinted at the vastness of the energy contained behind that lid.

Bres paled; his body grew taut with the discomfort, but he did not flinch. His own anger and need had given him the strength to keep up his defiance.

"Who am I? I'm the one who's kept the bloody de Dananns defenseless and in fear for all these years, that's who I am! I'm the one who's been risking my life to put down their uprising!"

"But you've failed, Bres," the hard voice shot back. "You have told us you would destroy them, yet your army was badly defeated at Tara."

"Army? Is that what you call that rabble of misbegotten beasts? I warned you that they'd have little chance if the de Dananns unified and regained their strength. You were supposed to help me. You were supposed to see to it that those Champions were stopped before they could organize the rest."

There was a long silence from the giant. When the voice spoke again, its sharp edge was dulled by a note of defensiveness.

"We attempted to stop them. We underestimated their strength. Lugh Lamfada and his companions have greater powers at their command than we had thought."

"Bloody right they do," Bres agreed. "So it's you who've failed in this as much as I." His arm shot up to point accusingly toward the crimson eye. "It's because of you that my forces have been thrown back. Now you've got to do something about it."

"You know that the resources of this Tower were not meant to be used in that way," Balor replied firmly. "It was up to you to control the de Dananns with the garrisons in Eire. This uprising should never even have begun."

"It never would have if you had let me destroy them when I wanted to, when they were weak," Bres countered. "But you refused. You wanted no confrontations. You wanted them just kept weak and passive. Well, they're not weak anymore, and they're surely not passive! And if you don't give me help—I mean real help—this time, Eire will soon be in their hands."

There was another long pause from Balor before he said flatly, "All right. Enough accusations. It's clear that we've both misjudged our enemies. It's time to see if our mistakes can be corrected. Salmhor, Bres, come with me. We must see Mathgen."

And the throne on which he sat began to move.

It pivoted to one side and rolled forward smoothly, leading the two men. They moved into a corridor that ran from the throne room to the open door of Balor's private lift. It was much larger than the one that had brought Bres up, and easily able to accommodate the Commander's massive form. He glided into it and the huge chair pivoted again, bringing him around to face the opening. After Bres and Salmhor had moved in beside him, he raised a gauntleted hand slowly from the chair's arm, shifted it forward, and depressed one of the controlling levers just inside the doorway. A shining metal door dropped down, a whining sound arose, and the room began to fall.

Balor's private lift slid down its shaft, the cables that lowered it humming and vibrating with the enormous weight they supported, the car clattering past level after level as it descended from the heights.

Helmeted soldiers guarding the lift access on a lower level heard the car descending, heard it squealing to a stop behind their particular door, and snapped to rigid attention as the door slid up. Closely followed by Bres and Salmhor, Balor rolled forth into another corridor, quite wide on this level, but with a ceiling barely high enough to allow the giant's passage.

Its only lighting was from banks of tiny, constantly changing light that clustered thickly upon both walls. Rows pulsed, columns flashed, lines ran in continuous, repeated sequences, or flickered randomly. Behind small, lighted windows of glass, wheels inscribed with complex designs whirled and rocked and spun.

Beyond the many open doorways they passed, more walls of light carried on secret rituals in the dimness of long rooms while tribes of square-cornered devices, squatting in row after row, answered with their own displays of light and supplied an eerie accompaniment to the dance with a constant symphony of hums and hisses, clacks and rattles. But none of this played to the benefit of any human audience. The rooms were deserted.

Balor's own nature was all the more emphasized in this surrounding, which suited him more than any human one. As he rolled forward, the shifting patterns of light flowed across the smooth metal of his body and reflected from the rounded helmet as if they were a part of him. The glowing red slit of the nearly shuttered eye seemed to draw a new intensity from this play of energy.

Ahead of them, another set of gleaming silver doors marked the corridor's end. And another set of the helmeted guards who flanked it snapped to attention at his approach, drawing their strange, globe-tipped weapons up across their chests. He rolled between them, the front edge of the throne driving into the doors, shoving them back.

He pushed through into a large, square room. Three of its flat walls were aglow with patterns of light. A fourth was blank and dark. Intricately constructed machines of polished metal stood about like a waiting company of armored creatures, appropriate pets for the likes of Balor. Though motionless, the shifting lights that glinted sharply from their assortment of appendages endowed them with a semblance of constant, jerky movement.

Balor glided past them, leading the two men toward the central feature of the room: a wide cylinder of glass that ran from floor to ceiling.

It was an enormous tank, brilliantly illuminated within by a round panel of glowing white at its top. The hard, clear glare fell upon the grotesque being that hung within the tank like a specimen of exotic marine life on display.

Chapter Five
METHGEN'S PLAN

But the being did not float there. It was suspended within a web of cables, tubes, and wires that seemed to grow from all parts of its body like tendrils, reaching out, intertwining, finally connecting it to a myriad of objects hung around it in the tank.

And it was no sea creature. Its limbs were bones thinly sheathed with a mottled, dead-white skin. Its head was a hairless skull with a stretched, parchmentlike covering that threw nose, cheeks, and chin into sharp relief. Still, the badly wasted form was recognizable as that of a man.

The tendrils that appeared to grow from him were, in fact, from the surrounding objects whose function it was to sustain his life. A metal shell encased his withered torso, pumping lungs that no longer worked alone. Tubes fed and drained fluids for a body unable to handle its own needs, and cables supplied the energy that urged the faltering organs to work on.

From bulbous objects embedded in the eyeless sockets, two more wires protruded, coiling up to a small box suspended above the head. As Balor and the two men drew near the tank, this box swiveled about, revealing a glowing circle of blue glass fitted at one end. This was directed toward the advancing trio like the stare of a huge, lidless eye.

At the same moment, the blank back wall of the room flashed into life.

A glowing haziness, like a fog lit by a full moon, filled the dark field. Then shadows appeared within it, wavering and undefined at first, but quickly taking on sharp outlines and vivid colors. In moments the blank wall had become a scene, an image of the three figures crossing the room as seen from the viewpoint of the staring blue lens.

The Commander rolled to a stop beside the tank, Bres and Salmhor on either side. Within the web, the skeletal being stirred slightly. The scarred gash that served it for a mouth began to move. But the voice issued from somewhere outside the cylinder of glass to fill the room, its breathless, sibilant tone made hollow by the device that artificially increased its volume.

"Greetings, Balor. I have been expecting Bres to visit us."

"He tells me that conditions in Eire are as you have foreseen, Mathgen," he replied. "We can regain control only by committing the Tower forces to a battle there."

Mathgen replied ominously. "I have always warned you to avoid just such a situation."

"Yes, yes," Balor returned, his voice an irritated rattle. "And until now we have managed to do so. But now there is no other choice if we mean to stop the de Dananns."

"Your arrogant confidence in the marvels of this Tower still blinds you," the other hissed. "I thought that by now you had come to fear Lugh Lamfada and believe in the Prophecy that he would lead the de Dananns in destroying your power."

"I fear nothing!" The iron voice cut in like a sword. "I have only come to believe that he could be dangerous. He has survived every attempt to destroy him. He has managed to begin this uprising and restore the de Danann strength. He has even managed to survive the full force of my eye!" The crimson glow behind the lowered lid flared at that memory. "I grant the possibility that he might cause some unnecessary damage to our forces. But his powers are only magic, as yours are, Druid. I am expecting *you* to find a way of dealing with him."

"There will be another dangerous enemy to deal with in Eire as well," Mathgen said. "Do not forget Manannan MacLir!"

"Manannan MacLir?" said Bres curiously. "The one who calls himself a sea god?"

"Yes," Mathgen answered. "He has been helping them for some time, I believe. A most intriguing being. I have been studying all the information that we have gathered about him."

The images on the wall behind the being wavered suddenly and then were blown away like clouds dissipated by a violent gust of wind. For Mathgen could use his sorcery and the vast technology of the Tower's creators to project far more than what the lens saw. He could create images from his own mind—or from the mind of anyone his magic let him probe.

Now he was forming a picture drawn from Balor's experiences. A soft green isle was appearing in the glowing haze. It grew clearer, larger, filling the wall. In its lush vegetation and its unspoiled naturalness, it was a place of striking contrast with the stark isle of the Tower.

"The legends about him call him a sea monster," Mathgen's hoarse rasp went on, "a dangerous and quite unfriendly being. He makes his home on this isle to the east of Eire, protected by a band of heavy fog populated with legions of deadly sea creatures. Yet, for some reason he chooses to secretly aid the de Danann cause, to come to Eire in a ridiculous disguise and risk himself for them."

"Disguise?" repeated an amazed Bres. "Who is this Manannan pretending to be?"

In answer, a new image formed upon the screen. It was of a lanky figure cloaked in a battered coat, a broad grin showing through a tangled mass of hair and beard.

"The Clown!" Bres cried. At first the revelation seemed impossible to believe, but then certain memories returned—of Gilla pulling the weapons from his coat, of Gilla holding off a dozen warriors with a display of extraordinary swordsmanship, of Gilla smiling inanely down at a mud-coated and defeated Bres. He realized the truth.

"Of course," he said. "He's always with that boy, always seeming so harmless, so awkward."

"He is a madman," Balor rapped out. "My last encounter with him convinced me of that."

"Perhaps. Or perhaps that madness masks a cleverness. And he is no charlatan. Though he seems to have few special powers in Eire, he does have great command over the forces of the sea. He could easily direct those forces against you."

"I would welcome another chance to match myself against him," Balor replied with assurance.

The lipless mouth twisted upward in a death's-head grin as Mathgen gave a faint cackle of laughter.

"Your confidence astounds me," he said, the wheezing voice taking on a mocking tone. "The last time he nearly destroyed you. Are you so certain you can defeat him now?"

"All right, Mathgen," Balor rumbled reluctantly. "MacLir could be a danger to us as well. That only means you must deal with them both. My forces must be able to sweep through the de Danann without risk."

"I can make you no promises about that," the wasted being replied. "I may have ways to remove these two from the fight, but Lugh Lamfada is protected by the Prophecy. So long as he chooses freely to be their Champion, I doubt he can be killed." The wheezing voice took on a more admonishing tone. "Listen to me, Balor! I tell you not to send your forces to Eire. It is not worth the risk."

"Not worth the risk?" Bres cried in anger and disbelief. "This is to save Eire, you bloody great insect. This is—"

"Silence, Bres!" the Druid said in a voice so deadly that the man of Eire fell silent. "You and your island are of little significance. It is the future of those in this Tower of Glass that must be considered. It can be a great future with great rewards. There is no reason to jeopardize it. I have another plan."

"No." Balor's reply was like a hammer stroke. "I will waste no more of our time with this sorcery of yours. Our reluctance to commit our forces to the fight has given the de Danann a chance to organize and restore themselves. More delay will only let them grow stronger. It is worth the risk to see them finished now. And you must help, Mathgen."

"Your mind is as unbending and mechanical as your form, Balor," Mathgen said contemptuously. "You will never understand the vastness of the supernatural domains. You can see only this sterile, frigid world of logic and machinery which your science has created."

"I understand that it is my machinery and my science that keeps you alive!" Balor retorted. "For that you must serve me!"

"Serve you!" the Druid managed to force out as if choking on the words.

There was a silence from Mathgen then. Salmhor and Bres expected it to end with a scathing response to the Commander's words. Instead, when the Druid spoke again, it was in a tone of acceptance, as if he had changed his mind.

"Very well, Balor. Take your forces to Eire. Perhaps it

will finally convince you that I speak the truth. I will do what I can to carry out your wishes."

"What will you do?" the dark giant asked.

"That knowledge is for me alone. My methods will come from my most secret skill in enchantments. I can tell you that knowing the Clown's true identity will be quite useful. Only Lugh and a very few de Dananns know he is MacLir. That will work for me. But I will need help. Bres, is your son Ruadan still loyal to you?"

"Yes," Bres assured him. "When I was captured in the battle at Tara, he helped me to escape."

"And is he still with the de Dananns?"

"I told him to stay with them in case his services should be needed by me again. No one suspects his true allegiance except perhaps his mother, Bridget. But she would never betray him."

"Good, for his services will be needed. With his help there will be no sea-god or Champion to keep the forces of this Tower from destroying the de Dananns utterly!"

"Then I am satisfied," Balor intoned. The red gaze shifted fractionally, coming to rest on the officer. "Sital Salmhor, you will pass orders to prepare the fleet for sailing."

"It will have to be soon," Bres put in. "Lugh and his bloody friends have discovered that we aren't planning to surrender. The de Dananns will not delay long in coming to finish us. They may be marching now!"

"Our captains must be ready to depart within one day," Balor ordered. "Have all the engines prepared and loaded aboard."

Salmhor's eyebrows rose sharply in astonishment.

"All of them, Commander?"

"All of them. And see that my own ship is readied as well. I'll be accompanying our forces to Eire."

"Yes, Commander," Salmhor acknowledged stiffly.

"As for you, Bres," Balor continued, the fiery eye shifting back to him, "you'll return to Eire and see that your companies prepare a secure landing place for us. Salmhor will accompany you. He will help you and provide a link to us."

Bres cast a sidelong hostile glance at Salmhor. The officer returned it with a small, chill, supercilious smile.

"Work together," the hard voice warned. "Make no errors in this!"

As soon as Balor and the two men had left his chambers, one of Mathgen's clawlike hands began to move.

The bony fingers curled inward very slightly, powered by all the strength left to the ravaged being. It was just enough movement to depress a switch fastened in the scarred palm.

In moments a smaller door in the rear corner of the room swung open, allowing four figures to enter. They strode to the glass column and lined themselves up before it.

They were soldiers of the Tower, thickly built, dark, large-featured men in the inevitable silver-gray. Their faces were hard, lifeless, and chill, as if they had been molded of lead. Only their eyes were alive, glowing with the same intense light of the lens that was Mathgen's eye, as if the souls of men no longer dwelt in these human forms, only the will of the creature in the web.

"You four have been trained to become my legs and my hands," the terrible voice rasped. "Now you will carry out a special task for me. Do you understand?"

Four heads nodded together.

"Then listen carefully. You will dress yourselves as de Danann warriors. You will go to Eire in one of their primitive sailing craft. You will enter the de Danann camp and contact a boy named Ruadan. With his help you will carry out my plan. Is that clear to you?"

Again the heads nodded in unison.

"Very good. Make *no* contact with Bres or Salmhor or any of the Fomor of Eire. After it is done, you will return directly here to me. Remember, great care must be taken in this. I want no interference! Balor wishes MacLir out of the way, and it will be done. But it will be done my way—and serve my ends!"

A massive object, its outlines masked by a covering of heavy cloth, rolled past Bres and Salmor. The hidden wheels on which it moved raised a din of clanking, like the rattle of swords on scores of iron shields, and this was accompanied by a deep, constant roar of the internal forces that propelled it.

Bres watched it pass with a look of irritation, as if the thing had been a cow plodding across his path. Then he strode on, ignoring the activity within the storage area. Hundreds of men were at work, shifting stores out onto the quays along with more of the strange vehicles. He was not about to reveal any of the awe he felt for all of this to the haughty Tower officer.

They passed out through one of the huge portals and onto the quay. The black ships there were being prepared for sea by their crews while other Tower men loaded supplies and weapons aboard them. Beside them on the quay a line of the shrouded vehicles was forming, their mysterious, hulking forms even more menacing in such a company. The combined low throbbing of their idling engines created a sound like continuous rolling thunder.

"How are your preparations proceeding?" Bres demanded as they moved along the quay past this line.

"We are exactly on schedule," Salmhor assured him primly. "Our ships will be prepared to leave by tomorrow night."

They stopped as a metal boom swung out from the mast of one of the black ships and over them, lowering heavy cables to rest upon the last vehicle in the line. These were quickly affixed to its body by a crew of men. The boom then ascended, the cables grew taut, and the vehicle rose from the quay. It lifted high enough to clear the warship's deck, then was swung inboard and lowered. More crewmen guided it to a resting spot, where the cables were disengaged.

"All of our machines are being brought out and loaded for this campaign," Salmhor said as the two watched this process. "I never thought that I would see such a day."

Bres detected a note of bleakness in the usually impassive voice.

"You don't approve of this, do you, Salmhor?" he said.

"You know my feelings, Bres. These machines have been carefully preserved for generations, to be used when the Tower moves to dominate the world again. They were not meant to be hazarded in campaigns to regain one island for a pack of defective and odious creatures."

Irritated by Salmhor's attitude, Bres wheeled on the officer.

"You really do amaze me, you and your bloody Tower attitude. I thought *I* despised the Eirelanders, but you're worse! I mean, they're your own people, your own blood, exiled by you because of some ancient malady, cast out from your 'perfect' Tower. They fight for you, work for you, supply you with materials and food, and you sit here in your ice mountain and look down on them as if they were flies swarming on a cow's hot dung!"

"Serving us is their function," Salmhor responded in a careless tone. "The preservation of the Tower, the protection of the pure blood, is the only thing of value. If all of them must be sacrificed to that end, it should be done." He turned to Bres. "It should have been done this time."

"Are you saying you disagree with Balor's orders?" Bres accused.

"Certainly not. Our Commander acts through necessity. You are the one who created that necessity. Now we are forced to rescue you."

"You're taking a great risk saying such a thing to me!" Bres warned.

"Am I?" the officer returned, unimpressed. "And how often have you assured us the de Dananns were weak, useless, unable to fight?"

"They have strength now," Bres countered. "And they have a fighting spirit I didn't expect to see in them."

"You sound almost admiring, Bres," Salmhor said, then smiled in a contemptuous way. "But then, I forgot you have their blood in you."

With that he turned and strode away. Galvanized by rage, Bres sprang after him, grasped his shoulder, and swung him forcefully around.

"Listen to me, you bloody, smirking prig! I'll take you with me because Balor wishes it. But I'll take none of your superior airs."

This outburst caused no ripple of concern in the officer's smug exppression.

"I am a soldier of the Tower of Glass," he answered smoothly. "My blood is pure. You are a mongrel, with the blood of those barbaric de Dananns in you. Destroying them won't change that. You'll never be one of us."

Before the outraged Bres could respond to that, Salmhor pushed away the restraining hand and gestured toward one of the nearby vessels.

"This is our ship, and the captain is waiting to sail," he said pointedly. "So, if you're quite through with this absurd argument, I think we should go aboard. You were in a hurry, I believe."

With that he turned and strode up the gangway into the ship. Bres stared after him a moment, fuming, before stomping up the gangway after him.

In moments the ship had cast off and was gliding across

the water of the little bay. Once clear of its sheltering rocks, a radiant white sail blossomed from the slender mast, and the sleek vessel soared gracefully away like a sea bird skimming low over the waves.

Not long after it had slid out of sight, four men emerged from the base of the Tower of Glass. They were clad in the tunics and bright cloaks of de Danann warriors. The hoods of the cloaks were up, shadowing their gray, immobile faces.

At a brisk pace they moved along the quay, passing the lines of dark ships and heavy equipment. Beyond them, a crude wooden fishing boat of Eireland was tied up, looking like a scruffy rat among a gathering of otters. The four men boarded quickly and put out to sea, headed toward the southern horizon . . . and the shores of Eire hidden just beyond its rim.

Chapter Six
THE FORCES GATHER

The meadows were like a soft black cloak studded with ornaments of bright gold. All across their gently rolling extent hundreds of fires sent up glowing yellow cones into the night.

These cheering blazes illuminated a scene of great activity. For the thousands of warriors of the Tuatha de Danann clans were gathered there, making their final camp and their last preparations for battle.

Around many of the fires, warriors were at their evening meal, the rich aroma of the stews and breads scenting the cool fall air. Others were at work, honing the blades of spear and ax and sword, seeing that shields and harness were in good repair. The martial sound of their clashing arms provided a sharp music to accompany the talk of fighting styles, weapons, and stragegy.

They were a handsome people, tall, lean, and naturally graceful in movement. Their features were long, slender, and elegant, the foreheads broad, the light eyes widely spaced. They wore their fair hair long—tied or fastened back at the neck in fighting. Their weapons matched them in their style, slender, finely made, but with no sense of frailness. With these gleaming weapons and their bright battle raiment, the warriors made an imposing sight in contrast to the ragged Fomor horde. In the firelight the brilliantly colored cloaks of the various clans made a shifting kaleidoscope of the entire camp.

On a small mound in the center of the army, a circle of timbers had been erected to provide an enclosure for the High-King. Another, larger fire burned within it, surrounded by the leadership of the de Dananns. Chieftains of the clans, Champions, High-Druids, and Chief-Bards sat upon rush mats and held their final council of war.

Among them were two of the Dagda's sons, two men who in looks and temper were as unlike as days in spring and fall. Angus Og was a bright, ruddy-faced, boisterous lad of a spirit with his father, ever of good will, ever ready to join in reckless adventures. But Bobd Derg, a Chief-Bard of the clans, was a lean, pale, and brooding figure, refusing to participate in this talk of war, glaring about at the others in sharp disapproval.

Beside High-King Nuada sat Findgoll, a High-Druid and most respected counselor. He was a tiny man, looking almost frail in contrast to the massive warriors. His head was large, making the face below the wide span of brows seem too small. A sharp chin and nose, shrewd little eyes, and a spirited temper gave him a foxlike air. On the king's other side and just behind him sat the Raven-Woman, Morrigan, silently watching the talk with glinting eyes. Wrapped in her black cloak, her body seemed to vanish against the dark, and her cadaverous white face floated there at Nuada's shoulder like a ghostly omen of the death that would come soon.

Their animated discussion of battle tactics was interrupted suddenly by the entrance of several figures through the opening into the enclosure. Nuada and the others looked up as the firelight revealed Lugh and his companions.

"My friends!" the High-King said, beaming with pleasure. He rose at once and moved to greet them along with Findgoll, Angus, and others of the company. But Bobd Derg hung back, not joining in as the arrivals were welcomed heartily and directed to spots opened for them at the fire.

"Have food and drink with us!" Nuada offered as they

seated themselves. "We were wondering when you would be joining us."

Lugh and his friends settled close to the High-King. Food and drink were passed to them, but the Dagda seized at once upon the latter, upending a great skin of ale to let the golden stream pour into the yawning chasm of his mouth.

Gilla eyed this performance critically. "Well, he's done for that lot," he said. "He'll never fill that bottomless well of his insides." He reached into his cloak—itself apparently bottomless—and hauled out another skin, which he passed to the others.

"You came here in good time," Lugh said. "We didn't expect you for another day. We've been scouting the Fomor army while we waited."

"Good!" Nuada said, much pleased. "What are they planning? How are they disposed?"

Lugh pulled a stick from the edges of the fire and sketched out a rough map in the dirt as he explained.

"There are some low hills just ahead. They slope down to the coastal plains. The Fomor are forming up their companies here, just to the east of their city. If we begin at dawn tomorrow, we will be upon them before midday."

"How strong are they?" asked Niet, one of Nuada's most trusted chieftains.

"Several thousand warriors," Lugh replied. "Bres has gathered every Fomor left in all Eire there. Even with the defeats we've given them, their numbers may be very nearly equal to ours."

"And with Bres driving the poor brutes, they'll likely fight until they're killed," Nuada said grimly, envisioning the forthcoming slaughter.

"It'll give us an interesting fight after all then," the Dagda said cheerfully, lowering the now-deflated skin. He peered around the fire. "Here, got any more ale?"

Reluctantly, the other chieftains passed along a second skin. Its contents were quickly following the first.

"You act as if you are eager for this bloodshed," a morose voice said. Bobd Derg sat forward, driven by his father's words to speak up for the first time. "There must be some way to end the violence, make a peace with them."

"By Danu, here it comes again," the Dagda said irritably.

"I know what you think, Father," the young Bard returned, not intimidated by the giant man. "But someone

among us must say this. Someone must remind us that we
came to Eire as a people of learning, of arts, and of magic,
who meant only to live in peace."

"For years our people believed that," the Dagda replied.
"It did nothing but sap away their will for fighting. They let
Bres and the Fomor frighten them into submitting to any
cruelty and giving up every bit of pride they had. Now that
they've finally proven themselves warriors and have nearly
battled their way to really winning Eire for themselves, you
want them to give it up?" He snorted derisively.

"I don't want them to give up everything else they have
been to become nothing but the crude, hard, and bloody
warrior that you are!" the Bard shot back, his lean body taut
and vibrating with emotion, his voice stretched to a high and
quavering note.

"Ah, it's ashamed I am to have such as you be of my own
blood," the Dagda said with disgust. "I want to hear no more
such coward's talk."

"No, no, my friend," Nuada said placatingly "He has a
right to speak, as we all do!"

The Dagda growled and snatched away the skin that
Gilla had finally gotten back and was lifting for a drink.

"Lugh, what are your feelings?" the High-King asked.
"You talked with Bres."

"Bres will never make a peace," the young Champion
said, shaking his head. "So long as the Fomor follow him,
he'll try to destroy us and take Eire for himself."

Nuada looked around the circle at his counselors.

"And the rest of you. Are there any more here who
believe we should not fight tomorrow?"

There were vehement denials from the gathering.

"We are ready to fight, Nuada," spoke up another chieftain named Febal. "Our warriors are eager for it."

Nuada nodded and rose. His voice took on a hard note of
finality.

"Then at dawn we will march. And with the strength and
courage of our warriors, tomorrow will see us masters of
Eire and free of the Fomor tyranny at last. Now, let's be
going to the clans to see that all preparations have been
made."

The circle of men rose too and began to make their way
out of the enclosure. Nuada looked to Lugh and his companions.

"There's no need for you to go with us," he said. "It's

enough you've done already. Stay here and rest a bit. We'll return soon and we can talk."

"I'll go with you," the Dagda answered. He shook the third skin and dropped it upon the ground. "There's nothing to do here."

He pulled up his huge bulk and, joined by his son Angus, moved off, apparently unaffected by enough ale to lay flat a dozen men. As they went out, Angus was eagerly demanding details of the adventure in the Fomor city, which the Dagda supplied in his dramatic, highly colored way. Morrigan also joined the High-King's company, fading into the darkness beyond the enclosure's doorway.

Bobd Derg was the last to go, watching the others pass, then turning to cast a final, dark look at Lugh before following the rest out.

"I don't agree with Bobd Derg's feelings," commented Lugh, looking after the melancholy Bard, "but I do admire his courage for facing the Dagda. I'm not certain I could."

Gilla lifted the flat skin and contemplated it sadly, as if it were a pet that had died, then stowed it back inside his coat. He said nothing.

Shaglan moved away and stretched himself out against the log wall of the enclosure. Very soon he was asleep. Aine moved closer to Lugh and they fell into a quiet talk. But Gilla didn't join in. He sat with his long legs crossed beneath him, elbows on his knees, chin resting in the cup of his hands, staring into the fire.

After a time Lugh noted his silence and the abnormal somberness of his expression. He nudged Aine and nodded toward the Clown. She looked, then shrugged, unable to guess what might be troubling him. Bothered by his friend's curious state, the young warrior was finally moved to speak to him.

"Gilla, what's wrong with you tonight? I don't think I've ever seen you in such a serious mood."

This seemed to draw the Clown from his trance. He shook his head but continued staring into the fire as if seeing some disturbing image there.

"I don't know," he said slowly. "I feel a great . . . mortality tonight. It's a feeling I've not had before."

He looked around suddenly at Lugh, his gaze holding the young warrior's, his voice taking on an urgent note. "Tell me, lad, that you'll continue to be Champion of the Sidhe until the Prophecy's fulfilled, no matter what it means!"

"You know I will!" Lugh answered, puzzled by this request. "Why would you even need to ask me that?"

"I just have a need to be certain in my mind that whether or not I'm about, you'll carry on."

"Whether or not you're about?" Lugh repeated, more confused. "And why wouldn't you be?"

"This isn't over yet, young friend. Anything can happen, even to me."

"If anything did happen to you, Gilla, I'm not certain what I'd do," Lugh told him, much sobered by his fatalistic talk. "You've helped me from the start, showed me what to do—"

"Ah, no, lad," Gilla said, stopping him, "you must never think that way. It was your own will that brought you here and your will that takes you on. You are the Champion. Just remember that so long as you follow your own heart, you'll know what you must do."

Aine, by this time, had had quite enough of the Clown's somber mood. "This is all ridiculous!" she said firmly. "We've come through everything up to now. Why should that change?"

Gilla regarded her with that same gravity.

"None of us, not even Queen Danu, with all her powers, can know what will come. Fate and feelings, chance and nature and human will all take a hand, and none has power over any of the rest. You remember that—and you stay very close to our young warrior."

He shook himself then, as if putting off some heavy cloak, and smiled—only a ghost of his usual grin—through his beard.

"Don't be taking the poor old fool too seriously," he said. "I'm just no good tonight. Maybe I'm getting a bit too old for such adventuring. It's time for a rest. A long rest."

He unwound his legs and climbed to his feet, stretching his lanky form. "I'll leave you two and take a walk around, I think. Maybe the high spirits of this lot will give a lift to mine." He headed for the enclosure's opening. "See you in a bit."

Lugh called, "Take care!" after Gilla as he ambled out, then turned to Aine. "He's gloomy enough. Do you think he's worrying about the battle tomorrow?"

She was still looking after him, her smooth face pinched by a worried frown. "I don't know. I've never known him to be the least concerned about a fight. He's always welcomed them. I think it's something else. It worries me."

She turned to him, her face close to his, her eyes shining with intensity, her words sharp with alarm. "Lugh, I think he really feels something is going to happen. Maybe he's had some premonition, about himself or"—she hesitated, then forced it out—"or one of us."

Lugh laughed at this, replying with that fearless certainty of youth. "Of course not! We've survived so much, we've got to survive the rest. You told him that yourself! Nothing can harm us."

"No!" she said fiercely, gripping his arms so tightly, he almost winced. "Don't say that, Lugh. We only think it's true because we've been so lucky. The one great fear I've had is that you might die before this all is ended, that your death might be some part of this awful destiny you are playing out."

He laid his hands upon her shoulders, the bravado gone now as he replied.

"I've feared your being harmed too, Aine, more than I've ever feared for myself." She opened her mouth to protest, but he went on, nodding in agreement with what he knew she would say. "I know. You'd never let me keep you from the fighting, and I'd never try. You're as much a warrior as I am, and as much a part of this. Still, there would be a great aching void within me if you were to be taken from me now."

"I know," she told him, and slid forward suddenly, throwing her arms about him, pulling herself close. He responded. Her head dropped back, her face rose to him, and he lowered his to meet her in a long kiss whose ardor rather surprised the young man.

Finally, short of breath, they pulled apart, though still locked in a close embrace. He started to speak, but stopped and coughed to clear the thickness from his voice before going on.

"Aine, we can't let this time go. We have so little together. If something were to happen, how could we let it all pass without . . . without . . ."

She shook her head. "No," she said, beginning what he expected to be a denial. "No, we can't."

"I understand," he began. "This isn't the time, the place, or—" He stopped abruptly, realizing what it was she had just said. "Would you say that again?"

"We can't let this time pass," she told him. "You're right."

His face lit up. "You mean, you want to . . ."

She laid back against a pile of sleeping furs beside the fire. "Yes," she said softly.

A wealth of impressions now combined to form one sensual image in Lugh's mind. The softness of the woman's skin glowing in the warm firelight against the plush, dark richness of the furs. The background of lances, swords, and shields stacked against the enclosure's inner wall, glinting with a bright beauty of their own.

He glanced over at the dog.

"What about Shaglan?" he asked.

"Never mind. He's asleep!" she answered impatiently. Then she lifted her arms toward him in invitation, speaking in a voice blurred by passion. "Lugh, don't wait. There isn't time!"

He needed no further urging. He moved forward, dropping down beside her. His arms slipped around the slender, yielding body and he pulled her close, feeling her against him, responding to his touch. He pressed his lips to hers again, this time with a youthful ardor fully unleashed. Her arms tightened around his neck.

"Well, the warriors are ready for some fighting, sure enough!" the Dagda bellowed, striding into the enclosure and letting a load of weapons drop to the ground with a tremendous clatter.

The young couple jerked upright at his entrance and looked toward him, brightly flushed with passion, embarrassment, and, in Lugh's case, more than a bit of irritation.

In behind the Dagda came Angus Og. This clever lad understood at once what they had interrupted. He smiled knowingly.

"Say, Father," he said, "I think that we . . ."

The Dagda ignored him, striding to the fire. He dropped his arm, letting the head of an enormous battle-ax fall to the ground between Lugh and Aine, the glinting edge slashing deep into the sod.

"What do you think of that, eh?" he asked with pride. "Goibnu the Smith made it for me. The finest metal, the finest work, and an edge that would take off a man's head so cleanly he'd not miss it till supper!"

The two looked up at the huge form looming over them, his big, weathered face split by a childish grin of delight at his new toy.

"Very nice," Lugh remarked with a singular lack of enthusiasm.

"What a weight it has!" the man went on ecstatically. "And what balance!"

He lifted it in one hand, swinging it about. The flat blade raised a wind and a *fwoomp*ing sound in its passage, flashing close over the heads of the pair. Then he abruptly tossed the weapon aside and dropped down by the fire, arms on knees, beaming at them.

"And how about you two? All ready for it then? I know you must be excited about tomorrow too. I can see the battle flush on you already. Can't wait, can you?"

Lugh glanced at Aine. She was clearly fighting not to laugh outright.

"I can't think of anything that would excite us more," he answered wryly.

Chapter Seven
DISAPPEARANCE

A nearly full moon broke from the shelter of a towering mountain of clouds, casting a chill glow across the dark expanse of sea, flecking the wave tops with light, throwing the troughs into blackness . . . and revealing the foaming wakes of a score of ships moving in exactly spaced formation toward the south.

The ships that drew these neat white lines across the surface were themselves almost invisible in the darkness. Their sleek black hulls, which sliced so cleanly through the waves, gave off only the faintest sheen, and the billowing, luminous sails that had swept them across the sea from the Tower were now lowered, for the coast of Eire was in sight. Like a pack of hunting beasts, the ships stole in upon their unknowing prey, powered by the forces throbbing deep within their hulls.

In the center of this formation moved a ship of much greater size than the others, both in its length and beam. In

its sharp prow a captain of the Tower stood, gazing toward
the dark line that marked the coast, intent upon a tiny point
of light that flickered there. He nodded with satisfaction and
turned toward a second officer at his side.

"That signal beacon marks our landing point," he said
briskly. "See that we remain on an exact course toward it."

"I will, my Captain," the other promised.

With this the captain turned and made his way back
along the deck. He had to move with some care, for the wide
expanse of metal was crowded with Tower soldiers. He stepped
over the legs of several dozing men, edged past another,
methodically inspecting the mechanism of his heavy crossbow, then went on through groups of others talking quietly or
giving their own weapons a final check. Unlike the de Dananns,
these men showed no sense of excitement or anticipation for
the coming fight, and there was no sign of fear in their well-
disciplined, set faces.

Toward the stern, the captain moved around a small,
square structure where a helmsman worked at the complex
array of devices that controlled the ship. He paused to repeat
his orders before going on.

Behind the steering-house he mounted low steps that
led him to a higher platform filling the wide stern. There the
massive bulk of Balor loomed above him.

"Commander, we are nearly to the coast on an exact
course to the landing point," the officer announced. "It is
visible ahead."

High above, in the dark mass that was the giant's head, a
light appeared, a curve of bright crimson like a sun breasting
the world's rim. The metallic voice replied: "Very good,
Captain. Have you received word on the de Danann forces?"

"Sital Salmhor has signaled us that Fomor scouts place
the de Danann army just to the south. They could attack as
early as tomorrow morning."

"Then the transport ships go in tonight. Have the machines unloaded as soon as possible."

"In the dark, Commander?" the captain asked, considering the logistics of such a feat.

"Have it done, Captain," Balor's voice clanged sharply.
"If the de Dananns arrive tomorrow, we must be ready to
deal with them and it must be a complete surprise."

"And yourself, Commander? Will you go ashore?"

"I will stay with the fleet until the battle is well joined.

Our ships must be kept far off shore until then. We cannot risk being seen."

The barrel head shifted, the red gaze coming to rest on the dark line of Eire's coast. The voice was lowered to a distant rumbling, as if Balor spoke only to himself.

"We *will* be ready. Now, it is only Mathgen's part in this that must be carried out." And the glow behind the lid flared brighter.

Firelight flashed sharply from the blades of the half-dozen daggers that Gilla the Clown juggled casually. His effort, coupled with his seemingly awkward movements, kept his audience in constant expectation of disaster. A large crowd of warriors had gathered from the surrounding fires, taking a bit of release from their talk of war in the lanky man's antics. They laughed and cheered with gusto as he staggered about, apparently keeping the deadly blades aloft only by luck.

With a flourish Gilla finally concluded his little act, the daggers flipped high, one by one falling into the baggy sleeve of his coat to disappear. The last he flipped up to balance for a moment on the tip of his jutting nose before whisking it away.

They urged him to go on, but he smiled and shook his head.

"Sorry, my lads, but I've got to be movin' on, so I do. Lots more to visit. But all good fortune to you tomorrow."

They gave him a reluctant but friendly farewell in return, and he ambled off, meandering through the camp, past the many fires and the busy crowds of warriors.

He was feeling in a more cheerful mood now. Mixing with these young men, doing his tricks for them to amuse them, had raised his own spirits. The old Gillaish grin had quite returned.

Soon in his wanderings he had reached an area where temporary forges had been set up. Here the smiths were at work, and would be through the night, making certain that every warrior of the army was properly equipped for the coming fight.

Some were shaping fine, slender spearpoints while others sharpened the thin, graceful curves of the longswords, or fit smooth wooden hafts to the lances. More were repairing or fashioning shields with heavy metal rims and layers of thick hide, or binding on sword hilts with rivets.

Gilla stopped to watch, especially intrigued by the master smiths who hammered out the finest weapons.

Goibnu, the chief smith, used his skills in shaping metal to hammer out a blade in moments, his blackened face fierce in concentration, eyes glowing like the coals of his forge.

Beside him Bridget wielded her hammer with a skill and speed that nearly matched Goibnu's. But she was master of many other skills, a renowned poet and miraculous healer of the sick and wounded as well.

Her face was curious, being divided into two very different halves. One side was that of a lovely woman, fair, soft, and smoothly drawn. The other was that of a hag, coarse-featured, skin creased and dried like ancient leather. Among the de Dananns, it was said that some accident had marred her, though the two faces seemed to match the two sides of her skills. No one knew that they also matched the cruel conflict that existed within her soul, the conflict she felt as a result of keeping the secret of Ruadan's true parentage from the de Dananns.

As Gilla loitered, watching the smiths, a young boy approached him somewhat timidly.

"Gilla Decaire?" he asked hesitantly.

Gilla looked around to see a youth whose innocence fairly beamed from his round, pale face. His beardless cheeks were thick with freckles and his head topped with a tousled mass of bright red curls.

Gilla knew the boy. He was often hanging about Nuada, acting as his aide. He seemed a fine, hard-working, if somewhat overanxious, youth. Gilla even managed to recall his name: Ruadan.

"What is it, lad?" Gilla said, smiling warmly. "You needn't be shy. I'm harmless enough."

"I've been seeking you all evening," the boy went on, more courageously. "Findgoll the Druid's wanting to see you. He says it's very important. Something to do with one called Manannan MacLir, he says. Only you can help with it."

The use of the name brought the Clown's attention at once. Findgoll was one of the few who knew his true identity. What he needed must be important indeed to have this boy mention it.

"All right, lad. Don't worry, I'll come," he assured the concerned youth. "Just take me to him."

The two walked quickly away from the forges—while behind them, Bridget stopped her work to watch, her eyes narrowed in concern.

Gilla climbed the high hill to the west of the camp, trying to keep up with the briskly moving Ruadan while not tripping in the darkness.

Near the top of the steep slope he paused and glanced back toward the camp. It seemed quite distant now, only a scattering of lights across the plain below. He looked up toward the thick darkness cloaking the hilltop.

"Is it so far out here that he wants to meet me?" he asked in some puzzlement.

"Aye, aye! It is!" Ruadan said in his best eager-puppy manner. "He told he you'd not want the others in the camp to know."

That was a logical enough precaution, Gilla decided. He shrugged acceptingly and clambered on in the boy's wake. A final effort brought them over the hill's crest.

It was topped, he found, by a dense knot of foliage, a little grove of trees and brush that showed as a dark fringe against the night sky. Ruadan led the way to a small break in this solid-looking mass and gestured with his arm.

"It's through here, sir. There's a little sheltered spot just inside where Findgoll's waiting."

Gilla moved past him, pushing into the bushes. They closed in behind him, and their darkness seemed to swallow him.

Young Ruadan waited a few moments, but heard and saw no more of the lanky Clown. A malicious smile twisted his innocent face into a chilling mask.

"That's one," he said, gloating over the ease of his victory. "Now for the other."

The camp had at last settled into sleep. The many fires had been banked against the morning. Save for the patrols walking the perimeters of the camp, the warriors slumbered in their wrapping cloaks.

In the High-King's enclosure, Lugh and his companions were at rest as well. But the young Champion's slumber was abruptly cut short by a whisper close beside his ear.

"Lugh Lamfada!"

He jerked up, a hand dropping instinctively to the hilt of

the sword that lay beside him. But in the faint light of the fire's embers he saw that it was only the boy Ruadan who crouched over him.

"What do . . ." he began, but stopped as the boy made an emphatic gesture for silence.

"Please, be quiet," Ruadan whispered. "You must come with me now. Gilla Decaire must see you. He said it is for the sake of Manannan MacLir." Ruadan leaned closer, whispering in even more urgent tones. "You must come quickly and you must come alone!"

The use of the Clown's true name was enough to convince Lugh. He cast a searching gaze about the fire. All the others were still asleep, all unaware of Ruadan. He looked longest at the peacefully sleeping Aine. The notion of telling her crossed his mind, but he pushed it away. Gilla had said alone, so alone he must go.

Silently, he arose and, taking up the Answerer, followed the boy out of the enclosure. They made their way cautiously through the camp, past the outer guards and up the slope of the hill to the west.

"He told me he must see you in secret," Ruadan explained. "He wanted none of the others to know. I was to see only you. He'd tell me nothing of what he wanted, but he said it was of a deadly importance."

Lugh listened in puzzlement as he followed Ruadan. It was odd: Gilla had given his true name to this boy and sent him on such a sensitive task. Still . . . the lad was right hand to Nuada, son to Bridget, well liked, and trusted by everyone. If Gilla needed a messenger, Lugh decided, then the boy seemed a fair choice.

It was with these rationalizations that he quieted his doubts and arrived with Ruadan atop the tree-crowned hill.

"Through here," Ruadan said, indicating a gap in the bushes. Lugh paused, then with a last shrug stepped forward, pushing through a screen of brush, and found himself in a small clearing.

He stopped there, for an instant frozen in amazement at what he saw before him.

In the center of the clearing Gilla Decair stood stiffly, seemingly embedded in a glowing column of blue-white ice!

It's a trap! Lugh realized, his hand flying to the Answerer. But before his fingers could close upon its hilt, a circle of light exploded in the ground beneath him, while another flared into being just above his head. From each streamed a sapphire glow, surrounding Lugh, joining together in a single tube of light that sealed him inside. He tried to battle free, but it closed around him in an instant, and it was like chill liquid turning to ice as it touched him, freezing his body, numbing his limbs, his flesh, his mind.

He felt consciousness slipping away and could do nothing to stop it. He fell into the heart of the fire of ice, and the sapphire flames consumed him.

From the darkness beyond the clearing four men moved in about him, their emotionless expressions made frigid by the blue glow from the column, their staring eyes glinting like ice.

Outside the grove of trees, Ruadan saw the flare of blue light within. It was done. He turned back toward the sleeping camp, his face twisting into a cruel smile of satisfaction. Now his father's army of Fomor would have no mighty Champion and no mystic Riders of the Sidhe to face. By the following night the Tuatha de Danann would be no more.

The rising sun was a swollen circle of pale white as it floated up from the east through a sea of heavy clouds. Its hazy light revealed the de Danann army, well involved in the process of breaking camp.

On the army's northern edge, Nuada stood in deep discussion with the Dagda and his son Angus. They were forming a van of the best companies, and the two older warriors were each hotly defending his own ideas of strategy.

Nearby, Morrigan sat on a cart's edge. With her long legs drawn up and her cloak about her she seemed more than ever like a great battle-raven. Dark eyes glinting with the expectation of the approaching carnage, she watched the warriors about her, nostrils flaring, as if she could already scent the hot blood.

Aine, with the dog-shaped Pooka trotting at her side, approached the little group. The men ceased arguing as she reached them.

"Ah, there you are!" said Nuada heartily. "We're nearly ready to move. We'd begun wondering where you'd gotten to." He looked beyond Aine and then back in a puzzled way. "Where's Lugh?"

"Aye. We figured he'd be with you for certain!" Angus said playfully, giving her a sly wink.

"I don't know where he is," Aine said. "I hoped he'd be with you. I can't find him, or Gilla either. I've been looking through the camp for them without luck. No one's seen either of them since last night. Have you?"

"Not I," said Nuada. He looked around at the others. "Any of you?"

The rest shook their heads in denial.

"Ah, don't be fretting about that pair," Angus said lightly. "You know what they're like. That Clown's always taking Lugh off on some strange notion. They'll turn up soon enough."

Aine knew that he was right. Gilla had more than once disappeared with no explanation to her, and Lugh had gone on dangerous missions, purposely leaving her behind. Still, she was angry. She had thought she had broken them of such foolishness. If they had done it again, Aine swore to herself, then the greatest danger they might face would be when they came back.

"Tell me, Shaglan," she asked the Pooka, "would you be willing to bite someone for me?"

"Let it go, Aine," the Dagda advised. "Likely they're just doing a last bit of scouting ahead. If they don't—"

But he was interrupted by a young warrior who now rushed up to them, panting hard, face flushed by excitement.

"My King!" he said breathlessly. "A large force has been seen moving toward us rapidly from the southwest. Hundreds of warriors!"

"Angus, alert the chieftains!" Nuada ordered. "The rest of you, come with me!"

At a run they moved around the camp to its southwest edge. There they found the warriors in that sector of the camp had already formed a large crowd and were gazing off across the plains. Some were pointing, and a murmur of speculating voices rose from them. Some shifted about, gripping their weapons uneasily.

The High-King and his companions pushed through to the front. They stepped into the open ground beyond and looked off toward the subject of all this intense interest.

A large body of men was moving across the plains toward them. They were in a tightly packed, wedge-shaped formation, point toward the de Dananns. That they were warriors was clear from the constant sparkle of light from their weapons and the faint but distinctive rattle of metal arms as they moved.

They were coming on at a quick and steady pace. As they drew nearer, their physical details became clearer. These were not Fomor, though they were massively built men, thick and dark. They were crudely dressed in furs and skins. Most had flowing mustaches and thick, long hair in loose braids. The weapons they carried were of a crudeness and size appropriate to the men. They presented quite a fierce and formidable appearance as they advanced like a herd of charging bulls.

"Firbolgs!" growled the Dagda, and his big hands tightened about the handle of his battle-ax.

For the Firbolg clans of Eire were longtime bitter enemies of the Tuatha de Dananns.

Chapter Eight
OLD FRIENDS

Though de Dananns and Firbolgs had been related in the distant past, events had separated them and made them rivals for control of Eire. Despite efforts on both sides to make peace, the treacherous Fomor had maneuvered them into war and in a final, bloody battle, the savage Firbolgs had met defeat. They had withdrawn their clans into the wild coastal areas of Eire and remained hostile to the victorious de Dananns, refusing their offers for a settlement. And soon after, with Bres's help, the much-weakened and war-weary de Dananns had themselves fallen easily under the ruthless domination of the Fomor.

"What in the sacred name of Danu do they want here now?" Nuada asked.

"I've not seen so many since the last battle of Magh Turiedh," said the Dagda grimly

"Could they be in league with the Fomor?" wondered Angus.

"They surely look ready for a fight," the Dagda answered. "We'd best be ready to give them one."

He lifted his ax into fighting position. All through the de Dananns massed behind them, weapons were being raised.

"We must shift our warriors into battle line," Nuada said. He turned to call out orders to the chieftains behind him.

But Aine had moved forward from the rest and peered intently at the Firbolg army. Suddenly, she whirled and cried out: "No! Wait! I don't think they're here to fight us!"

Nuada and the others exchanged puzzled looks.

"What do you mean?" he demanded.

"Look!" she told him. "See who's leading them!"

They did look again, this time focusing on the point of the great wedge. The Firbolgs were now close enough for individuals to be clearly identified. They were all bright-cloaked chieftains or clan shamans in their gaudy, feathered robes. At the very tip, beside a rotund shaman, strode a woman in a warrior's dress. She was of middle age but still quite handsome, boldly featured, strongly but not thickly built, with a braid of wiry gray-black hair. She moved with the proud assurance of a leader, and the golden torc of a chieftain was about her neck.

"Taillta!" the Dagda bellowed in pleasure and surprise.

Aine was already beaming with joy. She had never thought to see the Firbolg woman again.

Taillta was the daughter of MacErc, a powerful chieftain of the Firbolgs, and foster mother to Lugh. Not long ago she had returned to her people, determined to bring them peace—and a reunion with the de Dananns. Aine and Lugh had feared for her survival.

As she and the Firbolg army closed to within a spear's throw of the de Dananns, she lifted a hand. At once orders to halt were shouted back through the force and it slowed to a stop. For a long, uneasy moment the two hosts of warriors faced each other with the natural suspicions of longtime adversaries. Then Taillta strode forward, accompanied by the round shaman and a party of chieftains.

"Come, High-King," urged Aine. "We must go out and meet her."

Nuada allowed Aine to lead him forward. The Dagda, Morrigan, Angus, and Shaglan fell in behind.

Though the others stopped just short of easy sword-thrust range, Aine continued forward, hands stretched out in welcome. A broad smile came to Taillta's face.

"Aine!" she said, clasping the young woman's arms. "It is good to see you."

"We hoped you would come back to us," said Aine, "but we didn't know you'd bring all the Firbolg tribes with you."

"I've convinced them that the Fomor are as much our enemy as yours," Taillta explained. "They've decided—with only the gentlest bit of coaxing—that we must fight together."

Hearing this, Nuada moved forward to join them.

"Do you mean that you've brought these warriors to fight *with* us?" he asked, looking over the mass of hard men.

"We have been enemies too long," she told him. "My father and Lugh's father, your own Champion Cian, were friends. They wished our people to live together in Eire as equals." Taillta gazed into the High-King's eyes. "Tell me this wish is held by you and by the de Dananns, Nuada, and we will be allies."

"It is," he said firmly. "Since first we came to Eire we've wanted nothing more than to share in peace."

"Then when this battle is ended, do you pledge to a fair settlement?" she asked.

"I do," he promised, putting forth his hand.

Taillta took it in a strong grip. "Then we join you now as fighting companions—and may we soon become friends and brothers as well."

The Firbolgs raised a cheer of acclamation at this sign of accord between the two leaders. The Dagda moved forward to give Taillta his own hearty greeting and add his approval to this new bond.

"The Firbolg warriors are the finest I've ever faced," he told her. "It will be an honor to fight beside them this time."

"We have no time for celebrations now," Nuada said. "Taillta, the Fomor wait just ahead. If we mean to strike at them this day, we must move now."

"We've marched day and night to reach you in time," she said grimly.

"How many warriors have you?"

"Two thousand."

"Good," he replied. "They are all sorely needed. Can you draw them up on our western flank? We are nearly ready."

"I will," she agreed, and passed orders to her chieftains to re-form the wedge to the north. Nuada set his own warriors back to make final preparations for the march.

Taillta scanned the faces of the de Danann warriors about them and then turned to Aine.

"Where is Lugh?" she asked in puzzlement. "I thought I'd see him with you."

"He seems to have gone off with Gilla somewhere," Aine said, her irritation recalled. "On another of their little adventures, Angus says. I don't know whether to be angry or concerned."

Taillta only laughed. "They'll never change. But you know as well as I that wherever they are, they'll be back with us before the fighting starts. There are no others I know of who can take care of themselves so well as that pair!"

Had Taillta seen the pair at that moment, she would have realized just how wrong that statement was.

Lugh and Gilla, embedded in their tubes of blue-white light like fish frozen in a winter's pond, stood buried in the sand of a beach not far away.

Though totally immersed in the chilling medium, Lugh Lamfada was alive and conscious. He felt as if he had been submerged in an icy pool and forced beneath its frozen surface, though there was no sensation of drowning, of fighting for breath, only a numbness in his body. He seemed to be thinking all right. Quite as usual, in fact. And his eyes seemed to work, even if his gaze was locked in one direction and his vision clouded by a watery glow.

He could still see the cylindrical ice coffin of Gilla just in front of him, and the Clown within frozen in an attitude of alarm, hand on his sword hilt, mouth open, eyes wide. In fact, he decided, his friend's position was exactly the same as his own: they had clearly been caught in the same way.

And just as clearly, the Clown was alive, awake, and staring out of his own ice prison, unable to act.

Men moved about him, although Lugh could only see them as they passed through his narrow field of vision. They were heavy, somber-faced men, clad in the dress of de Danann warriors, but they seemed more like Tower soldiers.

Beyond Gilla he could see a small sailing ship drawn up to the beach. The men were making preparations of some kind aboard it, readying it to sail, he supposed. And there was little doubt they intended to take their prisoners along.

The idea that the Tower was involved quickly led Lugh to consider another disturbing possibility: More Tower forces might be planning to support Bres's army! If so, the de Dananns could be in grave danger.

From the angle of the faint sun it was well past dawn. Nuada's forces were certainly on the march by now. Soon they would be ready to engage the Fomor. But who—and what—would they face?

He had to get away, free Gilla, and warn his friends. He had to break free of this frozen light. It was created by magic, he guessed, and it would take magic equally strong to counter it.

That meant his sword, the Answerer, was his only chance. Given to him by Manannan MacLir when he had become Champion of the Sidhe, it held great power. Whether it would be able to help him now, he didn't know.

But to find out, he had to grip the weapon. Only by holding its hilt in his hand could its forces be awakened. He had reached for it before being enveloped in the blue light— but now his fingers were held motionless, embedded in the strange material, only a handbreadth from the sword.

He *had* to move his hand. Somehow he had to counter the magic of his prison with his own will. He began to concentrate upon his hand and on the sword, focusing all his strength on drawing closer to the hilt. His mind reached out to the weapon, trying to draw upon its mystic energies to help.

Nothing. His hand refused to budge. No added sense of power flowed to him from the sword.

Still, Lugh had little choice but to try again. He threw his will once more against the icy medium, concentrating all his strength on achieving just the slightest movement of one fingertip.

The four men now moved from their boat and approached the blue-white tube enclosing Gilla. As they came into Lugh's sight, his concentration was broken. A wave of despair washed over him. They were preparing to leave, to carry Gilla and himself away.

He watched the men lay out a net upon the sand. Then they unceremoniously tipped Gilla's icelike column over. It fell softly onto the sand and the net was pulled up around it. The four men took positions and gripped the net, heaving the encased Gilla up as if they were lifting a thick log.

Lugh watched in despair as they carried his friend down to their boat: without Gilla's plans, without the magical support of the Answerer and the strength of his comrades, he was nothing. He was no Champion, just a little boy playing a man's game. The sense of his own worthlessness threatened to overwhelm him.

The men reached their boat and two of them boarded it, swinging out a boom equipped with tackle from the mast. Ropes were lowered and the two still on the beach began to fasten them to the corners of the net. Soon Gilla would be hauled aboard, and then Lugh's turn would come.

Lugh's feeling of helplessness gave way to frustration, and then to rage. He could not let this happen! He had to reach the Answerer.

Anger surged within him like a wave of heat flowing through his limbs. He directed it toward his hand—and found himself succeeding! Like bright sun on the snow, the warmth radiating from his fingertips was actually softening the icy material before them. His hand moved.

Down on the beach the men finished hooking the ropes to the net. They stepped back, and one signaled to those in the boat.

Lugh's fingers pushed forward slowly, inching ever closer to his sword.

The ropes grew taut as those in the boat began to pull. The net rose around the blue-white tube. There was a hesitation as its weight bore on the rope, and then it lifted clear of the sandy shore.

Lugh's fingertips brushed the end of the Answerer's hilt.

Instantly, the weapon flared to life. A glow emanated from it, spreading through the surrounding material, suffusing the sapphire column with a golden radiance. And the power streamed into Lugh; surging up his arm and across him like a wave. Its intensity increased until his form was lost in brilliant light. Like the heat of a blazing fire, it began to melt the encasing blue-white substance, turning it to a liquid that suddenly burst, leaving Lugh free.

The men at the boat whirled toward him at the sound of the icy prison's demise. They found themselves looking at a now very animated warrior descending on them in a rush, a bright sword swinging in his hand.

"Get him aboard," one of them ordered the two in the boat. "We'll take care of the boy."

As those on the vessel continued to pull Gilla up, the

two on shore drew their own swords and started forward to meet Lugh's charge.

If the burly and highly trained fighting men of the Tower's elite expected to deal with Lugh easily, they were quickly disillusioned. The young Champion, in full battle fury, came upon them like a sea gale. Their first attack he beat back with an astonishingly swift series of blows from the Answerer. He slammed aside a killing stroke from one opponent, countering with a blow that drove the keen blade through the man's shoulder and deep into his chest.

As he went down, the second man charged in, seeking to finish Lugh while he was engaged. But the young warrior spun and sidestepped the rush. He jerked the Answerer free and swung it back, bringing his fist and the weapon's heavy hilt against the base of the attacker's neck. The man's forward momentum and the blow carried him stumbling on, to slam down heavily into the sand.

Lugh wasted no time finishing the stunned soldier. He broke into a run for the boat.

By this time the other two had gotten Gilla safely on board. They saw the young warrior so easily finish their companion, and prudently decided not to stay. Both grabbed up poles and began with haste to push the boat from the sand.

Under their combined force it backed quickly into the waves. It was already some distance out when Lugh reached the water and plunged in, determined to stop the vessel and rescue the Clown.

One of the two men leaped to the sail while the other began swinging his pole to keep Lugh back. The slender length of wood gave the young warrior a stinging slap against the neck, knocking him from his feet. He struggled up and splashed on, ducking under another swing and then leaping to grasp the pole.

A tug-of-war commenced, Lugh trying to pull the whole boat back, the soldier trying to free his pole. The man at the sail, seeing this, shouted in irritation: "Idiot! Let it go!"

The other obeyed, and Lugh staggered back and sat down in the water.

He was up again and wading out after the boat which still wallowed in the shore waves as the soldiers battled with the sail. When a splashing sound came from behind him he turned just in time to avoid a savage sword cut.

The man he had left stunned on th beach had recovered. Now, as his swing missed, he threw himself against Lugh, grappling at him with both arms to pull him down.

Lugh lost his balance and both men went over, sinking beneath the surface. Salt water burned in Lugh's mouth and nose. He felt the thick arms of the soldier tightening about him. He realized the man intended simply to use his strength and greater bulk to hold him under. He struggled, but his sword arm was pinned to his side and the man's whole weight was atop him.

In such a situation the ethics of fighting had very little value. He thrust his face forward and seized his opponent's broad nose in his teeth, crunching into it with all the strength in his jaws.

Involuntarily, the man's grip relaxed, and Lugh managed to bring the Answerer up in a short thrust that tore into the soldier's midsection. He rolled sideways in his death agonies and Lugh burst to the surface, gasping for air.

He got his footing and heaved himself upright, sea water streaming from him. He looked around for the boat, ready to take up the pursuit. But as the water cleared from his vision, he realized the vessel was now well out to sea, picking up speed under a spread of ballooning sail, slipping hopelessly out of reach.

He watched the ship glide away, carrying Gilla off to a fate he couldn't even begin to guess at.

Chapter Nine
THE FIGHT BEGINS

Lugh's anger over his failure to rescue his friend was short-lived. He could do nothing now to help the Clown, and another matter of greater urgency demanded that he act, and quickly.

"I'll come after you yet, my friend," he promised, looking for a last time after the departing ship. But he knew—he could almost hear Gilla's voice telling him—that his first duty was now to join the de Danann host.

It was late morning, and the battle might already have been joined. Lugh had no idea where he was. He could be at some distance from them, and he was afoot. He realized that there was only one way he might reach them soon. He would have to call the Riders of the Sidhe.

The wraithlike Riders, like the Answerer, were a power Manannan had given him when he assumed the role of Champion. The mystic sword controlled them. He lifted the glinting blade before him, pointed toward the west, and began the invocation that would summon the Riders.

In the heavy clouds rimming the horizon a strange disturbance began. As if a separate storm were rising, a section of the clouds began to billow downward. They shifted so violently, they almost seemed to boil. Their swollen bellies hung down, sagging lower as if to touch the earth. Then the swirling gray began to grow lighter as a glow appeared within them.

The clouds grew incandescent from the intense light that began quickly to rise to a brilliant peak. They burned with white fire, then burst open as if no longer able to contain such power. From the rent that now showed in the lowest clouds, a line of light appeared, slanting downward like a bolt of lightning. But it did not strike the earth. Instead, it turned to fly across its surface, skimming the ground, heading directly toward the waiting Champion.

As it drew nearer, its speed began to slow. The light softened and a rushing sound, like that of a coming wind, was heard, along with a faint, high jingling. Within the line of light shapes became visible. They were of sleek, lean horses stretching out their bodies in a run, and of tall riders, bent low over their horses' heads, sharp points of light flashing from the tips of their slender spears.

Soon they reached Lugh, and the troop of eerie horsemen drew to a halt. The enveloping glow faded from them now, like a fine mist falling away, leaving them clearly revealed. Each horse was of an almost luminous gray-white, long-limbed, and powerful. Each rider was cloaked in silver, a shield like a glowing moon upon one arm, a lance with silver rings about its shaft held upright at his side. All wore helmets of silver that masked all the face but the bright gleam of the unblinking gray eyes.

They sat motionless and silent in two columns of ten riders each. At their head stood another horse, riderless. Lugh approached it, sheathed the Answerer, and mounted, thus assuming leadership of this troop of unnatural beings.

"Now we must find the de Dannans," he told them. "Riders, follow me!"

He urged his mount forward. It broke at once into a gallop, the others falling in behind. In moments they were speeding across the countryside, the landscape passing in a blur of color, the horses' hooves seeming not even to touch the ground.

He would reach the de Danann army very soon. But in his heart Lugh wondered if it might already be too late.

The de Danann and Firbolg companies moved to the edge of the last ridge of hills. Below them now were the wide plains that edged the sea. The thousands of warriors made a fringe far along the ridge, sparkling with the light reflected from their shifting weapons. At the center of their line Nuada and his Champions reined in their horses and took stock of the situation.

Below them, across a wide expanse of level ground, the Fomor army was gathered along the shore. At a distance the black and ragged horde of awful beings looked more like a seething mass of insects. They had already fouled the fine green fields and white beach all about them.

Behind them, nearly at the water's edge, the Fomor had erected a high palisade of upright poles and wicker screens. It extended for some way along the shore. As Nuada had expected, the Fomor were still a vast and formidable force. Here, with their backs against the sea, they would likely fight with the fury born of desperation.

"Why have they chosen to meet us here, in the open, instead of at their city?" the High-King puzzled. "Attacking that warren would have been difficult."

"I don't know," said the Dagda. "They have erected some kind of defensive works there. Perhaps they're intending to withdraw behind it when we attack."

As Aine looked down on the enemy force, she felt the stirrings of uneasiness. Something was wrong here. She wished that Lugh and Gilla were with her now. Why didn't they appear?

"They are making no move," Angus Og remarked. "They aren't fools enough to attack us on high ground."

"Day is flying!" the Dagda growled impatiently. "There's no reason to delay. Let's go now and give them what they're wanting."

"No!" Aine protested. "Wait for Lugh and Gilla. You may need them."

Nuada shook his head. "I know your concern," he said understandingly, "but we haven't any choice. The Dagda is right. We must engage now, or the day may end before we can win a victory."

"Taillta," she said, appealing to her friend, "Do you agree with them?"

"I do," the woman answered grimly. "Sorry, Aine, but even if something has happened to delay them, we can't wait longer." She laid an assuring hand on Aine's arm. "Don't worry. I'm still certain they'll be turning up any moment now." She turned to Nuada. "I'll go now and join my own warriors. We'll attack on your signal."

The High-King nodded, and Taillta urged her mount away across the ridge toward the Firbolg contingent on the western flank. Nuada looked around at his officers.

"Pass the word to all companies. Be ready to advance—on my command!"

Below them Bres was watching the forces on the ridge from a walkway atop the wicker palisade. He smiled with satisfaction as it became clear that the de Danann forces were preparing to attack. Below him in the shelter of the barricades, a half-dozen of the Tower's black ships were drawn up. And along the shore, still wearing their heavy shrouds, sat twenty of the vast machines.

Their crews were ranged beside them in precise rows, awaiting orders to move. Salmhor paced before them, constantly scanning them with a critical eye, fussing with his pristine uniform, his expression one of complete disgust for this entire proceeding. Often he pressed a cloth to his mouth and nose in a vain attempt to close off some of the stench from the army massed just beyond the wall.

A Fomor warrior with a face that seemed to have melted and slipped down onto his shoulders appeared around the barricade and approached Bres. Salmhor gave him one look and turned away, shuddering with nausea.

"My King," the man called up to Bres, "The de Dananns seem about to move. What orders do you have?"

"The companies are to stand," Bres told him. "Let the

de Dananns come on. We want to lure them as close as we can."

"Aye, my King," he said, and hurried away. Bres looked to Salmhor.

"Is everything in readiness with you?" he asked

"Of course!" Salmhor answered sharply, indignant at such a question. "Your enemies' ranks will be torn open by our engines. Even this filthy rabble of yours should be able to deal with them then. If not, the rest of our forces are prepared to move in and save you."

The nasty, smirking attitude of the man nearly roused Bres to anger once again, but he fought it down. This was not the time for it. Instead, he answered in a hard and uncompromising tone.

"Don't forget—your bloody marvels failed me once before." Bres paused, making his voice even harder—"If they fail here, you'll be dying with the rest of us."

Stung by this criticism, Salmhor opened his mouth to give a reply. He was forestalled by a shout from beyond the wall.

"Bres! My lord, they come!"

"My turn now, Nuada," he murmured to himself as he watched them advance.

The combined force of the de Dananns and Firbolgs was a wave covering the field as they poured from the ridge. The clash of their arms blended with the sound of their battle cries to form a constant roar. Warriors ran forward, jostling one another for position, pushing forward eagerly to be the first to strike the Fomor line.

Bres watched until the last of them were down from the high ground, until the first of them were well across the plains and rapidly closing with his forces. He waited until he could see Nuada, riding at the head of his mounted troop in the heart of the mass. Then he turned and gave Salmhor the command.

"Now!"

The first warning the attacking force had was the sudden rise of a great rumbling, as of close thunder striking the earth. Then the wicker screens fell forward, crashing to the sand, giving the Firbolg and de Danann warriors their first look at the Tower's machines of war as they rolled forward, ready to attack.

They were vehicles of a type that few de Dananns alive

ever seen, or could even have conceived of, enormous, sharp-cornered, great boxes of metal set upon wheels, moving on tires twice a man's height. These protruded beyond the base of the metal boxes on long axles, allowing the machines to roll easily across rough terrain. Atop each box a flat deck was affixed, much like that of a ship, large enough to accommodate several men.

These vehicles moved forward smoothly in what seemed to the startled observers to be some magical way, for no draft animals were visible. The only clue to their locomotion was a deep growling from within each machine.

But most ominous were the appendages attached to the bows of each vehicle. A number were fitted with metal arms, hinged to fold outward on either side. Their bottom edges were lined with cutting scythes, scores of them set in a close row, edges to the front. They dropped down as the machines advanced, the blades just touching the ground, turning it in furrows as they cut along, clearly capable of chewing up whatever came into their path.

Others of the lethal engines had large, spinning wheels at their front. These were formed of wide, flat metal blades fastened to a central hub, like spokes, parallel to the ground and just above it. Still others had large metal pincers, like a lobster's claw, that snapped constantly as the vehicle moved, or wide scooplike blades edged with thick spikes, hinged to move up and down, ready to cut a man in two.

Twenty of the strange machines rolled out in a precise line and headed through the ranks of the Fomor army, who hurriedly parted to make a way for them. At an increasing speed they started toward the now-halted de Danann host, who stood staring at the incredible things with an amazement that turned quickly to alarm.

"What in the name of Danu?" Nuada asked.

"Magic from the Tower!" the Dagda roared. "I've seen them once before. They'll tear our men apart," he added grimly.

Already the machines were nearly upon the attacking force. The front lines of warriors launched a cloud of javelins at them. The weapons showered upon the upper structures, hitting a few of the soldiers there but not slowing the attack. The sharp points of some did penetrate the thick wheels, but were rolled down and broken off, having done no apparent damage.

And then the machines slammed into the foremost ranks.

The de Dananns and Firbolgs, so closely massed, could do little to get out of the way. Scythes mowed them down, plowing the lacerated bodies into the sandy earth. Paddle wheels sucked them in, thrashed them, and tossed the broken bodies out behind. The pincers and blades made their own bloody paths as they rolled inexorably on.

Nuada's army battled courageously, but they were like ants defending their nest from invading beetles. They slashed and beat at whatever parts of the monsters they could reach, but even the skillfully fashioned weapons of their master smiths were useless against the metal skins of the Tower machines.

Warriors who managed to evade the devices at the front tried boarding the vehicles, only to be kicked off or shot with crossbows by the soldiers on the decks.

As they forced their way deeper into the front of the host, those behind began to panic. The warriors around Nuada's party appealed to him for help.

"There must be some way to stop them!" Aine shouted over the roar of the machines.

"Kill the drivers!" the Dagda shouted back. "Look at that cage in the rear."

Aine could see them now, small canopies of metal strips forming a ribbed protective structure over a man seated behind a high console.

"The men in there control the things," the Dagda went on. "If we could reach them somehow . . ."

"We can," crackled the voice of Morrigan. Instantly, her body began to glow luminous with the beginning of her transformation.

"Good idea, Morrigan," Aine said enthusiastically, quickly grasping the woman's aim. "Shaglan, we'll go too. You must become a bird and carry me."

The helpful Pooka nodded and its dog-shaped body turned soft in its own shifting process.

"If we can stop even a few, we might save hundreds," Aine said. "Hurry, Shaglan!"

Morrigan had finished her own change, and her raven's form now rose from the horse's back, flapping into the sky.

"Nuada," the Dagda said, laying his massive hand on the High-King's shoulder. "We must withdraw."

"Yes," the High-King said sadly, looking around at the

chaos and destruction the machines were creating in his force. His brave warriors were fighting on, refusing to run, defying the enemy advance, but it was futile. "Yes, we must retreat before we are destroyed."

Shaglan had now assumed the shape of a strange, long-necked bird large enough to easily carry the slender woman. Taking up a lance, Aine climbed onto its back. It ran forward a few strides before spreading its huge wings and soaring up, banking away as it gained altitude.

As the two magical birds climbed and circled over the battlefield, Nuada passed orders to his forces to withdraw. It took little urging to convince the stalwart but nearly helpless warriors to quit the impossible battle. They turned and began a quick retreat back toward the high ground to the south.

But the slaughter did not end. Freed of having to force their way through the press, the machines now rolled ahead faster, catching the slower warriors and those who stumbled in their flight, driving the rest before them. It was clear that if their speed continued to increase, they would catch and overrun the army long before it reached the hills.

While the others withdrew around him, Nuada stayed behind. Stubbornly, he refused the Dagda's demands that he pull back. He would not go until he saw that all his companies had started their own retreat before him.

He stayed until one of the machines with a vast threshing paddle at its front started for him. Its driver had spotted the mounted man with the trappings of royalty and meant to have him.

"Nuada!" the Dagda shouted.

The king grudgingly obeyed. The two men turned their horses and urged them to a run that would carry them safely ahead of the spinning blades.

But one of the soldiers on the vehicle's deck chanced a shot at Nuada. It missed him, but sank home in the neck of his mount. The animal twisted up, neighing in agony. It fell sideways, crashing upon Nuada, pinning him to the ground. He turned his head—and stared into the swiftly approaching blades.

Chapter Ten
COUNTERATTACK

The Dagda had ridden on for some way before he realized Nuada was down. Wheeling his horse, he rode back to the trapped king.

He dismountd, knelt by the fallen animal, and slid his arms beneath it. With a heave he lifted the body, allowing Nuada to pull himself free. They rose quickly, only to find that the Dagda's horse had been panicked by the machine and was galloping madly away. That left nothing for the two men to do but run to escape the threshing blades.

They leaped away to safety as the voracious monster gobbled up the carcass of the horse. But the driver was determined to have his prey, and pressed his vehicle forward at full speed. It was gaining.

The Dagda had been forced to run before one of these metal beasts before. He did not like the feeling. Ahead and to their right he spied a large, weathered boulder jutting from the grassy plain.

"This way!" he told Nuada, leading him toward it.

The machine was closing in when they reached it. The Dagda stopped and seized the stone, larger than himself, wrapping his arms about it. His rage added to his already supernormal strength. In one yank he tore the stone from the soil, swinging it above his head.

"Here! Chew on this!" he bellowed at the thing nearly upon him, and launched the stone forward into the spinning blades.

It slammed against one blade, bending it badly, then fell through into the others, jamming them together. With a painful shriek of tortured metal the entire wheel ceased turning. The machine came to a halt with a tremendous jerk, throwing its crew from their feet.

The Dagda looked over his handiwork, nodded with satisfaction, then joined Nuada. Other de Danann riders, seeing their plight, had reached them now, and the two were quickly remounted, riding away to join the retreating force.

Above them the two birds were sweeping down, having chosen their own targets for attack. Morrigan's attack was direct. She shot in at the driver of a scythed vehicle that was nearly upon a large cluster of de Danann warriors. Drawing in her wings, she arrowed through the bars of his protective cage and went right for his face, raking his scalp and forehead with her talons.

He yelped with pain and lifted his hands from the controls to fight her off. The undirected machine veered sharply from its course.

The raven battered at him with her wings, one claw in his hair, one tearing at his face, while her sharp beak darted at his eyes. He screamed for help, flailing at her, his face streaming with blood.

But other soldiers were coming to help, drawing swords to thrust at the Raven-Woman. Two men were loading their crossbows with the short metal bolts. Morrigan had already experienced the accuracy of these weapons. She realized it was time to quit the fight. Relinquishing her hold, she gave an angry caw and soared away, just avoiding the bolt that whizzed through the place she'd been.

Though the man was free, he was blinded by the blood of his many wounds. His vehicle still ran on without control, heading across the path of a second Tower machine.

The second driver saw it coming much too late. He tried desperately to turn his machine away, but only succeeded in taking the impact broadside. The scythed vehicle smashed in, prow driving into the other engine's side, metal blades ripping into its tires. Hopelessly tangled together, both machines came to a stop, groaning and shuddering like two wounded monsters locked in a death struggle.

Aine, meantime, was directing Shaglan in at another of the machines in an effort to help Taillta. She had spotted the valiant woman trying to lure the attacker up a craggy knoll so that her brawny warriors might board it from the rocks.

They were having little luck. The machine could pivot with amazing speed, snapping its metal jaws at any who approached while the soldiers aboard shot down all who managed to reach its side.

The Pooka swooped in at these bowmen, wings out, and caught two of them across their throats, knocking them over the side. Startled, the other soldiers whirled toward him as he settled to the deck. The sight of the great bird, and the young woman upon it, took them rather aback—and gave Aine a chance to attack. She threw her lance, downing one man, then drew sword and dagger and leaped from Shaglan to confront the rest

A dozen more soldiers closed in, only to suddenly find themselves facing a very large and angry cat.

When Taillta realized what was happening, she led her own warriors in a unified attack. With the soldiers on the machine well occupied, she and several others managed to duck around the pinching jaws, gain footholds on the body's metal sides, and begin to climb upward. The soldiers trying to surround Aine and the Pooka were themselves quickly surrounded and overwhelmed by savage Firbolgs.

The driver at the rear, seeing his mates cut down, decided hastily to abandon his position. He leaped from the back of the moving vehicle, leaving it to roll off a steep drop on one side of the knoll.

"Jump!" cried Aine as she felt the deck begin to tilt.

All leaped from the upper side of the machine as it went over, crashing heavily onto its side.

They picked themselves up and looked down at the thing, upended like a giant bug, wheels still spinning uselessly in the air. Aine looked at Taillta and found the woman beaming in triumph.

"That was fun, wasn't it?" Taillta said delightedly. "Let's go after another!"

"I'm afraid it won't do much good," Aine answered darkly, looking around. For their little victoreis had done nothing to stem the relentless drive of the machines.

Far out to sea, the balance of the Tower fleet was hanging at the horizon line, waiting for some word. In the bow of the Commander's ship, a seaman intently watched a blinking light on shore. When its flashing ceased, he quickly moved back toward the vessel's stern, where Balor sat like a great idol of black iron, waiting.

"Commander," the man said, "we have a signal from Sital Salmhor. Our machines have shattered the whole de Danann line. They are pursuing the survivors inland. Bres had ordered the Eireland Fomor forward behind them."

"Excellent," the voice clanged. "Take the fleet in. I wish to see the end of this battle myself."

Orders were passed. The Commander's ship started ahead, leading the other ships in toward the coast. Slowly, the tiny figures swarming on the battlefield came into view.

At the same time, the battlefield was coming into Lugh Lamfada's view as well. He and the Riders of the Sidhe had just topped the southern hills and he was able to look over the scene on the plains below.

He was horrified by the situation laid out before him. The de Danann and Firbolg companies were in headlong flight. The machines of the Tower wheeled through the flying warriors, leaving wide trails of carnage behind them. The mainland Fomor were moving up in force behind them, ready to finish their opponents once they were thoroughly broken. And behind them, gliding in toward the shore, the rest of the black fleet of the Tower was visible.

Lugh watched in dismay. The Tower's whole force must be committed here. He hadn't really believed they would come to Eire. He had hoped that they had given up the fight. Why had they chosen to help Bres?

Then, as the ships moved closer to the shore, he was able to identify the familiar black form rising at the stern of the largest ship, and he had his answer. Balor was alive.

Balor! Lugh had been so certain the being was dead. He had last seen the giant swept away by a storm Manannan had created. He had thought his greatest enemy gone forever.

He was frozen for a long moment, staring at the dark figure. Fear of this giant swept through him as it had before, a fear so unreasoning, so stark and overpowering that it swept away his ability to think, seized him like the massive grip of the giant himself.

What if Balor landed? Nothing could withstand the force of that unshuttered eye. Lugh could see the crimson light of it even from where he stood. He knew what its energy could do. He had seen it lay waste a clifftop fortress. He had faced its full power with the Riders of the Sidhe—and he had barely survived. These thoughts ran in a wild tangle through his mind, and over them like a shadow lay his earliest memory of the terrible being as it moved forward to take him from the cradling arms of his mother.

Lost in his own thoughts, Lugh stared—until the sounds of the machines and the frightened men below drew his attention. Soon the army would be overrun, the machines cutting them off, leaving the survivors to the savage attack of the Fomor horde. Their plight recalled the young warrior. Afraid or not, it was his chosen task to be their Champion. He must do what he could to save them, or at least delay the metal horrors long enough for them to retreat safely. "Riders," Lugh cried, raising the Answerer high, "attack!" Balor would come later.

They swept down the slope toward the battle, moving into a line, the horses galloping exactly abreast, close together. Some of the de Danann warriors below saw them coming and sent up a cheer. It drew the attention of Lugh's comrades.

"Lugh!" cried Aine, and beside her Taillta cheered loudly.

Across the field Nuada and the Dagda reined in their troop and watched.

"He is striking directly for them," Nuada said. "But can even the Riders of the Sidhe stop those things?"

The Dagda only shook his head. "I don't know."

As Lugh's band drove in against the first of the machines, the de Danann warriors scrambled from his path. The lances of the Riders dropped forward in one graceful move to point at the vehicle as if they meant to joust with it.

The driver of the machine—fitted with the long, scythed arms—saw them come on and altered course to accept this strange challenge. The scores of blades chewed along through the sod, ready to devour the entire troop at once. A smile of cruel delight stretched the driver's thin mouth as he threw full power to the vehicle. It leaped forward.

The contenders closed rapidly, ready to engage. But with the metal destroyer drawing near, the tips of the Riders' slender lances began to glow, the light quickly increasing to the incandescent brightness of white-hot metal. These spots of brightness swelled to become blazing globes. Then, as if erupting from the contained energy, each shot tendrils of fire—like sustained bolts of lightning—that leaped across to touch the other points. In an instant all the Riders were linked by a fabric of light woven of the crackling, flickering strands. Lugh's horse had dropped back slightly from the others, and this silver barrier now created a shield for him.

The driver of the machine was puzzled by this odd light, but its fragility seemed no threat to him. It certainly would not stop the rush of his vehicle's blades.

But from this network of interlacing threads a single stream of power shot forward suddenly. It was a thick and solid column of glistening whiteness, like a geyser of water jetting from the earth. It crashed against the front of the machine, bursting there, fragmenting into a hundred tendrils of silver that sizzled across the surface of the vehicle entwining to create a glowing lacework shroud of energy.

The soldiers aboard were caught by it. As if they were strands of iron, the lights shot through them, impaling them, jerking them up and holding them in stiffened positions of agony so that they seemed to hang upon the lines. The force coursed through the inner workings of the machine, burning them out. From the instruments before the driver, a dozen bolts of energy leaped out, striking through his face, running up his arms, throwing him back in his seat, body rigid.

The Riders' power raked the vehicle from prow to stern, then abruptly died away. Released, the lifeless bodies of the crew dropped to the deck. The huge machine, its mechanisms destroyed, rolled softly, gently, to a final stop.

For a moment there was a silence across the battlefield as those of both sides watched in amazement. Even Lugh was startled by the spectacular effect. He reined in, bringing the Riders to a halt, and stared toward the stricken vehicle.

Though taken off guard by this unexpected force, the highly trained Tower soldiers were quick to react. After only a brief hesitation, the drivers of the other vehicles steered toward Lugh and the Riders, intent on overwhelming him by the sheer force of their numbers.

The rest of the de Danann force was now ignored. The warriors, realizing they were free of pursuit, stopped their retreat and gathered at the base of the inland hills to watch. On the far side of the machines the advancing Eireland Fomor also pulled up. All waited to see what would be the result of the strange duel developing on the plains between.

There Lugh Lamfada found himself at the center of a closing circle of the immense machines. He looked around him at the collection of whirling, snapping, and chewing blades converging, and wondered if the Sidhe could withstand them all.

"Good enough," he told himself, trying to feel optimistic. "At least I've gotten their attention."

Chapter Eleven
BALOR'S CHOICE

A second machine rolled in toward Lugh at full speed, the wheel of blades at its front spinning, eager to be the first to grind him up. But its driver reckoned without the Riders' speed. Their lances all shifted toward it, bringing their shield of light swinging around.

"Fire at them!" the driver ordered the soldiers on the prow.

Several of them lifted the crossbows and loosed the short metal darts. They struck the surface of the glowing barrier, slipped in, and were absorbed in a brief flash of brightness. The light had swallowed them as if they'd been dropped into a pond.

The driver's eyes widened in shock at this. Then he realized that the lance points were coming to bear on the front of his machine. The shield's glow was growing brighter in preparation for loosing a second blast of energy.

He wrenched at the controls, desperately trying to maneuver the machine from the oncoming force. But it had just begun to turn when the stream of light caught it, exploding against its front quarter, again sending the dazzling currents of lightning dancing across the surface of the machine. And, as before, this display of energy—beautiful and lethal—left the vehicle to roll to a stop, lifeless and smoking.

Some of the drivers of the machines had by now rolled behind Lugh's troop and were trying to come in at his rear while those before him kept him occupied. Seeing this, Lugh quickly ordered the Riders into a circle. There the light barrier became a silver ring, while Lugh, from the center, directed the Riders' power from point to point.

Bolts of the energy were fired very quickly now, first at those slipping in behind. One driver managed to wheel his machine away from the deadly stream. It shot harmlessly past his stern, spreading out and fading in the air. But a second machine, sweeping around its fellow to attack the Riders, was caught full on the prow and met the fate of the others.

This attack, however, allowed another of the scythed vehicles to safely reach the circle of Riders. Lugh heard the noise of it and turned to see it nearly atop them.

Above, the driver laughed triumphantly as he saw the Riders swept beneath the blades. He pictured them torn and ground into the earth. He expected to hear the screaming of the men and mounts, feel the tremor as the scythes gnawed at the bones. But there was nothing.

The machine rolled on over the spot. He turned to look over the side for the remains. What he saw behind him was the full troop, completely untouched.

Even in the brief time, Lugh's mount had borne him from the vehicle's path. The Riders themselves had stood their ground, letting the scythes run right over them. The unearthly beings simply dissolved into the air, allowing the blades to cut through, and then re-formed again when the machine passed on.

Now, as the driver stared aghast at them, they lifted their lances and unleased an energy bolt that burst against the vehicle's stern. A fourth Tower marvel rolled silently to a stop.

The rest grew wary now, turning off from the direct attack to circle Lugh's party. At Lugh's direction the Riders fired two more blasts of the deadly light at them. And although quick moves by the drivers managed to wheel the targets from harm's way, it caused all the machines to take up evasive movements as they rolled. Each of the drivers watched the others, uncertain what to do, waiting for someone else to initiate an attack, not very eager to make such a move himself. A stalemate.

At the shore Bres was shouting in fury at Salmhor.

"Your machines have failed! The rest of your force must land! Balor has to destroy Lugh now! Now, Salmhor! Do you understand?"

Salmhor did understand. There was no denying the truth of what Bres said. He ordered the message sent to his Commander.

But Balor needed no message from Salmhor to see what was happening. The smoldering glare of his crimson eye was already focused on the battle.

Mathgen had failed. And now, on the verge of an easy

victory, that boy had appeared again to give challenge. A third of his war machines had been destroyed, and further attacks on Lugh would surely mean the loss of more.

Only the intervention of Balor might turn the advantage back to his side again. But he would not enter that battle and face the young champion. He recalled vividly his last battle with Lugh and his Riders of the Sidhe. The fiery power of his eye had met their silver stream of energy. He had vanquished them, but only with difficulty, and Lugh had survived the eye's full force. No, he would not risk himself and the forces of the Tower. For all his doubts, he would still heed the Druid's grim warning of the Prophecy.

"Send a message to Salmhor," the voice boomed out. "Tell him to withdraw our machines. We'll waste no more of them here."

On the battlefield Lugh and his Riders were still turning constantly as he kept a close watch on the circling machines. He wondered how long it would be before they all came in at once.

Then, at the Tower ships along the shore, a bright light began blinking at a furious rate. Lugh noted this and wondered if it was sending a signal to the drivers to quit their delaying and get on with it. He prepared himself for a joint attack.

But instead, the machines all began to turn away! He watched in amazement as they swung about and rolled back toward the shore at high speed.

Bres was more than amazed. He was furious.

"What are you doing?" he raged at Salmhor. "You can't pull them out now. You've got to destroy Lugh! Destroy the de Dananns!"

"The Commander has ordered us to withdraw the remaining machines," Salmhor answered coldly.

"What?" Bres cried. "What about my army?"

"They will be useful in covering our safe withdrawal. You and they are now to be on your own."

Bres grabbed the officer's tunic in one fist, yanking him close. "You promised to help me. You promised you would destroy the de Dananns," he told Salmhor, adding menacingly: "You are not going to abandon us now!"

Four of the Tower soldiers moved forward, two on either side of Salmhor. They lifted crossbows threateningly toward Bres.

"I suggest," Salmhor said in an even tone, "you release me—quickly!"

Bres looked at the ready weapons and the determined soldiers and loosed his hold. Salmhor stepped away, tugging his tunic straight with a sharp gesture. His tones were warning.

"Don't try to interfere again, Bres."

In frustration Bres turned away from him to look out toward the battlefield again.

The machines were almost back to the massed Fomor now. These warriors, bewildered by this strange move, realized almost too late that the rolling vehicles were not going to stop. In a sudden panic they scrambled from the paths of the machines, staring after their rapidly retreating sterns uncomprehendingly.

Nuada and his champions watched too, realizing that the metal horrors were heading directly for the ships.

"Forward warriors!" he cried.

Swinging his sword above him, the High-King charged, the rest of his mounted troop behind him. The warriors of his clans saw him and charged forward.

"There go the de Dananns!" Taillta shouted to her men. "Will the Firbolgs join them?"

A roar of acclamation rose from the rough warriors and they too swept forward. The two forces were one as they headed across the shore plains again.

The Fomor army at first had no idea as to what was happening. The poor creatures stood like a great herd of stunned oxen, watching the machines depart, until the rising battle cry of the charging warriors drew their attention to the force now rapidly descending upon them.

Their leaders, caught completely off guard, were still struggling to determine strategy when the de Dananns and Firbolgs reached them, crashing against their whole line.

The Fomor closed ranks quickly under the attack and began their resistance. They were hard fighters—and they were fighting for their very lives. The two forces locked together in savage struggle. In the densely packed mass of warriors, there was barely room to swing a sword.

Nuada and the Dagda led a drive that forced deeply into the Fomor. Aine and Taillta with the Firbolgs slashed into their flank. But Lugh and the Riders held back, the young Champion unwilling to use the unnatural forces of the troop in fight that was now fair. This battle the de Dananns and their

Firbolg allies must win themselves . . . or their winning of Eire would mean little.

That victory would come soon, despite the stubborn resistance of the Fomor. They had not the strength alone to hold back the determined onslaught of their opponents. Still, they refused surrender, believing that their saviors of the Tower would come back to their aid at any moment.

In this belief they were to be disappointed. For while they struggled on, the machines continued rolling down to the shore.

Orders had already been passed to the waiting ships to prepare for loading. Bres was forced to stand by in helpless fury and watch the booms swing out from the ships' masts, the tackle rigged, the cables dropped to crewmen waiting on the beach.

As soon as the vehicles arrived by the ships, the loading process began, proceeding with the usual Tower speed and efficiency. Gangways were run out from the ships' sides and, while men from the ships hooked up the vehicles, the soldiers from them began to board. In moments the first machines were lifting from the sand, rising up to be swung onto the decks.

Bres turned from his observation of the battlefield and realized that Salmhor himself was starting up a gangway into one of the ships. He ran after the officer, shouting after him: "You cannot do this! These Fomor will be massacred. Eire will be lost."

Salmhor paused at the top of the gangway to cast a look of chill indifference back to Bres.

"It is better that your animals die than our soldiers," he told Bres. "And, frankly, I consider this overgrown isle of yours very little loss." He turned to go on, but paused to add as an afterthought: "Will you be coming with us? Or will you stay and die a heroic death leading your army, trying to save your Eire?"

Bres looked back toward the fray. The Fomor forces were clearly weakening. Taillta was directing a fierce attack by the Firbolgs, tearing the Fomor flank to ribbons, while Nuada's troops pierced deep into their center.

"I suggest you decide quickly," Salmhor prompted. "Your rabble will not hold much longer."

In fact, the Fomor warriors had finally realized that their erstwhile saviors were in the process of hurriedly abandoning them. This had quite a disheartening effect. They had already determined that they had no chance of defeating the attacking force alone. Now their only hope was about to sail away, and their last means of escape would go with it!

In hundreds they suddenly abandoned the fight, turned, and began to pelt back toward the beach.

"Here they come," said Salmhor. "We've no more time to wait." He glanced along the row of ships. The last of the machines were just clearing the ships' sides, being swung onto the decks. The last Tower crewmen were making their way up the gangways. He turned to the vessel's captain.

"We leave now!" he ordered. "Pull away at once!"

Bres decided. He jumped for the gangway of Salmhor's ship, running up behind a last party of crewmen.

Across the battlefield Lugh noted the familiar bright cloak of his old enemy as Bres boarded. He realized the man would escape again. Hoping to stop him, he led the Riders in a gallop, curving around the end of the fighters and into the confusing mass of Fomor fleeing toward the shore.

Lugh's comrades, meantime, found the resistance before them fading rapidly. In increasing numbers the Fomor were quitting and heading for the beach, determined to reach the vessels before they sailed.

The de Danann and Firbolg warriors at once charged forward, slashing easily through the last remnants of their enemies and joining this race for the beach.

With the speed of the Riders, Lugh reached it before any of his friends. His troop pressed forward through the mob of Fomor, so disordered and bent on escape that they paid no notice. The Riders managed to create an open way for him, but the tangle of warriors made the advance maddeningly slow. And the Tower ships were nearly ready to leave.

The last machines had been secured on their decks, the last crewmen boarded. The driving forces deep within the black hulls were rumbling to life. The Fomor, however, were swarming around the ships, leaping for their bows, crowding onto the gangways, splashing into the water to try to climb their sides.

"Take us out now!" Salmhor shouted, looking down on the horrible mass of beings surging around his ships. "And keep these vermin off!"

Tower soldiers acted quickly. The gangways were jettisoned, dropping scores of hapless Fomor into the sea. Pikes and swords and crossbows were used to brutally thrust back any who climbed the sides. On Salmhor's ship one wretched being managed to get a grip on the deck rail with his good hand and the crook of iron that served him for another. He looked up to see his leader, Bres, standing above. His popping eyes pleaded.

"Please, lord!" he cried.

Bres's foot shot out in a short hard kick to the warrior's face. He dropped back, leaving the hook dangling from the rail.

The ships were now all drawing back from the beach. The Fomor in the hundreds were wading out after them, screaming for rescue, staggering through the waves, pushing one another down in panic, climbing upon one another, creating a squirming snarl of beings in the water. From the attack of the de Danann and Firbolg warriors now descending upon their rear, they were defenseless.

Lugh and the Riders finally reached the water's edge, and again the young Champion found himself just too late. Salmhor's vessel had slipped clear of the beach and was backing rapidly into the open water, too far out to reach.

At the bow of the ship Bres stood, looking back over the final destruction of the Fomor army. As his eyes scanned the shore, they were stopped by the glowing troop of Riders. His gaze fixed on the young warrior at their front, the one who had again brought him to defeat. At the same moment, Lugh saw Bres, and the gazes of the two men locked. For an instant Lugh could sense the great despair, the feeling of loss that filled his enemy as he was at last driven from Eire. Then the moment passed, and the contact was broken.

All around Lugh was chaos, the struggling, screaming Fomor writhing in the surf like terrified beasts, their last resemblance to human beings gone from them as the de Danann warriors exacted final, savage revenge on the beings who had so long enslaved them. The waves seethed with the convulsions of the dying and washed a blood-tinged foam upon the beach.

Lugh had no stomach for the slaughter. He sat unmoving upon the gray-white horse, staring out after the departing ships. Those from the shore joined the balance of the fleet. Together the sleek black ships turned with the grace of

dancers and slid away, abandoning the poor, despised creatures who had served the Tower's ends for so long.

A hand touched his leg and he looked down to see Aine
and Shaglan beside him.

"Lugh!" she cried. "I didn't think you'd come!"

Though Aine smiled, Lugh could hear in her voice anxiety. He slipped from the horse's back to hug her close.

"I was afraid something had happened to you," she said.
She hugged him in return, then pulled back to look into his
eyes. Something was wrong.

"Where's Gilla?" she demanded, the tone of alarm returning. "Lugh, where's Gilla?"

"I'm sorry, Aine. He was taken," Lugh said bluntly,
unable to think of an easier way to tell her.

"Taken?" she repeated, not understanding. "Taken by
whom?"

He shook his head. "I don't know. But I'm afraid it has
something to do with the Tower of Glass."

They looked out toward the departing ships and the
black form visible upon the stern of one. Even at that distance they could still see the fiery glow of that deadly crimson
eye.

The small boat was made fast to moorings in the great
stone quays below the Tower. A dozen gray-uniformed men
moved at once to lift the chill blue cylinder from within it and
move it onto the platform.

"Careful, there!" Mathgen's henchman cautioned them
sharply. "That is a precious cargo. It goes to the Druid's
quarters directly. And his curse will be on anyone who
damages his prize!"

As the men moved with great care and greater dread to
obey, lifting the cylinder and carrying it along the quay, the
now-conscious Gilla found himself staring up the glistening
Tower.

For the first time he knew what had happened to him,
and he moaned inwardly at the thought of what the future
held. His only comfort was that Lugh seemed to have escaped. It was up to the young Champion now, and Gilla
prayed to Danu that Lugh's spirit would direct him the right
way.

Book Two
THE RESCUE MISSION

Chapter Twelve
RUADAN

The fire was a red-yellow pyramid that sent its light high into the night sky. Beneath it the Fomor city was dying, its vileness consumed by the purifying flames. The years of accumulated filth sent clouds of oily smoke roiling up as the fires that fed upon them swept through the warren of buildings.

It was a spectacular sight, filling the horizon, illuminating the countryside around. It shed its glow on the plains beside it, playing over it with an eerie, shifting light that added an even stronger atmosphere of strangeness to the already bizarre scene.

It was more like a view of some supernatural realm of lost souls than of reality. Under the grim eye of warriors with poised weapons, the grotesque citizens shuffled away from their blazing city in long lines. Some few of the miserable beings carried their meager belongings with them. The Fomor women dragged or herded along their misbegotten broods who often cried in their fear. A despairing wail rose over the whole file, joining in a single shrill lament for what was lost.

At a safe distance from the heat of the doomed city, these families of the Fomor warriors were joining an enormous sea of captives already formed. Along with the now-homeless citizens of the last Fomor stronghold in Eire were gathered the surviving few hundred of the fighters, now disarmed and drooping in attitudes of defeat. A tight cordon of de Danann and Firbolg warriors circled them like a briar bush whose thorns were made of iron. Nearby, workers were busily engaged in erecting a timber stockade that would become a temporary prison for the beaten race.

Lugh stood by a bonfire with Nuada and his comrades, watching the end of this sad procession as it crawled by. For all their brutality to the de Danarns, for all his own hatred and loathing of them, the young warrior still pitied them now. They were broken. They had lost their city and their possessions. Many of these women, no matter how awful they appeared, had lost their fathers, their mates, their children, that day. And soon they would be losing Eire.

"We have them all now," Nuada said, looking back along the line toward the city. "These are the last. Now that fire can burn that place away." He looked around at his companions and smiled. "Like burning out an infected wound with a hot iron. It'll make Eire clean all the quicker."

"Might have been better if this fire had taken care of this lot of bloody maggots as well," the Dagda remarked callously.

"What will happen to them now?" asked Lugh, watching a hunchbacked woman creep by, burdened with a clutch of spindly children who clung about her like great spiders.

"The few of their chieftains who are left have pledged never to disturb us again," Nuada told him. "For that, we'll let them sail away from Eire."

"But where will they go?" the young man wondered. "The Tower surely won't give them shelter or food."

"That's no concern of ours, lad," the Dagda put in. "Look, they're alive, aren't they? Don't be expecting any more charity from us. It was many a warrior who wanted to see them all slaughtered after their cruelties to us."

Lugh nodded. He understood the de Dananns' feelings. Perhaps this was fair. And yet he felt a sorrow for the Fomor of Eire, cheated by fate, betrayed by the Tower, and left to die.

He felt a hand slide into his and looked around to find Aine close beside him. In her eyes he saw a look of understanding and kindred sympathy.

From the direction of the burning city two de Danann chieftains now appeared and strode up to join the party with the king.

"We've driven all that we could find out of there," said the thin-faced one known as Febal. "The warriors are bringing them here."

"There were a few who managed to escape us," added the heavier, squarer chieftain known as Niet. "The fire'll likely get them. And we left this great, filthy swarm of them that were trapped in a sort of pen. Most terrible-looking monsters I've ever seen, even among the Fomor. We thought it'd be kinder to let them burn as well."

"Good work," Nuada told them. "When you've got the last of them gathered, see to the finishing of that stockade. At dawn we'll find what craftsmen there are among them and set them to work preparing their boats for sea."

The two chieftains nodded their agreement and moved away to organize their warriors for the new tasks. The High-King turned to the others at the fire.

"When the last of them sails away from Eire, then we can truly say that it is ours. Finally, we have the home we've sought all these years. The Prophecy has been fulfilled." He put a hand on Lugh's shoulder. "And we owe our victory to this young Champion."

"For you this is finished," Lugh told him grimly. "But for me there is something still left to do. I must try to save Gilla Decaire. And to do that, I've got to find out what happened."

"I can help you," said a voice from behind him.

He and the others turned as another pair of figures approached the fire. One was the woman smith called Bridget. And her sinewy arms were tight about the struggling figure of her son, Ruadan.

Her labors as a smith had made the woman more than a match for the slender boy. As they reached the fire she flung him violently forward and he fell heavily to his knees before the others.

He sat up, lifting a face pinched with fear toward the warriors. The red fire was like a flush of shame across his freckled white cheek.

"Ruadan!" Nuada said in surprise, recognizing his young aide. He looked to Bridget, who stood looming over him, her strangely divided face filled with despair.

"I've brought my son to you because he knows what has happened to your friend," she told Lugh, her voice blending grief and rage.

"This is the boy who told me where to meet Gilla," Lugh explained to the others. "It was because of him that I was caught!"

"I know nothing about it!" the boy wailed. "I was doing only as I was told to do. I didn't know anything would happen! I swear to Danu that I speak the truth!"

"No. You lie!" his mother spat out, leaning down over him threateningly. "I saw the four strange warriors come to you. I saw you go away with them. I watched you seek out the Clown and lead him from the camp. You led him into a trap just as you did Lugh!"

"Mother, please!" he cried, looking up to her with that young and guileless face, his voice pleading. "You have to believe me. I didn't know who those men were. I thought they were de Dananns. I did only what I was told to do. Please, Mother, how can you do this to me?"

"Maybe Ruadan is right, Bridget," Nuada said in defense of this boy whom he had so long trusted. "How can you be so certain he meant to betray us?"

She looked around at them, her face grimly set by the hard decision she had made.

"I know what he is because I know the truth about him," she said slowly. "I have kept the secret too long. He is the son of Bres."

"Bres!" Nuada gasped.

"I kept the secret because I feared that the de Dananns would hate him. I wanted him to grow up free of the evil that had touched his father. Still, his father reached him, and the Fomor blood in him must be strong. It was Bres that Ruadan turned to, not me."

She looked down at the boy, who knelt still, now frozen in shock at this revelation. Her eyes glistened with tears as she went on. "I tried to believe it was not happening. Finally, I could pretend no more. I came to realize that my son had been spying for his father all the time. He had passed on the plans of our rising. He had helped to free Bres after you had captured him at Tara."

Lugh looked down in wonder at Ruadan. He understood now why the Fomor had so often seemed to know their moves. This boy had nearly succeeded in bringing about the destruction of the whole de Danann race!

He gazed into the childlike, innocent face and sensed the kind of ruthless nature it concealed. Here was a fit son for Bres indeed.

"When I realized what he had done here, I knew I had to speak," Bridget went on. "He tried to flee when he found you had escaped. I caught him and I brought him here." She lifted a hand to point at Ruadan. Her voice tolled out the next words with finality: "My son is a traitor!"

Lugh now stepped forward. "Where is Gilla?" he demanded. "What did those men do with him?"

The lad turned toward him. He took up the whining tone of a frightened little boy again. "I don't know! My mother is mad! I had nothing to do with—"

In a single move the Answerer swept out. The bright point touched the smooth curve of the boy's upstretched throat. Lugh's youthful voice was edged with iron too as he cut Ruadan short.

"Your mother has condemned you with her own words. I have seen into your heart and I know she speaks the truth. Tell me what you know or you will die right now!"

Ruadan stared up, his cunning mind calculating Lugh's sincerity. He saw nothing but grim intent in the face above him. His own look of innocence vanished abruptly in a snarl of open rage.

"All right, 'Champion,' " he answered scornfully. "If I'm to die, I'll at least have the satisfaction of giving a last pain to you. You'll not be seeing your Clown again. The Tower has him now."

"So it is the Tower," said Lugh. "And he's not dead?"

Ruadan laughed. "He'd likely be better off if he were. But those men were to deliver him alive to their master."

"What, Balor?" asked the Dagda.

"No," said the boy. He grinned around at them with evil satisfaction. "Someone whose power is even greater. Someone who'll yet see all of you destroyed. Your own Druid, Mathgen!"

Lugh's comrades exchanged an apprehesive look at that. For all of them, the name invoked great dread.

"You're underestimating the strength of Gilla Decaire, boy," Lugh said. His gaze went to the faces of his friends. "If he is in the Tower, and alive, there is still hope!"

As he moved to address them, Ruadan was for a moment forgotten. The point of the Answerer slid away from the lad's throat. He took advantage of this to make a desperate move. He leaped to his feet and shouldered Lugh aside. Snatching a dagger from within his tunic, he charged for the High-King, his face twisted in fanatical rage.

"Death to Nuada!" he shrieked.

But then his triumphant shout turned to an agonized cry. His head snapped back as the point of a spear tore out through his chest. Instantly dead, he crumpled to the ground like something boneless.

The group of warriors looked from the stricken lad to Bridget. Her strange, divided face, set with her determination, was also streaked by tears. It was her own spear, the slender point fashioned by her own hand, that her strong arm had driven through her son.

"Now he has paid for what he has done," she said in a voice quivering with the emotion she controlled, "and so have I."

She moved forward and knelt by him. Gently, she pulled the weapon free and rolled him over. His face now seemed very young, very innocent, in death. She looked up to the king.

"I'll take him with me now," she said.

Nuada could find nothing to say. He nodded. She lifted the slender form in her arms and moved away.

"I'll go with her," the Dagda said, displaying an unexpected compassion.

"I'll go as well," said Morrigan. "She is a friend of mine."

Together this peculiar couple followed Bridget away through the camp.

Now the High-King turned to the rest, a look of puzzlement on his face.

"It's clear why the Tower might want you, Lugh," he said, "but it's very strange that they'd be after Gilla Decaire. What good can that Clown be to them?"

"We cannot tell Nuada that Gilla is really Manannan MacLir," Lugh said firmly, looking around the circle of his friends.

All of those who knew the Clown's true identity were gathered there: Findgoll, the Druid; the Dagda and his son, Angus Og; Morrigan; Taillta; Aine; and the now–dog-shaped Pooka. They had crept away from the encampment to meet on a rocky bit of shore well away from their fellows and out of sight. Now, seated in various degrees of discomfort on the heap of wave-scoured stone, they discussed the plight of their friend.

"I don't see why we need to keep his secret now," the Dagda said. "The rest should know all he's done to help us. We all owe him."

"It was the wish of Manannan that the de Dananns never know he was helping them in their uprising," Lugh reminded him. "To tell them now, when they've finally won their battle for Eire, would go against everything he's done."

"Why is it that they took him?" wondered Angus Og. "He must've seemed a harmless Clown to them, same as to us."

"I understood why when I saw Balor was still alive,"

Lugh told him. "He knew what powers Manannan had over the sea. He must have wanted him well out of the way before risking his fleet in an attack on Eire."

"He must have wanted you taken for the same reason," put in Aine. "He certainly knew about the Riders of the Sidhe."

"That explains why they captured him," the Dagda said, "but not why they'd bother keeping him alive."

"Remember, it was Mathgen he was to be taken to," Findgoll replied.

Mathgen! Lugh had heard much about this infamous High-Druid. Once a de Danann, he had used his magic in an attempt to seize the mystical isles of Tir-na-nog, the dwelling place of Queen Danu, the powerful sorceress who had befriended the de Danann people. But the Dagda, Morrigan, and Findgoll had managed to thwart his plans. Then they had thought him destroyed. Now they knew he still lived, using his talents for those in the Tower of Glass.

"That ice-blue shroud is a bit of trickery well within his Druidic skills," Findgoll went on. "You can be sure he has a reason for wanting MacLir alive. My guess is that he wants the secret of the sea-god's powers. That could be very dangerous for us. The Tower will still be wanting to see us destroyed. And Mathgen is likely after a bit of his own revenge."

"There's only one thing that we can do, you know," Lugh said with determination, looking around at his friends. "We have to rescue him."

Chapter Thirteen
A RESCUE PLAN

"Just what exactly is it that you mean by 'we?'" the Dagda asked carefully.

"Us," Lugh answered, waving about at the little band. "Those of us here." He grinned, adding with great camaraderie, "I thought of going myself, but I knew I couldn't keep you from coming along, so I decided not to try to stop you this time."

"You might have tried just a bit," Angus said, clearly not sharing in Lugh's enthusiasm.

"You want us to go into the Tower after him?" the Druid asked. "Just us?"

The Dagda shook his head. "It would be madness trying that. It would take our whole host to storm that bloody Tower. And that's the only way you'll get inside."

"If an army did go against the Tower, you know well enough what fate they'd be risking," Lugh countered.

The Dagda did know. It was many years ago that his people had first come to Eire, seeking a land that they might make their own. Then they had met the Fomor of the Tower. Balor had demanded tribute of them, but they were a proud race of warriors who would submit to no one. They had sailed out boldly to attack the Tower of Glass.

The images of that battle were still vivid in his mind: the sleek black vessels slicing through the lighter craft, the deadly bows of the grim Tower soldiers, and, finally, the crimson beam of Balor's single eye blasting the helpless ships into flaming wrecks. Only a handful of all of the clans had survived that terrible day.

For the Dagda, as for the others who had survived, the Tower was a place of terrible power. Even the defeat of the Tower's machines had not lessened the almost supernatural dread of it. To attack the mountain of glass or even penetrate its mysterious interior seemed unthinkable. And he realized that it was this old fear that was making him hesitate now.

"A direct attack would likely fail and cost Manannan his life," Lugh was saying. "But a small group could sneak in and take him out."

"I think he's right," Aine put in supportively. "Lugh and Taillta and I have been in the Tower with Manannan, and we escaped safely."

"Which only means that they'll be all the more watchful for someone trying it again," the Dagda said. "They'll likely have guards at every possible entrance. How do you think you'll get in?"

Lugh smiled. "I think I know of one way that they might not think to guard. Here, look at this."

He climbed from his rock and smoothed a patch of sand. With the point of his dagger he traced a simple picture of the

Tower. He indicated the levels, the central atrium, the lifts, the lower storage area, and the throne room of Balor.

"Aine, Gilla and I managed to sneak in once through these storage areas," Lugh explained. "But that would be the most dangerous way now. Of course, there are no openings into the walls of glass above."

"Then where do you think we can go in?" the Dagda asked.

Lugh tapped the top of the drawing with his dagger. "The roof. There is a doorway and a stairs leading down into the top level of the Tower. But they can't be expecting anyone to get in that way."

"And they're right in thinking that," the Dagda said. "Just how do you plan on our getting up there?"

"That I may be able to help us with," came the voice of the Pooka. He lifted his shaggy form from a hollow in the rocks, stretched, and moved down beside Lugh.

"Of course, he can become a bird," said Angus. "But how's he supposed to take us all to that roof? He would be days flying us one by one from Eire."

"I would alone," Shaglan replied, his mouth stretching into a wide canine grin. "But a clan of Pookas could do it in one flight."

"A clan!" the Dagda bellowed. "What, do you mean that we should trust ourselves to that lot of treacherous beings? They'd as likely dump us in the sea as help us."

The Pooka's smile vanished. Stricken by these harsh words, he dropped down at Lugh's feet, his body sagging.

"Hold on," Lugh protested. "That's not fair."

"Not fair?" The Dagda shot back. "It was that family of his who helped Mathgen when he betrayed us and tried to take Tir-na-nog for himself! They used that bloody bird form then as well. Flew the Druid and his army in to take Danu's palace. Now you think they'll do the same for us?"

"It's to atone for that wrong to you that I think they will help," Shaglan said sharply, rising up again as his hurt gave way to anger. "We were tricked into helping Mathgen then, as you well know. We've had our punishment for it too, losing our power to take the shape of men and being exiled to the wild places of Eire. There are others like me who want to win the friendship and trust of the de Dananns again."

"Shaglan has proven his loyalty to us, and you've accepted him," Lugh told the Dagda. "Couldn't you accept others too?"

"You've made a peace with the Firbolgs," Taillta reminded him. "Why can't you do the same with them?"

The Dagda wavered. He cast a look to Morrigan, who had watched silently from her rock like a dark statue. She nodded. He looked to Findgoll, and the little Druid smiled.

"It's time to be healing all our old wounds, my friend," he said.

The Dagda grunted, hesitated, then nodded himself.

"All right then. If Shaglan can convince these other Pookas to help us, I'll give my trust to them. But if I find myself falling into the sea, you won't mind if I do a bit of complaining on the way down?"

Shaglan's broad smile returned. "No fear of that. And I thank you for your belief."

"That's settled then," said Angus Og, who had no problems with the Pookas but was still somewhat uncertain about this plan. "Now, what happens after we fly to the Tower's roof? What do we do then?"

Lugh went back to the map. "Here," he said, pointing, "just at the base of the stairway from the roof, there is a special room that slides up and down the Tower."

"Slides up and down?" Angus said uncertainly.

"It's safe enough," Lugh assured him. "We can go to any level in the Tower without being seen. With its help we can strike very quickly, go in and out of the Tower before most of them even know we've been there."

"Simple," said Angus dryly. "We need to find only a single man in all that giant place."

"That's where I'll help," put in Taillta. "I was kept a captive there for a long time. I learned the insides of that Tower very well. I can take us anywhere we need to go."

"All we have to know is where to look," said Aine.

Lugh smiled at her. "For that we'll have to ask."

The Dagda was still shaking his head doubtfully.

"I don't know, lad," he said. "This sounds too much like one of the mad plans that Clown was forever coming up with. You're becoming more and more like him."

Lugh found this observation somewhat startling. He had never considered that himself. Was he becoming like MacLir? And, if he was, was that good or bad?

"Still," the big Champion continued, "we can't be turning our backs on one who's helped us, given us the magic to restore ourselves, saved us countless times—even if he is a madman with a great, foolish grin. No, lad. We're owing this much to him."

"Well, I suppose I'm game enough for it," Angus added in a stoic way. "We'll all die, of course, but I hadn't planned much for the rest of my life anyway."

"I love a positive spirit," Taillta said. "When can we go?"

"I can start out right away with Shaglan," Lugh told her, "but it will take some time to reach the Pookas."

"We'll need five more of them," the Dagda said. "One for Taillta, Aine, Angus, and myself, and another for MacLir, if we should get him out."

"We'll need six," Findgoll corrected hastily. "I'm going too!"

"That you are not!" the Dagda roared, heaving his bulk up from its rock and looming threateningly over the little man. "We'll need fighting skills for this, not your wizard's tricks! The last time we took you with us you were only in the way!"

The Druid jumped up, stretching his body up to its full height—which brought it only to the big Champion's shoulder. Still he faced the Dagda squarely, glaring up into the battered face with indignant rage.

"In the way, was I?" he shouted back. "And wasn't it my magic that saved your own life then? And isn't it Mathgen himself whom you're going to face this time?"

"He's right," Lugh said placatingly, moving up between the adversaries. "We may need the knowledge of another Druid to free Manannan. We have to take Findgoll."

Again beaten by the force of greater logic, the Dagda only snorted his frustration and plumped his body back down on a rock. Grinning in victory, the little Druid looked to Shaglan.

"Six it will be then, if you please," he said.

"All right," Lugh said. "Then we're all agreed. Shaglan, how long will it take to bring your family here?"

"Two days to reach the Burren lands, find them, and return," the Pooka told him.

"Then we should return in three," said Lugh. "There's another place that you must take me first."

"Another place?" Aine said in puzzlement. "Where?"

He fixed her with a searching look. "Do you remember

how Manannan was that last night? He must have sensed this. He told me that I would know what to do. I didn't understand him then, but I do now. The feeling's very strong in me. I can't deny it. I must go to Manannan's Isle."

With a faint whine of its mechanism, the glowing lens of Mathgen's eye swiveled around toward the door of his room as it slid open. The image on the screen behind the Druid's tank settled on the vast form of Balor as he rolled swiftly through. The lens pivoted to follow him, and the projected view swelled as he approached.

"I know what has happened, Balor," the faint voice rasped before the Commander could speak. "My powers brought me an image of the fight."

"You told me that Lugh Lamfada would be gotten out of the way!" the giant thundered accusingly. "You said that my forces could attack with little harm!"

"I told you that I would *try* to deal with Lugh," Mathgen amended. "I failed."

"Failed!" Balor's voice was vibrating the entire room now. "So half my machines are destroyed, the garrisons in Eire are destroyed, the island is lost, and the de Dananns are stronger than ever!"

"As I warned you, the boy has great powers," the Druid replied, undisturbed by Balor's rage. "And, as I recall, it was you who seemed to feel he was no threat."

This reminder of his previous blustering quenched much of the fire of the Commander's anger. The heat of his blazing ruby eye faded with it.

"Lugh is dangerous," the whispering voice continued. "But where I have failed you in one way, I have succeeded in another. And it may prove to be of greater importance to us both. It may make the loss of a few of your precious killing toys quite unimportant."

"Unimportant?" Balor repeated. "But they are a part of this Tower's future! They are intended for our use when we leave here and regain our power."

"Yes, yes," Mathgen hissed wearily, as if he had heard this pronouncement too often before. "I know all about the purpose of the Tower and the future of the pure Fomor race. I know that, if I am right, that future can be achieved more easily than ever before."

"Explain!" Balor clanged. "No more of your vague Druid rambling."

But before Mathgen could speak, the main door to the room slid open again. Bres strode through it, ignoring a harried Sital Salmhor, who trotted at his side, protesting his intrusion here vigorously.

The red eye of Balor and the Druid's blue lens both turned upon these two as they approached.

"What do you mean, pulling out those iron monsters of yours and leaving us?" Bres demanded angrily as he stepped up before the Commander.

"I told him he mustn't come here, that he had no right to question you," said Salmhor, his voice filled with his towering indignation at Bres's crude behavior.

"I have every right!" Bres retorted. "It was my army being left to the slaughter. It was my Eire being thrown away!"

"Our machines were being wasted," Balor told him flatly. "The force of Lugh Lamfada's Riders might have destroyed them all. There was no point in going on to save your creatures for you."

"But *you* could have destroyed that boy," Bress challenged. "You could have landed and dealt with him. Why didn't you use that so-powerful bloody eye on him?"

And then, a realization suddenly dawning upon him, he paused and eyed the giant being appraisingly.

"That's it, isn't it?" he said in a musing tone. "You weren't certain that you *could* deal with him yourself. You believe what Mathgen said about that Prophecy. You're afraid of him, aren't you? You're afraid he really might destroy you"

"Enough!" Balor rumbled threateningly. "You take a great risk to suggest that to me!"

"Yes, Bres," Mathgen's sibilant whisper put in more soothingly. "Balor has only learned to become more cautious. My own warnings are what have made him so. I understand the kinds of powers we face. I am better able to deal with them."

"Are you?" Bres shot back. "And what about the marvelous job you did in settling that boy Champion? It was little enough harm you did him!"

"A fact which only serves to demonstrate how difficult an adversary he is to deal with," the unruffled Druid told him. "I learned from it. The knowledge may prove useful. Balor acted correctly to withdraw. Had he listened to me earlier, he might have saved his machines. And," Mathgen paused, "if both of you will listen to me now, I may be able to show you how this minor defeat will be no hindrance to our final victory."

As it had with Balor, the Druid's cryptic statement served to draw much of the force from Bres's mood of belligerence.

"If you can perform some Druid trickery that can change this into anything but a disaster," he said sullenly, "then I'll call you a true marvel myself!"

"Very well," said Mathgen, and one skeletal finger moved to depress the lever in his hand.

The door hidden in the room's corner slid apart. The two remaining henchmen of the Druid moved into view, hauling a lanky figure forward between them. As they neared the tank, its hard glare fell upon the familiar features of Gilla Decaire.

The Clown blinked up into the light, then swept his gaze around at the alien setting.

"An interesting place!" he remarked congenially. "Is it hard to keep clean?"

"You may dispense with that absurd role of Clown," Mathgen wheezed out. "I am aware that you are really Manannan MacLir."

The prisoner looked hurt. "Oh, really? Now, that's not very nice." He leaned toward one of the Druid's men and said in a confidential way: "It was meant to be a secret, you know."

"Don't waste your foolish attempts at humor on me," the being in the tank hissed sharply. "And take off that ridiculous disguise!"

"What, this?" The Clown stroked his tangle of beard in an affectionate way. "But we've been together for so long! It's like a part of me. I'd feel quite naked without—"

"Take it off or I'll have it ripped off you!" Mathgen commanded.

The lanky man glanced right and left at the burly stonefaced guards, who seemed quite capable of doing such a thing.

"No! No! I'll do it!" he volunteered hastily. "They might tear off the wrong bits!"

The two released his arms and stepped back. He lifted his hands to his face. The onlookers watched with curiosity as he worked his long fingers through the mat of beard and dug them deeply into the flesh of his jowls. Then he pulled outward. The beard and part of the face beneath pulled slowly away with a faint tearing sound. He dropped the limp mass of flesh and hair, then yanked away part of his eyebrows and the sharp end of his nose. Lastly, he pulled the ragged mass of hair from his head.

The face revealed by this seeming violence was much less awkward and absurd, but still pleasantly unusual. The nose was still considerable, the eyes still bright gray. The face was squarer, the chin more pronounced, the forehead wider. The hair, of a distinctive silver-gray, was short and lay in smooth waves on the large head.

"Well, there it is," he announced with a triumphant air. "Do you find the 'true me' more acceptable?"

"The true you?" Mathgen repeated. The lipless mouth curled back in a ghastly, rotting smile. "The true you has yet to be revealed, old friend."

Chapter Fourteen
MANANNAN'S SECRET

The prisoner looked over the creature in the tank with interest.

"I've decided that you must be Mathgen, the Druid," he said thoughtfully. "You really don't look very well, you know. Perhaps if you got out more?"

"Still playing the fool?" Mathgen sneered. "Well, Manannan, I have learned a great deal about you from Balor's visit to your little isle."

The vast image of MacLir that had filled the screen behind the tank now began to waver, its colors dissolving, shifting, re-forming into the hazy green image of Manannan's home.

"Why, that's amazing," the tall man said, honestly impressed. "Can you do other tricks as well?"

"My own magic and the science of this Tower allow me

to project my own thoughts here, as well as those I absorb from others. But even my powers cannot penetrate mysteries protected by another's magic, as your island is. Still, Balor has managed to enter your domain, and the impressions he has brought me tell me much."

Other vague images swept across the screen in a confusing and somewhat overlapping procession. They included brief views of a strange mound of earth, a dreamlike landscape, and airy beings in bright garments.

"This dwelling place you call a Sidhe, the inhabitants you call your people, the powers you have given Lugh Lamfada—these all suggested something else to me," Mathgen went on. "I couldn't be certain of it until I saw you unmasked. I know you, and I know what you really are. You're no sea-god. Your power comes from Tir-na-nog!"

"Tir-na-nog?" Balor's metallic voice was sharp with impatience. "What is this about, Mathgen?"

"This man is a servant of Queen Danu," the Druid explained. "She has sent him to Eire to aid the de Dananns and see that Lugh fulfills the Prophecy!"

Balor had heard these names from Mathgen before. He knew that it was this powerful sorceress who had befriended the de Dananns long ago. It was she who had given them new strength, new knowledge, and new magic skills and sent them to make Eire their own land. Since the day one of his ships had found the ravaged body of Mathgen in the sea he had heard the Druid speak often of the marvels of Tir-na-nog's four shining cities. And since the de Dananns had appeared in Eire he had constantly heard the warnings of what a threat those Children of Danu might be to the Fomor power.

"But if he is from Danu, why has he acted in such secrecy?" Balor asked.

"The de Dananns are a very proud race," Mathgen replied, his husky whisper touched by scorn. "For them to know that the magic of their great patroness was winning Eire for them would be a tremendous blow to that pride. So Danu provided a guardian for them in the form of a mysterious god of the sea. Am I right, MacLir?"

"You are a very clever . . . ah, can I call you a man still?" the prisoner replied amiably.

"I know Danu's thinking very well," Mathgen told him, ignoring the insult. "Remember, I lived in Tir-na-nog. I had a command of magic that rivaled even hers!"

"I remember," Manannan said. "And I remember you used it to betray your own people and her trust in you. I'm afraid it makes you very hard to like."

"I am the one with just cause to hate," came the wheezing reply. "I meant to give the de Dananns power, a power Danu's people waste, hidden away on their tiny isles. We could have used it to conquer any land, move nature to our will, create vast wealth. And for my dream I was given this useless rack of bones, barely kept alive by these things that hang upon me like parasites. But now the time is coming for my revenge. Danu made one mistake in sending you here: She didn't know that I was still alive, that I would see through your attempt at a disguise."

Manannan listened patiently through his tirade, then nodded. "Yes, that's quite interesting," he said politely, "but I don't see where your having me will give you much revenge. The de Dananns have apparently won Eire. The war is over."

"The war has just begun," Mathgen hissed. "With the forces of this Tower I will go to Tir-na-nog. This time I will take control, and the Fomor will again become the great power they once were."

"As much as I dislike causing disappointment," MacLir put in affably, "I think I should point out that no one knows just where Tir-na-nog is. I mean, it is hidden, far out in the western sea, by a magic that makes my isle's cloaking fog seem tame. It can't be found—unless Danu allows it to be."

The gash of Mathgen's mouth stretched into its ghastly smile again. "It can also be found by the subjects of Queen Danu. And we have such a subject right here with us!"

The tall man laughed. "You have to be joking, Mathgen. You can't think that I'm going to tell you how to find it!"

"I do," came the whisper, "and you will, in time."

The men at Manannan's sides moved in and seized his arms. They forced him toward a large, complex device that glittered faintly under the shifting lights, a bewildering array of silver appendages that looked distinctly unpleasant.

The man pushed him roughly down into a curved seat in the center of this sinister contraption and secured his limbs with a number of heavy straps.

"Not too tight about the ankles now," he cautioned. "My feet tend to fall asleep."

"Jest for as long as you can, MacLir," said Mathgen. His

glowing lens swiveled to point toward the bound figure. The image of Manannan's face filled the screen behind the Druid's tank. "Soon, you *will* give up your secret to me. With my magic I can probe your mind, draw what I want from you. You have only to think of Tir-na-nog's location, even for an instant, and I will have it."

The face of the screen grew hazy, fading away into a strange, swirling whiteness crossed by a fine pattern of gray lines, much like a heavy rain, obscuring the view.

"My mind touches yours now, MacLir," the voice whispered. "Think of Danu. Think of your Blessed Isles. Tell me where they are. Show them to me now!"

The gray-white mist on the screen wavered suddenly, as if whipped by a sharp gust of wind. The watchers looked toward it eagerly, expecting to see this shroud lift and reveal the hidden isles.

The wavering grew more frenzied. Vague, tantalizing shapes started to form. They grew sharper and clearer, darker and larger. And then . . . they disappeared.

Manannan laughed. "I'm sorry, but that was so much fun! I really had you excited for a moment, didn't I?"

Mathgen's whisper sharpened to an angry wheeze. "You may have the power to defy me now, but when the pain courses through you, it will take all your concentration to control your thoughts. Then your defenses will break." The druid paused. "In time, my friend. In time."

One of the Druid's men moved in again. He lowered a helmet of silver metal over Manannan's head. Its visor dropped forward, shutting off his sight.

He had a strong feeling that things were going to become a bit difficult from here on.

The great bird flew on, tireless beats of its broad wings carrying it toward the east, soaring high above the open sea. The sky was brilliant, the sea a sparkling sweep. From his perch astride the back of the bird Lugh found it a delightful view.

He shifted his grip about Shaglan's neck and said with what enthusiasm he could manage: "I actually think I'm getting used to being up so high."

The Pooka chuckled. "I can tell. You're barely choking me now."

"Isn't there anything that you're afraid of, Shaglan?"

"Only losing control over my shape at some important movement. Forgetting myself and slipping into the form of a boar or a salmon while up here would be a nasty surprise."

"You would have to mention that, wouldn't you?" Lugh added unhappily.

Shaglan only grinned and flew steadily on.

Below them now appeared a strange wall of white, like a heavy cloud bank hanging on the sea. This was the band of fog that made a full circle about Manannan's Isle, a band so thick any ship that entered it quickly lost direction.

Within that swirling gray other dangers lurked: sea creatures of varied and fearsome kinds dwelt there, waiting to challenge any who dared to venture into their domain.

Lugh recalled his first visit to the isle and his voyage through that awful fog. He was glad he had Shaglan to carry him above the barrier this time.

Within its ring the sea grew clear again, revealing a wide circle of blue. And at its center, like a jewel set in this azure background, was the emerald glow of the sea-god's enchanted isle. Rolling meadowlands of lush green gave way gently to low hills furred thickly with trees, all softened by a hint of mist that gave the whole countryside a look of dreamlike unreality.

As Shaglan spiraled closer, Lugh directed him toward the meadows on the western side, just beyond the shore. There an odd feature of the land grew more obvious as they drew near, an enormous mound, quite high and smoothly rounded. It might at first have been taken for a natural hill save for its isolation in the level fields and its perfect, symmetrical shape. They spoke of something created by a power other than that of nature.

"Down there," Lugh said, pointing. "There's an opening in the top of the mound."

"I don't see anything," the Pooka replied.

"It's nearly invisible from outside, but it's there," Lugh assured him. "Just drop down slowly on the very top. You'll find it."

With some misgivings Shaglan obeyed, slipping down carefully toward what appeared to be a very solid bit of hill. Just as he was preparing to feel the jolt of hard earth against his feet, the ground faded away, dissolving like a ghostly image. They sank through, as if the hill were absorbing them, and disappeared into its depths.

It was a most peculiar sensation. One moment they were outside, then—with a curious, bewildering rush, like being spun around—they were suddenly inside. Above them was a clearly visible round opening showing the bright sky. Below and around them spread the interior of the Sidhe.

Lugh, as before, experienced a sense of awe at seeing this strange dwelling place of Manannan. And, as before, he was especially fascinated by its size. For although the mound was very large outside, it did not seem capable of encompassing so vast a space as now lay before him.

Under a cavernous dome of smooth earth the floor of the Sidhe appeared to contain a whole countryside of its own, complete with streams and ponds, vales and meadows and hills, forests of exotic vegetation Lugh had seen nowhere else, alive with strange and brightly plumaged birds that soared and sang among the trees. Herds of cattle and sheep grazed peacefully on its grassy plains. The landscape faded away to the hazy distances of the circle. The forms of human beings moved there as well. These were the inhabitants of this marvelous Sidhe, a people well suited to their surroundings.

They all seemed very young and were of a slender, graceful form and fragile beauty. He saw many of them as the bird sailed lower, some at work in the gardens, others with the herds, many at play or at music or in talk. In a little glade a pair of harpers were spinning out a lively air whose high, sweet, vibrant notes drifted up to him. And around the two danced women of the Sidhe, their bright, flowing skirts forming a shifting pattern against the grass.

But as Shaglan swooped around the Sidhe, these people began to take notice of their visitors. Activity ceased, and word passed quickly about until all were gazing upward.

Lugh realized they had been seen, and waved, afraid this peaceful folk might be alarmed. This appeared to have an immediate effect. The entire population began a movement toward the center of the Sidhe.

This was also Lugh's goal, for here was the hill that marked the focal point for the dwelling's life. It was a smaller version of the mound itself: a grassy knoll, neatly rounded, with a level area at its top. Here a circle of large, roughly hewn standing stones, evenly spaced like the prongs of a crown, sat on the brow of the hill.

At Lugh's direction the Pooka fluttered its way gently down toward a landing in the clear area within this ring of stones. As they came in, the inhabitants of the Sidhe closed in around the mound, moving up its slopes to form outside the ring. When the bird had settled, Lugh slipped from its back and smiled warmly around him. He received a wreath of bright smiles in return.

From one side of the circle a small group of the young people moved forward, passing through the stones and approaching Lugh. At their head was a young man whose features were sculptured so finely that Lugh had to term him beautiful. He raised a hand in greeting and addressed Lugh in a voice whose tones conveyed a sense of gentleness and peace.

"Welcome to you, Lugh Lamfada. We are glad to see the Champion of the Sidhe returning to us." A note of puzzlement then marred the serenity of his speech. "But where is Manannan MacLir? It is strange to see you here without him."

"I have bad news," Lugh said, then lifted his voice to address the whole company. "I have sad news for you all. Manannan MacLir was captured by the Fomor. I believe that he is now a prisoner in the Tower of Glass."

A sigh of regret, like the soft keening of a night breeze, ruffled through them.

"I intend to rescue him," Lugh announced firmly. "That is why I've come. When I stood on this mound and agreed to become the Champion of the Sidhe, Manannan told me that I would be forever of this place and its people. The last time I saw him, he said that I would know what I must do. Since he was taken, a strong feeling has grown in me that I must come here."

The young man nodded. "If that is in your heart, then it must be so. And if Manannan is gone, it means that now there is something we must do."

He turned from Lugh, raised his hands, and addressed those gathered about the ring in a voice that took on a new power and volume.

"My friends, Lugh has come to us. It is time for our help. We must raise the Call!"

With that the young man began to raise a chant, a low and crooning song whose words the warrior of Eire could not understand. The others joined him, their voices blending like strands of silver to create a fine, intricately worked harmony.

As it lifted upward, a new light began to shine down on

the mound from above. Lugh looked upward and realized that a great pool of light was forming below the opening, swelling until the upper portion of the dome was filled with it. It swirled there, a luminescent white, like a mist lit by the sun. And then a form began to take shape within it.

It was as if something were moving out of the white void, taking on shape and color as it came closer. The dim outlines grew clearer until Lugh saw that he was looking at a face, a beautiful woman's face gazing down at him with a benevolent smile.

The Sidhe's inhabitants knelt at once in honor to this vision. Only the young Champion remained upright, staring upward, silently mouthing the name of this being: "Queen Danu!"

Chapter Fifteen
LUGH'S RETURN

Lugh had seen the image of this mystical being twice before. As then, he now felt an aura of warmth and good will from her, as if she had been his friend all of his life.

"Lugh Lamfada," came the soft, clear voice, a song itself, "your return here means that the destiny you have followed has nearly reached its end. The fates of the de Dananns, the Fomor, and many others will be played out in these next few days."

"What will happen?" Lugh called. "Please, Danu, can you tell me?"

"No power can say what shape the fates will take," she answered. "Your own will and courage will decide. But my magic has shown that in your mission one instrument will be needed by you. It is the fourth gift of the cities of Tir-na-nog; the Spear of Gorias. Take it with you now, Lugh Lamfada, and all the hopes of the Blessed Isles go with you as well."

At these words the face above began to fade, receding into the mists. The young Champion, left rather bewildered by her cryptic message, shouted entreatingly: "Wait! Please! What is it that I'm to use this spear for?"

The answer drifted faintly back to him, as if already from a great distance. "When the time comes, you will know!"

And with that, Danu was gone.

In a moment the silver mist had dissolved away, revealing the dome above once again. But Lugh continued to stare up for a long moment at the spot where her face had appeared. He was wondering, in an irritated way, just what was the good of having such great magical powers helping him if they couldn't provide some knowledge that wasn't quite so vague!

A light hand touched his sleeve and he turned to find a young man beside him. The others of the Sidhe had risen to their feet and were regarding him expectantly.

"Are you ready to receive the Spear of Gorias?" the young man asked.

Lugh shrugged. He hadn't much choice but to take what had been offered him, for whatever it was worth.

"I suppose I am," he said.

His boyish host nodded and led the warrior toward the very center of the ring. Here was where the four gifts of Danu had once rested, waiting for the day they would be used.

Lugh looked over the spot, recalling his first sight of it. There, on a low, flat-topped stone, had lain the gleaming Answerer, which he now carried. Beside it had stood the tall, rounded column of stone called the Lia Fail—the Stone of Truth—whose roaring voice would proclaim a true king of Eire. This Lugh had carried to Tara to prove the right of Nuada to the High-King's throne, thus deposing Bres.

A fire pit in the third corner of the square marked where the Cauldron had sat. It could never be emptied of the miraculous stew that it contained. Lugh and his friends had survived many adventures to take it safely to Eire, where it had restored the strength of the whole de Danann host.

From three of the four shining cities of Tir-na-nog—Falias, Finias, and Murias—had these marvels come, each one a gift of its city's greatest sorcerers, given to aid the de Danann people in their struggle for Eire. Now only one gift remained, that of Gorias, fourth city of the Blessed Isles.

It hung by its shaft from a tripod of iron. Its head was submerged in a large black iron pot. So enormous was the energy that emanated from this spearpoint that the liquid around it boiled furiously all the time.

The young man accompanying Lugh stopped a respectful distance from this sacred object his people had so long protected here. Lugh stepped boldly closer and looked down into the pot.

The water was certainly boiling, he thought. He could not imagine the kind of heat that was somehow being generated there. The water rumbled and sputtered and crackled with the violence of the power it seemed barely able to contain.

He looked around to the young man who was watching him, still with that sweet, untroubled smile.

"This spear," he said, "it looks very . . . ah . . . hot!"

"Oh, yes," the other replied quite cheerfully. "Manannan has said that there is a power in that spearhead greater than any we could imagine and very deadly to anyone it touches. We stay well away from it ourselves."

"Oh," said Lugh, giving the thing another searching examination. It looked hotter than ever. "Well, I don't suppose he told you just how I was supposed to . . . take it?"

To his relief, this query was answered promptly.

"Of course! If you truly are the Champion who is to wield the spear, you simply take it. There is no danger to you."

"Really?" Lugh said, at first relieved. Then another point struck him. "But, ah, how do I know for certain that I really am the right one?"

"Why, you must be! Manannan himself proclaimed you so, didn't he?"

"I suppose so," Lugh agreed, but with a distinct lack of conviction. He had often doubted that strange being's sanity. He had as often questioned his own rightness as Champion. Well, he told himself, here was a fine chance to test both.

He put on what he hoped was a look of bold determination and stepped right up to the cauldron. The metal of the pot radiated a heat that he could feel on his legs, and the steam from the boiling liquid was nearly stifling. Just moments there would parboil his face. He had to move quickly. He stretched out a hand.

"Steady, lad!" cautioned Shaglan from across the ring.

He was steady. He shot his hand forward, seized the spear haft firmly in its middle, and pulled it up. It came free of the suspending tripod as it was lifted. The head came clear of the masking liquid, releasing the energy that had been contained.

A bright light flared up from the mouth of the pot. Its glare made the Sidhe about seem to grow dark.

But so far Lugh was safe. He felt no pain, no burn from this great force. After a moment he peeked cautiously out through the eyes he had squeezed shut and realized that nothing else was going to happen. He stepped back, bringing the spearhead clear of the pot, into the view of everyone.

The light concentrated in the head was like that of molten silver. Bright flares of light shot out about it as if it were a star. Flushed with triumph and relief, Lugh lifted the weapon high. The brilliant glow intensified to a nearly blinding point, pulsed, then faded back to a more reserved blaze, contained just within the head itself.

Surprised by this reaction, Lugh lowered the spear and looked curiously at the glowing point. As he did, his young host approached him.

"The Spear of Gorias has accepted you," he said in explanation of the phenomenon. "It has prepared itself for you to bear it."

One of the young women still outside the ring of stones now moved forward. When she reached the two, she bowed low and stretched forward her arms, presenting what seemed to Lugh a leather bag.

The young man took it and, in turn, passed it to Lugh.

"This covering has been created to cloak the spear's head and contain its power," he told Lugh. "It will serve this function for only a few days' time. Should anyone but you attempt to remove the cover or use the spear, its power will consume them. Do you understand?"

Lugh nodded. He did not hesitate in taking the cover, which appeared nothing more than a small sack with a drawstring. He slipped it over the head and drew it tight. Whatever magic it possessed certainly seemed sufficient to contain the weapon's enormous heat and light. It looked quite innocent now.

"Before you return to Eire, will you rest and eat with us?" offered his host.

"I thank you," Lugh replied, "but I must start back at once. If Manannan is alive, he is in grave danger. We will have to act as quickly as we can."

"Of course," the other said. "Though we do not understand the sadness and violence of the world you go to, we know that what you will do must be done. As Queen Danu has said, all of our hopes will go with you."

Lugh walked back to the Pooka, who eyed the spear warily as he prepared to mount.

"You'll keep that thing well away from me, I hope," it said.

"Don't worry," Lugh said, trying to sound assuring, "it's safe enough, I think."

"Very comforting," it answered. "Well, let's be off."

Flapping its great wings, the Pooka trotted off across the hilltop and launched itself from the crest, soaring out across the magical countryside before wheeling about and beginning its climb. Lugh turned to wave a final good-bye to the crowd still watching from the central mound. Then the Pooka was through the round window in the dome and out into the open sky again.

"Interesting place," Shaglan observed as they soared out over the ocean, Eire-bound.

"Too peaceful," Lugh added. "I don't think I could stand all that smiling and sweetness for very long."

The Pooka laughed. "Now you're sounding like MacLir."

"I suppose so," Lugh answered thoughtfully.

For some distance along the shore, boats were pulled up. All types and shapes of sailing craft were there, from small, hide-covered curraghs to large, wooden transport ships. Fomor workers, under the watchful eye of de Danann guards, had been collecting them, repairing them, readying them to carry the remainder of the Fomor horde away from Eire.

While Nuada and his chieftains supervised this mammoth undertaking, Lugh's companions gathered some distance up the coast in an isolated spot and awaited the return of the young warrior. They had said no word to Nuada about their going, hoping their absence would not be noted until their mission was well under way.

Now Findgoll, Angus, Taillta, and the Dagda sat about a small fire on the beach, making their own preparations to depart. The little Druid carefully went over the stock of precious magical supplies he would carry tucked in a pouch within his cloak. The three warriors went over the tools of their own trade, honing dagger, sword, and ax.

Farther along the beach, Aine sat on a flat rock at the water's edge. She stared out to sea, moodily casting pebbles into the surf. Often she turned her head to cast her gaze up toward the eastern sky.

Behind and above her, Morrigan was perched atop a large boulder. She sat cross-legged and was painstakingly at work honing the cutting edge of her longsword. Her sinewy arm drove the whetstone smoothly along the slim blade in long, easy strokes. Still, her glinting eyes flicked often to the back of the young woman hunched on the rock below. And something poignant in the scene of the lonely Aine and the vast sea seemed to touch the Raven-Woman, for she stopped her honing finally and spoke.

"Are you fearing that he won't come back?" she asked in her dry rattle of a voice.

It was a surprise to Aine to hear Morrigan speak. She had become used to the woman not speaking unless addressed. Aine twisted about to look up toward her, a strange, ominous figure, dark against the sky, the sword in her hands.

"It had occurred to me that he might try going himself," she replied. "You know how he is. I'm afraid he'll get the foolish notion that he has to do it himself and save the rest of us, particularly me." A faint smile touched her lips. "That's why I made Shaglan promise to bring him back here, no matter what he says."

"Are you certain that your fault isn't as great as his own?" Morrigan asked. "In your wanting to protect him, you treat him as a child. But he is a warrior now. A Champion. He has the right to choose his own way, alone."

These words troubled Aine. She began to protest, but couldn't deny that there was truth in Morrigan's words.

"Maybe you are right," she said. "But I haven't gone with him just to protect him. I want to be a part of what's happening myself! I'm a warrior too. This is my fight as much as his. I won't be left out!"

Morrigan considered her silently for a long moment, her dark eyes searching the young woman's face.

"You must do as your heart says," she croaked out at last, "but you can be too much the warrior, at the cost of everything else."

"What do you mean?" Aine asked.

The Raven-Woman rose, unwinding her long legs. She climbed down easily from the high rock, settling onto another close beside Aine. The young woman studied the odd being closely, puzzled by this sudden intimacy. She had never known the solitary, ruthless warrior to speak so much before. She had grown used to thinking of her as something other than human.

"It's long ago that I was wed to the Dagda," the husky voice began. "It was then that I thought I knew my own heart too."

Now Aine had an even greater surprise. The harsh voice of the raven had softened to a low-pitched trill of sound that was almost pleasant. And as Aine watched the gaunt face now turned to the sea, she saw it take on an expression that she had to call wistful.

"When our tribe left the eastern lands and came to Eire, I was a different being," she went on. "I was a young woman, not the thing of bones and tendons you see now."

Aine tried to picture a younger Morrigan. She fleshed out the cadaverous face and realized for the first time that the fine bone structure would have created a look of great beauty.

"I was a woman, a Champion's wife, but I wished to be a warrior too. When so many of our men were killed in the attack on the Tower of Glass, I vowed that I would be one to take their place. It was the Dagda who trained me, and I became as good in the fighting as any of them. I became more and more proud of my skill, more aware of the feeling of strength it gave me. It was my way to show my worth. So I trained the harder. I came to think of nothing else. My life became the challenge to prove myself better, harder, more deadly than any other. I became lean and strong and fast. But it wasn't enough. I still lacked the true temper of a Champion."

Aine now found herself caught up by this story, fascinated with the life being revealed to her by this enigmatic woman.

"When Queen Danu's people brought us to Tir-na-nog," Morrigan continued, "they offered to teach us some of their magic skills. I asked that my woman's spirit be changed for one more ruthless, one which loved only the sound of battle, the scent of death, the taste of blood. They gave the magic to me. It consumed me utterly. The spirit of the black battle-raven filled my body. The woman that I was died, and with it died all of my love for men."

"And the Dagda?" Aine wondered.

"Our love died too. He saw it happening, but there was nothing he could do. So I gained what I wished, but I became a creature that feels for no one else, who loves only to fight and to quench its thirst in a victim's hot blood. A mate with death I am. And sometimes there is a great loneliness in me. . . ."

The voice trailed off. The gaunt woman sat silent again, staring out at the sea, but with her gaze fixed on something far beyond it, something lost past time's horizons.

But this lasted only a moment. Then the eyes dropped from the sea to the gleaming blade still clutched in her lean hand. She started, shook her head, and came back into the present. She turned her head to fix a searching look on Aine.

"Do you understand me? Act for yourself. Do whatever you feel you must do. But consider what might be lost to you in the doing of it."

"I understand, Morrigan," Aine told her gravely, "and I will consider. But I think that in one thing you are wrong. The feeling for others hasn't all been taken from you. I hear it speaking from you now."

At this, the most curious thing of all happened. A smile touched the Raven-Woman's face, filling it with a warmth and life Aine had never seen before. For an instant she could truly see the vital young woman Morrigan had once been.

The smile vanished quickly, however. It was wiped away as the gaunt being jumped up, jerking her head about and stiffening.

"Listen!" she said. "I hear the sound of birds!" She scanned the eastern sky, then lifted a hand to point. "Look there!"

To the east, a formation of birds had appeared. They were formed into a tight V, and angling sharply downward toward the seashore as they came. As they approached, Aine realized that the birds were a peculiar assortment, and very large. She peered up at them hopefully, finally seeing what she sought: the figure of a human rider upon one's back.

"It's Lugh!" she cried with joy. She rose and started at a run along the shore toward the point where the birds were coming down. The others began moving toward it as well.

Shaglan was the first to flap in to a landing, and Lugh slipped from its back to greet his friends as the other birds dropped down around them.

Aine reached him first. In a burst of exuberance she threw her arms about him and hugged him tightly. Lugh was surprised by this spirited display from one who usually strove to appear in control. He looked at her in puzzlement.

"What was that for?"

"Just happy to see you back," she said, beaming.

He smiled in reply. "I'm happy to see you as well,"

The others had joined them now. With one arm about Aine's shoulders, Lugh lifted the other to gesture at the company of enormous birds.

"Shaglan has succeeded," he said triumphantly. "The Pookas will take us. We start for the Tower of Glass tonight!"

Chapter Sixteen

INTO THE TOWER

Manannan MacLir's head was twisted violently to one side, the muscles of his face and neck strained taut. His whole lanky form was tensed rigidly in its bonds as Mathgen sent power coursing through the diabolical contrivance that held the prisoner. The energy flared across the surface of his skin with a faint crackling.

"Release your mind, MacLir," the soft, insidious voice demanded. "Just for a moment! Give me what I seek!"

On the great screen behind the lighted tank a confused montage of images flickered—distorted forms, vague hints of landscape, a shifting array of colors—and nothing was indentifiable.

"Surrender to me, you stubborn fool," Mathgen urged. "Surrender or I will destroy your mind. I'll wipe it utterly away."

Though Manannan's face was drawn tight in the agony of concentration, he still managed to turn his head upright. His eyes opened and fixed upon the Druid. Then he smiled.

The images vanished suddenly from the screen. At the same time, the energy crackling across the prisoner died away. Manannan's body relaxed as much as possible in its uncomfortable seat. He took several breaths, then managed to speak.

"Tired?" he asked, trying to sound disappointed. "I was just beginning to enjoy it."

From the far side of the room Balor rolled forward to stop by the tank.

"What is the matter, Mathgen?" he demanded. "You told us two days ago your powers would break his will."

Mathgen's voice was a sharp hissing as he replied angrily. "He is very strong. He seems able to block any attempt by me to probe his thoughts. He is very unlike the rest of Danu's people, very unlike anyone I have ever known."

"That I have already been made aware of," Balor shot back, the metal voice a rattle of impatience. Waste no more time on him. Let me be rid of him: at least we will have one less enemy to deal with."

"No," the Druid protested. "Not yet. Eventually he must submit. I will find a way."

"Will you?" Balor asked. "I wonder. I have had my own experience with this stubborn being. Likely you will kill him before you learn anything. Be finished with him."

"I will not!" the harsh voice returned more stridently. "We have the key to Tir-na-nog right here. We cannot lose it now."

"It is a chance for your own restoration that you are afraid to lose," the giant said. "You have lived too long with the hope of that and the dream of this fantastic land."

"Tir-na-nog is real," Mathgen insisted. "Its powers are real. They go far beyond anything you can understand, far beyond what your great science has conceived."

"I have believed your tales for many years," the dark being rumbled. "I have listened to your warnings and did as you said to protect my Tower. Now I begin to wonder if this company of devices that keep your mind alive has begun to fail."

"The powers of Lugh and of this MacLir come from Danu. You've seen them. You know they are real. I can give them all to you. But you must give me more time!"

Balor was silent for a moment. Then the voice clanged out slowly: "All right. Do what you wish. But make something happen—soon."

"I will," the Druid promised. "I will."

The Tower was visible below now, glistening like ice in the reflected white light of the moon. The flight of birds sweeping toward it from the south was nearly above it. Their riders gazed down, carefully scrutinizing the stark, alien building as they circled slowly over it.

They made a most unusual-looking group as they sailed on the night winds. The Pookas' bird forms were of quite varied type, with no two similar. And it was clear from the bizarre nature of the shapes that the Pookas were a clan with great imagination and a strange sense of humor. It seemed to young Lugh that the beings had made it a contest to see which could create the most outlandish shape.

Aine's bird looked like an enormous pelican, with a ridiculously large beak that made its body seem small. Taillta rode something rather like a duck, save that its head and legs were those of a cat. Angus Og looked very uncomfortable aboard a rubbery-looking bird with a round body, stubby wings, and a long, long neck that flexed like a snake as the thing flapped along, while Findgoll's mount was more bat than bird, with huge leathery wings and fur and pointed ears. But the Dagda's transportation was the most dramatic of all. Its shape was that of a gigantic winged reptile. Twice the size of the others, it carried its weight with a massive spread of wings like the sails of a warship, switching a long, scaled tail restlessly behind it. It made an appropriate mount for the huge Champion, and the only one capable of lifting his bulk.

Lugh rode Shaglan, whose own, familiar bird form was the least exotic of the lot, to the young warrior's relief. Just off his shoulder the smaller raven shape of Morrigan winged along. Because of her size and dark color, she had been designated as the one to go ahead and spy out their chosen landing site. Lugh waved to her and pointed down toward the rooftop.

She responded at once, banking and sliding away, making a long spiral down and over the Tower. She swept low over the roof, turned, and passed over it again. Then she swung back upward, pumping with her wings to pull herself to the level of the others again.

She glided in next to the Dagda this time, holding position there while she launched into a long series of squawks, clicks, and rattles.

The Dagda had long before learned to interpret these sounds. He listened, then he lifted a hand to sign his information to the rest.

Two fingers raised indicated two guards on the roof. Lugh nodded in understanding. The guards must be silenced before the entire flock descended. He waved to Aine, gestured for her to follow, and leaned forward to murmur to Shaglan: "All right. Our turn now."

The Pooka began to drop down toward the Tower, the large-beaked bird following closely. The distant square of the rooftop grew until the figures on it became visible. The two were clearly lookouts, posted on opposite sides of the roof, east and west, patrolling and keeping a watch out to sea. Neither one had noted the danger directly above.

Lugh turned to Aine and gestured to the eastern guard. She nodded. The two whispered, "Now!" and dove swiftly in to the attack.

On the western side of the Tower roof, the bored lookout gave up his survey of the dark void and stretched himself. He turned and glanced across at his sole companion on this lonely vigil, so far away across the broad expanse of roof that no conversation was possible.

The other man was watching his sector with apparent diligence. A real stickler for the job, that one was, the watcher told himself complainingly. Now, his last mate, there was a fellow who would drop the job for a bit and have a little talk to break the monotony. And what was the harm in that? There was never anything to see out there. No reason not to take a break now and again. But could he convince this new lad of that? He could not!

He sighed and looked back out into the dark expanse. It was the boredom that was the worst, he thought. He'd actually begun to hope that something—anything—would happen.

A faint whooshing sound rose suddenly from somewhere. He looked around in puzzlement. The wind? Or some air escaping from one of the roof vents? No. It seemed to be in the night beyond the Tower. From above. He peered up into the sky.

A huge shape swept up suddenly from the darkness beyond the Tower's edge and skimmed low across the rooftop. A widespread wing, thick as a mast, struck him across the back of his neck and flung him forward. He slammed down on the hard surface and lay stunned.

On the roof's far side the noise alerted the other guard. He swung around to see the bird swoop by and realized that his companion was down. He opened his mouth to shout out an alarm, but from above a figure dropped upon him.

The weight struck his back, driving him forward and

down. As he hit the rooftop, hands thrust his head forward. It bounced against the surface and he went limp.

The first guard was now trying groggily to sit up. As he did, his uncertain gaze fell upon an amazing sight. Two giant and peculiar-looking birds settled lightly to the rooftop before him. From the back of one a young and pretty woman slid and moved toward him.

This, he thought to himself, was a bit more excitement than he had really asked for. He sat, bewildered, staring up at her as she approached. She smiled at him in a regretful sort of way.

"Sorry," she told him as the sword in her hand flashed out. The flat of the blade struck him alongside his head. He fell back again, unconscious.

Lugh, meantime, had seen that his own man was out and was securing him with thongs. Aine quickly did the same. As they worked, Shaglan flew upward to inform the rest that the rooftop was secure. Soon the other Pookas were fluttering in to a landing.

Morrigan quickly effected her transformation to a human shape. Shaglan made his own shift into the familiar form of a large dog. Lugh softly addressed the rest of the Pooka clan.

"Thank you, my friends. Now you must wait here for us. If all goes well, we should return here soon. If anyone of the Tower comes here before that, fly away, circle, and watch for us."

"And if you don't return soon?" asked the lizard-like being.

"If we aren't back here by dawn, wait no longer. It means things have gone wrong. There'll be nothing you can do."

"It takes great courage to enter this place of ice," the Pooka told him. "Good fortune to you."

Lugh gestured to his companions and they crossed the rooftop to a low square structure. In one side was set a single door of metal.

"This is the way in," Lugh whispered. "A stairway leads to the top level of the Tower. The chamber with the lifting room is at the bottom. A corridor leads from it to Balor's chamber. There may be guards there, so we must be quiet. Are you ready?"

All nodded. Their weapons were out and ready in their hands.

Lugh seized the handle of the heavy door and pulled. He had feared finding it locked, but it moved easily, swinging outward. He pulled it fully open, revealing the narrow stairway leading down into the Tower. It was dark, but a faint glow filtered up it from some light below.

Lugh started down, moving cautiously, the others close behind. The metal stairs made no protesting sounds at their weight, and they reached the bottom silently. But another metal door barred their way, and through a narrow crack along its lower edge came a line of light from the room beyond.

Slowly, Lugh eased the door open just enough to peer into the chamber. Across from him was the high, wide corridor to Balor's room. To the left was the shining metal door to the Commander's private lift. Lugh only glanced toward it and then pulled back. Two of Balor's elite guardsmen stood flanking the lift, their strange, globe-tipped weapons up before them.

As they were staring rigidly ahead, up the corridor, they had not seen Lugh. But they certainly would if he tried to move into the chamber, and would give an alarm before they could be silenced.

But this possibility had been forseen by Lugh. He turned and signaled to Shaglan, who moved up beside him. He crouched down to whisper into the dog's ear.

"There are two more. You know what to do."

The Pooka nodded and moved past Lugh, thrusting its head boldly out into the chamber. It gave a faint hiss.

Hearing it, the nearest guard turned his head to look, then stared in astonishment. Shaglan's head had gone through a quick bit of metamorphosis as he stuck it out. The man was now looking at the head of what seemed to be a horse.

Brown eyes peered at him from above a large, soft-looking nose. A wide mouth was stretched back in a broad grin. As he continued to stare, it slowly winked one eye. Then it withdrew.

The soldier was somewhat perplexed by this. He was fairly certain no horse could have gotten onto the roof without his knowing it. He didn't think a horse could have even fit on the stairs.

He considered mentioning the strange vision to his companion, but decided against it. The other guard would only think him mad. Still, for his own peace of mind, he had to check.

He sidled along the wall to the stairway door, then turned in a quick move and yanked it open. The stairwell was very dark. He stepped forward, peering up. A hand shot out from the darkness and jerked him forward.

There was a clatter. It drew the attention of the other guard and he realized that his companion had vanished. But the door to the roof was open! Where had the fool gone?

Irritated, he left his post and strode to the open door. He stepped to the stairs, looking up, ready to call out to the other angrily. But the words died in his throat as several swordpoints thrust out from the darkness to touch him at various vital parts.

"Don't move or make a sound!" Lugh warned. "Come in here!"

The man obeyed and was pulled onto the stairway. The door closed behind him. In the darkness he could see the intruders very little, but he could feel the weapons.

Morrigan moved forward and relieved him of his weapon. This she set down gingerly on the stairs. She had had experience with these spears once before. She knew the globes contained an energy that could kill with a touch.

"Now," Lugh said in his most ruthless tone, "I am surely going to kill you right now unless you tell me where Mathgen can be found."

The guard found this a fair enough trade for his life. "Level two," he said quickly.

"Thank you," Lugh said, and nodded.

From behind, Angus lifted the man's silver helmet and tapped him skillfully on the skull with his sword hilt. They caught him as he collapsed and pulled his body up the stairs, bound it, and left it beside that of his companion. Lugh then led his little band out into the chamber.

Closing the stairway door, he looked up the corridor to Balor's throne room. There was no sign of movement. No sound.

"We're safe, at least until the guard is changed," he whispered.

"Which I hope will not be soon," the Dagda murmured back.

"We'll have to move quickly," Lugh said. "This way!"

They moved to the lift door. Lugh turned to Taillta.

"Now it's your turn. You know how these work."

She stepped up to the switch beside the door and flicked it. The silver door vibrated and then slid up with a faint clattering.

"I could have guessed at that much myself," the Dagda remarked.

"There's nowhere to go from here except down," she replied. "Inside, everyone."

They moved into the room. The Dagda came last, shuffling in reluctantly and looking around suspiciously.

"I don't much like the idea of being shut up in here," he said.

"Wait," Lugh told him. "You'll like it even less."

Taillta examined the row of levers just inside the door and finally selected one near the bottom.

"Here we go then," she announced, and gave it a flick.

First the door slid down, causing the Dagda to start uneasily. Then the room itself shook, groaned, and began to drop. The sensation was unpleasant, especially to one who had not experienced it before.

"You're right," the Dagda moaned. "I don't like this at all."

"I find it very stimulating myself," said Findgoll, who seemed quite excited by the whole adventure. "Where's your courage, warrior?"

The Dagda's usual retort to this would have been a biting one. But now, when it felt as if his stomach were rising up into his throat, he couldn't bring himself to speak.

"Careful now," Taillta cautioned. "I think we're nearly there. We're slowing down."

As the lift clanked to a stop on Mathgen's level, the two guards flanking the door there snapped to rigid attention. The door slid up and they waited, expecting the black giant to roll past. But nothing happened.

Afraid to move, the guards kept their stiff postures for a while longer. Then they turned their heads to exchange a puzzled look. Finally overcome by curiosity, they turned and nervously peered around the edge of the door into the lift.

At the same moment, hands shot out to grasp the startled men and yank them into the lift, out of sight. There were some brief sounds of struggle, and then figures emerged. But the two guards were not among them.

Lugh Lamfada led his companions cautiously along the corridor, with its walls of flickering lights.

Though the corridor looked empty, the warriors kept alert for Tower soldiers, moving very slowly and stealthily, weapons ready. Findgoll, on the other hand, was more absorbed in examining the wonders of this place. He looked in fascination at the shifting patterns on the lighted panels as they passed, stopping at times to stare at some device.

"Come along, Findgoll," Lugh urged.

"If I could just examine one of these things," the little Druid murmured. "If I could understand how their magic works . . ." He rubbed his hands together nervously, as if the temptation to stop and touch one of them were nearly overwhelming.

"No time, Findgoll. Sorry," Lugh said. "And we've no idea what our meddling might do. Come along!"

Findgoll sighed regretfully and followed.

They moved on up the long corridor, past room after room, all devoid of humans. Then, far ahead, the doors that marked the end of the corridor came into view. And, with them, the figures of two more guards.

"Now what?" asked Angus Og.

"We can't sneak up on them," said Lugh. "The best attack now is a direct one. Come on." And he started toward the guards at a run.

The two men stared in bewilderment at the strange group charging toward them: by the time they realized they should defend themselves, Lugh's band was upon them.

"Watch those globes!" Morrigan warned as she dove in on the guard to the right with Angus.

"Get on through those doors," the Dagda said as he moved toward the guard on the left, lifting his ax. "We'll take care of these!"

With Aine beside him Lugh drove against the doors, leaping through into the room beyond, weapons up, ready to engage any more soldiers there.

But there were none. They found themselves looking across a vast room, empty but for several strange metal contrivances that glittered under the banks of flashing lights.

Then the one blank wall ahead came to life. A flood of lights and colors washed across it, wavered, steadied to a clear image. They realized that they looked at an enormous picture of themselves, weapons in hand, faces frozen in expressions of astonishment.

"Greetings," came a hissing, insidious whisper, seemingly from everywhere at once. At the same moment, the dark column in the center of the room grew suddenly white as its lights flashed on, revealing the horrible creature suspended within.

"I am very glad to see that you have come, Lugh Lamfada," said Mathgen. "Welcome to the Tower."

Chapter Seventeen
IN MATHGEN'S LAIR

Having disposed of the two guards outside, the rest of Lugh's party now burst through the doors into the room. They stopped short when they saw the being ahead.

"And you've brought some of your companions with you," the awful voice went on. "So many of my old friends too. I enjoy the chance to meet with you again."

Recovering from their initial astonishment, the party moved forward, staring now in rather morbid fascination at the wasted being who, somehow, still lived.

"Mathgen?" asked Findgoll, trying to find some resemblance in the skeletal form entangled in the web to the man he had known.

"Findgoll, my fellow Druid. Don't look so surprised. What you see is the result of what you did to me, with the help of Morrigan and the Dagda."

"We can finish what we started right now!" the Dagda growled, and started forward, lifting his great war-ax.

"I don't think that would be very wise," the hoarse voice warned sharply. "If you try to harm me, I'm afraid you may cause difficulties for another comrade of yours."

A square of light in the ceiling beside the tank grew suddenly bright. Its hard, white glow bathed a gleaming contraption sitting below. It revealed the familiar, lanky form strapped there.

Lugh took a step forward, but another warning came from the Druid.

"No, young Champion. Take no more steps. I assure you, he will die if you do."

"Never mind about me, Lugh," Manannan shouted. "Destroy him! Get away!"

"You will see your friend dead first," Mathgen promised. "And none of you will survive to leave this Tower. Help has already been summoned. In the meantime, I can keep you here. I have powers that you cannot stand against."

"I can," Findgoll challenged. "I beat you once before."

"Little fool! Your simple magic was never equal to mine. And now, I have used the forces within this Tower to amplify them to a level you cannot begin to comprehend. Watch!"

The device that held Manannan began to hum. From a score of points around it crackled a blue-white light. The strands of it shot across the prisoner's body, throwing a glowing aura over him. He jerked back with the pain, his body stiffening.

"Stop!" cried Lugh. "What are you doing to him?"

"You see," the whisper went on calmly, "I can bring any degree of pain I wish to him. I can increase the power . . ." The aura of light increased in intensity. Manannan's body convulsed in agony. ". . . until I reach a point that will cause death. So, decide now, young Lugh. Surrender to me and you will live. Defy me and MacLir will die, with your own deaths following soon after."

Lugh looked in desperation from his companions to the tortured Manannan. He thought of the spear of power strapped to his back. Its flaming head would surely pierce that monster's tank and destroy him. But to kill Mathgen also meant the possible sacrifice of all of them.

His mind whirled with the complexities of his choice. But one thought came through clearly: No matter what fate expected of him, he would not risk his friends. He would not condemn Manannan MacLir.

"We must surrender," he said quietly to the rest.

He quickly sheathed his own bright Answerer, unbuckled the harness, and let it drop to the floor. The spear followed. Aine's weapons clattered to the floor next, and then the others slowly dropped their own. The Dagda came last, letting his heavy ax thud down with great reluctance.

"Very good," Mathgen congratulated them. The blue

aura sizzling about Manannan died away. "To stay alive is always the wisest choice."

The main doors to the room pushed open then. Mathgen's two henchmen rushed in, leading a squad of helmeted Guards. They quickly encircled the little band of invaders.

"Collect their weapons," he ordered the soldiers, "and be quite careful with that sword of our young Champion." The lens swiveled down to point at the Answerer. The image of it grew to fill the screen. "I sense a great deal of magic linked to that weapon." The lens shifted again and moved the focus to the spear. Even with the cover, the great heat it was generating appeared upon the screen as a distorting haze around the head. "That spear too. Some kind of powerful energy is contained there."

The weapons of the group were quickly collected. One soldier gingerly picked up Lugh's spear and sword.

"Take anything that you find on the Druid too," Mathgen directed. "Although what feeble magic he could do would be of little harm to us."

"Feeble magic?" the little man shot back. "At least I have the ability to move about, not hang like a carcass for the drying!"

"That may not be the case for much longer unless you remain still," Mathgen threatened.

Fuming, the Druid fell silent while a soldier searched him, pulling several vials from his tunic.

"Good," Mathgen said with satisfaction when all had been collected. "Now, let us examine these weapons of yours. Guard, unsheath that sword!"

The man handed the spear to one of his fellows and pulled the Answerer slowly from its sheath. The fine, slender blade glowed brightly even in the dimly lit room. On the Druid's screen it seemed to flare like an aurora, with great arcs of multicolored light arching from the point back to the hilt, flowing again up the blade. The guard looked from the weapon in his hands to the display on the screen with dismay, clearly afraid of the strange force he held.

"Danu's magic certainly courses within that metal," Mathgen wheezed. "It was the smiths of Murias who forged such a weapon, I would guess." The lens swiveled suddenly to Lugh. "What powers does it have, boy? What does it do for you?"

Lugh stayed silent.

The being in the tank gave a soft bray of laughter. "Never mind. I'll discover its secret in time. Guard, place it on that table carefully."

This the guard was very happy to do, resheathing the sword and laying it softly on a nearby metal table.

"And now, this spear," said Mathgen, the focus of his glass eye switching to the other weapon. "No doubt it is another of your gifts from Tir-na-nog?" As before, the heat it generated was visible on the screen as a bright haze about it. "Most interesting. There is a very unusual form of energy centered there. And what is its purpose, my young Champion? What marvelous tasks does it perform for you?"

Lugh continued to stare at the wasted Druid without reply.

"You remain stubborn? Well, its use should not be too difficult to guess. Its appearance is quite innocent. To conceal what? Shall we see? Guard, loosen the edge of that covering so we can see the head."

The guard hesitated. He was already very aware of the intense heat radiating from the spear's concealed point. But he was more afraid of the creature in the tank than of this unknown. He complied. Delicately, he loosened the drawstrings on the cover slightly. With a finger he eased it slowly back until the lower edge of the spearpoint was exposed.

Instantly, a blinding flare of intense silver light exploded from the point, swelling outward, swallowing up the guard before he could act. He stood, terror-stricken, as the light engulfed him, consumed him totally. His hand released the edge of the cover and it fell back. The glow was cut off as if a door had slammed shut. The spear dropped, clattering to the metal floor. The man was gone.

Those in the room stared at the fallen spear, transfixed by this demonstration of awful power, blinking their eyes to recover from the searing brightness.

"So, it *is* dangerous," came Mathgen's whisper, displaying no emotion above a clinical interest. "There is enough force in that spear to destroy hundreds of warriors, a fleet of ships, perhaps even the Tower. Or, is it meant only for me?"

Lugh still kept up his stubborn silence.

"Manannan has trained you well, I see," the Druid said, amused. "We'll waste no more time with this now. One of you others, place that spear with the sword!"

The guards exchanged nervous glances. No one moved

at first. Finally, one braver spirit crept to the weapon with great reluctance. He looked fearfully at the spear and at the place where his fellow had stood. At last he leaned down, took the wooden haft firmly in one hand, and tugged the drawstring very tightly closed with the other. Giving an audible sigh of relief, he carried the weapon to the table and placed it beside the Answerer.

"You're as great a monster as you ever were," Findgoll told Mathgen angrily. "You sacrificed that poor man on purpose!"

"It takes sacrifice to learn, old friend," the hissing voice returned. "And now that we've rendered your little band harmless, we can discuss some new sacrifices—from you!"

"What do you mean?" Lugh demanded. "What are you going to do?"

"I intend to ask you for your help," Mathgen replied.

Across the room, the main doors swung inward again. This time they admitted the familiar form of Sital Salmhor, his normal air of restraint gone now in his alarm.

"What's happened here?" he cried out. "We were told you were under attack!"

"No danger," Mathgen soothed. "Our invaders are well in hand."

The officer stopped and regarded the captives.

"So, our enemies have come to us!" he said, his haughty manner returning. "They make things easy for us, Mathgen." He smiled with a malicious pleasure at young Lugh. "You took too great a risk at last, didn't you? We should have known that you would come to rescue your comrade. We can always rely upon your acting from your foolish sense of loyalty."

"Their arrival was most expedient," Mathgen told him. "They may even have saved MacLir's life. I had nearly given up on him. Now there is a new chance that we can discover what we seek."

"Don't be playing with us, you rotting bag of bones," the Dagda roared. "Tell us w' t tortures you've planned out for us! You've had enough years hanging there to think some lovely ones out, I'm sure!"

"It may surprise you," the sibilant voice answered mildly, "but I intend no real harm to you. I would, in fact, see that you were all released, if you would help me. I want only one thing. Your friend MacLir has been rather stubborn about providing it to me. But if one of you could divulge the information, or convince this ridiculous clown to do so, you could go free. All I wish is the location of Tir-na-nog."

The Dagda snorted derisively. "The Blessed Isles? Tell you where they are? What, so you can take Balor and his black ships there? Not likely."

"It would do no harm to you," Mathgen reasoned. "You have Eire. You would be left alone. That I would promise."

"You'd promise?" said Findgoll, hooting with laughter. "And who would believe your promise, traitor? We know you only want Danu's power for yourself. Don't be treating us as babes!"

"I thought perhaps you might be sensible for once," said Mathgen, the hissing voice taking on a burr of irritation. "Still, I expected your denial. I have other ways of learning what I need to know from you."

The lens that served as his eyes turned slowly across the little band, the image of each sliding into view upon the screen and pausing as he scrutinized each one.

"Young Lugh—what is there in your mind, I wonder?"

At these words Lugh felt a sudden pressure inside his skull, like a fist tightening about his mind, squeezing it. On the screen a burst of light wiped away the picture of the room. New images formed, a tangle of impressions. With a shock he recognized there scenes of his own life! The isle where he'd been hidden for so long, the destruction of his home by Balor's eye, the gleaming Tower of Glass, Gilla's Sidhe, and Aine in warm firelight, violent fights, breathless chases, the Fomor city, the battle on the shore, all flicked by at an incredible speed, ending with the terrible image of Mathgen's skull-like face.

Then the force was suddenly gone, releasing him. He staggered backward a pace before catching himself. On the screen the scene of the captives and the room wavered back into view.

"As I thought," Mathgen said in a dismissing tone. "You are only a boy, playing out a role." The lens shifted to focus one by one upon the others. "And the rest of you: Taillta? You are a Firbolg. Our fine de Danann heroes? No, I sense nothing there." The face of Aine moved into view. She stared boldly into the lens. It paused.

"Young woman," said Mathgen thoughtfully. "You are no de Danann. Yet you have helped them, risked your life—why? Who are you?" The image moved in on her eyes until their clear, gray brightness filled the screen. "Strange. There is something there. Something . . ."

Again the screen exploded with light. As it did, Lugh saw Aine stiffen, throw back her head, close her eyes. He knew that the Druid was using his powers to probe her mind as his had been.

"Let her alone!" he cried, starting toward her.

Two guards stepped before him, raising the globes of their weapons to block his way.

"Stay back, boy!" Mathgen warned.

Enraged, Lugh ignored him, shoving forward between the guards to reach her. But the globe of one weapon touched his shoulder. He felt a pain jolt through him, knocking him sideways as if he had been struck a heavy blow. He fell limply, shaken, weak, his arm tingling and numb. He looked up helplessly toward the trapped girl, unable to rise.

On the screen another montage of images was whirling by. Lugh recognized views of Tara, of their fights together, Manannan's Sidhe, himself in firelight. And then there were scenes he didn't know: hazy views of lush and pleasant countrysides, of hills crowned with shimmering cities that seemed worked in gold like finest jewelry.

"That is Tir-na-nog!" Mathgen said, his voice a wheeze of rising excitement. "You know! You are Manannan's sister!"

Chapter Eighteen
MATHGEN'S VICTORY

"Fight him, Aine," MacLir shouted to her. "Block him!"

But the girl had been caught by surprise. The Druid had invaded her mind before her mental defenses could be brought up. She struggled, her slender body vibrating with the strain. But the images of the pleasant land and the shining cities grew sharper as Mathgen forced her to concentrate upon it.

"There is Tir-na-nog," came his loathsome whisper, insinuating itself into her thoughts. "Remember it. Dwell upon it. Return there in your dreams. Tell me how it can be found."

His magic probed deeper into her mind, like searching fingers, violating her most private secrets. Inwardly, she was revulsed, but she could do nothing to force the invader out. On the screen appeared a view of the sea. To the watchers it appeared as if one were skimming low across the surface at great speed.

"Very good," said Mathgen. "Now you are going there. It lies just ahead. Home. You are going home."

In the projected scene a fog now came into view, lying like a pure white scarf drifting on the waves. It grew rapidly, filling the screen, blocking out everything with a swirling cloud.

"Aine!" Manannan shouted at her desperately.

The fog was thinning out, tearing away. The scene abruptly cleared. Ahead, the dark coastline was visible.

"Tir-na-nog!" Mathgen cried triumphantly.

At that the image on the screen vanished. Aine felt the power withdrawing from her mind. Her strength drained from her and she sagged to the floor.

Defying his own pain and weakness, Lugh rose to his feet and, before the guards could move to restrain him, crossed the room to her. He knelt down, lifting her in his arms. She was alive, but her breathing was labored. She moaned softly.

"Aine!" he breathed, terrified that she was dying. "Aine!"

Her eyes fluttered, then opened. She stared up at him, bewildered at first, then she recognized the face above her. With a great relief he saw a faint smile touch her lips.

"Your concern touches me deeply," Mathgen hissed sardonically. "But the girl is unharmed. She tried to resist, but I moved too swiftly. For an instant the memory of her Blessed Isles was there, and it was enough. The location of Tir-na-nog is now mine."

"Little enough good it will do you," Findgoll said. "Danu will never let you control her powers."

"You know as well as I that there is little she or her people can do to stop me," the wasted being replied.

"Now, Mathgen," Salmhor said harshly. "Destroy them! They have been leaders in the de Danann rising. They are too dangerous to be left alive."

"I don't agree," said Mathgen. "They are quite harmless now. I think the forces of the Tower can manage to safely hold them, don't you, Salmhor?"

"If you wish," he said. The Tower officer pivoted. "Guards, take our captives to the lower cells."

"But not young Lugh," Mathgen put in quickly. "Leave him with us. The others may all be taken away, and MacLir as well. Release him."

Mathgen's two henchmen moved quickly to unfasten Manannan's bonds. Aine had by now recovered most of her strength and began to rise. Lugh helped her to her feet where she stood, yet a bit unsteadily, his supporting arm around her shoulders. As the guards closed in, he pulled her protectively closer and lifted his other arm to fend them away. The shining energy globes moved forward.

"Be careful, boy," Mathgen warned. "You'll only be the cause of your companions being hurt. Let her go and move away from the others."

Lugh glanced around at his friends, all under the threat of the strange weapons.

"All right," he agreed. "But Taillta will see to Aine."

He waited until the Firbolg woman had moved in to put an arm around the girl. Only then did he release her and step back, holding his hands up before him in a sign of acquiescence.

Now free of his bonds, Manannan rose. Wincing from a certain soreness in his limbs, he crossed to the others, stepping up by his sister.

"Are you certain you've not been harmed?" he asked with concern.

She gamely smiled at him. "Except for a roaring headache."

He looked up toward the being in the tank. "And what have you planned for Lugh?" he demanded.

"Have we finally found a way to stop your jesting?" Mathgen said, the whisper filled with amusement. "I am amazed."

"Carrion! Just tell me what you intend!" Manannan shot back angrily.

"Nothing that will harm him, I assure you," the unruffled voice replied. "But keep in mind—his continued safety depends on your peaceful cooperation . . . as yours does on his. Guards, take them out!"

Submit the little band did, but not without some hostile looks at the guards who now herded them together. Soon, under Salmhor's command, they were being led away.

As they passed out through the main doors of the room, they cast final glances back toward Lugh. He looked a small and lonely figure there beside the awful being suspended in the tank.

Lugh felt a sense of isolation and despair filling him as he watched his comrades disappear. He tried to fight it down, turning defiantly toward the Druid.

"And now what happens?" he asked.

"Nothing, for the moment," Mathgen told him. "You have had a long and wearing night. I would like you to accept the Tower's hospitality." The gaze of his lens shifted to his two assistants. "You will see that our young friend is made comfortable in one of our treatment chambers. Bring food to him as well."

The men bowed in reply and moved up to flank Lugh.

"Remember, the lives of your companions depend upon you," the Druid reminded him again.

He said nothing more as the two led him away, out through the smaller rear door of the room. The gaze of Salmhor followed him out, then swung toward Mathgen, filled with puzzlement.

"What are you about?" Salmhor demanded. "You have what you wanted from them. You said that they were harmless to us now. Why keep them alive?"

"The Prophecy protects that boy," the Druid returned. "I have pulled some of his teeth, but I cannot be certain what other powers he may have. There are forces no magic of mine or machine from this Tower can defeat." Mathgen paused before continuing. "Fate is a landslide. Once begun, it carries all before it."

"Fulfillment of the Prophecy depends upon Lugh's free choice to become Champion and aid the de Danann cause," the Druid explained. "If *he* could be changed, brought to renounce his mission, and turn against the de Dananns, then nothing would hinder us in seizing Danu's power!"

"How could Lugh possibly be brought to turn against his own people?" Salmhor asked, openly skeptical.

"Balor knows how," Mathgen answered cryptically. "It is time for him to tell that boy the truth!"

The door of the lift slid up and the little band of captives was prodded out by the compliment of guards. They had made only a brief downward trip this time, but the environment before them was far different from that above.

Clearly, they were far beneath the Tower, in the lower

levels of the foundations sunk deep into the rock of the tiny isle. The corridor with its walls of lights had been replaced by one of blank, smooth stone, lit by widely spaced squares of light in the low ceiling. There was a strong feel of dampness there, and a pungent odor of decay.

They moved along the corridor and soon came into a square room. From each of its other sides a similar corridor ran away into gloom. Its walls were of the smooth white stones and unadorned. Its floor was made of dark metal, like that of the ships' hulls, badly worn by time and streaked with the red-brown of rust. It was empty save for a single metal table on the far side of the room, lit by a radiant panel in the ceiling directly above it. Behind the table sat the room's single occupant.

He was a thick, soft-looking man with tiny eyes peeking above the high, round cushions of his cheeks. His expression and his sagging posture spoke of overwhelming boredom until the prisoners entered. Then he sat forward, eyeing the unusual group with interest, an interest that changed to surprise when he realized that Sital Salmhor was with them.

The man leaped to his feet so quickly that his belly jiggled, and he threw himself into a position of rigid attention, head up, chins pulled tightly in. An attempt to pull in the stomach as well proved futile.

Salmhor ordered the prisoners to a halt and stepped forward, addressing the man brusquely.

"Warden, these Eirelanders are to be kept here—in the name of Balor himself!"

"Yes, my Captain!" the other returned, stiffening even more at the sound of the giant's name.

Salmhor ran a critical eye up and down the warden. He noted the stubble on the sagging jowls, the unkempt uniform, the stretch of the tunic over the protruding stomach with disapproval.

"Is this the appropriate appearance for a Tower officer?" he demanded.

"Well, sir," the warden began nervously, "I . . . ah . . . well, hardly anyone comes down here, sir, and especially not an officer of your rank, sir," he finished lamely.

"There is no place in the Tower for sloppiness, Warden," Salmhor snapped. "Clean yourself up, man! Don't let me see you this way again!"

"Yes, my Captain!" The man was vibrating with tension now.

"And see to these prisoners properly! Nothing must go wrong. Balor will hold you personally responsible if it does, Warden. Do you understand?"

"Yes, my Captain."

"We have their weapons here too," Salmhor told him. He signaled to a pair of the guards, who moved forward. One was laden with swords and harness. The other staggered under the burden of Balor's ax.

"I will see to them, my Captain," the warden assured him.

Under Salmhor's direction the guards dumped the weapons on a pile against one wall. Then the officer's attention returned to the still agonizingly rigid warden.

"Very well, Warden," he announced. "Now you may put the prisoners into the cells."

"Yes, my Captain. At once!" the man replied.

Clearly relieved at being freed from his uncomfortable pose, he moved away from the table. Just beside it was a rank of long metal pieces. To the prisoners they looked like nothing so much as a dozen broad-bladed swords, points embedded in the floor. The warden stopped before them, lifting a pudgy hand to lay on the black-bound grips of one. He looked toward Salmhor.

"Now, sir," he said, "if you could have them moved up just a bit?"

Salmhor barked the orders and his guards herded their knot of captives forward.

The warden watched this process carefully. After the group had advanced several paces into the room, he lifted a hand.

"Stop!" he said. "That's far enough. Now, my Captain, if you and your guards could just step clear?"

The prisoners looked around them as the guards backed away, bewildered by this peculiar strategy.

It was Manannan who noted the mark on the metal floor, the thin line edged with rust. It was Manannan who realized that this line formed a square that his little band of comrades now stood within. And it was Manannan who suddenly understood what was going to happen now.

"What is this?" the Dagda demanded in alarm.

The warden shoved his handle forward. The long metal

piece shifted, pivoting at its lower end. There came a loud, sharp clattering from beneath them. The floor began to shake.

"Steady!" shouted Manannan. "We're going to . . ."

The word *fall!* trailed away as the floor dropped suddenly from beneath them. A huge metal panel, hinged at one side, swung downward and back. The prisoners slid sideways, then fell over the edge, plunging from sight.

The warden pulled back on his lever. With more clattering, the door swung upward again, clanging to a close.

"There, sir. That's done it!" the warden announced with satisfaction.

"You're certain there's no way they can escape?" inquired Salmhor. "Those Eirelanders may have some little tricks."

"No worry there, sir," the man assured him. "There's only this one way out of there. No one's ever escaped."

"And what if we want to get them out?"

"There's the ladder, sir!" he said, nodding to a long metal device laid along one wall. Its black metal rungs and supports were thick with rust. "It's never used, though. As far as I know, no one put down there has ever come back up again!"

Down below, the members of the little band were struggling—accompanied by a great deal of cursing from the Dagda—to untangle themselves and get to their feet.

Their new surroundings were far from promising. This room was much smaller than the one above. A single, grimy square of light beside the metal door above them provided the only illumination. Three walls were of the smooth black stone. The fourth was pierced by a doorway beyond which only darkness lay.

The musty odor was much stronger here, as was the humidity. Dampness shone on the smooth walls and streaked their one-time whiteness with yellow stains.

"I smell death here," cawed Morrigan, her glinting eyes shifting nervously about.

"We're not dead, anyway," Manannan commented positively.

"Alive, maybe, but buried just the same," Angus replied in a glum way.

"Now, lad, don't despair," the tall man said encouragingly. "Something will come up." He looked to the Dagda. "Do you think you can do something about that door?"

The huge warrior studied the metal panel carefully. It was the height of two men above him, and its bottom surface showed no gaps, no handles, no hinges.

"By Danu," he swore, "I don't see a way I could get that open from here."

"How about the walls?" Angus suggested.

For reply, the Dagda stepped up to one of the smooth surfaces. They seemed formed of a single mass, showing no joints. He drew back a massive fist and drove it against the stone, grunting with the power of the blow.

There was a loud *thwock* of its connection, followed by a pained exclamation from the big warrior. He looked down at the bruised flesh of his knuckles ruefully.

"No damage at all," he said, "unless it's to the bones of my poor hand."

Morrigan had been standing silently to one side, wrapped as usual in her dark cloak, nearly invisible in the faint light. But now she came to life, wheeling sharply about, her gaunt figure dropping into a defensive posture, her glittering gaze directed toward the black doorway.

"Listen!" she rasped. "Something's coming!"

They all turned toward the opening. Nothing could be seen there, but the sound that had alerted the keen-eared Morrigan was now loud enough to be heard by all the band. It was a shuffling, dragging sound, as if something were being pulled or was crawling across the floor. And it was growing louder rapidly. Whatever produced the sound was most definitely moving toward them.

"It appears we're not alone in here," Manannan observed—quite unnecessarily.

From the rear of Mathgen's chamber Lugh was escorted along another corridor. The walls of this one were bare of the flashing lights but lined with doorways set at short intervals. Each opened, he noted in passing, into a tiny room, all identical, clean, square-cornered and sterile, furnished with a small bed and metal table.

It was into one of these rooms that he was finally pushed by the burly men.

"Stay here and rest, and no trouble from you," one said curtly. "We'll bring food in a while."

They backed out, swinging closed a metal door. He heard the sound of a latch being thrown outside.

It took him only a moment to look around the room. Except for the bed—a metal-framed contrivance with a thin mattress of cloth—and the table, the room was featureless. There was no decoration of any kind on the spotless white walls, no color in the white bed covering, no mats upon the stark white floor. All was bathed in a hard, wintery glare from a large square of light in the ceiling. It all made Lugh feel rather chilly.

Dispirited, he dropped down on the bed and began to lay back. He was stopped by the desperate shriek of a tiny voice: "Don't do that, please!"

He was back on his feet in an instant, looking around him in alarm. Then he froze as a peculiar feeling began to steal up his back. Tiny feet, and clawed ones too, were crawling up his spine!

His impulse was to tear the garments from him and smash whatever had crept into them. But then the small voice came again, pleading: "Don't do anything too violent now. It's me, Shaglan!"

Shaglan! He nearly laughed aloud with relief. Lugh stood patiently, ignoring the urge to scratch, while the Pooka proceeded up his spine, across his shoulder blade, down his arm. Finally, from the edge of his sleeve, a tiny quivering pink nose poked out. Long whiskers followed, and then the rest of the mouselike creature.

Lugh sat down again and Shaglan clambered down onto his knee.

"It's a great relief to be out of there," it said, busily smoothing down its ruffled fur with tiny paws. It seems like days I've been clinging in the hem of your cloak by claws and teeth."

Lugh now realized that in all the confusion of their capture, no one had noted the Pooka's absence.

"What happened to you?" he asked.

"Well, when I saw that we would be trapped, I thought I might be more useful if they didn't know I was along. While that thing in the tank was busy with you and Manannan, I shrank myself down to this and climbed up into your cloak to hide."

"You're a clever Pooka," Lugh said, smiling, "and I'm glad to have someone with me." He looked up and around the room, and the smile faded. "But look where I've brought you. I've gotten you caught with all the rest." He shook his head sadly. "It's quite a mess I've made of this, bringing all my friends here to save Manannan. I've only made things worse."

"Ah, lad, don't be so hard on yourself," Shaglan said, trying to cheer him. "We all wanted to come. And it was right to want to rescue MacLir."

"I was a fool," he said, refusing to be comforted. "I had finally convinced myself that nothing could stop us, that I really was the great Champion of the Sidhe. I thought Danu's power had made me invincible."

"Lugh, we all thought the same," the Pooka reasoned. "We've come through so much else."

"Well, Bres was right this time," Lugh said bitterly. "We took a risk too great."

"I could change into some immense ferocious beast," the mouse suggested. "That could get us free."

"It could likely get the rest of them hurt too," Lugh said. "No, my friend, this time I'm afraid they really have us." His eyes clouded with worry. "I only hope Mathgen spoke the truth when he said that the others would be unharmed."

Book Three
AGAINST THE TOWER

Chapter Nineteen
NUADA DECIDES

The High-King of the clans of the Tuatha de Danann strode out from his wooden enclosure and stopped at the rim of the hill to look out over the scene spread below.

It was a fine, brilliant day with a sharp western breeze scudding a few billowing, flat-bottomed clouds across the sky as if they were ships under sail. The morning sunlight slanted across the wide shore plains that stretched away before him, clearly defining every object with long shadows, black against the bright emerald glow of the fields. Beyond, the waters of the sea were a glinting sapphire.

Toward the west there was a flaw in this jeweled landscape. A great scorched patch on the earth marked the remains of the last Fomor stronghold in Eire. It was still sending faint spires of smoke up from its smoldering, blackened ruins.

Directly ahead of the High-King, a vast encampment covered the plain between hills and sea. It was composed of the combined forces of de Danann and Firbolg warriors, clustered about hundreds of small fires. They formed a vast circle at whose heart was a second ring. This one was formed of logs and served to keep enclosed the survivors of the once powerful Fomor clans of Eire. Inside that circle of timbers many hundreds of the monstrous creatures were now packed, like a herd of cattle bunched in its pens to await the slaughter. But they weren't to die, at least not at the hands of their conquerers. Their fate was to be exile.

Stretching far along the shore were the vessels that would carry them away. In the past days since their defeat, the Fomor—under the watchful eye and prodding spears of their new masters—had gathered every sailing craft they could. There were many scores of them now, and of many kinds and sizes. Nearly all had been made ready for sea. And even now a large company of de Danann warriors was escorting Fomor from their stockade to get on with the work.

Very soon Eire would be free forever of this pestilence that had blighted it so long. Then the de DanNanns and their new Firbolg allies could begin the real work of living and growing, creating their own culture here.

That notion should have pleased Nuada. It was, after all, what he and his people had been seeking for those many years. Since Nemed had led their clans here from the east so very long before, it had been the one dream that had sustained them: to have their own land. Now that dream had finally come to pass.

Why, then, did he have this feeling of something not complete? Where pride should have filled him there was a hollowness. Instead of the spirit of success, the specter of failure haunted him. He had led his people to restoring themselves. What made him so dissatisfied?

He shook the feeling off. The day was invigorating, and there was much to do. It was time to begin meeting with his advisors to decide the best manner for sending their captives off. The only difficulty was that several of his council's most vital members appeared to be missing.

The day before he had slowly become aware of the absence of Findgoll, the Dagda, and Morrigan. He had told himself that they were likely busy in the camp and he had simply missed them. Today he determined to look for them, and to that end he left the hillside and moved down into the sprawling encampment.

He moved from fire to fire, from clan to clan, telling the others of his chieftains and Druids about the need to meet. Always he asked about his comrades and always was the answer the same: no one had seen them. In the sectors where the Firbolgs had made their camp, he received another surprise as well. No one there had seen Taillta since the day before.

He worked his way methodically through the entire camp, finally reaching the shore. Fomor were now laboring hard to caulk hulls, set masts, repair sails. He stopped to watch, his mind filled with an odd foreboding. He was sure now that his friends were not in the camp. But where had they gone?

It was nearing midday when the birds appeared.

Nuada was in consultation with a group of chieftains about the security arrangements for boarding the Fomor.

They were interrupted by a voice raised some distance away, shouting something above the din of the workers. This cry was taken up by others and spread rapidly. The king and his chieftains looked about to see what was the cause of this alarm. They realized that men along the shore and on the boats were pointing up and out to sea.

The attention of Nuada went there too. He saw nothing to excite interest at first—just a small flock of birds coming toward them. But then he realized that there was something very peculiar about them indeed. No two of them were alike. In fact, some of them didn't even appear to *be* birds. And they were certainly extraordinarily large.

"What in the Blessed Isles are those?" asked the chieftain called Febal.

"I've no more idea than you," Nuada told him. "But they seem to be coming down here. Come along. Let's find out what this is about!"

The bizarre flock was angling steeply down now, heading for a clear spot of beach just beyond where the ships were drawn up. Nuada and his group made for this at a rapid stride, arriving as the creatures began to settle from the sky.

They joined a large mass of curious warriors who had already formed. But they kept well back from these strange and threatening-looking creatures, leaving them isolated in a half-circle of space at the water's edge.

The winged beings were quite wary themselves, pulling into a tight group as they landed, glancing around at the surrounding warriors with nervous movements.

"What do you think they want here?" Nuada asked.

"Do you think they're dangerous?" asked the chieftain called Niet.

Their questions were soon answered, for the scaly, lizardlike creature with leathery wings crawled forward from the rest, lifted its head high on its slender neck, and addressed them.

"We seek Nuada, High-King of the Tuatha de Dananns," it said in formal tones.

Though a bit surprised to hear it speak, Nuada still moved boldly out to stand before it.

"I am Nuada. And who are you?"

"We are of that clan you know as Pookas."

This name raised an immediate and sensational response from the gathered men. A loud rumble of collective outrage was heard, and several sharply voiced threats were clearly audible. But this Nuada quickly silenced with lifted hands.

"Certainly you know the feelings of my people toward you," he said.

"We do," the other replied. "It is because of our past wrong to you that we've come here, hoping to change your feelings toward us. It was our brother Shaglan who told us this might be done."

"Shaglan has been more than a friend to us," Nuada said. "He has regained our trust through his loyalty."

"We hope to do the same," the winged lizard said earnestly.

"It will take more than the word of a traitor's lot like you to do that," Niet shouted angrily. "Shaglan has risked his life for us."

"We understand. And that is why we gave our help to the friends of Shaglan. Last night we flew them to the Tower of Glass."

Exclamations of shock and disbelief arose in the crowd. Nuada, however, too clearly understood now what had happened.

"Let me guess," he said heavily. "Did these friends include the Dagda, Morrigan, Taillta, and the Druid Findgoll?"

"Your Morrigan had no need of our help, but we carried the rest, and Lugh Lamfada, Angus Og, and the woman Aine as well."

"Of course," said Nuada. "I should have known they would try such a scheme."

"What are you saying?" Febal demanded. "Is what this Pooka says true?"

"It is, I'm afraid. All of them have been missing from the camp. I've no doubt of where they've gone."

"But why would they risk themselves by going to the Tower?" the chieftain asked.

"To save Gilla Decaire," the king said angrily. "I knew that Lugh Lamfada had sworn to stand by his friend. I should have realized that the others would join him."

"They've gone to save the Clown?" Niet said, sounding surprised. He found it difficult to understand why all of them would become so foolhardy over that gawky lunatic.

"It's impossible," argued Febal. "How could that small group attack the Tower themselves?"

"They meant to sneak into it," the Pooka explained. "We

flew them to its roof and they went inside. They planned to find this Gilla and return here before you'd even known they'd gone. We were to wait until sunrise for them. We waited much longer. They never returned."

"Never returned?" said Nuada sharply. "What happened?"

"We've no way to know that. Likely they were caught, maybe killed. We are sorry. We came to you, thinking that you should know their fate."

"I still don't see why we should be taking the word of this traitorous pack," growled the unforgiving Niet.

"We might have just gone home," the Pookas' leader answered in an offended tone. "We had fulfilled our agreement faithfully. Yet we chose to come here." The long neck swept the lizard head about as it looked over the gathering. Its voice became chill and hostile. "But I see the way of it. I see the mistrust still in your eyes. We have already suffered greatly in punishment for our crime. Still, you demand that we prove ourselves to you. It is too much. Our task is ended. We will not seek your friendship anymore!"

With that, the great creature lifted its saillike wings. The others followed quickly. They raised a great flurry of wind with their pumping wings, driving the gathered warriors back as they rose up.

Slowly, they flapped higher over the shore plains, then turned to soar away inland. Nuada looked after the flock of strange beings until they disappeared over the southern ridges. He felt a deep regret at their abrupt departure.

"We should not have treated them so harshly," he told his people. "It took great courage for them to come to us."

The warriors, however, had forgotten already about the Pooka clan. They now crowded around their High-King, eager to find out what this news meant.

"All right," he said, raising his hands to quiet the clamor of questions. "Listen to me. I have no doubt that this is true. It means that we have lost many of our greatest friends. Our Champions Morrigan and the Dagda are gone, as is the High-Druid Findgoll. And gone with them is Lugh Lamfada, who more than any other has helped us to regain our freedom."

He looked out toward the sea's northern horizon, seeing in his mind the chill, gleaming shaft hidden behind its rim. His voice took on a new certainty as he continued.

"I think that you all know as well as I what must be done

now. It is time for us to go against the Tower of Glass, to save our comrades or to take our revenge!"

"This is absolute madness!" complained Bobd Derg loudly. "We don't even know if any of them are still alive!"

They were at council in the High-King's enclosure, a wrangling mass of over a hundred chieftains, Champions and Druids of both the Firbolg and de Danann clans.

"It's your own father and brother than you're condemning with your words," Niet accused.

"My father lives for such adventures," he shot back. "Angus is the same. If they got themselves killed this time, it's the kind of death they wished. It's no reason for any more of us to throw their lives away going after them."

"It's nothing to do with their bein' alive or dead to me," put in Goibnu the Smith. "It's the revenge that we must take against the Tower. We all know it was them behind the cruelty we've suffered from all these years. They've got to pay for that!" His eyes flashed a fire of hatred as hot as his forges.

"Aye, and they'll not let us have Eire in peace," added another chieftain. "They sent those metal beasts of theirs here to destroy us. How long do you think we'll wait until they try something against us again?"

"They'll destroy us surely if we go against the Tower," Bobd Derg countered. He raised his voice so that it could be heard above the arguing of the rest.

"Please, all of you, you must listen to me!" he called in tones filled with all the passionate intensity that could be imparted to it by a trained High-Bard. The other voices faded. "All of us here know what will happen if we try to attack that Tower! The younger warriors grew up with the dark, bloody tales of destruction that their fathers told them. The weapons of the Tower are vast. They are beyond what we can imagine or what our magic can create. Think what their few war engines did to us! Without the miraculous help of Lugh Lamfada, we would not have survived! But the forces we would face this time would be much greater. The black ships of their fleet alone would slice us apart. And then there is the dreadful flaming eye of Balor himself!"

The men listened and they remembered the lurid tales. But since the restoration of their strength and their defeat of the Fomor in Eire, a fighting spirit had filled them. They

were not easily to be driven into doubt and fearfulness again
by such words.

"Their iron monsters took us by surprise," Niet shot
back with great bravado. "If we had been prepared, we could
have beaten them."

"Aye! Aye!" Goibnu added with gusto. "We know what
we'll face this time! We're stronger and we have the skills and
knowledge which we learned from Danu. We can find ways
to fight them. And we can win!"

A general cheer of acclamation greeted this, but the response of Bobd Derg was violent and harsh.

"You are truly fools if you think that. What mad compul-
sion makes you wish to fight? We have what we sought. We
have won Eire! There is no need for more!"

"There is a need," said a quiet but forceful voice. "I
understand that now. This is what must be."

Everyone turned their attention from the Bard to their
High-King, who had until this moment stood quietly at one
end of the group, listening. His face was set in lines of
certainty. His piercing gaze swept around to meet the eyes of
every man as he continued.

"I came to Eire first with Morrigan and the Dagda, with
Findgoll, Diancecht, Macha, and Goibnu and so many other
of those sons of Nemed. Few are left now of that band, and of
that few, some of those comrades closest to me are in that icy
Tower. But that is not the reason that I choose to go against
its might. I will go because I know that this battle had to
come, that we have not truly won until we have defeated the
forces there. Do you see? That is the true meaning of the
Prophecy. Not that we free ourselves of the monstrous race
that enslaved us. Not that we win Eire for ourselves. But that
the power of the Fomor race be destroyed. And its power lies
out there, in that Tower of Glass.

"But it was said in the Prophecy that Lugh would lead
us," pointed out the tall, aristocratic Druid named Meglin.
"How are we to act without him?"

"Lugh *has* led us," Nuada answered. "He has brought us
to this point. He has shown us the way that we must go.
Now, finally, it must be up to us. He has fought enough
battles for us. It is time that we fought the final one alone!"

There was a roar of agreement from the others. Weapons
were drawn and brandished in the air. Bobd Derg's protesta-
tions were drowned out and, defeated, he slunk away.

"I will ask no warrior to go unless he chooses," Nuada told them when the cheering had died. "This will be a hard battle, and I will lead no man who does not freely follow me."

"How will we go against them?" asked Febal.

"We will use the vessels gathered here. They are nearly ready to sail and will hold hundreds of fighters. It will be the task of Goibnu and his craftsmen, of all our Druids and other men of skills, to devise the means to help us win this fight!"

"What about the Fomor prisoners?" another chieftain wondered.

"I would hope that our Firbolg cousins would keep the watch on them until we return," Nuada said, looking to their chieftains.

"Wait, High-King," protested a burly Firbolg chief whose flowing mustaches were braided at the tips. "With all respects to you, you're not leaving us out of this. Remember, it's our Queen who's a captive too! Seems only fair that we go along with you."

"It's our fight with the Tower that must be finished," Nuada reasoned. "Your people have already done much. Why risk yourselves?"

"Risk?" the warrior repeated, and grinned. "Why, we look at it as a chance to fight. You can't deny a Firbolg that!"

Nuada grinned in reply. "All right. Any warrior who wishes to join us is welcome. Those who choose to stay in Eire will watch the Fomor until we return."

"*If* you return," Bobd Derg muttered darkly as he moved out of the enclosure.

Behind him, Nuada was now briskly giving orders.

"All right, my lads, we must be at work then. We must strengthen the largest ships for battle, prepare our arms, find ways that we can fight. If we mean to go, then by tomorrow we must be ready to sail against the Tower!"

Chapter Twenty
THE TOWER'S LIFE

The lift door slid upward, and Lugh Lamfada, escorted by Sital Salmhor and two of the helmeted guards, stepped out onto the wide floor of the vast atrium that served as a core to the Tower. Lugh looked up from its center. The levels stretched away far above him. The separate bands of white and silver that marked each gallery seemed to grow smaller with the distance, shrinking the space enclosed down to a tiny, lighted square.

It had the beauty of stark simplicity, of clean line and symmetry, Lugh thought. But it was a beauty lacking any sense of warmth or life.

He found this impression strengthened by the inhabitants of this icy realm. The gray-uniformed people about him seemed nearly identical, moving with the same brisk precision, faces set alike in disciplined blankness. To Lugh they seemed scarcely human, more like metal statues animated by the Tower's magic, serving it with the same mindless efficiency as its other machines.

"On the levels just beneath us are the systems that power the entire structure," Salmhor was saying in his most prim and austere voice. "These systems were created by our ancestors many years ago, when the Tower was built. They are self-sustaining and will supply our needs forever."

"Then, did your people intend this as a refuge for you after the rest of your civilization had collapsed?" Lugh asked. Despite his predicament, his youthful curiosity was aroused by this strange place and its history.

Salmhor gave him a hard, appraising look. "So, you have heard something of our past?"

"I've heard some legends spread by the Eireland Fomor," Lugh explained. "They say that a monstrous evil created by your own magic turned upon you and destroyed most of your race."

"I suppose that is the way a primitive mind might interpret what happened," Salmhor answered with a superior air. "Our own science did bring about our near extinction. Its creations infected our people, and the infection spread quickly. Nothing could stop it. So this building was created. Yes, you were right in calling it a refuge. It was to isolate, protect, and nurture a carefully selected group, the finest elements of our race. Here they could safely live until the plague had spent itself, and then begin the task of rebuilding."

"But your plague must have run itself out many years ago!" Lugh said. "Why have you continued to keep yourselves shut away here?"

Salmhor raised a disapproving eyebrow and his tone grew sharp. "That is none of your affair," he said, and moved away. The guards urged Lugh along after him.

"The legends say that the blood of those in the Tower was also tainted by the curse," Lugh prodded. "That means even your hiding away here didn't completely save you, doesn't it?"

Irritated, Salmhor stopped at the far side of the atrium and turned on Lugh again.

"We do think we're a clever boy, don't we?" he said in exasperation. "Very well, yes! We did have a problem with genetic . . . ah . . . failures here for some time. But we have reversed that degeneration."

"By keeping those who were normal here while the rest were exiled to Eire."

"We have kept a pure Fomor race here," he said in a lordly manner, "and it has grown stronger. Now, come along. There is a great deal more you are to see."

Once more he led the way, moving around the outside of the lower level, pointing up various corridors leading into the inner rooms.

"On this and the other lower levels are the facilities that provide services to the Tower," he explained. "Kitchen and dining areas are here as well as general stores for clothing, supplies, and equipment. Just above is the level for medical services."

"I saw them," Lugh reminded him. "They seemed deserted except for Mathgen."

"Our people are very healthy," Salmhor told him curtly. "We'll go up to the central levels now."

They had made a circuit of the atrium by this time,

arriving back at the lift. A group of Tower people who had clearly been preparing to board it instead stood respectfully aside for Salmhor as he ushered Lugh aboard. With only the two guards they started upward.

"Tell me, why are you showing me all of this?" Lugh asked. "When they shut me away in that little room, I didn't expect you'd be coming to give me a tour."

"I've no idea," the man answered stiffly. "I simply do as the Commander ordered. It is not the practice of a Tower officer to question him."

"No," Lugh said with a little smile. "I'll bet it's not."

The vibrating room pulled them up the shaft for some distance, letting them out on a level about halfway up the Tower. As they walked along the gallery, Lugh glanced over the rail. The atrium floor now equaled in size the square of ceiling high above. Other than that, this level was identical to the lower ones: a smooth white inner wall pierced at regular intervals by corridors.

"On these levels we have our training areas," Salmhor told his charge. "We develop the many skills necessary to create those who can serve our ends with greatest efficiency. It is with such ideally bred and educated people that we will repopulate the world."

"With Mathgen's help," Lugh added.

Salmhor sniffed scornfully. "We need no help from his sorcery or from the supposed magic of this Tir-na-nog. Our own strength makes us superior. Let me show you."

They rounded a corner of the gallery and entered one of the corridors. Along its sides were many doors, and from behind them came the sounds of voices and what Lugh easily recognized as the clash of arms.

"Through here," Salmhor invited, swinging one of the doors open.

Lugh moved through into a large, brightly lit room. Under the hard white glow of the radiant ceiling panels, scores of Tower soldiers were engaged in the grueling task of training for war.

As Salmhor entered behind him, a voice somewhere shouted a loud command. Immediately all activity in the room ceased as the men pulled themselves to rigid attention.

"Get on with your normal activities!" Salmhor ordered. "We are here to observe."

Just as quickly the men resumed their work.

Lugh watched in fascination. In the room's open center, two facing lines of men were at a carefully choreographed play with swords and long knives, painstakingly working through a series of feints, parries, and attacks under the watchful eye and sharp tongue of an instructor. Along one wall, a dozen more practiced with the deadly metal crossbows, sending the short bolts whizzing to the hearts of man-shaped targets. Still other soldiers were engaged in wrestling, in use of spear and ax, or in exercising. Lugh was especially intrigued by one group, who seemed to be desperately fighting off ponderous machines that were pulling and pushing at them with metal limbs.

"What are those things doing to those men?" he asked. "Is it torture?"

"Those devices are used to strengthen them," Salmhor said, shaking his head over this barbarian's ignorance. "It is important that every soldier of the Tower be at his peak physically."

Lugh could well believe the truth of that. The bodies of the soldiers training about him all seemed well-muscled and as hard as the iron of a skillfully forged sword.

But as they moved about the room, Lugh found himself at a loss to understand the attitude of these men. The way they instantly responded to commands, their rigid discipline, their mindless laboring, were aspects alien to him. The Firbolg and de Danann warriors he knew were, in contrast, wild, emotional, and highly individualistic, fighting with their own unique styles, following no man's orders except by their own choice. These Tower men lacked all separateness. The uniforms, the close-cropped hair, the sameness in build, in movements, in facial expression, reinforced his impression that they were identical.

"We have other areas devoted to preparing our people for other tasks," Salmhor explained with pride. "Men are trained to crew our ships, to service the Tower, to manufacture weapons and supplies. Each one is prepared from childhood to be a perfect soldier of the Tower. He is ready to sacrifice himself for the Tower's good."

"Why?" Lugh asked bluntly.

Salmhor cast a pitying look at him. "You really don't understand, do you? The Tower's purpose is all that matters. Without it, there is nothing."

"There are a few other things I'd rather have, thank

you," said Lugh. He was thinking of fiery sunsets playing against high cliffs that reared up from the wild sea, of soft meadows fragrant with spring rains, of mist-shrouded hills that all seemed to hide wonderful mysteries. And as he compared Eire's natural charms with the stark and artificial surroundings of the Tower, he wondered for a brief, wistful moment if he would ever see those charms again.

Salmhor disregarded his comment. "Come along!" he ordered briskly. "I will show you the living quarters now."

Lugh went along without coaxing from the guards this time. He had actually become eager to learn more about life in this amazing place. He had already discovered things that he had never considered before. But none was as great a surprise to him as what he saw next.

The lift took them up several more levels. They got off at another identical gallery, walked along a similar unadorned, brightly lit corridor. This time, however, the doors they passed opened into rooms filled with children!

It was a most astonishing discovery for Lugh because he had never imagined finding children living in the Tower. It seemed fit only for the grim, gray-clad soldiers of Balor.

Each of the rooms they visited held children of a different age level. Their activities were always carefully supervised by several adults. Most of these adults, Lugh noted with great interest, were women.

Like the men, the Tower women were largely sturdy in build, their features somewhat broader than those of the de Dananns, but not unpleasant. They dressed in the same simple tunics and trousers as the men, hair cropped short or tied back tightly, expressions just as sober.

In the rooms of smaller children there was a great deal more activity. Still, Lugh observed that the natural tendency toward independent action in even the youngest was severely repressed. Games were played, but with a gravity, a care, and a regimentation that both astonished and distressed Lugh. It seemed to him quite unnatural.

And for the older children there was yet more discipline. Youths went through rigorous physical training or sat in rows on hard benches, backs stiff, heads high, listening attentively to lessons recited by droning instructors.

"This certainly looks exciting," Lugh remarked dryly. He recalled his own carefree, enjoyable childhood. "What is it that they do for fun?"

"Fun?" echoed Salmhor, giving him a curious look, clearly not understanding what he meant.

"Never mind," Lugh told him. "You've already answered me."

As they went on he became aware that when the children reached about the age of twelve, the mixing of boys and girls in the classrooms ended. He saw only males in the older groups, engaged in early training for warfare.

"What happens to the girls?" he asked Salmhor.

"They are sent to separate training at this point," the officer explained. "While the boys are now moved to a single quarters where they will be schooled together, the girls remain with their mothers to learn their own duties in the Tower."

"What are their duties?"

"They help maintain the Tower's functions, as everyone else does," he answered vaguely. "Let us move along."

All this was making a gloomy impression on Lugh. The children here were taught to lose any sense of their separate identities, and though their presence should have added a note of warmth and humanity to the icy nature of the Tower, they only served to make the young warrior feel all the more an alien here.

"How many children are there here?" he asked as they moved back onto the gallery.

"Several hundred," Salmhor answered. "Their quarters and those of the women are on several of these upper levels." He waved a hand up and down the atrium.

Again Lugh glanced over the rail. The floor below had now dwindled to a tiny patch. The ceiling above was very near. They were only a few levels from the top now.

"What about the men?" he enquired. "You didn't mention where they stay."

"Their quarters are somewhat farther down the Tower," Salmhor said curtly. He was obviously tiring of answering questions from this naive boy. As they reached the lift once more, his voice filled with relief. "I think this concludes our little tour. We'll now continue on up to the top. Balor is waiting for you there."

Balor! That name renewed Lugh's apprehension. What had the dark giant in store for him now?

They rode up to the highest level and started across the gallery toward the Commander's throne room. Lugh glanced down from the height and found with some pleasure that his old fear of it was nearly gone. Flying with Shaglan had helped him after all.

This thought reminded him of the Pooka. He lifted a hand to the waist of his tunic and patted the small warm lump. He felt it squirm and heard a faint voice complain: "Not so roughly, please!"

Salmhor, striding before Lugh, shot a suspicious look back toward the young man.

"What was that?"

"Just humming a bit," Lugh assured him, trying to smile innocently.

Salmhor shook his head irritably over this strange lad and went on.

They reached the anteroom to Balor's quarters. Lugh waited anxiously as the guards swung back the doors and ushered the two men forward into the Commander's presence. Now, finally, he would discover what this odd treatment by his captors was all about. Somehow he didn't feel that the experience was going to be a pleasant one.

He strode into the huge room at Salmhor's side. Ahead of them sat the towering black form with its blazing slit of eye. Beside the giant's throne stood Bres, his hate-filled gaze fixed on the young Champion. As the two reached the room's center, Salmhor signaled Lugh to halt.

The ruby beam of the single eye shone on Lugh. He could feel the uncomfortable warmth of it prickling on his skin. He fought to contain the tremor of fear and return Balor's gaze fearlessly.

"We have discovered the guards you attacked," the metal voice hammmered out. "We know you entered the Tower from the roof. How did you come to be there?"

At the cold words Lugh's fear of the being rose up and threatened to overwhelm him. But then an image came to him of MacLir, facing danger with that careless manner and that inane smile. As before, the spirit of Lugh's mentor strengthened him. He would handle Balor as Manannan would.

"We flew," he replied, putting on what he hoped was an insolent smile.

"Did you?" said Balor, clearly not amused. "Bres feels it was some Druidic magic. Is he correct?"

Lugh shrugged. "You're wasting your time in this. I'm not telling anything to you. If you want information, I suggest you try torture. You're very good at that. Otherwise, let me join my friends."

"Not quite yet," said Balor. "We have more to discuss." The eye shifted fractionally, bringing its crimson gaze to the officer. "Salmhor, have you done as I ordered?"

"My Commander, we have shown the boy through the Tower," Salmhor answered in his best subservient tone. "I have explained its functioning to him, at least to the extent I felt he could comprehend."

"He has seen the living quarters and the children?"

"He has."

"Good, Salmhor." The eye moved back to Lugh. "It is important that you see our life here, see that those of the Tower are simply human beings, not monsters."

"But, why?" Lugh asked, even more bewildered than before. "You have what you wanted from me and from the rest. You have no more use for us. Why bother to keep us alive? Why show me your Tower?"

"Because," the voice rumbled slowly, "if you understand us, realize what we truly are, it will be much easier for you to accept that you are one of us yourself!"

Chapter Twenty-One
BALOR'S STORY

Lugh managed to give a derisive chuckle at that. "You've got to try something better. You surely can't expect me to take you seriously."

"You are the son of Ethlinn, my own daughter," the iron voice clanged on. "The blood of the pure Fomor race runs in your veins."

Bres, wide-eyed with disbelief at this unexpected revelation, was now listening with intense concentration. Lugh, however, was taking the giant's words with a great deal less seriousness.

"I've heard that tale from you before," he responded, struggling to keep up his flippant air. "If you're trying to confuse me with it, you'll fail. I couldn't be grandson to such a monstrous thing as you. It's impossible!"

"What I tell you is true," Balor replied. "Your father was the de Danann Champion, Cian, but your mother was of this Tower. He stole her from here and carried her to Eire. When she was finally returned, she had a child. That child was you."

Lugh reeled. If this was true, it explained the dream of the Glass Tower that had come often to him in childhood. It also explained why Manannan had always avoided telling him much about his mother.

And with this realization came another. He turned his head and met the astonished, searching gaze of Bres. Again he felt that peculiar linking between them and, for the first time, understood its source. In the blending of two bloods within them, they were alike. For all their differences, they shared this single characteristic, and it gave each a unique insight into the other's soul.

But even as he was forced to accept the truth of the Commander's words, he found a new resolve not to be shaken by it.

"And if I do believe this, why should it change my feelings toward you?" he retorted, his pretense at nonchalance abandoned in favor of open defiance. "It was still you who killed my mother and father!"

"I killed your father, yes. He came again to take both of you. This time I fought him on the rocks below us. He managed to take away the power of my legs. I managed to take his life. But while we fought, Manannan MacLir was able to spirit you away. Your mother died of grief over her lost child."

"You lie!" Lugh accused. "She died because you kept her a prisoner here."

"You were told that by MacLir," Balor countered. "She loved the Tower. It was against her will that Cian took her away. She wanted her son to take his rightful place as a leader of the Tower. For many years I searched for you to bring you back, but that treacherous 'sea-god' had hidden you away too well with Taillta and her clan to guard you."

"You meant to destroy me as you destroyed all of Taillta's people and the home where they raised me," Lugh said vehemently.

"It was not meant that you should be harmed," Balor

explained. "Our intent was only to rescue you and keep MacLir from using you."

"Using me?" Lugh said sharply. "What do you mean? He helped me!"

"He controlled you," the giant rapped out. "He knew the Prophecy that only the son of Cian could lead the de Dananns and destroy the Fomor power. He meant to see that you fulfilled that Prophecy. So he hid you away until you were grown. He kept you safely out of my reach, isolated and ignorant of the truth."

"But why?" asked Lugh, fighting to keep a skeptical tone against such a devastating notion. "What would he gain?"

"Control of you. Because the son of Cian might fulfill the Prophecy only if he chose freely to do so. Don't you see? Manannan feared that if you knew about your Fomor blood, you would choose to join us instead of helping the de Dananns. That he and his Queen Danu could not allow. No. They needed you to be their instrument for destroying us."

Could that be true? Since his first meeting with the Master of the Sidhe, he had felt manipulated. Often he had thought Manannan too much in control. Was it possible the being had tricked him and turned him to some end against his will? And what about Aine! His beloved Aine! Was she capable of condoning such an act? The image of her ruthlessness in summoning the rats returned to him and he recalled her saying that she would do whatever necessary to achieve success.

His instincts and experience told him to reject such ideas. Even so, his former assurance was weakened by a nagging doubt. When he launched another argument, it lacked much of the force of his earlier attempts.

"Even if Manannan did keep this secret from me, you can't convince me that it was for evil ends. He let me see conditions in Eire for myself before asking me to make my choice. I know how brutal you were to the de Dananns. The decision to help them *was* freely made by me, and I would make it again!"

"We in the Tower had no intention of causing suffering to the de Dananns," Balor told him. "We did not know what savages our poor exiles had become. It was Bres who was meant to keep them in control. My only intent was to keep the de Dananns from challenging us. We might have taken all our forces to Eire long ago and annihilated them as Bres wanted. I was against that."

Bres was clearly not pleased by the direction of this conversation. He cast a hostile glance up at the towering figure.

"I want you to understand clearly that there is no good or evil here," Balor continued. "That's why it was important for you to see the Tower. You had to be convinced that we are not out to destroy the de Dananns, that we are only trying to survive, as they are. We could be at peace with them."

"And what do you want from me?" Lugh asked cautiously.

"You know the whole truth now. You know that you are as much Fomor as de Danann. You cannot choose one side over the other. You must deny the Prophecy, and it will be ended. Manannan will not be able to use you any longer. We will all be free of it."

"And what about the de Dananns?"

"We will make a peace with them. They will have Eire without our interference and we will have the seas without their challenging us. You can become the peacemaker. You are a leader of them. You have their trust. You could insure peace."

"Wait!" Bres protested. "What about me? You promised Eire to me!"

"Silence, Bres," Balor warned sharply. "You must know that you could never return to Eire again."

But the former High-King's outburst had drawn Lugh's attention to him. Now he stared intently at the man, an understanding of what was happening here coming suddenly clear to him. And with that understanding, any doubts that Balor had managed to create were swept away.

"I see," he told the giant. "You want to make another Bres of me. You want me to keep the de Dananns docile and no threat to you. You still fear the Prophecy!"

"No!" Balor rumbled. "We fear nothing. We wish only to avoid needless destruction. We want peace!"

"You talk about peace to me while you've used every kind of treachery and cruelty you could. You've killed my parents, destroyed my home, tortured my friends. You would have slaughtered the de Dananns if you'd had the chance. And now you want me to believe that you meant no harm? You showed me your Tower, hoping to convince me of your humanity. You meant to have me feel that there is no good or evil in this, that I can't make the choice between you. Well, you failed. This Tower is filled with beings of iron and ice, not people. And it's not my mission as Champion I'll deny, it's the Fomor blood in me." He held out his arm, fist clenched, veins sharply defined beneath the light skin of his tensed forearm. "If I could drain it from my veins, I would!"

He drew himself up, striking a defiant pose, staring into the glare of that crimson eye. "You're the evil here, and I'll do nothing to help you. So, if you mean to end my part in the Prophecy, you'd best destroy me now!"

He expected that he had invited a scorching blast from the eye with his bold speech. He was surprised and relieved to discover that he was wrong. For a long time Balor's shuttered gaze rested warmly upon him while the giant sat silent and motionless, as if in contemplation. When he finally spoke again, his tones were a flat, low clattering instead of a thunder of rage.

"It's clear that I need to waste no more time on you," he said. "If you wish to be a de Danann, then you may join them." The eye moved to the officer waiting beside Lugh. "Salmhor, see that he is taken to the cells."

With that, the enormous throne began to roll, turning to cross the floor and disappear into the hallway leading to Balor's lift. He left the young warrior and the others staring after him, all taken somewhat at a loss by his speedy acceptance of Lugh's rejection.

Salmhor recovered first, moving in to grip Lugh's elbow and tug him away.

"Come along then. You heard the Commander's order. And no difficulties from you, or it will go hard for you and the others."

Lugh had no choice but to allow the officer to lead him back across the room and out the doors. Their two guards fell in behind again, weapons at the ready as they started out toward the atrium.

Bres followed, catching them as they reached the gallery.

"So, boy, you had me dethroned, cast out of Eire as a halfbreed. And now you know you are no different," he said scornfully.

"I am different," Lugh said. "I could never act as you have toward the de Dananns."

"It's the Fomor blood, boy," Bres told him. "It's too strong. You may fight it, but it will take you too."

"And destroy me, Bres? As it did your own son?"

"What?" said Bres, taken sharply aback. "What do you mean?"

"His own mother revealed the truth," Lugh told him bluntly. "He's dead. Your hatred took his life just as it lost you Eire."

The man was left stricken, staring after Lugh as the young warrior and his escort marched on to the lift. As they entered and Lugh turned to face Bres, he spoke again.

"I am sorry. But what I've learned has only proven to me that the Fomor blood doesn't have to control. You've let it happen, Bres. You could still choose to fight it. Think, man: what has it gained for you?"

Salmhor activated the lift and the silver door slid down, cutting off Lugh's view of Bres's anguished face.

The beach was now swarming with workers busy upon the scores of ships. But it was now de Danann and Firbolg craftsmen who worked upon them. The Fomor were all shut away under heavy guard.

As Nuada moved along the line of larger vessels he noted the progress with satisfaction. Since dawn they had accomplished much. Now, as the sun began its final plunge into the western sea, huge bonfires were being set along the beach so the work might continue on into the night. In the glow of a sunset that paved a gold-flecked highway of light across the waves, he watched the men adding a wicker defensive bulwark to the sides of a wooden barque.

"It's coming along very well," remarked one of the chieftains with him. "By morning we should have enough vessels ready to carry nearly our whole army."

"We'll have to have," Niet put in, grinning. "There's hardly a warrior of the de Danann or Firbolg clans who doesn't want to come. We'll be having to order some to stay behind and mind the captives, and you can be certain we'll hear loud complaints from them!"

They moved on along the shore, coming to the timber sheds that marked the makeshift smithy that had been swiftly erected. Here every de Danann skilled in metal-working was feverishly laboring over anvils and forges.

Goibnu, seeing the High-King's retinue approach, moved to meet him.

"How are your people doing here?" Nuada asked.

"We've replaced every weapon lost already, my King," the man told him, a proud smile glinting whitely in his blackened face. "We'll have the extra weapons ready by dawn."

"And what about that other task?"

"I'm at that myself. Look here." The smith held up a short length of chain. Each of its links was of forged iron, heavy and thick.

"Will they work?" Nuada said, examining them with interest.

"Will they work?" The smith looked offended. "I'll have you know my finest skills are in that. All the tricks in working metal I learned from those in Tir-na-nog I'm using to fashion these links. There's not a metal in Eire or in that Tower can match their strength. Don't you be fearing about that. They'll do the job all right."

"Goibnu, I've no doubts about your skills," Nuada said, smiling. He handed the chain back and added more gravely, "But they'll do us little good unless we can close with the Tower ships."

"That," said Goibnu pointedly, "is a problem for the Druids. My own bit will be ready by dawn."

Nuada noted Bridget at work, beating away spiritedly at a length of glowing iron. He nodded toward her.

"How is she faring?" he asked Goibnu softly.

"She's working the grief from her," he answered. "She's forged more longswords than any two of my others, and every one a beauty. But there's much sorrow and much hate hammered into the blade of every one, I can tell you. I'd not wish to be a Fomor facing the cut of one of them."

Nuada nodded in understanding and left the smith to get on with his work. He and his chieftains moved away from the shore now, back through the thick scattering of smaller boats toward a cleared area just beyond.

Here, within a circular stockade, the bright-cloaked Druids fluttered about a collection of steaming cauldrons like a flock of nervous birds. A smell at once acrid, sweet, and putrid filled the air, and the varicolored plumes of smoke rising from the pots combined to form a yellow haze that hung above.

Meglin, the haughty High-Druid, rushed to welcome Nuada, smiling ingratiatingly, bowing low.

"Is this unusually humble behavior on your part to warn me that you've not succeeded yet?" Nuada asked suspiciously.

"Oh, no, my King," Meglin assured him quickly. "We believe that we have found something to help."

"Fine," said the king. "Then tell me what you have."

"You know, my King, that during our long repression by the Fomor, our skills became disused," the Druid explained apologetically. "But we have been practicing with great diligence. I think we can say now that they are restored."

"You mean that, thanks to the fine instruction of Findgoll, you finally recovered your powers," Nuada corrected.

Meglin sighed. "Yes, I suppose so," he agreed reluctantly, hating to admit to the superior magic of the little Druid. "But, now that we are restored in our own right, we are quite capable of work just as skilled, as you will see."

He led the High-King's party toward one of the fires. They passed a boyish-looking Druid who was prodding in a dispirited way at what seemed to be a sheep lying on its back, all four legs stiffly in the air. Nuada looked at this with some puzzlement.

"What's he doing with that dead sheep?" he demanded.

"Ah, that's young Ce," Meglin explained briefly. "He needs more practice. He can never conjure anything alive! But here! This is what you want."

He pointed down, with an air of pride, into the thick, yellow-green substance boiling in a large cauldron.

The High-King looked down at it dubiously. "That? Why, that looks like pea soup!" He bent forward and sniffed. "Smells a bit like it as well! What's that supposed to do?"

Meglin at once assumed a scholarly tone. "Well, we knew that our danger lay in the Tower ships simply running us down before we could engage them. We had to devise a way to get our vessels alongside theirs without them being able to see us."

"I know all that," Nuada said. "Tell me what you've done, please! There's no time."

"Very well," Meglin said indignantly. "The elements we've blended here should raise a mist that will cloak our fleet."

"For how long?"

"Only a brief time. It can't be used until the very latest moment."

"And will it work?" Nuada asked, fixing the Druid with a piercing stare.

"It will. We're certain!" he assured the king.

"You had better hope so," Nuada said. "Because you're coming along to see it gets used properly. And if it fails, you'll be swimming home right along with the rest of us!"

Chapter Twenty-Two
THE PRISONERS

The floor opened beneath Lugh Lamfada, dumping him suddenly down onto the hard floor below.

He found himself looking up toward the smirking face of Sital Salmhor as the metal door swung to again, shutting him within the cell.

He got slowly to his feet, rubbing a bruised backside. A faint stirring within the folds of his tunic reminded him of the Pooka.

"Shaglan! Are you all right?" he asked anxiously.

"As if you care!" the little voice replied irritably. "Jumping about and nearly falling on me!"

"Sorry. I didn't plan that one myself. They've dropped us into what must be those cells of theirs."

A small, pink, quivering nose poked out of Lugh's tunic, followed by a glinting pair of eyes.

"It's not a pleasant sort of place, is it now?" the Pooka commented.

Lugh agreed. In the dim light he could see nothing but the faintly glistening stone walls. But where were his friends?

"We'll have to look for the others," he said. "There's a corridor up ahead. It seems the only way to go. Why don't you stay hidden while I do a bit of exploring?"

"If you think it's best," Shaglan said resignedly. "But

don't make it much longer. You've been wearing this tunic just a bit too long for me, lad."

"Very funny," Lugh said, and poked the tiny head back out of sight. Then he began to move cautiously along the shadowy corridor.

The glowing panels set in the stone roof were coated with ages of grime and spaced at wide intervals. Between their faint pools of light Lugh felt his way along the walls in darkness, peering ahead intently, watching for movement, hearing only the pounding of his own heartbeat. He proceeded in this way for what seemed like ages, stopping at several points to listen.

Suddenly, he stumbled.

Something caught his foot and he fell forward before he could catch himself. He threw his arms forward to soften the impact as his body crashed down onto something that crackled like a pile of dried twigs. He rolled to one side and found himself looking into the black sockets of a skull.

That brought him smartly to his feet. He stood looking down at the skeleton that lay stretched across the passage floor, nearly invisible in the dark. It was much the worse for his tumble into it, as many of the brittle bones snapped.

"Sorry," he said, and then recalled his passenger. "Shaglan?"

"I'm all right," the little voice replied. "I'm getting used to it. Where are we now?"

"I don't know," said Lugh, "and I'm not certain I want to."

With some understandable dread, the young warrior crept to a turn in the corridor and peered around it.

The passage ahead was choked with bones. Whole skeletons lay stretched upon the floor just before him. Beyond them was an amazing display of hundreds of individual bones. They had been built into elaborate and cleverly engineered structures, some reaching up to the ceiling. And in the midst of these towers sat a pyramid of faintly gleaming skulls whose scores of eyeless sockets seemed to stare at him.

He was returning this stare in an astonished way when a hand dropped onto his shoulder.

He whirled around, knocking it away. He found himself facing what seemed at first to be one of the skeletons sprung to life. But a closer look told him this was a living man, although the difference was slight. He had little more meat on his bones than the dead.

He was very old, Lugh saw, and stooped, his hands knobbed and bent. A wispy gray beard hung far down his chest. His head was bald save for a ragged fringe. His clothes were tattered remnants about his frail limbs. Still, Lugh recognized them with surprise. They had once been a uniform of the Tower.

He had cowered back in fear as Lugh turned on him, and the young warrior now addressed him in soothing tones.

"I won't hurt you. Who are you?"

The man recovered. Realizing that he wouldn't be struck, he now took on a shrill, belligerent tone: "Lobais is my name, boy. I came here to help you, and I didn't plan to be hurt for it!"

"You surprised me," Lugh explained. "I've just been put down here."

"I know! I know! We heard the clang of the doors. That's why I came after you."

"I'm looking for some friends. Would you know if they're here?"

"Yes, yes," he said impatiently. "I'll take you to them. We'd have been there now if you hadn't gone wandering into the wrong passage."

"What is this place?" Lugh asked.

"What it looks like, boy," he answered curtly. "Not even the dead escape these cells. You're lucky you didn't find a storage area for the newly dead. That isn't so pleasant."

"Who was it that piled the bones so carefully?"

"Me. There's little else to do down here. Now, come along!"

Lugh was weary of being ordered about, and he didn't know if he could trust this strange and wretched creature. Still, he didn't wish to be left here. So as the little man began to shuffle back along the passageway, he fell in closely behind.

They turned back into the main corridor, and traveled along it for some way, past two side passages, and finally emerged into a larger room.

Here they found gathered several score men whose uniforms all announced them to be of the Tower. These uniforms were in various stages of deterioration, as were those who wore them. Some of the men were in as sorry a state as Lugh's new acquaintance. Others seemed young and in good condition, their status as prisoners evident only in the filthy state of their clothing and their sprouting beards.

But Lugh gave these men only a sweeping glance. His attention was quickly drawn to a far corner, where his comrades sat.

As they saw him enter they sprang up with exclamations of relief. Aine ran to him, taking his arms and peering anxiously into his face.

"Lugh!" she said. "Are you all right? We were afraid that they were doing something terrible to you."

"I'm not hurt," he assured her. "And what about you?"

"Nothing has happened to us except that we've met a few fellow captives here," Manannan said. "And this place is certainly lacking in real comforts."

"But where's the Dagda?" Lugh asked, looking around for the familiar hulking shape.

"He's wandering about through all the passages," said Angus. "He can't stand the thought that he can't smash his way out of here. He's determined to find a way to escape."

"He could spend a lifetime about that," said one of the men in Tower dress. "No one's ever escaped from these cells."

Lugh looked at him with curiosity. He was a young man, swarthy and roughly handsome in features, stocky and powerful in build. From his condition he could not have been there long. Lugh's gaze went from him to the others who watched him, some few with interest, most with apathy.

"Who are these men?" he asked.

"I'm sorry," said MacLir. "You haven't met our new friends." He indicated the young man. "This is Eab, once an officer of the Tower forces." He nodded toward Lugh's guide. "Lobais you know. He was once in charge of maintaining the powers that make this whole place work." He waved a hand around the room. "The rest are men like them, once loyal members of Balor's companies."

"Why are they here?"

"They learned too much," MacLir said cryptically. "Here, see if you can find a dry place to sit. We'll tell you what we've learned. It will explain a great deal."

They all dropped down upon the smooth, damp floor. As Lugh arranged his cloak beneath him, he felt the stirring within his tunic. The tiny head popped out.

"So you've forgotten me, have you?" it said irritably.

"Shaglan!" cried Manannan with delight. "We'd guessed that you must have hidden yourself somehow. Welcome back."

The being peered around him at the surroundings. "Well, is it safe to come out now?"

"It's safe," Lugh told it.

Shaglan crawled out and then pulled himself up the outside of Lugh's tunic.

"Ouch! Careful with the claws," the young warrior said, wincing.

"I'll just sit here a bit if you don't mind," it announced, perching on his shoulder. "I need to work the knots out of my limbs." And it began to stretch its small body.

The Tower men watched this performance with fascination.

"So you were telling the truth about that Pooka thing," said Eab, quite amazed by it.

"Certainly!" Manannan said. "I'd like you to meet Shaglan, a truly marvelous being. And the young man holding him up is Lugh Lamfada."

Eab now eyed Lugh with a new interest. "You mean, you're the one Balor was seeking all those years? The one all that great fuss was about?"

"I'm afraid so," Lugh admitted. "But tell me why you're all here. What have you done?"

"We've tried to be free of this place, that's what," the soldier answered bitterly. "You see, there are some of us who've realized the whole Tower is as much a prison as what we're in now. Oh, the soldiers get out at times, but only to fight at Balor's orders. The rest are locked away here, some never smelling the outside air or seeing anything but the sea beyond those glass walls. It's worst for the women. Most of them never leave their quarters high up the Tower. And their only real purpose is to breed."

"Breed?" repeated Lugh, recalling the children he'd seen.

"For the good of the 'Pure Fomor Race!' " the man spat out as if it were an obscenity. "The population of the Tower must always be increased. So the women are forced to mate at the command of our leaders. And it's a sorry woman who's found to be barren!"

He nodded at the hopeless men around them. "Many of us here have women and children up there that they love. We can't be with them. The Tower controls their lives. We tried to raise a rebellion but we failed."

"Are there many others besides you?" Lugh asked.

"Some. Most accept the Tower's will. They've never known anything else. And there are others who would fight, but they're afraid. Balor and his guard are too strong."

Lugh felt great sympathy for this man and the other helpless victims of Balor's tyranny. But it also pleased him to discover that some independent spirit still lived in the people of the Tower. The Fomor blood in him was not, after all, devoid of humanity.

Still, there was one thing he didn't understand.

"You talk as if you expected to be trapped in the Tower forever," he said. "I thought your purpose was to leave here and reoccupy the outside world once you were strong enough. Wasn't that going to happen soon?"

Eab shook his head. "No. That was a lie. It's been spun out to us for generations as an excuse for them to keep their control of us. If anything, the opposite is true."

"What do you mean?"

"That's the most incredible thing we've found, Lugh," MacLir put in with great enthusiasm. "This Tower is dying!"

"What do you mean?"

"It's wearing out." He pointed to the old man. "Lobais here is the first one to discover it, I think."

"I did that!" he agreed, bobbing his head vigorously. "I was the one that cared for the great systems that keep the Tower alive. For years I did that, tending them as if they were my children. They were the only love I had, and I knew every bit of them like no one else!"

"I thought that the Tower was built to sustain itself without needing any care," said Lugh.

The old man grinned, showing his toothless gums. "Ah, that's what they wanted everyone to think. But it was me who kept things working, just as my father did." He tapped his narrow chest proudly. "It was Lobais who kept the Tower well!" His old face crumpled then, and he went on in sorrow. "I did, at least, until one day I saw the truth. I knew that no one could save it anymore. It was all getting old, you see. Just too old!"

He looked around them, tears showing in the drooping corners of the old eyes, voice quivering as he went on. "It was all right before when it was only little things to be fixed. But it was bigger ones every day. The ones who had created it all had gone long ago. We'd lost all their knowledge over the years. There was nothing I could do but watch it start to come apart. The mistake I made was telling others. That's why I was put here."

"Do you see, Lugh?" said Manannan. "It explains why Balor has tried so hard to avoid a fight. When the de Dananns came to Eire from Tir-na-nog, Mathgen must have warned Balor they could be dangerous. He feared the skills and magic Danu's people had given them. He convinced Balor to fear them too. Balor might have challenged the de Dananns then, but he knew the Tower was weakening. So he listened to Mathgen and decided not to risk damage to his forces. Instead, he used trickery and fear to keep them in control. Their old fear of the Tower and the monstrous look of the Fomor exiles were enough to convince them to submit. Then it was the job of Bres to weaken them by starvation and humiliation and pain so they'd have no will to fight. It worked—until you came along."

"Of course!" said Findgoll. "Mathgen's sorcery revealed the Prophecy to him, and he convinced Balor that they must keep it from being fulfilled. But they failed. Lugh survived."

"He deposed Bres and helped restore the de Dananns," Manannan put in. "Then he helped them win Eire." He laughed delightedly at the thought. "Ah, that great pile of iron must have been convinced of the truth of the Prophecy then!"

"Well, if he was, he's certainly not worried about it anymore," said Lugh ruefully. "Not with all of us here."

"And the way to Tir-na-nog open to him," added Aine.

That robbed MacLir of his glee. "It does look as if we've run into a little snag in our weaving there, doesn't it?" he admitted. "Apparently even Danu couldn't foresee a turn of events like that."

"I don't understand why you're so concerned about it," Lugh said. "With all the powers Danu and her people are supposed to have, why can't they just destroy the Fomor if they try to seize Tir-na-nog?"

"You don't understand the people of the Blessed Isles, lad," Findgoll explained. "They are people of peace. They could never use their magic to harm another living thing. They'd die first themselves."

"And they will if Mathgen reaches those Isles," the croaking voice of Morrigan put in.

Angus looked at Manannan with curiosity. "But you're of Tir-na-nog too, aren't you? You're certainly not like that."

The tall man gave a little sheepish grin. "Yes, well, I'm afraid I'm a bit of an odd one there. I was an outcast, to be honest, until Danu needed someone to come and help you. So, you see, there's really no one who can correct this little problem other than our stalwart band."

"Except that we're not much good shut away here," said Lugh.

"It could be worse," Manannan said, his usual buoyant mood returning. "I mean, we are all alive, and all together here. Balor obviously thinks he's won. He doesn't consider us any more threat to him. That means we're free to act."

"Act how?" asked Lugh.

He grinned. "At a guess, I'd say the first thing we have to do is get ourselves out of here!"

Aine looked at him in disbelief. "Brother, playing a madman for so long has finally made you one." She lifted her hands to indicate their grim surroundings. "Have you noticed where we are?"

"No one leaves here," Lobais put in darkly. "Not even the dead!"

"Is that so?" Manannan said, eyeing the Pooka. "Well, I think our friend Shaglan may be our way out!"

From the corridor a huge figure now appeared, striding into the room. It was the Dagda, and his face was knit in a scowl of frustration after a fruitless search for some means of escape. But his battered face lit with joy at seeing the young warrior.

"Lugh!" he said heartily, moving toward the others, hand out in greeting.

Lugh rose and turned to meet his friend, putting out his own hand.

But as the Dagda reached him, the expression of this warrior who feared no danger froze with horror, eyes wide as he stared at Lugh's shoulder.

"Look out there, boy!" he bellowed suddenly. "There's a rat on you!"

And before Lugh could stop him, he had launched a swing of his arm, palm open, that slapped Shaglan away.

The tiny form flew across the room, giving out a pained squeal. It plumped to the floor, tumbled, then lay still.

"Filthy beasts," the Dagda remarked in disgust to the audience, who stared, frozen with shock.

Aine recovered first. "That was the Pooka!" she cried, rushing toward the stricken creature.

Lugh and the other followed, quickly surrounding the little bundle of fur as Aine crouched beside it.

"I didn't know!" the Dagda said in distress.

"How is he?" Lugh asked anxiously.

With the greatest care Aine unrolled the rodentlike form and examined the little body.

"I can't tell!" she said in anguish. She looked up at Lugh, tears welling in her eyes. "Oh, Lugh, I don't even know if he's alive!"

Chapter Twenty-Three
THE FLEET SAILS

The morning air was chill and scented with the sea in a bracing combination. An even layer of clouds, like a smooth gray woolen cover, lay across the sky. But the winds were fair and steady, and the sea was calm. It was a fit enough day to sail, Nuada decided.

He stood in the prow of the largest of the ships pulled up along the shore and looked around at the rest of the fleet, ranged on either side. The work of the long night had readied them for the sea and prepared them to take on the Tower's black ships. He turned back to the beach, where the thousands of de Danann and Firbolg warriors were now gathering, ready to begin boarding.

Nuada stepped to the edge of the ship and looked down at the crowd below. As the warriors became aware of the High-King, the talk and the clatter of their arms died away. They stood silently, expectantly, looking up toward him.

"My warriors, my friends," he said, "our fate lies waiting for us now. But whatever happens, we ourselves have chosen to face it." He ran his gaze across the sea of upturned faces, all glowing with the battle-light. "Many of you never meant to be warriors. You came to Eire for peace, to find a place to practice your skills, to tend your herds, to learn, and love, and grow. But you've learned that to have that place you must be ready to fight for it."

He raised a hand and pointed out into the Northern Sea. "Beyond that ridge of waves lies the Glass Tower. We sail now to face an enemy more powerful than any you have seen before. But until we face that enemy and see its power destroyed, we will not have won. Eire will not truly be ours. Are you ready to join in this final battle for our land?"

A bellow of acclamation from thousands of throats was their response. Its volume nearly deafened Nuada. Swords and lances began to bang against shields in a clamor of noise that quickly settled into a rhythm, joined by a rising chant: "Nuada! Nuada! Nuada!"

The courageous spirit was an invigorating draft to the High-King, filling him with a vitality he had not felt in many years. He beamed with pride, letting the wave of sound wash luxuriatingly over him for a time. Then he raised his hands for silence. The cheering faded.

"You have answered as I knew you would. Now it is time. Warriors, board your ships! We sail for the Tower!"

With a last roar to proclaim their zeal, the crowd began to move. Under their chieftains' orders, clans were divided and directed toward the vessels. Nuada watched the process from the deck of his own ship, pleased by the continued ardor of his men.

"Nuada!" said a voice, and he turned to see Physician Diancecht approaching.

He was the greatest healer of them, and the oldest of the de Dananns. A tall man of aristocratic bearing, he exhibited little sign of his age except in the whiteness of his hair and the slight stoop in his shoulders. In his movements and skills he showed the boundless energy of a youth.

"I have prepared a hospital to receive our wounded here," he told the High-King in his brusque, efficient tone. "With our healing methods we should be able to save any warrior who returns here alive."

"We'll do all that we can," Nuada promised.

"That won't be enough!" Diancecht snapped back. "That's why I'll be going with you, and the other healers will go in other ships. You'll need our skills with you."

"You can't go!" Nuada protested. "You'll be needed here!"

He brushed this aside with an impatient gesture. "Enough of us will remain behind for that. If you do survive the attack, we can help hundreds return safely. If you don't"—he shrugged—"well, there won't be much reason for us to be waiting here, will there?"

Nuada saw the determined glint in the old healer's eye and knew it meant no argument would work. He laughed. "Fair enough, old friend. And I can't say I'm not pleased to have your company."

He spoke sincerely. Diancecht was one of the few of Nuada's close comrades left.

The physician moved to stand beside him and look over the ship's wicker bulwark at the men passing below. They watched in silence for a time, both lost in their own thoughts. Then Diancecht spoke gravely.

"Does it have to be done, Nuada?"

"It does," he said with certainty. "I've known it since we defeated Bres's army."

"What do you mean?"

"Before that day I'd thought it was our need to win Eire that had brought us here. But when the land was ours at last, I knew it wasn't enough. It wasn't the need to have our own land that drove us, it was the need to regain the spirit we'd once had as a people. We lost that spirit long ago, when we were defeated at the Tower. You were with us. You remember our pride then. You know what happened. Ever since then that fear has been with us—and until we overcome that fear, we will not regain our pride."

"You are their king, their leader," the other said. "It is your decision that has brought them to this. There's no feeling in you that you might be wrong?"

Nuada shook his head. "I failed them once. I let Bres take the kingship and I watched as he destroyed our people, drained away our will and strength. I didn't act then, but I will now. I will not fail them again."

Diancecht looked down on the faces of the warriors moving by. There were so many young faces, still beardless, filled with eagerness.

"Many will die," he said bluntly. "All of us may be destroyed."

"I would rather die with the knowledge that we had redeemed ourselves than live with the sense that we had not," Nuada told him.

The old healer turned a searching gaze upon his friend. "Are you certain that this isn't to redeem yourself?"

Nuada met his gaze squarely. He considered a moment, then lifted his right hand before him.

"You see this hand? It was you who restored it to me and with it the chance to restore the rest of my life. And I have used that chance to ease the pain I felt through all those years I sat helplessly, hopelessly watching our people made slaves by the Fomor." He curled the hand into a tight fist. "But I swear to you, Diancecht, that I did not do this just to redeem myself. It was done for our people too. Danu knew. She knew that we would have to do this if we ever meant to be our own again. You understand, don't you? Of all the rest, I had hoped you would most clearly understand that this must be done."

After a brief hesitation the healer sighed and nodded. "Yes, my old friend. I do understand. I remember too what it was like before, hiding in the mountains with the hunted few who had escaped, praying for some salvation that we feared would never come. From the first time I met young Lugh and he gave me the courage to restore your hand to you, I knew what we were beginning, and I think I knew that it would have to end at that Tower of Glass."

"Thank you, my friend," said Nuada, laying his hand upon the other's shoulder and smiling warmly. "I value no one's support more than your own."

Then a figure moving up the gangway into the boat caught the High-King's eye. He looked more closely, sure he was mistaken. The lean figure was familiar, but it was clad in warriors' trappings, carrying shield and spears, a longsword strapped at its waist.

"By Danu!" Nuada said in astonishment. "Look there!"

He moved across the deck to accost this individual as he stepped aboard, looking him up and down.

"Bobd Derg?" he said, still disbelieving. "Is that you beneath that iron?"

The Bard shot him a chill glare, pulling himself up stiffly.

"For a very long time I have argued against this madness," he said with great passion. "I have hoped that our people would choose not to become involved in this savagery and give up trying to live in this harsh land. I have only wanted them to return to the harmony and beauty of Tir-na-nog. They would not listen. Now I see that they mean to go through with this and will likely be all killed. Well, if that's what is meant to be, I will not stay here and watch you go."

"But you're a Bard!" Nuada pointed out. "A man of peace!"

"I am also the son of the Dagda, remember. That means I was trained as a warrior, and well-trained, I may add. I am going!"

"And welcome!" Nuada said heartily, slapping him on the shoulder. "Your father would be proud!"

"An honor I find most abhorrent, I'm afraid," he replied.

"You were a fool to have given up so easily on that boy," the being in the tank hissed angrily.

"Be careful, Mathgen," Balor warned. "You take a risk to call me that. The boy would not be changed."

"But you might have kept at him!" the Druid argued. "You might have brought him to me! Perhaps my powers could have confused his mind, at least convinced him not to serve the de Dananns."

"I tell you, he would not be changed!" repeated Balor sharply, his voice echoing in the room like the striking of a metal drum. "It makes no difference in any case. I am convinced now that he has no other powers to use against us. You were wrong to be concerned. No matter what his choice, this absurd 'Prophecy' is ended."

"What have you done with him?" Mathgen demanded.

"He is safely imprisoned with his comrades."

"Balor, I tell you again, you must deal with this boy and with the de Dananns!"

A tinge of scorn warmed the gray color of the giant's voice. "I will not heed your fearful ravings any longer. I have finally realized that they were false. I might have destroyed the de Dananns long ago except for you. Now I will act!"

"What do you mean?" asked Mathgen.

"I have given orders that my ship be made ready. We are going to sail for this Tir-na-nog of yours at once. And your Danu help you if the tales you've told me of its powers are as false as your warnings."

Mathgen answered this threat in a voice wheezing from rage and indignation. "Its secrets will make you more powerful than you could dream. Then you will know how inferior are the great forces of your Tower!"

"Indeed!" Balor replied, unmoved. "Well, after we return with all this magic, we will deal with our prisoners and the de Dananns. Preparations will be made for you to be moved aboard. I hope you survive the trip."

"I will, knowing that my regeneration lies at its end," Mathgen assured him.

The main doors to the room suddenly opened, and Salmhor rushed through.

"Commander, we have received a report from one of our sentry vessels," he said briskly as he came to attention before Balor. "An enormous fleet of sailing craft—several hundred they estimate—is approaching us from Eire."

"The Fomor," Balor answered, unconcerned. "We already knew they were readying ships to leave Eire."

"No, Commander," Salmhor told him. "Our captain says these ships were crowded with armed warriors. He is certain that they are de Dananns."

"De Dananns?" Balor repeated quietly, as if to himself. "Can they be so mad as to come against the Tower again?"

Him head swiveled toward the Druid again. The iron voice rang with a triumphant sound. "You see, Mathgen? They make it easy for us! They are coming here. We have only to wait for them to come and be destroyed."

"Balor, take no chances," Mathgen warned once more.

"There are none to take. When this is finished, we will leave for your Blessed Isles."

"Shaglan, please wake up!" Aine pleaded, working over the motionless rodent form. She really didn't know what to do. She had at least determined that he was still breathing. But it was impossible to see how badly he was hurt. She tried prodding his small body gently with a finger. He gave a faint moan and stayed unconscious. She tried wiggling his legs. They fell back limply.

"I wish I had my potions," Findgoll said helplessly as he watched. "I might have done something."

"Finished him off, most likely," the Dagda put in as he peered anxiously down at the Pooka.

"That kind of talk I'll not take from a great ox who flails away at his friends without a thought at all!"

"I said I was sorry," the Dagda muttered in a subdued way. "I just hate rats!"

"Try rubbing his stomach," Lugh suggested.

Aine gave him an impatient glance. "That puts animals to sleep. It doesn't wake them up."

Manannan MacLir was sitting removed from this, his lanky form propped as comfortably as possible against the chill wall. He watched the little huddle of his comrades around the stricken Pooka with fascination.

"You know how ridiculous that looks, of course," he finally remarked. "All of you trying to nurse that tiny beast."

As one they turned to look at him, their expressions all of outrage at his apparent heartlessness.

"Well, you're no help, that's certain," Aine responded caustically.

"My sister, you're the expert on animals. I'm sure you're doing whatever can be done. And I don't really think it's so serious as you're all afraid it is."

"How can you be so bloody certain!" the Dagda demanded.

"Pookas are very pliable, and very tough," MacLir explained. "Quite difficult to harm. They tend more to bounce than to break. He'll be all right."

Manannan's prediction seemed to come true at his words. The little animal stirred, shook its head, and looked up. The bright beady eyes fixed in anger on the massive warrior above him.

"A fine thing!" he cried bitterly. "I take on this unpleasant form. I'm nearly suffocated, almost squashed, and tied in knots to help you. And what do I get for it? Smacked down by a monster is what!"

"Calm down, Shaglan," Lugh soothed.

"I meant no harm," the Dagda assured it earnestly.

"You know we all love you, Shaglan," Aine added, stroking the furry body softly.

"I quite like that," he told her, the anger fading from his voice. He got carefully to his feet, shaking the small form thoroughly.

"Well, nothing seems damaged," he announced to the relieved company. He gave the Dagda a grin. "I suppose one can't expect to take on this kind of shape without running some risk. No fault of yours."

"Just don't be taking on any insect forms," Aine cautioned, "or you'll find yourself being trod upon."

"He may have to," said Manannan, climbing to his feet. "I'm afraid my plan for escape depends on our friend's ability to make himself small."

"What do you mean?" asked Lugh.

"There may just be a way out of here, for him," Manannan explained. "Like the Dagda, I did a bit of exploring. The place is sealed up quite tightly, but there are some openings. Come with me."

Shaglan hopped into the hand Lugh extended. The little band, joined by Eab, Lobais, and some other of the curious prisoners, followed Manannan back into the corridor. As they went, he told them what he had found.

"There are a number of small metal doors set in the wall, high up, by the ceiling." He indicated a number of these thin black panels as they moved along. "I've no idea what they're for, but they're tightly sealed."

"I can't pull them off or punch them in," put in the Dagda. "Too hard."

They turned into the first of the side corridors they reached. Lugh expected it to lead to another storage place for corpses. Instead, it entered a small, bare room with a stone trough along one wall. Above this was a small, square opening.

"This is how the prisoners get their food," he explained. "A chute slants upward from here to the level above. They simply pour it down into this trough. Fine food too! Rotted vegetables, bones, gristle, moldy bread. These starving men eat as if it were a king's feast." He smiled at the Pooka. "You, Shaglan, only have to nip up there and find a way to get that door opened for us. It's very simple."

"Simple?" the Pooka said, eyeing the hole suspiciously. "For a start, how do I know where this comes out? What'll be waiting there?"

"Well, there is one other choice," Manannan MacLir said. "There's a bigger hole down through the floor in that other corner there. You can guess what that's used for. You could try getting out through there if you'd rather."

"No, thank you, MacLir. I see your meaning." The little creature sighed. "It'll be this way then."

"There's some kind of a hinged door above," MacLir said, peering up the shaft. "But there's quite a large crack about it. I can see light beyond. If you can take on some sort of slender form, you should be able to squeak through. Pardon my humor."

Lugh obligingly held up the Pooka so it could examine the opening too.

"It might be slick going. But I've something that should work. Here, put me down."

Lugh deposited him carefully upon the floor. At once the being began to change. But its transformation was a very peculiar one. It lost its form, becoming quite soft. One end then swelled outward suddenly, sprouting a snout, bristling whiskers, and curled tusks, while the rear portion shot out into an long, thick, green-scaled tail distinctly reptilian. It was an alarming-looking combination, and the captivated audience all started back a little in surprise.

"Shaglan, what's happening to you?" asked Lugh.

"Oh . . . sorry," the being grunted, and began to squirm madly as if in a struggle with himself. "I . . . can't quite . . . control this thing," it gasped out as it fought. "That swack on the head seems to have muddled me. Hang on. I'll get it."

He wrenched himself about violently, and the two ends both began to shrink again. Soon they had been reduced to the form of a small, sluglike creature.

"There!" its tiny voice announced with relief. "That's it. This should work."

"That problem won't happen again, will it?" asked MacLir.

"No, no," it answered crossly. "Just thrown off stride a bit. Hard to concentrate with a thudding headache. But I'm in control now. Just put me up the chute."

Lugh looked at the slimy-looking creature, then smiled at Aine. "Go right ahead."

"Coward," she said, and offered her own hand to the Pooka.

He wiggled aboard and she lifted him to the edge of the hole. He slid forward and crawled quickly upward, the sticky feet of the creature giving him good purchase on the steeply inclined metal surface.

When he reached the trapdoor, he had no difficulty pushing the small, soft body through the crack, and continued on toward a square of light not far above.

There was only one problem, he suddenly noticed. The chute he was climbing had apparently begun to shrink.

And then he realized that this wasn't the real problem. The truth was much more disturbing—and much more deadly. He had begun to swell!

Chapter Twenty-Four

ESCAPE

He didn't seem to be able to control the swelling. His only chance was to get out of the chute before he became jammed in it and expanded to a point where he was crushed. He slithered upward with desperate speed, heading for the square of light he hoped marked the upper end.

His body was inflating rapidly now. And he seemed to be sprouting limbs, but of what he couldn't tell. His head was expanding too, the nose stretching out ahead of him.

He scrambled madly upward, working with all he had and all that was being added on to him. He was bumping against the sides, then scraping along, forcing himself through the metal tunnel that would soon strangle him. The end was just ahead of him. Beyond it was a larger space. No time for caution. He launched himself through the opening.

In the small room a single Tower worker had just wheeled a cart filled with garbage through the door. It was his task to feed the prisoners. But he pulled up, staring aghast at the sight before him.

From the opening to the chute something horrible was emerging. It was a thick, fluid mass, swelling out like rising bread dough gone mad, pouring to the floor. As it plopped down, it took on a form, turning before his astonished gaze into a huge, fat, gray-skinned beast that filled half the room. It sat there on its broad haunches, peering at him from tiny brown eyes. And then its wide mouth opened, showing flat white teeth. The tiny ears twitched, and it spoke. "A tight squeeze there!" it observed.

The worker bolted, leaving the cart. Shaglan looked after him, hoping the man would find his experience too unbelievable to want to give an alarm. He couldn't do much about pursuing him anyway in his present form. He had to do something about getting into a more useful shape. He wasn't even sure what he was now.

It was a difficult process. He realized that the blow from the Dagda must have thrown his systems off more than he'd thought. After some experimentation and a good bit of hard concentrating—which only made his head throb all the more—he got his form pared down to that of a large, fierce and sinewy lionlike beast.

Much more satisfactory, he thought. Now, if only I can stay this way.

He peeped out of the room, looking along a dimly lit corridor that ran to a turning not far away. There was no sign or sound of anyone coming in this direction. If that worker had gone to alert someone, they weren't hurrying to check. He set off to find his way back to the entry room for the cells.

As he moved stealthily along, a faint note, like that of a horn, began to sound repeatedly somewhere above him. What, he wondered, was happening now?

On the quays of the Glass Tower, the blaring alarm was calling a vast force to assemble.

The black ships of the Tower's fleet were moored there in precise line, sleek and lethal instruments of war ready to slash through any enemy. Before each the crews and companies of soldiers were drawn up in perfectly dressed ranks. In their silver-gray uniforms they looked a single, well-honed weapon.

The last of the men moved swiftly into line. The officers at their front cast a final look of inspection over them. Then they were called to attention as the claxon ceased, the last note echoing away from the Tower across the sea. All eyes fixed rigidly ahead as the immense, dark form rolled forward from the blackness of the Tower's interior and onto the quay.

He came to a stop, Salmhor and Bres flanking him. The thin red glow beneath his lowered lid played slowly across the ranks as the head pivoted. All felt the heat of the ruby beam as it washed over them, reminding them of its power.

"This day will be one of greatness for our Tower," his iron voice tolled out. "It will mark the end of the de Dananns and a new beginning for our race. Soon we will fulfill the goal our ancestors set for us. We will again become the great civilization we were so long ago.

"The Tuatha de Danann believe that they can challenge us. You will show them that they are wrong. You will show them the full might of the Fomor." The lid rose a fraction, revealing more of the energy pent there. The voice grew harder. "You will destroy them. Any man who does not give his full measure for the Tower will face my wrath!" These last words crashed like lightning upon them. But none dared flinch.

Balor turned his head to Salmhor. "Take them out now, Captain," he ordered. "Let the de Danann fleet come within sight of the Tower before you engage. And, Salmhor—let none escape. Do you understand?"

"Yes, Commander," the officer replied briskly. He stepped forward and snapped orders to the other officers.

"Board the ships! Prepare to get under way!"

And, like the mechanism of one of their machines, the Tower soldiers moved instantly to obey.

Balor pivoted and began to roll back toward the Tower. Bres fell in beside him.

"What is my part in all this, Balor?" he asked the giant.

"You will accompany me to my chamber," the giant replied. "From there you can watch the final destruction of the de Dananns that you've wished for so long. That should please you."

Bres followed, but there was no pleasure showing in his face.

"Do you think Shaglan can get us out alone?" Aine asked Lugh.

The two sat in a corner of the large room, separated from the other prisoners. Their comrades had started back along the corridor toward the chamber of the outer door.

Lugh shook his head. "I don't know," he said darkly. "It won't be easy for him, all alone."

She gave him an evaluating look. "But that's not all that's bothering you. What else is wrong?"

"It's nothing to trouble you with," he said.

"Yes, it is," she insisted. "It's this terrible predicament we're in." She pulled her legs up tightly to her, dropping her head to her knees, her voice sharp with anger for herself. "It's my fault too. I'm the one who gave the secret to Mathgen. I was the weak one."

"No!" he protested quickly, slipping an arm about her shoulders. "Aine, you couldn't help that. It was me bringing you to this danger that caused it."

"Actually, it was me, being careless enough to let myself get caught," said another voice.

They looked up to see Manannan standing over them, Taillta at his side. They sat down with the young couple.

"Dear sister, no one can blame you for what happened," he assured her earnestly. "We all underestimated Mathgen's powers. Even our powerful Danu." He grinned. "Now, be a good, stout chap and steady up!"

She had to smile in return, and her spirits lifted. Not so Lugh, whose own expression remained glum.

"What about you, lad?" asked MacLir, turning to the young warrior. "You didn't tell us what it was they did to you up above."

Lugh contemplated the big, lean, friendly face of his comrade and mentor silently for a moment, uncertain how to reply. Then he decided that it must be said, gotten into the open and cleared from the way. He stated it flatly.

"Balor told me who my mother really was."

MacLir sobered. "Oh, I see. I thought it might be something like that."

"I didn't want to speak of it with the others here. It's still hard for even me to believe it." He fixed MacLir with a probing look. "But it is true, isn't it?"

The man nodded. "Yes, it is."

"I wasn't going to speak of it," Lugh said, "but I have to know about it. Manannan, why didn't you tell me?"

"Listen to me, Lugh," said Taillta. Moving closer to him, she laid a hand upon his arm and spoke with intensity. "Your mother was my friend. She was as fair and warm and kind-hearted a woman as I'll likely ever meet. She hated the Tower as much as these poor men here do, and she was just as much a captive. She loved your father and went with him willingly. His death was the greatest sorrow in her life. But she had a final happiness too, knowing that at least you had escaped. You've got to believe that you are as she would have wanted you to be."

Lugh knew that he could never doubt Taillta, the one who had raised him, been as a mother to him, protected him at the risk of her own life many times. A new sense of comfort filled him, banishing his last fears. He smiled warmly and placed his hand on hers.

"If Shaglan has made it through, he could be getting that

door opened any moment," MacLir said in a brisk tone. "I think we'd best be there and ready to act if that happens."

They agreed and rose to go. As they entered the corridor, Lugh held back, letting MacLir and Taillta go ahead. He put a hand on Aine's arm to slow her.

"I had a doubt about Manannan up there," he said. "I had one about you too. I thought that maybe you had tricked me." He colored with chagrin. "It was foolish. I know you'd never do that to me. The idea was with me only for an instant. Still, I wanted you to know."

She smiled ruefully. "Don't think of it. It's my own fault, always having to seem the one in control, trying to be harder and tougher than you. I can see why you'd fear my tricking you. You've a right not to trust me."

"No!" he said fiercely, pulling her around to him, looking down into the depths of those brilliant eyes. "I do trust you. I love you."

She looked up at him, seeing the truth of it in his eyes. It filled her with an exhilaration she'd never known, and she could no longer hold her own feelings back.

"And I love you," Aine said.

They moved together, their lips meeting in a kiss that neither wished to break.

"I don't mean to interrupt," Manannan called from ahead, "but we are in a rather awkward situation now."

Reluctantly, they broke away from each other. Lugh sighed regretfully. Aine gave a laugh.

"It's all right," she said. "We've gotten used to it."

Shaglan moved cautiously through a maze of storage rooms, seeking the chamber that held the prison door. He was rather surprised that no one was about. So far the worker was the only one he'd seen.

Finally, he heard voices ahead. He eased silently down the corridor on his cat's feet, peered around a turning, and found himself looking into the very room he sought.

Before the warden's table two guards were holding the worker he'd met between them. He looked very unhappy.

" 'E said 'e saw a great monster oozin' from the pipe, Capt'n," one guard was explaining, trying to keep a sober face. "We thought him mad, of course."

"Likely," the warden agreed. "But you checked on it anyway?"

"Oh, yes, sir," the second guard responded quickly. "There was no sign of anything at all. It's my own feeling that this one's been drawing on his drink ration a bit too often."

The warden fixed a baleful glare upon the worker. "Is that it? Are you drunk, man?"

"If I was, would I have reported this?" he wailed. "I know it sounds mad, but I saw it."

"Coming up the food slide to the lower cells?"

"Yes, Captain. A walloping great beast!"

Through this, Shaglan was examining the row of huge levers beside the warden's table. Somehow he had to get to them, find the right one, and pull it. Maybe if these guards left, he would have a chance.

"This does sound impossible," the warden said after considering. "Still, there are some Eirelanders down there. I've heard they can do conjuring, create illusions, that kind of thing." He considered a bit longer, then spoke with decision. "We'll take no chances. Take him to Balor. Let him decide if this means anything. Meantime, call more guards to search this whole level."

The Pooka had to act now. Once Balor was alerted and more guards were swarming through the level, there would be no chance to rescue his companions. He leaped out across the open floor, heading directly toward the guards.

The officer behind the table saw him first and shouted a warning. The guards whirled to find the huge cat upon them.

Shaglan took no time for subtlety, using his strength and speed savagely. A single swipe of the claws tore the throat from one guard, spraying the hapless workman with blood. He screamed and ran. Shaglan let him go, pivoting to spring upon the other guard as he tried to bring his weapon up. The man went down with Shaglan on his chest. The animal's great jaws clamped upon his head and closed. He went limp.

Shaglan released him, swinging around toward the man behind the table. He was standing now, staring in shock at the scene. The Pooka fixed big, dark, glittering eyes on him.

"Let my friends out of your cells or I'll tear you apart as well," he growled in his best ferocious tones.

"You talk?" the man gasped out. "What are you?"

"Never mind!" snarled the cat. It crept forward, head down, teeth bared, threatening. "Open that door now!"

The man stood unmoving for a moment. His eyes darted

around the room as he assayed his chances. Then he made a decision.

Moving with a speed that took Shaglan by surprise, the warden snatched up a sword from behind the table and jumped to the bank of levers. The Pooka started forward, rising to put his front paws on the table. But, seizing one of the levers, the man barked a warning.

"Hold on, you! No closer now! This lever will flood the cells below. It'll drown everyone there. Stay back or I'll throw it!"

Shaglan hesitated, wondering if by a quick move he could reach the warden before he could act. Then noise behind him made him look sharply around. The guards from the lift, alerted by the screaming workman, were charging into the room, weapons ready.

Seeing help arrive, the warden grew brave. He lunged forward, driving his sword toward Shaglan's chest. The Pooka caught his movement in the corner of one eye and jerked aside. The blade slid past and the man fell forward, his soft belly colliding with the sharp table edge. Before he could recover, Shaglan cuffed him hard on the side of the head with a backhand swipe of one enormous paw. The warden staggered back, colliding with the row of levers.

His consciousness failing, he groped out blindly, got a tenuous grip on the lever he sought, and collapsed against it. His bulk shoved it forward. It squealed in protest, but it moved.

Shaglan, now occupied with defending himself against the two guards moving in cautiously, was unaware of the warden's action until a distant rattling and grinding noise began to rise from beneath the stone floor, making it vibrate. And with it came another sound, an ominous sound that his sharp ears easily recognized.

The sound of rushing water.

Chapter Twenty-Five
A LITTLE WATER

As they moved along the corridor toward the door, Lugh and Aine became aware of a metallic rattling. It seemed to come from all around them, and they paused to look about for its source.

Aine spotted it first, pointing toward one of the metal panels high in the wall. It was sliding slowly upward.

They moved closer, trying to make out what was happening. They hadn't long to wait to discover the truth. For as the lower edge of the metal cleared the stone below it, a stream of water shot forth, catching Lugh across the forehead and knocking him back with its force.

Aine pulled him out of the way, and he shook the water from his eyes.

"Look there!" Aine cried, pointing back along the corridor. From each of the small doors spaced along the walls another stream of water was gushing, the flow increasing quickly as the doors rose higher.

Ahead of them it was the same. But out of the spray that now filled the corridor, figures emerged: MacLir and the rest of Lugh's comrades.

"They're flooding this entire level!" Manannan shouted over the roar of water. "Come on! We've got to get everyone down to the door. It's our only chance!"

They moved back up the corridor into the jets of water. The Dagda simply bulled past them, and the rest tried to duck under. But before they reached the main room, they met the Tower men headed their way. They had reached the same conclusion as MacLir: there was only one way out.

Lugh and his friends began to help the weakest of the men along. Lugh took charge of Lobais. The Dagda slung two others across his shoulders and plunged back along the corridor, leading the way.

It was harder going now. The doors were fully open,

each pouring a stream of water in with such tremendous force that it slammed against the opposite wall. The corridor was crisscrossed with them, turning it to an obstacle course.

To make it more difficult, the water was also beginning to collect, to fill the floor and rise. In moments it was ankle-deep, creeping swiftly upward toward the knees. It made walking difficult, especially for some of the older prisoners. But they continued to splash on, making for the outer door along what now seemed an endless corridor.

"Where's this coming from?" Lugh shouted to Lobais.

"The sea!" he shouted back. "Can't you taste the salt of it?" There are flood valves all along the Tower's base."

"How deep will it get?" Lugh asked.

"We're below sea level!" the old man answered, and made a gesture above his head that explained the rest.

Finally, they reached the entrance chamber. Above them the metal door was still tightly closed. There were no sea-doors here, no punishing jets of water, but it was flooding in from the corridor, already up to their waists.

"Everyone together!" MacLir shouted. "Form a tight circle! Get the weakest in the center!"

All of them crowded in, collecting in a pack in the middle of the room. Lugh's company and the strongest of the prisoners formed an outside ring, linking arms. The others huddled within this, somewhat sheltered from the rushing water, hanging on to one another to keep from being swept away.

The waves were boiling in around them now, crashing against the walls to burst and shower them with spray. As they swirled around Aine, something was washed hard against her. She struck out angrily at the loglike object and it rolled over sluggishly. A bloated white face with staring eyes and open mouth came into view.

With a cry of revulsion Aine shoved the rigid corpse away. But others appeared, the inhabitants of the storage rooms, disturbed from rest by the flood and carried here. They swirled around the circle, ghastly bits of flotsam, bumping and rubbing their decaying bodies against the living prisoners.

"It won't take long to fill at this rate!" MacLir remarked as the water reached his chest. For the shorter Aine this meant it now lapped her chin.

They looked up toward the metal door. It showed no sign of opening.

"Curse that Pooka!" bellowed the Dagda. "What's happened?"

"Maybe he's dead!" said Angus.

"He'd better not be!" Manannan said wholeheartedly.

He wasn't, but he was finding it a struggle to keep from becoming so.

The two guards were wary, fast, and highly trained. They split up as they attacked, coming at him from two sides. One would drive in to attract the beast his way while the other tried to come at him from behind. The Pooka was forced to lunge back and forth constantly to keep them away. He knew that if one of the charged globes they wielded even touched him, it could kill.

Still, he couldn't allow them to keep him tied up. He could hear the water rushing into the cells below. He knew that at that moment his friends might be drowning. He had to save them somehow.

He made a risky move. He backed until he was against the metal table. Then he made a quick feint left and right to make both guards flinch away. As they did, he turned and sprang over the table.

The lion's agile body served him well. Before they could recover and come around after him, he was at the levers. He hooked a claw into the warden's fat belly and dragged him off the lever he had pushed. It stayed thrown over. He wrapped both paws around it and tugged. It wouldn't budge. The mechanism was jammed open. The flooding couldn't be stopped!

His friends would have to be gotten out. He looked at the other levers. Which one opened the door? No time for experimentation. The only answer was to throw them all.

But he got no chance. The guards were on him again.

While one moved around the table to come at him, the other leaned across the metal top as far as he could and swung at Shaglan with his globe-tipped spear.

The Pooka pulled back, but he was not quite quick enough this time. The metal sphere grazed his shoulder as it whizzed past.

Even this light touch was enough to release the energy contained within the weapon. It violently jolted the lionlike form. As the tingling sensation ran through Shaglan, it seemed to drain his strength. He collapsed limply to the floor, eyes glazing, body heaving with labored breaths, tongue hanging from his open mouth.

The second guard moved in more slowly now, looking down at the fallen beast warily.

"Think he's out?" he asked apprehensively.

"Coward! What're you waiting for!" the other shot back. "Be certain he's finished!"

The guard nodded and moved forward again, the globe dropping toward Shaglan.

In the cells the water had now reached a level well above the prisoners' heads. They struggled to stay afloat, treading water, clinging tightly together to keep the weakest up. Still, some had already sunk beneath the surface or been swirled away by the rushing flood. The rest continued to battle on desperately, trying to survive, hoping that the metal door above them would swing open.

When Lobais surrendered to his fatigue and sank below the water, Lugh pulled him up. He struggled to pull free.

"No! Let me go!" he pleaded wearily. "We're finished anyway!"

"Hang on!" Lugh told him. "You've survived this long. Stay alive. There's still a chance!"

He looked upward to the door, fighting off his own rising despair as he thought beseechingly: Please, Danu, let there be a chance!

Above him the deadly globe had dropped to just above the Pooka's chest. But in a swift and unexpected move the creature rolled sideways, under the shining sphere, into the guard's legs.

The size and resilience of the lion's body had saved Shaglan from being more than momentarily stunned. Now he took the man by surprise, lifting up beneath him as he rolled.

The guard toppled forward, slamming down upon several of the levers at once, throwing them over.

The metal trapdoor clanged and then dropped inward, its lower edge splashing down into the water.

"He did it!" Lugh cried out in jubilation.

"Someone's got to get up. Get the ladder down here!" Eab shouted.

"Lugh! You do it!" the Dagda told him. "Here! On my shoulders!"

Lugh understood what he meant to do. Quickly, he pulled himself onto the warrior's broad back.

"Crouch down and be ready!" the Dagda said. "I'm going under!"

He let himself sink, their combined weight pushing him to the bottom. He felt the floor beneath his feet, bent his knees, and pushed upward with the full power of his legs.

He exploded from the water, his whole torso lifting clear of the surface. At his highest point Lugh jumped, stretching his arms above him.

He caught the lip of the opening and hung on. Slowly, he pulled himself upward and peered cautiously over the edge.

Beyond the metal table Shaglan was battling to keep the second guard away from the levers. The first one still lay across them, unmoving.

The Pooka was having no difficulty with only one attacker, until a strange sensation crept over him. The man seemed to be growing suddenly. With dismay Shaglan realized what was really happening. He was shrinking!

The shock from the charged globe had not helped his already unstable condition. He had lost control of his form again and was changing. But into what?

The guard, watching this transformation with astonishment, wasn't sure. What had been a large and very savage cat now looked more like some kind of fat, piglike creature, covered with shaggy hair, and neither large nor savage.

He started to close in on this thing, but stopped as a sound reached him. He turned to see Lugh Lamfada pulling himself up over the edge of the doorway.

Determined to stop this escape, he turned away from the now-harmless-seeming Pooka and headed toward Lugh. But Shaglan was not to be ignored. He dashed forward—with good speed for all his rotund figure—diving between the man's legs.

The guard cried out as he tripped, staggered, then fell forward, dropping onto the shining sphere of his own weapon.

There was a sizzling sound and a loud crack. He jerked once and then rolled sideways off the globe, revealing a smoldering black patch on his chest.

"Good work, Shaglan!" Lugh told his friend. He ran to the metal ladder against the wall and hauled it to the edge. Metal flanges in its end matched grooves in the stone floor.

He slipped the ladder in and dropped its length down into the water that was now churning not very far below.

The prisoners began to climb out, the weakest sent up first. Lugh's comrades were the last to leave the nearly filled cells, with Manannan bringing up the rear.

He clambered out onto the dry level, his lanky form streaming water, still grinning broadly.

"Shaglan, I knew you could do it!" he said heartily. Then he caught sight of the piglike creature and stared in mixed amusement and surprise. "I mean, you are Shaglan, aren't you?"

"I don't see any humor in this at all," the being responded coldly.

"Oh, sorry! Sorry!" MacLir said quickly, much abashed. "You did a fine job. Congratulations."

The others had discovered that their weapons were still piled against the wall. Quickly, they each found their own.

"Ah, it's good to feel that weight again," said the Dagda, giving his ax a swing. He looked to Lugh and the Pooka. "What about other guards?"

"I saw only the four," said Shaglan.

"That's all they keep on this level," Eab said, joining them.

"What do we do now?" asked Lugh.

"I'd say we should get out of this dreary place as soon as possible," MacLir replied. He turned to Eab. "Is there another way out of here besides that lifting room? Some way we won't be colliding with more of your people?"

Lobais spoke up at that. "I know a way! I know every bit of these lower levels. Spent my life crawling about in them. I can take you up a way that likely no one knows about but me."

"All right then," MacLir said, beaming at the old man. "I knew that something would turn up." He looked around at the rest of the soaking and bedraggled group of prisoners. "And what about you fellows?"

"We want to escape from here as much as you do," Eab told him stoutly. "It seems that our best chance now is to stay with you."

Manannan looked around at his friends for signs of agreement. All of them nodded. They were in this together now.

"Good enough!" he announced. "If everyone feels up to it, we should begin."

"I wish I had my Answerer," Lugh said regretfully, watching the others strap their weapons on.

"Here," said Eab, lifting one of the guards' globe-tipped spears and offering it to the young warrior. "Use this."

Lugh looked down at the burned spot on the guard's chest, then eyed the weapon with distaste.

"No, thank you," he said. "You are very welcome to that!"

"The warden had a sword," Shaglan told him. "Behind that table."

As Lugh went to fetch it, Manannan spoke to him in assuring words. "Don't worry, lad. We'll be fetching your weapons soon enough."

The young warrior pulled the weapon from the senseless warden's hand, then looked back to MacLir and nodded, his youthful face set in grim, determined lines.

"It's time to make another visit to Mathgen," he said.

"What?" cried Eab in disbelief. "You mean to go back up into the Tower? That's madness!"

"Very likely," MacLir agreed, smiling affably. "But we've a thing or two that we mean to finish there."

The Tower of Glass rose slowly into view.

At first it was a sharp flicker of light on the horizon, steadying quickly to a constant gleam. It grew brighter, larger, resolving into a shaft of brilliant white that continued to rise upward as if something were being thrust out from the surface of the sea.

The men of Eire looked wonderingly toward it as their ships sailed closer. Very few of them had ever seen this icy marvel. Until now it had been only a terrifying image drawn by the elders' colorful tales, a scene in childhood nightmares. Now, at last, it lay before them, stark and menacing.

To Nuada it was much more than a legend. He had been in the forefront of battle that day, beside their leader Nemed as they sailed against the Tower. He thought of how filled with war fervor, how arrogant about their fighting skills they had been. He looked around him at the young men filling the ship. Now, after all the years of fear and weakness, that fighting spirit had finally been renewed.

Though this filled him with pride, the dark memories of that other day still haunted him. He saw the shattered boats, the hundreds of bodies drifting in the waves, the men screaming as the crimson beam from Balor's eye swept over them, turning them to flame.

Silently, he prayed to Danu that he was not leading his people to that same end.

Something else was showing on the horizon now. A row of tiny spots had appeared.

"There they are, my King," said Niet, moving up beside him. "The Tower ships."

Nuada knew that well enough. He had pictured what they would look like. It was exactly as it had been before.

"They'll wait for us there," he said. "They'll wait until we come close, and then they will come upon us like wolves tearing through a helpless flock."

"So they think," said Niet with a malicious grin. "This time we'll surprise them."

"That we hope," the High-King replied. "Have the word passed now. Everyone must be ready."

He watched his chieftain carry his orders to the other men and signal it to the ships on either side. He saw Goibnu examining the great wooden capstan set into the deck and wave across to Bridget, who stood beside a like one in the vessel running close beside them on their port side. His gaze ran over the warriors readying weapons and taking places along the wicker bulwarks and ended in the prow where Meglin the High-Druid stood with his cauldron of hopefully magic brew.

He wished that his old comrades were here now: Findgoll and Morrigan and the Dagda, who had fought beside him so long ago, and his eyes were drawn back to the Tower of Glass. It seemed impossible that they could still be alive in there.

Chapter Twenty-Six
IN THE TOWER'S HEART

Lugh and his companions crawled along the grime-coated tunnel single file, on hands and knees. At their head scrambled old Lobais, his frail body revitalized by this return to his own realm.

"They don't know these ways, those young pups don't!" he cackled with glee. "No. They don't know. Ah, but then, they don't know anything at all." And at these words his voice grew suddenly sad. "Too bad. Too bad. The poor, old Tower."

Lugh, crawling right behind him, hoped their guide was more sane than he sounded. It was possible that his long imprisonment had affected his mind and he was leading them into danger. Still, they hadn't much choice but to follow on and hope.

They had been in an absolute maze of these burrowlike passages for what seemed like days now. The knees of all the party were scraped raw and their backs ached. But the old man went on merrily, taking turn after turn as if he knew where he was heading.

It was tight going. The round tunnel—the Maintance Way, Lobais had called it—was narrow enough for a start, but its inner surface, save for a narrow path, was lined with cables and metal pipes of various sizes that ran along its length. These were often clustered or laid upon one another so thickly that the fugitives found it difficult to squeeze through.

In spots there were also additional dangers.

Lugh now understood what the old man had meant when he'd said the Tower was dying. The mood of clean, precise symmetry created by the levels above contrasted sharply with the decay below. The pipes were often thick with rust, some cracked or crumbling apart. Many cables were corroded or frayed as well. Lobais cautioned them often to avoid touching these places, explaining that substances and energies moved through them that could be deadly.

His warning was graphically demonstrated at one point. A pipe had split, letting a brown liquid ooze out and drip over the cables on the wall below. One cable, nearly worn through, was reacting violently. It crackled and spit, sending showers of sparks across the tunnel, filling the already fetid air with an acrid smell.

No one needed a warning to be cautious in slipping by this place, keeping as far away as was possible in the cramped space.

As they moved on they slowly became aware of a vibration and a deep, slow, throbbing sound. It came from ahead of them and increased in force rapidly as they went. It reminded Lugh of nothing so much as the labored pounding of an enormous heart.

Abruptly, the tunnel came to an end. A shaft rose from it toward a lighted space not far above. A metal ladder up one side offered the only avenue. This the old man began at once to climb, his string of followers close behind.

They emerged into a vast square room, several stories in height, larger than Tara's main hall in extent. In the center of this space squatted rows of immense objects. To young Lugh they seemed at first like graven images of monstrous gods within a temple, fit objects for the worship of those who inhabited the Tower.

But these were not silent, inanimate statues. These were things that rumbled and growled and shrieked in numberless, discordant voices connected by a single, strong rhythm. And they moved too their myriad levers, valves, and wheels, working away in some elaborate, mysterious ritual.

Impressive as this sight was to Lugh's party, the cautious warriors' first interest was security. They scanned the area carefully for soldiers, weapons ready.

"Don't worry," Lobais told them. "They seldom come here now. Come along!"

He started forward. Findgoll quickly fell in beside, plying him with questions about the wondrous machines. These the old man answered readily, with a distinct note of pride for the children he had tended so long.

The others followed as they moved up a wide avenue between two rows of the machines. While the Tower men seemed indifferent to the marvels, the visitors from Eire stared up at them in open awe.

Those to their left were the largest, dwarfing the company of humans. Great humps of gray-black rose up over a story. Their flat sides were pierced by fans of slits through which large wheels could be seen, whirling around with a high, humming sound. Across from them, sharp-cornered units of the same metal were covered with a complex array of devices whose function Lugh couldn't begin to guess.

Ahead of him Lobais was explaining with great gusto how energy was produced on the left and transferred to the right, where it was sent out to all the systems in the Tower. Findgoll was nodding and making noises as if he understood every word, but the young warrior found it quite incomprehensible. The Dagda fixed a curious eye on the odd pair.

"They seem to get on well," he said.

"A common interest does it," MacLir replied.

The Dagda snorted derisively. "That's well enough for the Druid, but it's doing us little good." He raised his voice to call out: "Findgoll, leave off your talking now. We've no time. We've got to know where to go next."

The little Druid shot him a sour look but fell silent. Lobais pointed upward.

"There," he said. "That's the way you'll need to go."

They looked. In one corner a ladder ran up the wall to a small doorway just below the ceiling. There was a similar arrangement in the opposite corner.

"Those openings will take you to the stairways leading to the upper levels," Lobais explained. He looked to the group of Tower men. "And if you want to escape, you'll find other doors there that will take you to the outside, right at the shore."

"Maybe you can capture a boat and get away," Lugh suggested.

"And what about you?" said Eab. "You're still determined to go up there?"

"We have to," Lugh told him. "There are many more in danger than ourselves."

Eab looked around at his fellows, then faced the little band from Eire again, his expression determined.

"Well, look here, my mates and I have been discussing this. There's more than just us involved here too. We've got family and friends up there. We can't just run away and leave them behind. We want to go up there and see if we can't get them out."

"I congratulate you on your courage," said MacLir, "but you'll be taking quite a risk. You know what kind of opposition you'll likely run into."

"No worse than you'll be facing," Eab replied.

"He may be right there," the Dagda said. "The whole Tower could be alerted by now. I wish there were some way we could divert a bit of the attention from us."

"But there is a way!" Findgoll said excitedly.

They all turned puzzled looks to him.

"These devices here!" he explained, holding out both hands toward the machines. "They supply the Tower with the force that makes all its magic work. If something were to disrupt their functioning, wouldn't it create a distraction for those above?"

"It would throw them into absolute chaos!" Eab said with delight. "Brilliant idea!"

"What do you mean?" wailed Lobais, suddenly frightened. "You can't mean to damage these machines!"

"Certainly!" Eab told him. "Think of how they'd panic. They might not even see us sneaking in." He stepped closer to the old man, his voice urgent. "You can do it, Lobais. You can show us how to make them quit."

"No!" he cried, cowering back. "You don't realize what you're saying. These machines, they can't be mended. If you destroy them, they'll never work again."

"So much the better!" Eab said, all the more eager. "Don't you see? The Tower would be useless. They'd have to abandon it. The rest of our people would be free!"

"Don't do this!" Lobais pleaded. "Not to the machines!"

"What are you talking about?" Eab demanded. "They left you in those cells to die. You must hate them too."

Tears filled the old man's eyes. "These are my family, my friends!" he sobbed. "All I've had. I can't let you harm them."

"Ah, you're mad!" Eab said impatiently. "Now, you help us, old man, or it'll be hard for you."

Lobais drew up his frail body stiffly. His face set itself defiantly.

"I won't help you, and there nothing left that you can do to change me."

Eab glared at him, then turned away angrily, frustrated.

"What now?" asked MacLir. "It'll be a bit difficult for us to damage all these contraptions."

"We don't need to," said Findgoll. He walked to a smaller, metal square at one end of the row. "Lobais told me that this one controlled the working of the rest."

The old man's face sagged in dismay. "Traitor!" he shrieked.

"It's for the best," Findgoll told him. "The lives of a great many are at stake."

"No! You won't do it! You won't!" Lobais cried, and ran to the machine, throwing himself before it defensively. He watched in terror as the others closed in around him.

"Take him away, Angus," MacLir said. "Gently now."

The young warrior grasped the man's thin shoulders and

pulled him to one side. He tried to struggle but realized it was futile. His body drooped in defeat as he watched them advance purposefully on his charge.

"There's some kind of door on the side," MacLir observed.

"Let's have that off for a start!" said the Dagda. He lifted his ax and brought it against the center of the panel.

It was thin metal and buckled easily. The big man put a hand through the gap opened at one side, gripped the edge, and in a single move tore the whole door loose.

He exposed the inner working of the mechanism, an intricate mass of wires and pipes, whirling cog wheels, and fluttering valves.

"It's likely a delicate sort of task to undo the wizardry of a thing like this," Manannan remarked, bending his tall form double to peer inside.

"Nothing like it!" the Dagda announced carelessly. "Here!"

He snatched the globe-tipped spear from Eab's hands, pushed MacLir aside and, before they could protest, slammed the weapon into the works with all the force of his great arm.

It plowed deeply into the complex of parts, ripping cables, jamming moving pieces, coming to rest with a flare of light and a ripple of tiny explosions. The machine's reaction was immediate. It began to make chattering and coughing sounds as if it were convulsing. Other small explosions flared erratically throughout its interior. Wisps of white smoke began to rise from it.

"That should do it!" the Dagda announced, grinning with triumph.

"Astounding!" gasped MacLir, staring at him in disbelief.

"You great, brainless bull!" Findgoll scolded. "You might have killed all of us doing that!"

The Champion shrugged. "It worked, didn't it? Now, let's be moving before we're caught here!"

There was nothing to do but agree. The party began to move quickly toward one of the ladders.

But as they started away, Aine noted that Lobais had stayed behind. She stopped Lugh and pointed back. On being released by Angus, he had sunk down where he was and now sat huddled on the floor, gazing forlornly at his stricken machine.

Aine went to him, Lugh following.

"Lobais?" she asked softly. "Won't you come with us?"

He shook his head. "No," he answered in a lifeless voice. "I've nowhere to go."

Lugh touched her arm and urged gently: "Come along. There's nothing to do here. Maybe it's best for him."

Sadly, she agreed. They hurried after the rest, climbing up the metal ladder to the high doorway.

As they went through, they looked back for a last time at the old man. He still sat there, between the rows of machines, a tiny figure amid his titanic brood.

The sinister black ships drifted on the waves, waiting, waiting while their prey sailed closer.

Nuada watched them fixedly as his vessel drew near. Soon, he knew, they would begin to move. The sleek ships would leap suddenly forward through the waves and fly toward his clustered fleet like metal bolts shot from the Tower crossbows. It was only then, only when they were about to tear through the frail boats, that he could give the command to act.

"Be prepared with your magic, Meglin!" he called to the Druid in the bow.

Meglin obeyed. With the help of several warriors, the heavy cauldron was lifted up to a position on the very edge of the bow and held there. His move was a signal to the others. In each of the large vessels spread out across the front of the fleet, another cauldron was hoisted to its place.

Nuada looked back toward the waiting ships. There was still no sign of movement. His hand gripped his sword hilt tightly. What was keeping them? If they didn't attack soon, the Druid magic might not have enough time to protect them.

On the command ship of the Tower fleet, Salmhor too watched carefully and wondered. He asked himself just how mindless these barbarians were. They kept coming on and on toward what they *had* to know was their destruction. It was just as it had been in Eire. He would let them come on until they were very close. He wanted them so close that when his ships tore through them, they would have no chance to run.

He could see them quite clearly now. He could see the warriors crowding the decks, the sunlight glittering from their weapons. So many warriors! How futile. Only that many more bodies to float in the ocean swells.

He turned to the ship's captain.

"It is time," he said. "Signal the others. Everyone is to attack now."

From the deck of the ship directly ahead, Nuada watched the Tower fleet start forward and smiled in grim satisfaction.

"Here they come!" he called out. "Meglin, your time is now! Praise Danu if it works!"

The Druidic pot was tilted, the thick substance oozing out, plopping down into the waves. In the other ships this action was repeated instantly. The white wakes churned the concoction into the sea.

The reaction was an immediate one. From the water there arose a great billow of black smoke, as if the sea had gone to flame. The clouds began to roll up, swelling rapidly all across the fleet of ships, swallowing them up. In moments there was nothing to be seen of them.

Sital Salmhor watched this dark curtain of smoke grow with a surprise that turned to contempt. What did these ridiculous primitives think they could do to help themselves with such an absurd trick as this?

"What are your orders now, sir?" the ship's captain inquired.

"The same," Salmhor replied. "Keep speed up. We attack."

"But we can't see them!" the captain pointed out.

"It makes no difference," the other snapped. "They are still in there. Drive right through that smoke and we'll run them down anyway."

"All right, my warriors, be ready!" Nuada called to the men. "Brace yourselves. If they're coming on, we'll know it soon enough!"

He drew his own sword and took a tight grip on the mast. He prayed he had judged the character of his enemies correctly and that the Fomor wouldn't be suspicious of the clouds and break off their attack.

His prayers were answered: the black ships plunged into the wall of thick smoke without slowing. Salmhor stood in the bow of his own vessel, peering out through the swirling gray to see the hapless de Danann vessels as they were driven beneath the metal knife edge of the prow.

He saw a dim shape looming ahead just to port, then another to starboard, the outlines of two large sailing ships drifting toward them under ghostly swells of sail. His ship would pass between these leading vessels, missing both, but that was all right. There were many more beyond.

He watched the ships gliding up on either side. His ship was almost between them now. But what was that ahead? A black line, almost invisible in the smoke. Something that was stretched from ship to ship, just above the water.

They were nearly on it now. He whirled and screamed a warning to the captain: "Reverse! Reverse! It's a trap!"

But he was too late. There came first a shrill metallic rasping across the prow, and then the ship jerked suddenly to a stop, throwing the unprepared crew heavily to the deck.

Chapter Twenty-Seven
THE SEA BATTLE IS JOINED

From his room atop the Glass Tower, Balor watched with growing displeasure.

"So, perhaps those fools have learned something," he commented as the cloaking black rose from the sea. "But not enough to save them."

Bres, watching from beside the Commander, said nothing. He stood silently staring down at the sleek ships as they penetrated the billowing curtain of smoke, waiting expectantly for them to tear out through the far side of the clouds in victory.

But they did not reappear.

"That little fog seems to have stopped your so-mighty ships, Balor," remarked Bres, unable to keep a tinge of derision from coloring his words.

Balor did not miss it. "Careful, Bres," he rapped out. "The Tower ships cannot be stopped by their magic. It is only some feeble attempt by the de Dananns to hide themselves."

"We'll know soon enough," Bres returned.

Inside the Druid's magic cloud the Fomor ships had plunged headlong into a de Danann trap, turning their devastating attack to chaos.

All of the lead ships of the Eireland fleet had been linked with chains forged by the hand of Goibnu. Left slack to hang beneath the surface as the two fleets closed, they had been cranked in by capstans in the cloaking smoke.

The Fomor ships had been caught across their prows, as Salmhor's had been. Even with their metal hulls and their power, they had been unable to break the links formed by the smith's great skill, hardened by the magic learned in Tir-na-nog. Some had ridden over the chains, pushing them down. There they had been dragged below the hulls, only to fetch up in the steering and driving mechanisms at the stern, fouling them. Other of the ships had pushed forward under the urging of powerful engines, dragging the linked Eireland ships for some way before coming to a stop. But this forward motion had only served to pull the enemy vessels more tightly together, leaving the Tower ships even deeper in the snare.

Two de Danann ships had been struck in the initial collision of the fleets. One had been torn open and sunk. The other, severly damaged, was slowly foundering. But for the rest, the plan had worked. Now, with the deadly black ships stopped and the ships from Eire well tangled with their foes, the real fighting began.

From the de Danann and Firbolg ships came a flurry of grapples. Hundreds of ropes fell across the Fomor decks to further enmesh them. And then, hard upon them, came the warriors of Eire, climbing across or leaping the gaps from ship to ship, swinging weapons and shouting piercing war cries, falling upon the stunned Tower soldiers.

The highly trained Fomor recovered quickly and acted to meet the attacks. Defenses were organized to repel the borders while men were sent to cut the grapple lines in an attempt to free the black vessels from the tangle.

But none of the Tower ships was able to pull away. Even Salmhor's vessel, more powerful than the rest, was unable to move. Though its engines were reversed, it couldn't pull clear of the de Danann ships now jammed hard against its sides. From its rear deck Salmhor peered intently into the roiling black, trying to discern what was happening there. He could hear the clash of arms and the shouts of men, but all sight of the battle was hidden.

Inside that shrouding smoke a nightmare conflict was being waged. Desperate to keep the Tower's forces from escaping, the Eireland warriors were swarming onto their ships, unmindful of risk in their fervor to engage the enemy. But that enemy seemed little more than wraithlike figures flitting through the shifting clouds. The faint glitter of swinging weapons was often the only clue as to where the fighting was, and those on both sides were hard pressed to know if the dark forms looming before them were friends or foes. Most fought in their own tiny, very personal realm, only vaguely aware of the much larger conflict being waged around them.

Soon, however, the darkness began to fade, the short life Meglin had warned of over. As quickly as it had been born it died. As its fabric shredded and dissolved, the whole scene was revealed.

For the first time the Fomor realized their entire fleet was embroiled.

"They are more clever than I expected," Balor said in an odd, low, introspective way.

It caused Bres to glance up sharply at the giant form. Had he detected a note of worry there? He looked back toward the ships, at the de Dananns he had once ruled, now fighting courageously against the supposedly invincible black fleet, attacking so savagely the Tower forces that had once struck terror in them.

"Can they defeat your ships?" Bres asked.

"Impossible!" clanged Balor. "They will be destroyed in time. My ships will fight themselves free, and that will be the end."

"What if they don't?" Bres challenged. "What if the de Danann ships get through?"

"If any of those vessels get past my fleet, I will destroy them myself," the giant announced, "just as I did once before."

"Why not use your eye now?" suggested Bres. "Wipe them all away!"

"No. The press is too close. My own ships might be hit. We must wait to see if any of theirs do break through."

The massive head swiveled slowly, bringing the crimson gaze toward the helmeted guardsmen at the doors.

"Get your captain here," he ordered. "Have him bring more men. I will be moving to the rooftop at once!"

"Yes, my Commander," one of them answered briskly, and then left the room in haste.

The giant's blazing eye swung back toward the scene of battle.

"If any of those de Danann ships sails clear," the iron voice rattled, "it will become a blazing pyre for everyone aboard!"

Unaware of the battle raging outside, Lugh and his companions made their way cautiously up the stairway.

They expected to encounter Tower soldiers, but made their way to the second level without encountering anyone—a particular surprise to the Tower men.

"With the lifts so crowded and always breaking down, there are many who use the stairs," Eab said. "It's very odd."

"Let's not question it," Manannan urged. "Let's just be glad and keep moving."

At the landing to the second level they eased the door open and peered out. Like the stairway, the galley seemed amazingly deserted.

"Your luck seems to be holding," said Eab. He pointed across to a hallway on the far side of the atrium. "The way to Mathgen's chamber is over there. It may be that you can get over to it without being seen. Stay away from the rail, back against the inner wall." He glanced back to his fellows clustered on the stairs below, then added: "Say, you know, going against that Druid could be a bit rough. My mates and I, we'd be willing to give you some help."

"We're grateful," Manannan told him, smiling warmly, "but this is a matter we have to settle. You've a task of your own."

"What will you do?" asked Lugh.

"We'll go up to the training levels," Eab said. "We can get weapons there. If we can take them by surprise, we might have a chance."

"A chance to be killed," said Lugh. "You'll be outnumbered, and you're unarmed. You're the ones who need help."

"We can't spare any, boy!" the Dagda growled. "We'll need every sword against that Druid!"

"These men are fighting the same enemy as we are," Lugh argued. "We owe our help to them, and we can't abandon anyone else who wants to escape this terrible place."

"He's right!" put in MacLir, and the others added their voices in agreement. Reluctantly, the Dagda was forced to agree as well.

"All right, lad. I suppose we could spare a hand or two."

"I'll go," Taillta volunteered. "I know what it's like for the women trapped up there."

Lugh understood her feelings. This brave woman who had raised him, hidden him, risked her life often for him, had once allowed herself to be captured to save him from Balor. She had remained a prisoner of that icy Tower until Lugh, Aine, and Gilla had rescued her.

"I'll go as well," said Angus.

"Time I was off on my own." He grinned at the Dagda. "You'll have to stay with them, Father. They'll be needing you."

The big warrior gave an uncharacteristic display of warmth at that, throwing his arms about his son in a great hug.

"You just see you stay alive, boy," he said in a low rumble.

"Of course I will. You trained me, didn't you? We'll meet you on the shore outside the Tower."

Lugh moved toward Taillta for a like farewell, but she raised a hand.

"No time and no need for that," she said brusquely, "We'll see you soon."

With that she started up the stairway, followed by Angus, Eab, and the rest of the determined Tower men.

Lugh and his comrades watched until they had all climbed out of sight. Then they pushed open the door and moved stealthily onto the gallery.

As Eab had advised, they stayed close to the inner wall, sidling as quickly as possible around the atrium to the corridor. From here Lugh led the way, Salmhor's earlier tour having shown him how to reach the Druid's lair. They followed the narrow hall past the rows of tiny rooms. It led them to a small antechamber. The rear entrance to the room of Mathgen was at its far side. Still no one had appeared to challenge them.

"Well, we've made it this far easily enough," said MacLir softly.

"Maybe too easily," returned the Dagda. He nodded at the metal door. "He could just be waitin' in there for us."

Manannan shrugged. "It doesn't matter much if he is. We've got to go in."

"It'd be a help if those bloody systems of theirs would do

a bit of breaking now," the Dagda grumbled, shooting Findgoll a nasty look. "They've shown no sign of it yet."

"You're the one who chucked the bloody iron into the works!" the Druid fired back. "Don't blame *me* if it didn't work!"

"Ah, you shouldn't have listened to that mad old man!"

"No more, my friends," MacLir said placatingly. "It was a chance we took. If it doesn't work, then it doesn't. I suggest that we direct our hostility toward Mathgen."

"And how do you suggest we attack him?" asked Lugh.

"The direct way is the best I think," MacLir said with confidence. "We go straight in at him and smash into that little glass realm of his before he can raise his defenses." He looked to the giant warrior. "Dagda, can you throw well enough to hit the thing?"

"Just give me one clean chance!" he answered, shaking the heavy weapon in his hand.

"Good. Then we'll go in together. You go right for him. Morrigan, Aine, Shaglan, and I will deal with any guards who might be in the way." He turned his attention to the young Champion. "Lugh, I think your task is to recover your weapons."

"Nothing will stop me from getting them," Lugh said grimly.

"I'm sure of that," MacLir replied, smiling at Lugh's intensity. "Just don't get ahead of us, all right?"

He looked down at the Pooka with uncertainty. Despite Shaglan's best efforts, he had retained the same furry, piglike shape since their escape.

"You might be safer here," the tall man said apologetically. "You're not really in . . . ah . . . *shape* for a fight, if you know what I mean."

"Give me a chance!" the Pooka told him irritably. "I haven't been able to concentrate yet. Hold on!"

They watched, exchanging doubt-filled looks as the being closed its eyes and tensed the rotund body. For a moment nothing happened. Then, slowly, the form began to waver, soften, bulge, and stretch. It grew and slimmed, its limbs becoming sleeker, its muscles sinewy. The hair shrank back to a thick tawny coat and the head took on the catlike features it had worn before. Shaglan was a lion again.

"That's a relief!" he said wholeheartedly. "I was afraid I'd be stuck forever in that horrible form."

"Marvelous, Shaglan," MacLir congratulated him. Then his gaze moved on to little Findgoll.

"I know what you're thinking," the Druid said, seeing the look. "Don't be trying to leave me behind either! I'll face Mathgen with you. You may need my help."

"More likely we'll trip over you!" the Dagda said.

"Never mind!" MacLir said quickly, forestalling another exchange. "He's a right to come too."

"Are you certain this will work?" Aine asked her brother with a certain skepticism.

He grinned broadly at her. "Dear sister, have you ever known one of my plans to fail?"

"Often!" she replied.

"Well, no one's perfect." He shrugged. "Come on. Let's visit the dear old Druid again."

With that he thrust open the metal door and the little band charged through into the room.

On the far side, Mathgen's two henchmen were bent over the metal table, gingerly holding up the sheathed Answerer. The lens that served Mathgen as an eye was directed at the sword, and a vast image of the weapon filled the lighted screen.

But at their entrance the lens whirled around toward them, the image of the sword sweeping away to be replaced by one of the invaders.

"Quickly!" MacLir shouted. "Get him now!"

The Dagda leaped forward, launching his ax in a hard throw. It sailed across the room, well-aimed for the center of the tank.

But a handbreadth from the curved glass surface the cutting edge seemed to strike something else. It turned, skittering along the side, flying away from the tank at a sharp angle to crash into the lighted panel on the wall beyond. There was a sharp explosion, crackling like lightning, and a shower of sparks from the section torn open. Across that section of the wall a swath of the tiny lights winked out. For a moment the ax hung there in the gaping wound, then it dropped free, clattering to the floor.

"Oh, oh," said MacLir.

"So, you managed to escape," hissed the malevolent voice. "But you never should have returned to me."

"You will never use the secret to Tir-na-nog, Mathgen,"

MacLir announced. "We are going to stop you here and now!"

"That is very heroic talk, considering you have no means to do so," the wasted being returned. "As you see, I am shielded by the energies of this Tower. You, on the other hand, are completely vulnerable. Let me show you."

And with that, the gleaming devices that had sat motionless around the room began to move.

The little band looked around at them in surprise. They were closing in from all sides, rolling forward on small wheels. From their metallic torsos, limbs were unfolding, extending a variety of lethal-appearing instruments.

"My closest allies," Mathgen explained. "Their purpose was to assist the healers of the Tower, long ago. Now they serve me and do as *my* power wills. Right now I am willing them to perform their skills on you."

The warriors set themselves in defensive positions as the contraptions closed in and prepared to parry the attack.

"Get behind me!" Lugh commanded Findgoll, pulling the little Druid back into the shelter of the others' swords as the devices rushed at him. One thrust a small, whirling saw-wheel toward him, but a swipe from Aine's blade knocked it away.

Then Lugh and his comrades were very busy. A glinting array of jointed metal limbs tipped with weaponry hemmed them in. Fine-bladed knives, whirling drill points, snapping pincers, saws, tongs, and slender probes all jabbed in at them with incredible speed. It took all the warriors' skills and dexterity to fend them off.

The weaponless Dagda looked for a chance to seize one of the metal creatures, but small blades flashing on its half-dozen arms threatened to shred him if he moved too close. Shaglan too found his opponents much too fast for even his cat's reflexes to counter. All he could do was dodge the attacks and snarl in frustration.

Slowly, they pulled back as the things advanced, forming into a tight defensive ring.

"This situation seems a bit familiar, doesn't it?" remarked Manannan. "Seems to be a habit with us."

"Except that before we're always had some way out!" growled the Dagda.

"Just keep them off," Manannan urged. "Something will turn up."

A hoarse cackling of dreadful laughter came from the ravaged Druid within the tank.

"Struggle for as long as you wish," he told them. "I'm enjoying this! I thank you for returning to me. It gives me the pleasure of finally dealing with my old friends myself!"

Chapter Twenty-Eight
DESTROYING THE DRUID

In the depths of the Tower the stricken heart of the complex was beginning to convulse.

The initial damage caused by the Dagda was multiplying itself. Systems designed to repair and sustain themselves were failing under the stress of age and of this terrible injury. More explosions came. More units broke down amid smoke and flares of released energy. Their failure threw yet more strain on other portions of the mechanism. These struggled to maintain their function, and then went into death throes themselves, creating more explosions, more fiery displays, more rents and cracks in the machinery.

The chain of breakdowns, once begun, spread quickly to the other portions of the vast plant. Great surges of unbridled power swept upward through the Tower. Aging units there meant to contain and use the energy began to overheat, explode, and burn. Devices that depended upon the energy for their lives began to weaken, malfunction, or fail.

On the soldiers' training level, high above, two helmeted guards patrolling the corridors paused as the overhead lights flickered.

"What's that about?" one said uncertainly.

"Just some shifting in the Tower's works," the other assured him confidently. "Nothing to worry about."

The two moved on, out of the corridor, rounding a corner into the central gallery.

They walked into Taillta and Angus Og.

Before either man could cry out or throw up a defense, the two warriors had struck. Single, skillfully aimed sword thrusts found the hearts of both guards. As they fell, Taillta and Angus moved in to seize the globe-tipped weapons.

Taillta signaled toward the door to the stairway. At once the escaped Tower men began to move out onto the gallery, Eab at their head.

Taillta handed him the power-spear she held and edged cautiously toward the outer gallery rail. She peered out across the atrium. No one was visible on the other sides of that level. She moved closer to the edge and looked up and down the atrium. No one seemed to be moving on any of the levels. She listened. Only a vast silence filled the chill white space. It was as if the Tower were truly a frozen world—or a deserted one.

Eab joined her, looking up and down the atrium himself, then shaking his head.

"I don't understand," he said. "Even in sleeping or dining periods there are soldiers moving about."

"A Firbolg never questions good fortune, he only uses it!" she told him tersely. "Where do we go now?"

"This way," he said. "There will be weapons in the training rooms."

They moved up a corridor away from the atrium. Dividing their party, they began to burst into the training rooms. They were deserted too. Quickly, the rebel soldiers armed themselves from the racks of practice weapons.

"We should sweep the rest of this level for Balor's guards," Eab said. "Then we can move up to the family quarters."

But these plans were interrupted. As they moved back into the corridor, the bright squares of glowing white in the ceiling flickered and then faded almost away. They were left in twilight under a pale luminescence like that of a mist-shrouded moon.

From out of one of the other training rooms another group of the rebels suddenly poured, their expressions frightened. Behind them the room was filled with an intense but wavering light.

"Eab, one of the illuminators in there burst!" a man called. "It's showering the place with fire!"

"It's the systems!" he said, looking around to Angus and Taillta. "They're beginning to fail. Come on!"

He led the way back to the atrium. The once-glowing space was gray in the half light. But in many places up and down its levels, the intense white-gold spots of other fires were visible. And from below, many threads of smoke were rising, joining in a rapidly thickening cloud.

"I hadn't thought that this might happen," he said in distress. "If there are greater fires below us, they could trap us up here." He looked toward the higher levels. "We've got to get to our families now and get them out of here!"

"Then let's go quickly," Taillta said, "before there's no way down."

In Mathgen's chambers, Lugh and his band continued their desperate battle. The fighters were managing to hold their own, but only by expending tremendous amounts of energy. They were beginning to tire, while the machines fought on with unlessened vigor.

The sharp gaze of the Raven-Woman caught a movement to one side. One of the things was slipping behind the Dagda while his attention was fixed on another before him. It was nearly upon him, moving with lightning speed, but her own reaction was faster yet.

She slammed away the flailing arms of the device before her and leaped to protect the Dagda. She was only just in time to save him, thrusting her own slender body before him as a shield. The long, gleaming probe meant for him instead drove deeply into the shoulder of her sword arm.

With a sharp cry of surprise and pain she jerked back, freeing herself from the instrument. But her arm, stilled by the wound, went numb, and her sword slipped from her nerveless fingers. As she staggered back, the Dagda realized what had happened. Bellowing with rage, he swung a foot up, catching the device's body and knocking it away. He threw a supporting arm around Morrigan and shouted to the rest.

"Morrigan's hurt!"

Instantly, the others shifted their defensive ring to protect her from attack. Without the Raven-Woman's fighting skills, however, the situation seemed all the more hopeless. The evil Druid's glinting instruments knitted a dazzling but deadly garment of silver with the speed of their darting movements.

The image on Mathgen's screen moved in close on the agonized faces of his victims as he savored their last moments.

Then, abruptly, the thousands of lights twinkling in the wall panels about the room flickered and went out.

Mathgen was distracted momentarily, and his control of the attacking devices was interrupted. Their movements slowed. Their arms dropped limply to their sides.

Lugh saw his chance to act. He leaped forward, shoved between two of the mechanisms, and charged directly toward the table that held his weapons.

Mathgen's two men had put down the Answerer and drawn their own swords at the entrance of Lugh's group. But the sudden loss of the lights had thrown them off guard. Before they could act to stop him, Lugh had dived between them, seizing the hilt of his weapon.

He swung it around, the heavy scabbard slamming into the temple of one man, knocking him from his feet. The scabbard flew off as Lugh then swept the Answerer back. The exposed blade glowed brightly, forming a blazing arc as it swooped down to parry a thrust from the second man.

The powerful blow knocked the other sword away. A return cut laid open the man's chest. He staggered back and fell.

"That will do you no good, Lugh Lamfada!" came Mathgen's wheezing voice. "You will still die with the rest!"

His control now recovered, the Druid sent two of his metal creatures scuttling toward Lugh. The others took up their attack on the young warrior's companions with a redoubled fury.

There seemed to Lugh nothing else to do to save his friends. He slipped the Answerer into his belt and took up the Spear of Gorias. He would have to use it to destroy Mathgen, no matter what the risks. He moved a hand to the ties of the leather covering.

"No!" MacLir shouted to him, fending off a thrusting knife with a deft parry. "Lugh, you can't use that!"

"What?" said Lugh, looking toward the tall man in disbelief. "How else can we fight him?"

Now it was Findgoll's turn. Mathgen's reaction to the failing lights had told him that the evil Druid's control of the machines had to be absolute for them to act effectively. He knew what could be done.

"The vial, lad!" he called. "Throw the vial at him!"

"Vial?" Lugh repeated. He looked at the tabletop, where lay a collection of the tiny, stoppered bottles that had been taken from the little Druid. But there were a half-dozen!

"Which one?" Lugh asked, and with some urgency as the two contraptions were nearly upon him.

"Throw them all!" Findgoll advised.

He did. Ducking away from one attacker's spinning saw blade, he slung the spear across a shoulder, swept up all the bottles in both hands, and hurled the lot toward Mathgen's glowing cylinder.

They smashed against the protective shield and tumbled in shards to the floor. But from their mingled contents there arose a self-conjured force even Findgoll had never seen before. There was a violent flurry of blizzard whiteness intertwining with the oily blackness of a moonless night. These two commingled and seemed to wrestle with a steaming, blood-red haze. And through this—twining, coiling, always flowing upward—was a stream of spectral figures, fantastic beasts and birds and serpents, their ghastly forms fluid, elongated, writhing in obscene couplings as they rose.

The air filled with the ghastly sounds of them: the gibbering and shrieks, the mournful cries and manic laughter of tormented beings.

As alarming as was this misbegotten bit of sorcery, it served the purpose Findgoll had intended. Its curtain rose before the ravaged Druid's haven of glass, floating up before the blue lens that was his eye. And across the image on the screen there drifted a like projection of the glow, obscuring the picture of the room and its occupants.

As Mathgen's intended victims faded from his view, the movements of the metal attackers became more haphazard, more hesitant.

"That's blinded you, you cursed traitor!" Findgoll cried in triumph to his old adversary. "Try to direct your creatures now!"

"You won't escape me," came the hissing reply from within the roiling clouds. "You won't keep me from Tir-na-nog. I will still destroy you all!"

His machines began to move with an even greater speed, but in a frantic way, as if they had gone mad. They struck out blindly with wild swings of their jointed arms, sweeping around in aimless circles, one pair colliding and attacking each other, tangling their long limbs.

By some lively movements, those in the little band were now able to avoid the devices. The Dagda found it easy to come behind one, seize it by the metal torso, heave it up

from the floor, and fling it against another. They came together with a most satisfying crash, both tumbling to the
floor, their bodies smashed, their bent limbs still waving
feebly like those of crushed insects.

He was so pleased with this effect that he seized another
one, lifting it high above his head.

"Dagda! The tank!" shouted Manannan, pointing to the
glowing column visible within the magic haze.

He understood. Shifting his direction slightly, he cast
the machine toward Mathgen's cylinder with all his power.

It smashed against the curving glass surface, its metal
body buckling from the force of the impact. Then it dropped
to the floor.

"Don't you learn, fools?" wheezed the Druid. "You can't
hurt me that way."

But he was wrong. Though the protecting force was
enough to keep the blow from breaking through the cylinder,
nothing could totally protect the glass from such a massive
shock. At the point where the machine had struck, there was
now just the tiniest, finest hairline crack.

It did not remain so long. Once the integrity of this
single, curving wall of glass had been violated, the entire
structure began to go. From the one crack, others began to
radiate, spreading out in a rapidly growing web across the
glass.

Like an avalanche begun by a pebble's fall, the effect
multiplied. Cracks snaked up and down and around the cylinder. In seconds, the whole surface was covered with an
intricate network of lines.

Within the cylinder were pent enormous forces, the
powers meant to keep Mathgen alive. But the weakened
structure was no longer able to contain them. They pressed
outward in all directions, bowing the surface of the glass, the
strain making it shudder.

Fissures opened. Jets of air shot outward with a sharp
whoosh, stabbing through the haze like a sword blade. A
foreboding rumbling began, growing swiftly louder.

"Get down!" Manannan warned. "Quickly! Protect
yourselves!"

They went down on the floor with only an instant to
spare. Mathgen shrieked, "No, no!"—and then his voice was
drowned out by a thunderous explosion as the whole cylinder
gave way at once.

It burst like an enormous bubble, its glass shattering into unaccountable tiny shards, blooming outward in a spectacular, glinting flower, spraying walls and ceiling. There was a fine, high, musical tinkling as the bits settled, and then there was silence.

Lugh rose dizzily. His bare skin was cut in scores of places, but he was otherwise unhurt. He shook off the fine coating of pulverized glass and looked around him. The explosion had blown away the magic haze. Where the cylinder had been there were now only the tangled remains of the cables, tubes, and wires that had formed Mathgen's life-sustaining web. And within it hung the tattered remnants of the traitorous Druid himself.

The man who had used the Tower's forces and his own magic to cheat death for so long was finally, unquestionably dead.

But the little band had not escaped unharmed. While the others arose, brushed debris from themselves, and stared at the massive destruction, Manannan lay still.

Realizing this, all moved quickly to him. Lugh gently rolled Manannan over. He was unconscious, his lean face very pale, but he was breathing.

"We've got to get him out of here," Lugh announced. He glanced toward the awful scraps of Mathgen dangling in the web. "There's nothing left to do here."

"Can you carry him?" Aine asked the Dagda.

"And easily? Not like a bag of fish?" added Findgoll.

"Of course I can," the big man said, scowling.

"How about you, Morrigan?" Lugh asked the Raven-Woman.

"It's only my arm," she answered tersely. "I can manage well enough."

A shattered wall panel across the room crackled and flared suddenly with light. Smoke began to seep out from within its damaged works.

"I think we'd better be going then," urged Lugh, "before something else happens."

The Dagda scooped up MacLir and cradled him in his arms as he would a babe. Lugh, Aine, and Shaglan led the way out of the devastated room, back up the corridor toward the atrium, the stairway, and the way out of the stricken Tower.

Chapter Twenty-Nine
BREAKTHROUGH

From the deck of his ship Sital Salmhor watched as the barbarians from Eire ravaged his proud fleet.

For all their hardness and training and discipline, the Fomor soldiers found themselves unable to fight off the onslaught of de Dananns and Firbolgs. These warriors seemed to have gone mad. They fought as individuals, throwing themselves fearlessly, savagely, upon their enemies, their faces aglow with battle fervor.

The deadly bolts of the Tower crossbows showered upon them, but could not drive them back. The neat, well-ordered ranks of Fomor soldiers could not stop them. Warriors slashed into the lines, shredding any attempt at a defensive formation. The Fomor found themselves caught up in free-for-alls, fighting separately. The decks of the black ships glittered with the swift, constant movement of weapons, roared with the crash of arms, grew slippery with the wash of hot, wet blood.

Slowly, the entangled vessels of the Tower were being overrun by the men of Eire. Scores of smaller boats moved up to join the fight.

On the broader deck of Balor's vast ship the Tower men were falling back before the furious assault of the de Danann warriors. They poured aboard from two vessels drawn tightly against each side of the prow by their connecting chain.

Their attack was led by Nuada, determined to himself have the honor of taking this greatest of the black fleet. The High-King slashed boldly into the defenders' ranks, sending them staggering back before the ferocity of his massive sword strokes.

Salmhor had withdrawn to the elevated stern deck of the vessel, there to look down upon the battle from behind a protecting wall of elite Tower guards. He watched in mounting agony as his soldiers were driven back. Who were this scum, this undisciplined, primitive rabble, to sully his fine men?

The regular Tower soldiers had been driven back to the center of the deck. There they were fighting valiantly to hold a line. But more de Dananns were swarming aboard, throwing themselves into the Fomor midst with savage battle cries and flashing weapons. The formation was starting to disintegrate under this constant punishment.

Salmhor would show them. He would show this horde that they were yet no match for the true might of the Tower. They would be surprised!

"Captain, take your men forward!" he ordered the leader of the guard's company. "Sweep these vermin from the ship!"

The officer saluted smartly and barked the command to his men. A hundred of Balor's elite fighting unit, resplendent in their pristine uniforms and shining silver caps, marched forward, throwing their globe-tipped weapons up before them in a single, practiced move.

As they moved into the fray, the line of deadly power spears had an initially devastating effect on the de Dananns. Warriors touched by the shining globes were propelled with tremendous force back into their fellows as if they had been struck a massive blow. The de Dananns began to retreat in panic before the measured advance of the guardsmen.

From the safety of the high stern, Salmhor smiled in satisfaction. This was as it should be. As he'd known, the Tower soldiers were proving themselves superior.

But his glee was short-lived. Nuada had learned of these strange weapons from Lugh and his comrades. He understood how their assault could be countered. Shouting to his warriors not to retreat, he pressed forward again, slashing about him with renewed vigor. Though more dangerous, the power spears were also far clumsier than a good longsword. He parried their attacks easily, his own quick, powerful return strokes clearing a way before him. He was a gale, blowing the dried leaves before him, sweeping a path into the guardsmen's ranks.

Seeing his fearlessness, his warriors were quick to follow him. They slashed into the Fomor, tearing the opening wider. The advance of the Tower men wavered, stopped, and fell apart, collapsing into a tangle of wildly flailing separate parts. And through the thickest of the fray swept Nuada, his tall, lean figure dominating the rest, his flashing sword sweeping around him, face glowing with the battle-light, mane of gold hair flowing behind him, the grand image of some wrathful battle god.

Salmhor was nearly mad with outrage. The finest of the Tower's men were being destroyed, degraded, humiliated before his eyes! The torn bodies of wounded and slain soldiers tumbled to the bloody deck like so many butchered cattle, their superiority stripped away by the disgrace of loss. The rest fought on, but with no confidence, struggling now only to survive before this withering blast, fear etching their once-sure, once-stolid faces. How, he thought, could this be happening?

And then his eye fell upon Nuada. All his attention focused on this one man who led the attackers on. Here was the man who had done it! Here was the one who had thrown his peerless soldiers into disgrace! Here was the man who had dared to challenge the mighty, the untouchable Tower of Glass! This one man became the object of all Salmhor's despair, all of his rage, and Salmhor determined that this man had to die.

Nuada was fighting in a tight mob just before the raised rear deck. The remainder of the Tower fighters were jammed against this platform now, battling vainly to keep their enemies away. Seeing a bowman in the crowd below him, Salmhor

His vigor reassured the warriors. Diancecht understood bent down and snatched the weapon from his grasp. It was loaded. He swung it up, leveling the bolt upon the tall figure.

In the crowd close beside the High-King, Bobd Derg was slashing his way through the soldiers with a verve and skill that would have delighted his father. Suddenly, they found themselves with no one to face. They had reached the rear deck, and only dead and dying men lay about them. Bobd Derg's gaze swept the deck on either side for new enemies, then rose to the platform above. He saw Salmhor leaning forward, the bow lifted, aimed at Nuada.

Shouting a warning, he jumped forward, swinging his sword up in a desperate attempt to stop the Fomor officer. But he was too late.

With a grunt of satisfaction Salmhor jerked the bow's firing mechanism. The metal bolt whizzed unerringly to its target. It sank home, burying half its length in Nuada's side.

As the High-King staggered and fell back into the arms of his warriors, Salmhor gave a cry of victory. This was his revenge! But then something struck him. A sharp pain ran through him. He felt weak, his arms dropping limply, the crossbow clattering to the deck. His head dropped forward and he looked down at the sword blade protruding from his chest. A spreading stain was discoloring the immaculate, wrinkleless tunic of his uniform.

He looked up at Bobd Derg, eyebrows lifted in a final show of indignation over this lout's effrontery. Then his body sagged and he fell to the deck to lie amid his men.

Bobd Derg yanked his sword from Salmhor and ran to his king. Nuada lay motionless, apparently unconscious.

"Quickly, get him back onto our ship!" he ordered the shocked warriors about.

At once a half-dozen men lifted the High-King and carried him from the fight.

Gently, he was passed across the gap to his own ship. There Diancecht was already hard at work treating the many wounded who filled the deck. The old physician moved quickly to his comrade. He directed the warriors to lay Nuada carefully down and knelt beside him to examine the wound.

"Well?" demanded Bobd Derg anxiously.

"It has done damage inside him," Diancecht said bluntly. "Still, he could survive. If we can keep that bolt from shifting, keep him quiet until we return to Eire, I may be able to remove the bolt safely."

"No!" came the protesting voice of Nuada.

The High-King was now fully awake. He sat up. The physician tried to push him back.

"You must lay still, Nuada!" he said. "You're badly hurt."

"Am I?" Nuada replied. His hand swung up and grasped the weapon's protruding end. With one swift move he jerked it free, flinging the bloody shaft away. Then he hauled himself up, waving off the warriors who tried to help.

"I am all right!" he assured them. "I will not leave this fight."

"Nuada, you cannot do this!" Diancecht protested with vehemence. "You can't realize what damage you've caused yourself by that rash act. If you stay quiet, there is still a chance."

"Back, Healer!" he warned ominously. "This is my fight. Nothing will keep me out."

He drew himself erect and stood steadily, one hand pressed tightly to the wound. He smiled at Diancecht in a triumphant way. "You see, old friend? I am fine. Nothing can stop us now, no matter what."

His vigor reassured the warriors. Diancecht understood and moved back.

Nuada swept a scrutinizing gaze over the black ship. It was now in their hands, the last of the Tower men cut down ruthlessly by de Dananns wreaking vengeance for the wounding of their king. He looked around at the rest of the embattled fleets. On many of the black ships it was the same: the decks heaped with dead, the remnant of the Fomor soldiers surrendering. On other ships the battles still went on, but in each case the outcome was clear. The proud Tower fleet was broken.

"We are finished here," he announced. "Now we will go against the Tower itself. Cut loose the chains. We sail on!"

The warriors were ordered back to their own ships. Goibnu and the other smiths knocked loose the massive clamps that had kept the magically forged chains fixed to the decks. The chains pulled loose and sank forever beneath the waves, their job done. The Eireland vessels drifted free, then started forward as the wind caught at their sails. They glided ahead at an increasing speed, all courses set directly for the Tower.

Behind them they left the Tower vessels wallowing helplessly in the swells, their sleek, black metal sides streaked with the red-brown of the blood running from their decks.

The large metal doors set in the rooftop vibrated, then parted with a piercing skreel of metal, swinging up and away from each other on massive hinges. They were being pushed up by a square object rising slowly from the interior of the Tower, Balor's private lift.

The metal box shivered and clanged to a halt. Its door slid upward to reveal the giant being. He rolled forward, Bres striding out briskly at his side. Behind them, four guardsmen and an officer emerged from the lift. The four were carefully carrying a singular object: a long glass rod as thick as a man's leg.

The officer halted the four men beside the lift. Balor's wheeled throne carried him on to the southern side of the vast expanse of rooftop, slowing to a halt at the very edge. Bres moved up cautiously next to the Commander and peered—without a great deal of relish—out at the scene spread so spectacularly below.

It took no careful evaluation to determine how the sea

battle was going. Most of the black ships were clearly drifting and powerless while the Eireland vessels were pulling away, gliding toward the Tower. The white billows of their scores of sails dappled the smooth blue surface.

"So, they have somehow managed to break through my fleet," rumbled Balor. "And now they seek to challenge me! Well, that will be their final act. I will finish them."

His head swiveled toward the officer. "Captain, have the rod brought here," he demanded. "You must prepare to lift my eyelid all the way up."

Bres looked in surprise from the glass rod to the giant. "Is that what that thing's for? Can't you open your eye alone?"

"This body has served the Tower for many years," Balor replied. "Lately it has sustained some . . . injuries. . . ."

"What you mean is you're bloody well near helpless, don't you!" Bres said sharply, realizing the truth. "You can't move, can you? No wonder you were afraid to enter the battle in Eire!"

"I am not afraid!" Balor shot back. "It is true that in my most recent encounter with Manannan MacLir I did lose much of my function. But the power of my eye is undiminished. Watch, Bres. You will soon see it burn your de Dananns away!"

The door to the stairway burst open. The escaped Tower rebels poured out onto the gallery. Led by Eab, Angus, and Taillta, they charged around the atrium, now hazy with the rapidly increasing smoke.

On the far side, a dozen guardsmen moved to challenge them. They had no chance. The escaped men, fighting now for the liberty of themselves and their families, overwhelmed them in moments. Eab took the group on to the main corridor into the living quarters. It was closed by a heavy door fitted with a bolt. From beyond it could be heard frightened cries.

"Look at this! Balor's had them locked in!" Eab said angrily. He slammed the bolt back and hauled open the door.

Released smoke puffed outward. A group of women clutching terrified children staggered forward.

"Thank you! Thank you!" one woman sobbed. "We were trapped. There are so many fires!"

"We must get them all out!" Eab told his men. "Some of you, go through the rooms. Find everyone!"

They moved into the corridor beyond. The darkness and the smoke made it a nightmare place. While some men directed the women and children out, others began a search of all the rooms.

Eab moved purposefully along the corridor, clearly intent upon some goal. Taillta and Angus stayed with him.

Around a corner and up another corridor he finally stopped, throwing open a door. In the small chamber beyond, a woman sat upon a bed comforting two small and fearful children.

As he stepped into the room, she looked up at him in surprise. But this quickly changed to amazement as she recognized the young officer.

"Eab!" she cried.

He quickly crossed the room to her, kneeling by her and clasping the three at once. Her eyes filled with tears of joy as she hugged him back.

"Oh, Eab!" she said. "It is you! But how can it be? How . . ."

He pulled back and looked into her eyes. "Never mind how. I'm free. I've come to take you out of here. We must go quickly!"

"But the guards!" she protested.

"There are none left to stop us," he told her, rising and getting them to their feet.

"Of course!" she said as they moved to the door. "That's why they locked us in. Balor must have sent the guardsmen with the rest."

"Sent them where?" asked Taillta as the little group passed into the corridor.

Becoming aware of the peculiar dress of Taillta and Angus, the woman gave them a rather searching look before replying.

"Why, off in the fleet is where. They've been sent off to fight another great fleet coming toward us from the south."

"From Eire?" said Angus. He exchanged a look of concern with Taillta. "Our own people?"

"I think we'd best go find the others," the Firbolg chieftain suggested. "Now!"

Chapter Thirty
THE EYE OF BALOR

The four soldiers shoved upward on the glass rod. Its slotted tip was set against the lower edge of the thick metal visor that shuttered Balor's eye. The men heaved, heaved, heaved in rhythmic unison at their captain's cadence. At first their efforts seemed unavailing, but at last, very slowly, the lid began to rise.

With a faint high shriek of metal on metal, it slid reluctantly upward. Gradually, the blaze of the single eye, like a blood-hued, bloated sun in a dusky sunset, was exposed.

"Keep going! Keep going!" Balor commanded impatiently. "It must be completely clear of the eye!"

At last, as the visor's lower edge rose above the pupil, it gave a loud clack and stopped.

"All right," he said. "It is at its highest point. Remove the rod!"

The men withdrew gladly, sweating profusely from the labor and the intense heat of the exposed ruby eye.

"Now I am ready," he hammered out. The barrel head inclined forward. The crimson gaze dropped toward the approaching ships.

Bres also looked down toward the tiny spots.

"They seem so far away!" he observed. "Are you certain you can hit them?" He had not seen the legendary eye of Balor in use before.

"Do you see that small boat sailing ahead of the others?" Balor asked.

"Yes, I do," Bres answered. The slender, sprightly craft had easily outdistanced the rest of the fleet.

"Then, watch!"

The eye shifted to it, held it in the crimson gaze. The orb flared brighter, brighter, its glow becoming so intense that Bres looked away. It reached a peak, and then a single ray of the ruby light shot out from it, like a solid column, expanding slightly into a cone as it stretched away, angling sharply downward toward the little boat.

Those aboard the craft never even knew that they were struck. As the beam fell upon them, the boat became in that instant a flaming pyre for them.

From the bow of his own vessel, not far behind, Nuada watched the boat blasted to a flaming wreck. His eye went from it to the Tower's roof. He was already certain what he would see there.

Yes. There he was. The black giant, just as he had been those many years before. But this time his people were coming as a strong force, not a scattered remnant, and this time they were attacking, not fleeing for their lives. The de Dananns would never retreat in fear again.

On the rooftop Bres was gaping in astonishment. He had never imagined that Balor's eye was capable of releasing such incredible destructive power.

"By Danu!" he gasped out.

"This is none of your Danu's childish magic," Balor told him in an irritated, clanking way. "This is the power of the Fomor, the might of the Tower of Glass. And now—"

But he was interrupted. The door of the stairway down into the Tower burst open. A guardsman staggered out onto the rooftop. His helmet and power spear were gone. His uniform was badly disheveled and he seemed near exhaustion.

"Commander!" he managed to get out in a choked voice.

"What is it?" Balor demanded, the smoldering eye still fixed on the attacking fleet.

"There is rioting! In the family quarters!"

"Rioting? What are you talking about?"

The young guardsman struggled to explain. His words spilled out in a jumble. "It is . . . very confusing. There are fires . . . and smoke. Many lights are out. The lifts as well. Women and children are escaping from their levels . . . pouring down the stairs. We—we couldn't stop them!"

"Captain, take your men and go with him," Balor ordered impatiently. "See what he's raving about. Take care of it."

"Yes, my Commander," the officer briskly replied. He called his men to attention and, taking the harried guardsman in tow, disappeared down the stairway into the Tower.

Bres looked after them with some vague anxiety.

"Are you certain it's all right?" he asked Balor.

"It is nothing," Balor answered with finality. "My only interest now is in seeing to these de Dananns."

The eye shifted slowly, the deadly gaze sweeping across the surface of the sea toward another approaching boat.

"I will not make this quick for them," he told Bres. "I will destroy them very slowly, one by one, as they draw near. They will feel agony for what they have done to my fleet."

"And if they turn and run?" asked Bres.

"Then I will sweep them all away at once!" the iron voice replied.

Lugh and his companions moved cautiously out of the stairwell into the Tower's cavernous storage room.

Still unaware of the battle raging outside, they expected that at least here they would have to avoid Tower soldiers. But the enormous place seemed deserted.

It was beginning to fill with smoke. So far only a thin veil of it hung in the air like a light fog, adding an extra touch of eeriness to an area already darkened by the loss of most of the lighting systems.

They crept along very cautiously, peering around constantly at the ominous-looking piles of stores. They heard no sounds except a distant rumbling and an occasional louder detonation from below as the Tower's machines continued their self-demolition at an ever-accelerating rate.

It was with relief—and a certain surprise as well—that they finally reached the far side of the storage area and passed out through one of the huge doorways onto the stone quay. Here they found a partial answer to the Tower's seeming emptiness. All the ships of the Tower fleet were gone.

"What's happened to them?" Aine asked. She looked around at the young Champion in concern. "Oh, Lugh, could they have sailed for Tir-na-nog already?"

"We'd best be worrying about ourselves right now," the Dagda pointed out with great logic. "We can't be staying here. Let's find some kind of boat."

"We can't leave without Taillta and Angus," Lugh said.

"We won't have to," said Findgoll. "Look there!"

They turned back toward the Tower. From the doorways into the storage level woman and children were now emerging, guided and helped by the escaped Tower rebels. And two faces in the crowd were particularly familiar ones.

"Taillta! Angus!" Lugh called.

Seeing their comrades, the two moved from the mass of refugees and ran to them.

"You made it!" Lugh said happily. "And you managed to get them free as well."

Taillta and Angus did not return his joy. "There's no time for that," Taillta said grimly. "An attacking force is headed here—we and I think it's ours."

"So that's where their fleet's gone!" said Aine.

"Has Nuada gone mad?" bellowed the Dagda. "And all the rest of them as well? Those Tower ships will tear ours right apart. I know. Can't we stop them?"

"It's too late, I think," said Angus, pointing out to sea. "They're already coming back."

It seemed that he was right. Sails were now visible as many ships swept around the end of the long, curving peninsula that sheltered the bay and made for the Tower harbor.

"But those aren't Tower ships!" said Lugh. "Those are fishing boats and traders and curraughs! Those are Eireland ships!"

"Incredible!" said Findgoll. "Somehow they've gotten past the Tower ships."

"They're coming here!" said Angus, giving a loud whoop of delight. "They're coming here to rescue us! The Tower's done for certain now!"

A crimson streak of light shot down, angling sharply across the sky before them. As they watched in horror, it struck the foremost of the incoming vessels—a fishing boat. In an instant it was ablaze.

They whirled about, their gazes rising to the source of the red beam. Above the top edge of the Tower they could glimpse only a black barrel shape and a glint of ruby light. But that was enough to tell them who was there.

"Balor!" said Lugh. "He can destroy them all!"

"Alone?" asked Angus.

"I've seen the power of his eye blast apart a fortress," Lugh replied. "He must be stopped somehow."

"But how?" the little Druid asked.

"The spear!" said a faint voice.

It came from Manannan. The lanky being still cradled in the Dagda's arms was now awake.

Lugh moved to him, alarmed by his wan face and his obvious weakness.

"Manannan, how are you?" he asked anxiously.

He managed a smile, but it was only a poor, pale copy of his usual broad grin. "It takes more than a thump on the head to do me, lad," he said, and then grimaced with pain, adding, "although I have been better. But never mind me. It's you! You've got to use the Spear of Gorias against Balor. Don't you see? Its power must be meant for his destruction."

The young warrior realized that he was right. Danu knew he would have a use for it. What other purpose could there be for such a weapon?

"Only you can do it now!" MacLir went on. His voice was growing fainter, but his great will forced the words out. "It was meant to come to this, all of it. And you were meant to come to this as well." With a great effort he lifted an arm, laying a lean hand on Lugh's shoulder. "It is time for you to act . . . Champion of the Sidhe."

Exhausted by this effort, he sagged back in the Dagda's arms.

"Rest, Manannan," Lugh told him. "I made a vow to you. I won't betray it now."

He pulled the spear from his back and looked at its covered point. Then he turned toward the Tower of Glass, his gaze lifting to the giant at its top.

Aine saw the determination harden his youthful face. She moved to his side, gripping his arms.

"Lugh, what are you going to do?" she asked.

"I've got to go up there," he said.

"No!" she cried. She pulled him toward her and spoke with urgency. "Lugh, you can't do this. You can't face Balor. He'll destroy you."

"If that is part of my fate in this after all, then it will have to be," he told her stoically.

"But it doesn't have to be," she argued.

"Unless I choose," he added. "And I choose this." He smiled and touched her cheek. "You know as well as I that it must be this way."

She held his earnest gaze a moment. Then she nodded sharply. "I know," she agreed reluctantly. "But you will not be going up there alone."

"None of us will be going up there at all!" put in Taillta. "Those lifting rooms are useless, and you'll never make it up those stairs in time. There's no way to reach him."

As if to reinforce this, a louder, more ominous rumbling came from the Tower's depths, accompanied by a series of sharper explosions. Smoke began to gush in greater volume from the open storage bays. A rising stream poured around the upper edge of each doorway, flowing up the side of the Tower in rippling yellow-gray streams.

"There is one way," said Lugh, his gaze falling upon the lion-shaped Shaglan.

The being sighed. "I should have guessed as much. All right, lad. One more time then."

"Sorry, my friends," Lugh told the others. "It seems that this time I've no choice but to go without you." He looked to Aine and grinned. "Even you. And if you want to know the truth, I'm glad of it."

"Lugh . . ." she began.

"Sorry," he said quickly. "There's no time now." His smile widened. "But then, there never really has been, has there?"

He looked back to Shaglan. The Pooka was still struggling with his shape, apparently caught somewhere between the lion's body and a bird's, the head beaked, the sinewy torso now feathered but still lacking wings.

"Shaglan, hurry!" he urged.

Another beam of crimson light shot downward from the Tower—and another vessel burst into a ball of flame.

"This is difficult enough without being rushed in it," the Pooka said irritably. "Ah . . . there. I've got it."

Wings sprouted from the sides, growing outward and unfolding like a spring leaf from a bud. The magnificent span was complete in moments. The being, however, still had the shape and four clawed feet of a lion.

"What about the rest?" Lugh asked a little apprehensively.

"No time for details," the Pooka said. "It'll work. Hop on!"

Lugh obeyed, and with a short run along the quay, Shaglan was airborne.

Lugh's companions watched them as they swept out over the waters of the bay, swung about, and started to climb toward the Tower's roof.

"Never enough time," Aine said softly, with regret. Then she added in a more forceful voice: "Danu, you had better help him!"

As Shaglan laboriously pumped his way upward, the Tower began to tear itself apart in greater earnest. The smaller fires on many levels were begetting larger ones. The increasing heat was igniting whole sections of flammable materials at once, with incredible force. Far up the Tower, above the quay, an explosion blew an entire glass panel outward. Shattered glass and flaming debris showered down on the refugees.

"We've got to move away from here!" said Taillta. "Get these people as far from the Tower as possible!"

With the assistance of Eab and the other Tower men, they began to herd the women and children out onto the long, curving peninsula of rocks that sheltered the mouth of the bay, the farthest point on the little island from the Tower walls.

On the rooftop, the frequent tremors had also made Bres aware that something very wrong was happening beneath him. While Balor's deadly eye was setting ablaze another vessel, he took a glance over the roof's edge and down the sheer side. Far below he saw thick smoke pouring out through a blasted panel. And as he watched, another panel several levels higher exploded outward, long tongues of flame licking out behind it.

"Balor!" shouted Bres. "The Tower is burning. We must leave here before we're trapped."

"The Tower cannot be harmed!" Balor thundered. "It will last forever. But the de Dananns will be destroyed!" And the eye fired its crimson ray again, turning another hapless craft to blazing wreckage.

Shaglan had by this time managed to flap his way up to a height well above the Tower's roof and just to its north. Lugh could see Balor, his broad back turned to them.

"Good work, Shaglan," he congratulated him. "Let's go in now. Swing around him so I can cast the spear right at his eye. And get in close! I'll have only one try!"

"Close!" said the Pooka unhappily. "Naturally. Well, hang on!"

He started to turn left to make a wide curve and dive in at the giant. But as he did, a peculiar and now-familiar sensation began stealing over him.

"Ah Lugh!" he cried. "I'm changing."

"What?" The young Champion looked down at the water so far, far below. His own greatest fear was being realized as well. "Stop it!"

"I can't—I've lost all control again."

"Try to hold on!" pleaded Lugh. "The roof is nearly under us. Just get us to the roof!"

The Pooka concentrated. He put his whole will to holding the shape of the wings as he stroked forward desperately. He barely managed to get above the roof as his form dissolved, the wings losing their stiffness and sagging uselessly. As the roof came quickly up, he braced himself to take the impact.

Shaglan slammed down, legs buckling under him, body crashing onto the roof. Lugh was thrown forward, over the Pooka's head, and tumbled across the hard surface. The spear, knocked from his grasp, skittered away, coming to rest against the opposite edge and very far away.

Dazed, bruised but conscious, Lugh managed to pull himself up to his hands and knees. As he did, he realized that some one was standing over him.

"Oh, no," he said wearily, lifting his head and looking up at Bres smiling down at him, naked longsword ready in his hand.

Chapter Thirty-One
THE SPEAR

Lugh rolled back as the sword slashed out at him. It whooshed harmlessly past and he managed to scramble to his feet and pull out the Answerer before Bres could strike again.

They faced each other, Bres still grinning.

"Somehow I expected you, Lugh Lamfada," he said. "I knew they should have killed you."

"Don't try to stop me, Bres," said Lugh. "I need that spear. I have to destroy Balor."

"Of course," he replied with mock graciousness. "Go and take it."

Lugh made a quick feint to the left and then leaped the other way in an attempt to get around Bres. But the man was wary and fast. He shifted to block the young warrior, driving in with a quick flurry of blows. Forced onto the defensive, Lugh fought back, the Answerer flashing as he parried rapidly.

The two warriors were closely matched. Bres's age was balanced by greater experience. His weight and strength compensated for Lugh's greater agility. Their exchange was furious but futile.

When both thrust in together, their hilts met and they locked together, muscles straining, faces close. Lugh tried to use the opportunity for a bit of reasoning.

"Please, Bres, help me!" he said. "The de Dananns are your people too. Don't let them be destroyed."

Bres laughed. "You expect me to help you? Because of you I lost my son—my throne—my Eire!"

He drove forward with his shoulder, knocking Lugh violently back. The young warrior staggered but recovered, setting himself to face Bres again.

"You lost those things," he fired back. "You tried to be a Fomor. You let that blood control you. It's lost you everything in Eire, and now the Fomor are lost as well."

"No!" Bres said. "It's you who's lost. The de Dananns will be wiped away, and I'll be free of them."

He attacked savagely again, pushing Lugh back with a series of powerful blows. Lugh managed to fend him off, but he was weakening. The escape from the cells, the battle in Mathgen's chambers, the explosion and the crash onto the roof, had left him worn and cut and bruised. His whole body cried out in agony from the continued exertion. He fought on stubbornly, calling on all the strength left to him as the ruby eye of Balor moved on, blasting ship after ship. But he was losing. With every step he was forced to retreat, his chance for success became more remote.

Suddenly, he was at the edge. His foot struck the raised border and he felt himself falling backward.

To save himself he was forced to throw his arms out and back, flailing away to regain his balance. He managed to do it, but at a great cost. For Bres was able to drive in close to him while he was off his guard and knock the Answerer from his grip with a hard, two-handed stroke.

"Now, young Champion," Bres told him slowly, savoring each word. "You are going to die!"

"Don't do this, Bres," Lugh said. "It will mean the end of everything for you. Destroying the de Dananns won't free you from them. They are a part of you. They're all that you have left. Bres, I'm like you! I know the Fomor blood doesn't have to win. You could choose. Choose now! The Fomor are finished. Don't finish the de Danann side as well. Help me save something!"

"Destroy him, Bres!" the voice of Balor rumbled from across the rooftop.

They both looked toward the giant. Their fight had finally drawn his attention, and he had brought the crimson circle of his eye around toward them. More vast than ever, his square, stark form silhouetted against the sky, he loomed up above the roof of his Tower, a monument to its existence, the image of an ancient creator god holding captive his own sun. The blazing disc appeared to seethe with the vast energy Balor now held back within it. Even across the wide roof, the intense heat contained there washed over the two men, nearly scorching them.

"He is our greatest enemy!" clanged Balor. "The only danger left. Destroy him."

"You are mad!" Lugh shouted at him. "You have nothing! Your Tower is destroyed. Your soldiers are dead. Your people have escaped your slavery and fled. The Prophecy was true. Mathgen was right. You have lost."

"You lie!" the giant thundered. "This Tower cannot be harmed. The Fomor power can never be destroyed. Bres, kill him now, or I will do it!"

Bres looked from the dark giant to the young warrior, meeting Lugh's searching gaze. Once more they saw into each other's minds, probed deeply into each other's hearts. For that moment their spirits fused, and through Bres's memory surged images of all the treacherous acts he had committed, all the horror and death he had created against the de Dananns for the sake of his Fomor blood, all he had done to prove himself truly Fomor and earn the glories that Balor had promised. He saw clearly now that they had all been futile, and how the dark giant had used him, destroyed him, for the good of the Glass Tower.

His sword dropped to his side. He turned toward Balor. And in Bres's eyes, a final understanding glowed to life.

"No!" he said defiantly. "I will not kill him. This is enough."

Freed of Bres's weapon, Lugh began to move just as the ruby eye flared and the beam shot toward them.

Bres was caught full in the stream of fire. In that same instant he became a blazing torch. But Lugh was able to dive away from the lethal beam in time. He landed rolling, staggered up again, and ran across the rooftop toward the spear.

The barrel head of the giant began to swivel, swinging

the gaze of the eye around after him, but he stayed ahead of it. He reached the spear and snatched it up, tearing frantically at the strings of the leather cover.

The head turned, turned, as the crimson gaze slipped toward him.

He got the strings untied and tore the cover from the head. The glowing silver force of it flashed out to form a halo about it as he lifted it and turned to face Balor.

The eye was already upon him, the force within it pulsing, building to its discharge point.

The beam of light fired out toward him as he cast the spear. The magic weapon slashed into the jet of energy. It clove through the waves of ruby light. The coursing power parted about it like a flood parting at a stone, forming two separate streams that curled out to the sides and away from Lugh, dissipating harmlessly in the air.

The spear plunged in, cutting through the beam, striking the very center of that eye.

The magic of Tir-na-nog and the science of the Tower met in a last confrontation, a final test of strength. It destroyed them both. They burst together in a mingling of blood-red and silver light, swelling up and out in a geyser. The concussion shook the rooftop of the Tower of Glass, and the shock wave knocked Lugh Lamfada to the hard surface, senseless.

As Lugh's comrades and the refugees of the Tower made their way out along the rocks of the peninsula, the explosion from the roof drew their attention back to it. They looked upward in time to see the headless black form of the giant topple back from the edge and out of sight.

"Lugh's done it!" Findgoll exclaimed.

"Now he and Shaglan have only to get away," said Aine, watching the rooftop hopefully.

"If they're still alive," Angus added. Then he glanced toward Aine and colored.

Another explosion in the lower levels of the Tower sprayed glass and wreckage far out over the rocks near them.

"We've got ourselves to be thinking about now," said the Dagda sharply. "Come on!"

They continued toward the point, but Aine glanced back often, praying she would see the familiar form of the Pooka rise from the rooftop with Lugh astride it.

On the incoming fleet Nuada and his warriors had also

observed the destruction of Balor. Their reaction had been a blend of amazement and joy.

"His head just burst!" said Bobd Derg, his poet's gift for words gone in his awe. "How did it happen?"

Nuada shook his head. "I don't know, but it's saved us! Now we go straight in. Make for their harbor."

"Look there!" another warrior cried, pointing. "There are people moving out onto that bit of rocks. Women and children, I think. They must be coming from the Tower!"

"Why, that's the Dagda himself with them!" said Bobd Derg. "I can't mistake that figure."

"And the Morrigan too," Nuada added. "By Danu. So they *are* alive." He turned and shouted to the ship's helmsman: "Head in there, toward that point! Quick now. We've got to pick them up!"

On the rooftop young Lugh once again struggled to his feet. I should be getting used to this by now, he told himself. But it was getting harder each time, and this last battle had nearly finished him. His body was screaming in protest as he moved his battered limbs. His ribs all seemed caved in, his head throbbed, and he was having difficulty getting his legs to move quite as they should.

He cast a quick glance at the blackened pile that had been Bres, then stumbled across the roof toward the smoking body of the fallen giant. The barrel head had been completely blown away, taking off much of the upper shoulders and chest with it. Inside the huge chest a large cavity was revealed. And something was within it. He peered closer, realizing it was a human form.

There, nestled in a tight metal cave, almost a part of the surrounding assemblage of machinery and gadgets, was a very old man. He had been killed instantly by a deep gash through the high dome of his head. It had streaked his long white hair with thick tresses of blood.

Another explosion within the stricken Tower made the surface beneath his feet shake violently, and it recalled Lugh to the present. He had to get away from here, and very soon.

Then he remembered Shaglan. The Pooka's huddled form still lay where it had crashed to the rooftop. He ran to it.

"Shaglan!" he said anxiously, laying a hand upon it. "Shaglan, are you alive?"

The landing had apparently arrested the being's form-shifting. Save for a beak and a feathered body, it was now mostly lion again. It shifted, moaned, and lifted its head to regard him with irritation in its large, dark eyes.

"I am," it said sharply, "and no thanks to this poor body of mine. Curse that Dagda! This is all his fault too!"

"Can you fly?" Lugh asked hopefully.

It tried to move itself, but grimaced with pain.

"Sorry, lad. There are parts broken inside me that I didn't know I had. And maybe I didn't before. Anyway, I can't even stand, much less fly, and I can't even begin to change my shape at all."

There came another, heavier explosion, from just below this time. Smoke began to seep up around the edges of the useless lift and pour from the open doorway to the stairs. Balor's level of the Tower was now afire too.

"Lugh, you can't help me," the Pooka told him earnestly. "Leave me. Get away yourself."

"I wouldn't leave you, Shaglan," Lugh replied. Then he shrugged and laughed. "Besides, there's no place I can really go."

He rose and moved back to the edge of the roof, peering down. He could see the people of the Tower moving from the tip of the Rocky peninsula into the water. Ships of Eireland were sailing in as close as possible and taking them aboard.

"At least the others are getting safely off," he observed. He looked back to the Pooka and spoke regretfully. "It really is my fault that you're here, Shaglan. I brought you into this."

"No, no, lad!" the being protested. "You brought me nowhere. It was always my own choice. I wanted to make amends for my clan's wrong."

"And that you've more than done," Lugh told it, moving back to its side. "We would never have won without you. The de Dananns haven't a warrior more loyal." He sat down and put an arm across the broad shoulders of the being.

"You know," Shaglan said thoughtfully, "I suppose there is something to dying heroically and all that. And we're surely going to do it in a grand and glorious way. But, to say the truth, I think I'd much prefer staying alive."

"So would I," Lugh admitted, thinking longingly of Aine.

Far below, the last of Lugh's companions were being pulled aboard Nuada's ship. Other ships had moved in to take the people of the Tower off of the rocks. Diancecht was already examining MacLir and Morrigan while Nuada greeted his comrades.

"I never thought to see you alive again," the High-King said. "But what about young Lugh?"

"It was he who destroyed Balor," the Dagda told him. "Flew up after him on that Pooka!"

"Where are they?" the king asked. "Did they escape?"

"We haven't seen either of them," Findgoll told him. "They must be still up there."

All eyes went toward the rooftop of the Tower, now almost hidden in a surrounding curtain of rising smoke. More explosions were coming from the base as the main power generators and the fuel sources deep below the Tower began the convulsions of their final death throes.

"They must be trapped," said the Dagda. "They would have come down by now."

Aine stared up at the dying Tower, her worst fears realized. She remembered . . . her first meeting with Lugh as he faced Bres in Tara's hall, their daring rescue of Taillta from the Tower, their desperate battle against Balor in Manannan's Sidhe. She recalled her agony when he lay dying in the Burren and she used the power of Danu to save him. And now, after all of that, was he not to survive this final act? She wanted to scream out at the unfairness, to demand that Queen Danu save the gallant young warrior, or do something herself. But there was nothing to do now, except to stand staring helplessly. Morrigan moved close to Aine and slipped her good arm about the girl's shoulders in a gesture of comfort.

But then, a movement in the sky above the Tower caught the Raven-Woman's sharp eye. She stared and then lifted her arm to point.

"Look there! What's that?" she called.

Aine's gaze followed her pointing arm. She realized that a formation of strange creatures was sweeping down toward the Tower's roof.

"It's the Pooka!" she cried with joy, her hope renewed.

"By Danu!" said Nuada. "They came back!"

They watched as the creatures settled to the rooftop. In moments they were lifting away again, two of them carrying a large form in their claws, a third with a figure astride its back.

They rose and wheeled sharply away from the Tower, winging out across the sea.

They were away with little time to spare. Moments later

the enormous power systems went in a final chain-reaction of explosions that rose to a single, tremendous discharge of energy. The smooth walls of the foundation were ruptured, crumbling apart as they blew outward all around the base. Deprived of its footing, the structure of glass above it began to collapse.

It was as if the interior supports had been shattered all at once. The Tower settled downward, level by level, sinking slowly, gently, with a peculiar sort of final grace into its broken foundation. The great, smooth, perfect walls of glass shivered, splintered, disintegrated into a fog of tiny bits as they were compressed. A great wind puffed outward from it, pushing away the fleet of Eireland ships. The roaring that accompanied it was like the crashing surf of all the seas combined.

The last moments of the Tower's death were shrouded by smoke and dust and debris billowing out and up around the bottom levels as they caved in. The din of it echoed across the waves and faded. The clouds drifted away and the remains of the Tower of Glass were revealed.

There seemed very little left to mark where the gleaming fortress had thrust up so boldly from the sea. Without its panels of glass it was only a pile of twisted metal and broken stones. The symbol of destruction that had haunted the dreams of the Children of Danu for so many years was gone.

"Now it is truly finished," Nuada said. He turned and smiled at his comrades. "I am at peace, my friends."

With those words he sagged forward. The Dagda moved quickly to catch him, easing him to the deck. The others moved around, but there was nothing for any of them to do. Nuada, High-King of the Tuatha de Dananns, was dead.

Chapter Thirty-Two
THE PARTING

The torch was thrust deeply into the piles of sacred yew and oak. The flames began at once to crackle up through the dry wood, quickly encircling the bier.

The body of Nuada lay upon it, clad in the bright trappings of a warrior. His face was relaxed into peaceful lines in death. His open eyes stared fearlessly upward into a clear and brilliant sky.

The High-Druid Findgoll stepped back from the funeral pyre and turned to face the gathering of Druids. Behind them rose the great burial mound where the ashes of the High-King would soon be laid with due sacred ritual. He raised his hands and the Druids began a low and mournful chant that drifted across the countryside of Eire like the sound of wind keening in the treetops.

Some distance from the mound, near the banks of the flashing river called the Boinne, the chieftains and the Champions of Eire watched this ceremony solemnly. Among those of this impressive gathering were Lugh and his comrades, all now healed by the miraculous powers of the physician Diancecht. Beside the young Champion stood Aine and MacLir, the lanky man once more in the disguise of Gilla the Clown.

"He saw his people restored and his own life redeemed," Manannan spoke softly. "He died a warrior—and High-King of a warrior race. He wanted nothing else."

With the chant concluded, the gathering of warriors began to break up and move away. Only the Druids would remain now to await the dying of the flames and the moving of the ashes to their last resting place within the central chamber of the mound. Many of the warriors mounted their horses and began the ride back to Tara. The Dagda, Taillta, and some others lingered to talk in a small group. Lugh,

Aine, and Manannan walked along the river to where a peculiar group of winged creatures waited.

The clan of Pookas still retained the form of the flying beings they had used to rescue Lugh. Shaglan, his shifting ability restored, had transformed into the familiar hound shape.

"They're all starting back toward the Burren lands now," Shaglan told his friends as they approached.

"But you could stay," Lugh told them. "You would be accepted here now."

"Maybe," replied the great dragonlike Pooka. "But there are many long years of distrust to be overcome. Although we've made a start, it will take time before we're part of the de Dananns again as Shaglan is. For now, we'll go back to our lands. But if the men of Eire need us again, they can ask for our help. Good-bye to you—and good fortune."

With that, the flock of them turned away and, with a great flapping that raised a torrent of wind, rose up into the sky and soared away. Only Shaglan stayed behind.

"So, you've decided not to go?" asked Lugh.

"Not I," he answered, stretching his mouth into a canine grin. "I've grown much too used to human company, and to you. I'll stay with you a bit longer, if you'll have me."

"With the greatest pleasure!" Lugh told the being heartily.

"I'm glad you're staying, Shaglan," MacLir put in. "As for me, I think the perfect time for leaving has come."

"You're leaving now?" Lugh said in surprise.

The tall man shrugged. "Yes, well, it's over, isn't it? The Prophecy's been fulfilled. Things all worked out according to my plans."

"According to your plans?" Aine said, fixing him with a critical glare.

"Well," he said, discomfited, "perhaps there were a few unexpected turns. But we came to the right end eventually. So, I can be off, Lugh, and you can get about living your own life, quite free of my interfering for once."

"But where are you going to go?" Lugh asked.

"I don't really know. Not back to Tir-na-nog, that's certain. It's a depressingly peaceful sort of place. And that Sidhe of mine's not much better. All that restful beauty!" He shuddered at the thought. "No. I was thinking that I'd travel a bit, see more of the world. There must be others out there needing help. There may be more Balors and more Towers of Glass."

"Sounds like great fun," Lugh said, smiling. He looked to Aine. "And what about you? Will you be going with him? You told me once that you would when this was done."

"No," she said firmly. She faced the tall man squarely. "Sorry, brother, but I've spent my life adventuring with you. I think it's time to consider other things." She turned back to Lugh, her voice taking on a warm and urgent and impassioned tone. "Lugh, I want to stay here too, if you want me. The de Dananns will be building a real life for themselves in Eire now. You'll be a part of that, and I want to help you."

He took her hands and held them tightly within his own. He looked down into those intense, brightly glowing eyes.

"Dear Aine," he said with amusement, "you don't really mean what you're saying. I know you. You are a woman, but you are a warrior as well. The adventuring means as much to you as to Manannan. You mean to give it up because you love me. But if I love you, I can't ask you to. It would only bring us both unhappiness."

She was stricken by his words. She stepped back from him, jerking her hands away. Her voice turned frigid.

"You mean you don't want me? After all that we've been through, after freezing and burning and fighting together, after all the times I've saved you, after what we've said to each other, now you don't want me? When I throw away my pride! When I offer myself! Why you contemptible—" Her hand went to her sword hilt. "I ought to cut out your heart right now!"

"Wait!" Lugh said hastily. "That's not what I meant at all." He glanced to MacLir for help, but the lanky Clown was only smiling, apparently vastly entertained. "Please, Aine," the young man went on, "just let me explain. I . . ."

But before he could go on, the familiar booming voice of the Dagda interrupted him.

"Ah, there you are!"

Coming along the riverbank toward them was a contingent of leaders of the de Danann and Firbolg clans. The Dagda and Taillta were at its head, with Angus, Bobd Derg, and the Morrigan close behind.

As they reached their comrades, the Dagda stepped forward, facing Lugh with a distinctly formal air that seemed ill-suited to the giant warrior.

"Lugh Lamfada," he said in a slow and solemn way, "we of the combined clans of Eire have met in council. We have decided that the person most fit to succeed Nuada is you. We ask you to become the next High-King."

Lugh laughed. "You're joking! You want me to be king?"

"Both the Firbolgs and the de Dananns want you, Lugh," Taillta told him. "You would ensure a lasting peace between us."

"I'm no king," Lugh replied with great sincerity. "I've never even felt myself a Champion! No, my friends, I can't be your king. My life is my own now, and it's going to remain so." He lifted a hand toward the Dagda. "Here is your new High-King. I can't think of anyone better suited. And I'm certain he'll work with you, Taillta, to share Eire fairly with your people."

"What? Me High-King?" the giant warrior said, taken aback.

"A fine idea," Taillta endorsed. "He was my own choice." She smiled and winked at Lugh. "I told them you'd never accept the kingship anyway!"

"That you did," the Dagda agreed, looking curiously at Lugh. "But what is it you're meaning to do?"

"That I was just about to explain to Aine here," he said, turning to grin at the young woman who had stood by, seething, through this exchange. "I intend to do a bit of traveling with her and this mad Clown."

Her anger vanished as she realized what he was saying. Her face lit with a renewed happiness as she moved to him again.

"Is it true?" she asked.

"Of course!" he assured her laughingly. "It's what I was trying to say before. Aine, I grew up on a tiny isle, thinking there was no other world." He looked toward the figure of the Clown. "It was Manannan who showed me there was more beyond the horizon than I could imagine. He's given me a spirit for adventuring like his own."

"You always had it, lad," the lanky being replied with his old, foolish grin.

"So, I won't ask you to stay here with me," Lugh told Aine. "Instead, I'll ask if you'll have me with you."

"You know the answer already," she said, abandoning all restraint, throwing her arms about him in delight.

*   *   *

Tara's hall now saw a celebration the like of which had never been in Eire. It was a joyous time, honoring the heroes and the new High-King, but there was sadness in it too, because it was a farewell for Nuada—and other departing friends as well.

The morning after dawned with that crystal clarity known only to the fall. The sky was brilliant, cloudless blue, the rising sun a sharply defined disk whose rays cast the autumn meadows in a gleaming gold, throwing long shadows behind the four making their way eastward from the Beautiful Ridge.

They made quite a peculiar-looking little band. The gawky Clown led, sitting atop his rickety cart, steering the single, tiny pony along. Beside the pony happily trotted a very large and very shaggy dog, while behind the cart there rode a young couple, horses close, heads bent together in intimate conversation.

From the high ramparts of Tara of the Kings, a gathering of their comrades watched them go. None could remember a leave-taking so difficult.

"I will miss Lugh," said Angus Og sincerely. "What will we do for adventures now?"

"It's Aine I'll think of," rasped the Morrigan softly. "I hope she finds her happiness."

The Dagda was surprised by the note of human warmth and sorrow in her voice. He lifted a hand and placed it on her shoulder in a comforting way. She left it there.

"They'll all be missed," he said. "That madman and that strange Pooka as well."

"Ah, but it's not for ever they're leaving us," the cunning little Druid said in a knowing way. "When there's a need in Eire, I think we'll be seeing our young Champion and our Master of the Sidhe again."

AFTERWORD

This novel, like those I have written earlier and those I am now developing, is based upon elements drawn from the Celtic mythology of Ireland. My primary purpose in developing these stories has always been to make that ancient literature, so rich with fantasy and adventure, better known to modern readers. It has been a source and inspiration for much in Western civilization from King Arthur to our present sword-and-sorcery books and films.

My stories come mainly from three separate groups of Irish mythology called cycles. With two of these cycles—the Red Branch Cycle of Cuchulain and the Ossian Cycle of Finn MacCumhal—I have tried to stay as faithful to the elements of the myths as possible. However, in the Cycle of the Tuatha de Dananns where Lugh Lamfada is the central hero, I have had to depart somewhat from this approach.

This most ancient group of the Celtic myths is rooted in the most primitive of tribal beliefs, created perhaps thousands of years before Christ. The stories are often vague, fragmented, and tangled, filled with obscure references and mist-shrouded figures once meant to explain the Celtic cosmos and the origins of the gods. The many versions of the tales are often far different, even contradictory. Their elements are many times too unbelievable.

In my attempt to create a coherent story and a credible one, I decided to build my plot around the one narrative that was similar in most versions of the myth, regardless of the variations in detail. This concerned the young hero, Lugh Lamfada. The son of a Fomor princess and a de Danann Champion, he is hidden away until adulthood. Then, with the help of Manannan MacLir and the Riders of the Sidhe, he returns to Eire to help the de Dananns, destroy the Fomor power, and kill Balor.

In other areas of the myth I found it necessary to interpret the elements, and some intriguing points in the ancient tales suggested to me the approach I finally used. First were the references to the enormous Tower of Glass and to the eye of Balor which could destroy all its gaze rested upon. They seemed more elements of science fiction than ancient myth. Were they attempts by a primitive people to explain technological forces? With this in mind, I found the description of the Fomor as grotesquely deformed taking on a new meaning. Had some disaster caused it? To provide an explanation that encompassed all these factors, I made the Fomor a remnant of an earlier, scientifically superior civilization, putting their science in a direct conflict with the supernatural powers of the de Dananns.

The tale of the Children of Danu is not complete. It goes far beyond the adventures of Lugh Lamfada recounted here. Their earliest days, their gaining of magic from Danu and their return to Ireland, form another exciting story. So does the saga of their later battle with the invading Milesian tribes for control of Eire. It is the loss of this battle that will send the proud de Dananns into the hidden places of Eire to live and become the gods and fairy races to men. And it is in these hidden places that many in Ireland believe the "Others" still dwell, making themselves known to men in the forms of Pooka, Leprechaun, and Banshee.

The name Banshee, by the way, is derived from the word *Sidhe* (pronounced "shee"). Although it originally is applied to the hidden underground palaces of the Tuatha de Danann, it eventually becomes a name for those who inhabit these places. Thus, today "Sidhe" is used synonymously with the name Tuatha de Danann to refer to the supernatural race. The word *Banshee* combines *Ban* (meaning "woman") with *Sidhe* to give us the name of this eerie woman whose wail foretells the death of one of Ireland.

It is this element, this link between the most ancient myths and the still-existent folklore and artifacts in Ireland, which I feel is the most fascinating aspect of learning more about the Celts. For what they were and believed, their romantic spirit is still very much alive today, not just in Ireland, but in all of Western civilization.

ABOUT THE AUTHOR

KENNETH C. FLINT became interested in Celtic mythology in graduate school, where he saw a great source of material in this long neglected area of western literature. Since then he has spent much time researching (in the library and abroad in England and Ireland) those legends and incorporating them into works of fantasy that would interest modern readers. His novels to date include *A Storm Upon Ulster, Riders of the Sidhe,* and *Champions of The Sidhe.*

Mr. Flint is a graduate of the University of Nebraska with a Masters Degree in English Literature. For several years he taught in the Department of Humanities at the University of Nebraska at Omaha. Presently he is Chairman of English for the Plattsmouth Community Schools (a system in a suburban community of Omaha). In addition to teaching, he has worked as a freelance writer, producing articles, short stories, and screenplays for some Omaha-based film companies.

He currently lives in Omaha with his wife Judy (whose family has roots in Ireland) and his sons Devin and Gavin, and he is hard at work on his next novel.

Coming in 1986 from Bantam Spectra Books—

A major new historical novel
featuring Irish Mythology's
most compelling hero

FINN

by Kenneth C. Flint

From one of fantasy's most popular new
authors comes an exciting new adventure,
brimming with action, humor, sorcery, and
romance, the story of Ireland's most popular
hero—Finn McCumhal.